WHAT PEOPLE ARE SAYING ABOUT

The Milhavior Chronicles

"I recommend this first book of the *Milhavior Chronicles* . . . The main characters are well-drawn and engage the reader's sympathy. The setting is realistic with descriptions that awake images in the reader's mind . . . I haven't enjoyed a fantasy as much as this one in a long time."

- Donita K. Paul, author

"If you enjoy epic fantasy, the mythic battle between good and evil, a fast-paced plot, and the entire process of hero-making - don't miss this book!"

- C.K. Deatherage, author

"I liken this book to the feeling you get after a friend has recommended an obscure movie you've never heard of - only to find it's one of the best movies you've ever seen . . . *Sharamitaro* is a real find, a gem! . . . I'd recommend this book to anyone who enjoys fantasy novels."

- Brian M. Rook

Sharamitaro

Book I
of
The Milhavior Chronicles

by
Jonathan M. Rudder

Athor Productions
PO Box 652
Granite City, IL 62040
www.athorproductions.com
info@athorproductions.com

Published by:

Athor Productions
PO Box 652
Granite City, IL 62040
USA

First Softcover Printing, December 2001, Infinity Publishing.com (ISBN 0-7414-0890-2)

Second Softcover Printing (revised), December 2002, Athor Productions (ISBN 1-932060-00-6)

Copyright © Jonathan M. Rudder, 2001
All Rights Reserved
Cover Art: Jonathan M. Rudder*
Designer: Jonathan M. Rudder

Neither the artist, the author, nor the publisher make any claim to any and all third-party 3D models, textures, or other materials used in the creation of the cover art. All copyrights for third-party materials belong to the individual creators and/or producers of those materials. Used under license. The artist only claims the copyright of the finished derivative art.

Printed in the United States of America

ISBN 1-932060-00-6

No part of this publication may be reproduced, stored in or introduced into a retrieval system, or transmitted, in any form, or by any means (electronic, mechanical, photocopying, recording, or otherwise), without the prior written permission of both the copyright owner and the above publisher of this book.

This is a work of fiction. Names, characters, places, and incidents are either the products of the author's imagination or are used fictitiously, and any resemblance to actual persons, living or dead, events, or locales is entirely coincidental.

*To Rebecca, James,
John, and Ellie,
Look to the Dawn,
and all is possible.*

Milhavior – West Lands

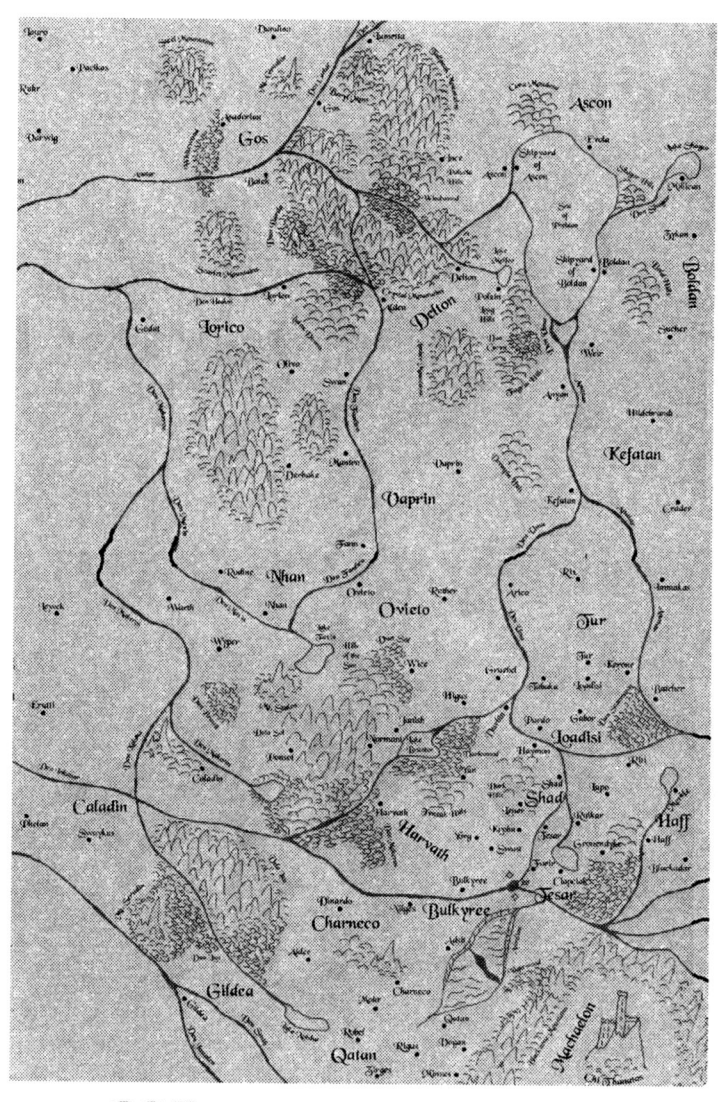

Milhavior - East Lands

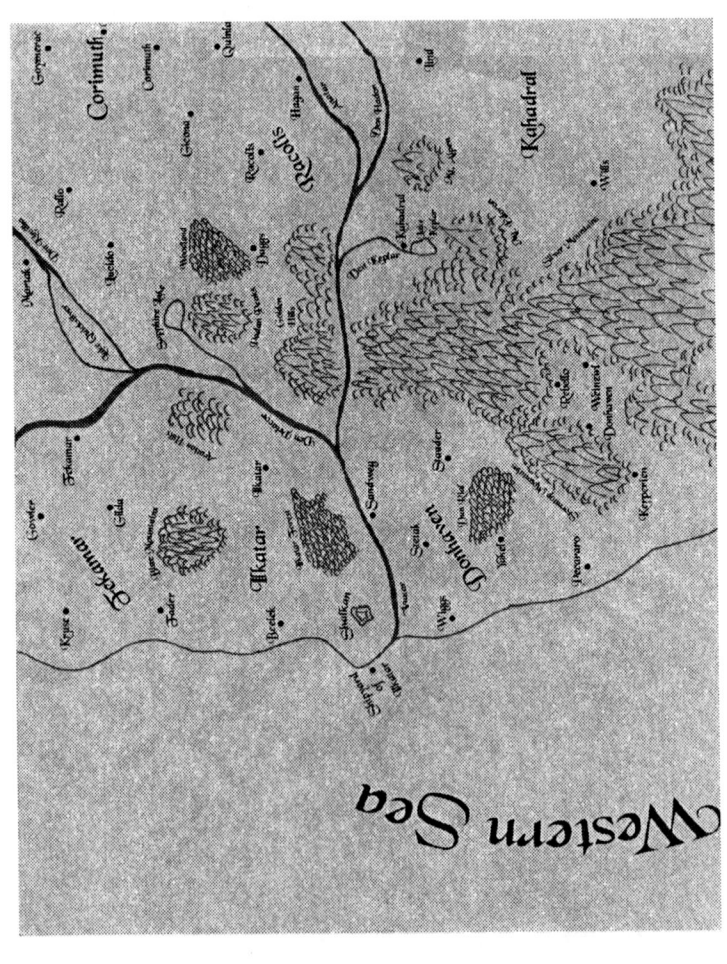

Milhavior – Northwest Quarter

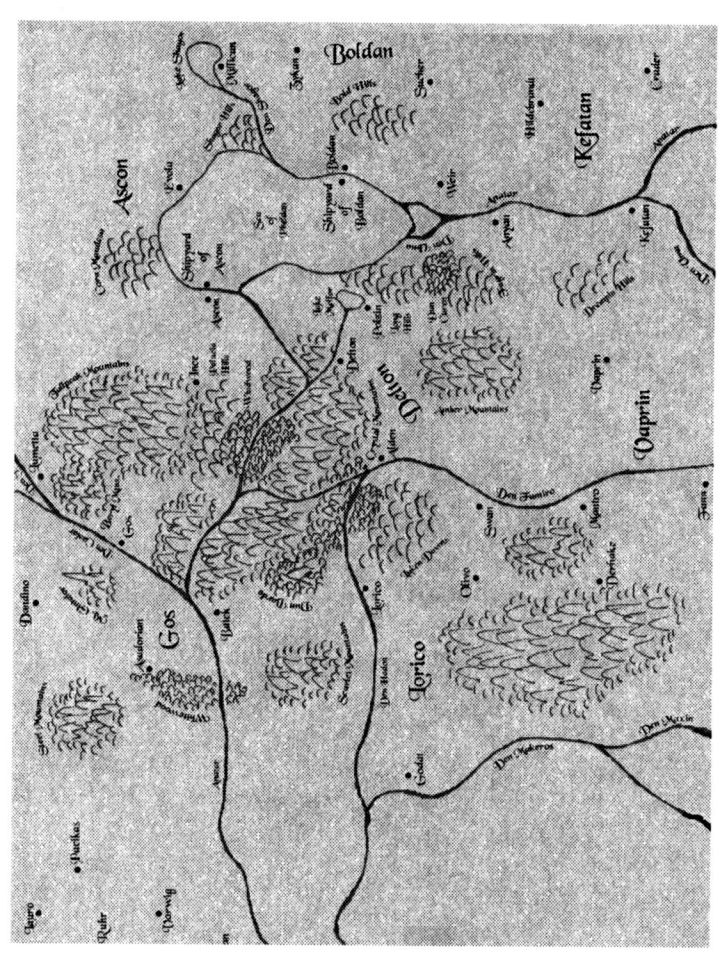

Milhavior - Northeast Quarter

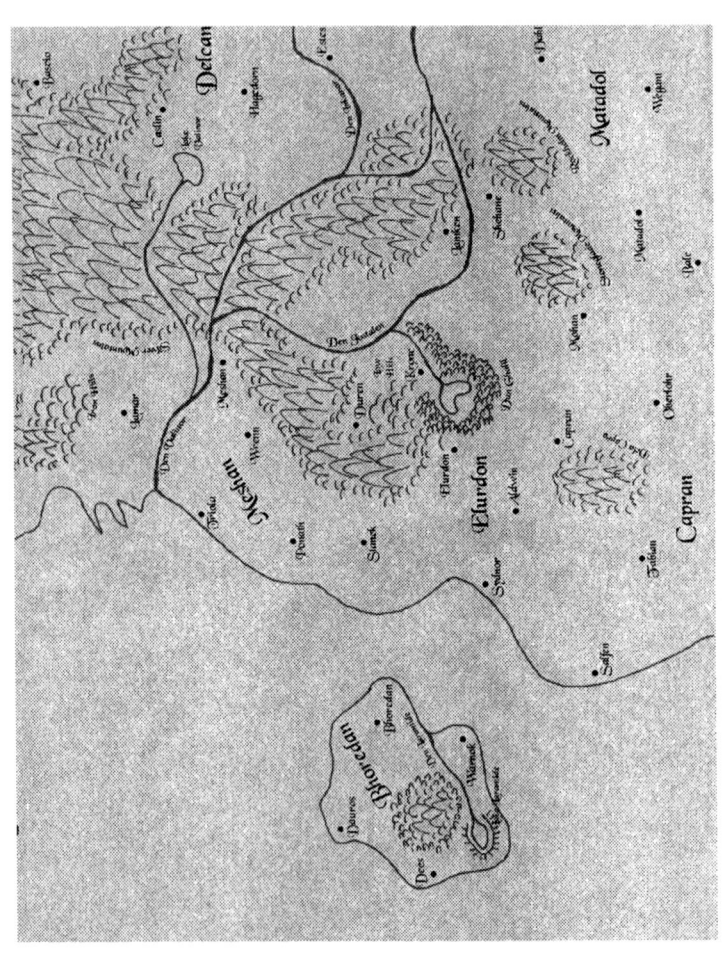

Milhavior - Southwest Quarter

Milhavior – Southeast Quarter

Prologue

During the Third Age of this world, a great war ensued in Mingenland of old. The Deathlord Thanatos came forth from his dark Realm into En Orilal, the Mortal Realm, promising power and immortality to all those who would serve him, knowing that if he could sway the balance there, it would be only a matter of time before the High Realm would fall to his dominion as well. In the barrens of Machaelon, north of Mingenland, he built a great tower, called in the Athorian tongue Chi Thanatos, Tower of Death, to be his seat of power in En Orilal.

The young races of Men and Dwarves were easily deceived by his promises, and many were swayed to his banner. The Deathlord began to muster his forces at Chi Thanatos, intent on sweeping all who defied him from the Mortal Realm. He knew, however, that to overcome, he would have to slay the Dawn King Elekar, Lord of the High Realm.

Therefore, he commissioned the Dwarves to forge Denaseskra, the Black Flame, a sword of unspeakable Evil. Forged of the black Elvinmetal, Crorkin, from which even the slightest scratch meant inescapable death, Thanatos believed that Denaseskra could bring death even to the Lord of the High Realm. Knowing that Elekar would come to face him in the Mortal Realm, the Deathlord prepared a trap at Chi Thanatos.

The Elves allied themselves with those mortals who refused to turn against the Dawn King, forming a great host which the *Annals of the Ancients* call the Alliance of the Free Kindreds. The Alliance chose three leaders, one to represent each of the races. For Men was chosen Ascon, a humble, yet worthy servant of Elekar. The Elves chose Joahin and made him Rasheth, or chief, of all Elves. The Dwarves took Graemmon Laksvard as their warlord.

For years, the Alliance waged a bloody campaign against Death's Legion, the combined forces of Men, Dwarves, Dark Elves, Kubruki, and other beasts of Darkness. Eventually, the Alliance's strength faltered. Death's Legion, joined by a host of Dragons, wrought havoc upon Mingenland, driving the Alliance to near-extinction.

Finally, as Thanatos predicted, Elekar did indeed come to lead his faithful against the Deathlord. But he was aware of the Deathlord's plans, and he was prepared. Though Elekar came in mortal form, the Legions of Thanatos could not stand before him. Even the mighty Dragons fled his wrath. But not all was as it seemed. As the Alliance drove Death's Legion back into Machaelon, to the very foot of Chi Thanatos, the Deathlord sprang his trap.

A great legion of Deathless, the soulless shells of mortals animated by the Shadow of Thanatos, surrounded the Alliance. Thanatos called for the surrender of his enemies, pledging that if the Dawn King gave himself up freely, he would spare the mortals. To the dismay of his followers, Elekar agreed and was taken into Chi Thanatos.

Many mortals despaired that the Lord of the High Realm would sacrifice himself and leave them unprotected against the vengeance of Thanatos, but Ascon remained with his King until

Elekar was taken into the Tower of Death. Ascon returned to his people and encouraged them to trust the wisdom of the Dawn King, but few now would listen.

The Dawn King was taken to a parapet and bound to the Black Altar. There, Thanatos drove Denaseskra through Elekar's heart and into the stone beneath until only the black hilt could be seen. As the blood drained from Elekar's body and death came, the Shadow of Thanatos fell across the world, smothering all in its grim embrace. Many then wept, for they believed Darkness would reign forever. How could Dawn come if its Light had been extinguished?

In the days following, Thanatos would come to the parapet where the body of Elekar remained pinned to the altar by the black blade of Denaseskra. He would mock Ascon from the balcony, gloating over the corpse of his foe, delighting in his victory, for there was none left who could stay his hand. On the fourth morning, the Deathlord ascended to the parapet, intending to send forth his Legion to destroy the Alliance, but was met by fear.

The Black Altar stood empty, but for the sword of power he had used to slay his enemy. The Dawn King had come in mortal form into En Orilal, but he was by nature immortal and no weapon made by mortal hands could slay him. Not only had he defied the bonds of death, but he had also transformed the sword. The blade had become pure Gloriod, which is called Silver-gold in the Common Tongue, the strongest and most powerful of all Elvinmetals, unbreakable by any amount of force.

Enraged, Thanatos pulled the sword from the altar and his hand was scorched by a white flame, for his dark power had been driven from the weapon, and the living fire of the Dawn had replaced it. In dread, the Deathlord threw the sword from the tower. As the weapon plunged to the ground below, burning with white fire, a great crack of thunder rent the air, and the sword vanished, as did the Shadow of Thanatos. Chi Thanatos crumbled in the light of the new dawn, ending the brief reign of the Deathlord in the Mortal Realm. Thanatos himself was banished once more into the Black Pits of Hál, the Death Realm.

The Dawn King returned for a little while among the people of Mingenland, and many followed him once more. And he divided the lands to the north and west of Machaelon and Mingenland among the race of Men, and he made those who had remained loyal to him through all tribulation the Kings and nobility of that land. And Ascon, most faithful, was given to be the High King over all. The forests of that land, Elekar gave to the Elves, for many wished to remain among the mortals to teach them the ways of the Dawn.

But to the creatures that served Thanatos, he gave only a curse: all beasts of Darkness were banned from the light of the sun on pain of death. Hearing this, the Lords of the Dwarves knelt before Elekar and begged his forgiveness for the evil which they had committed in forging Denaseskra. The Dawn King took pity on them, but would not absolve them of all blame. Instead, he placed a different curse upon them: that they would fear the light of the sun and dwell in the depths of the mountains. But their curse would be lifted one day, for Thanatos would return to the Mortal Realm, and Denaseskra would appear again in the hand of Ascon. From thenceforth the sword would be called Denasdervien, the Living Flame.

Near the end of the Third Age, Ascon and many of his people vanished from Milhavior, but before his brother Evola could take the throne, a Wizard of the Dawn King came to him and told him that he and his heirs could bear only the title of High Steward, for his brother's heir would return, though another would come before him to prepare the way, bearing the Living Flame, and by the hand of the Heir of Ascon would Thanatos be driven once more from the Mortal Realm.

I am Berephon, son of Runyan, Bard and Loremaster of Milhavior. I have stood beside the Bearer of the Flame of Elekar and have seen the prophecies fulfilled. This is his story. Hear it now and learn, for there is no Darkness that Light cannot pierce, no Death that Life cannot overcome.

Chapter 1

A furious wind blasted down upon the darkened landscape as lightning struck and thunderclaps echoed through the grim night skies. There would be no sailing for the ships lying in harbor at the Shipyard of Ilkatar, for none could survive such a rough main as the Western Sea was that night. Not even the great warships of Bhoredan, renowned as the mightiest vessels in all of Milhavior, could sail through that raging torrent.

Tempests as terrible as that were not common to the region, and the folk of the fishing villages spread along the coast of Ilkatar believed that they augured of ominous things, such as the Plague which ravaged the lands of Milhavior for nigh unto sixteen years. At one time, they had believed storms like these to be omens of pending doom from the sea-god, Heil. In later years, Heil and the other gods had been abandoned by all but a few of the Ilkatari. Most had embraced the teachings of the Analetri, the Sea Elves, who served the Dawn King, Elekar.

Even so, the coast-dwellers remained somewhat wary of the unnatural, and this weather was anything but natural. Whether or not the mysterious beliefs of the Elves held any truth mattered little: the winds of this storm did indeed bear tidings.

"Ach! Like the very Winds of Hál these be!"

The elderly man turned his greying face away from the window of his workplace in the Shipyard's kitchens and moved back to the small table at the center of the room.

Gwydnan was only a simple kitchenhand, though he could have been mistaken for the Shipyard's Master by the elegance of his raiment: a handsome, white tunic and black waistcoat, with sable trousers to match, and shiny, black leather boots, apparel not common to men of his lowly position. This, combined with his neatly-combed, snow-white locks—thinning though they were— and the chiseled wisdom of his face, made him appear more a stately gentleman than a hardened commoner.

He had been, at one time, a man of high position at the Shipyard. Only recently had he been assigned to work in the kitchens. Before the sudden change in status, he had served nearly twenty-six years at the docks as the Chief Dockmaster's assistant, having begun his employ at the Shipyard at a self-proclaimed age of sixty-three . . . though it was generally agreed that he was much older. He was, of course, greatly put out by his apparent demotion to kitchenhand, but there was nothing to be done about it, and he well understood that. There were other responsibilities attached to his change in position to which he was more suited than any of the rough hands at the docks.

Kanstanon, a lad of eleven summers, remained at the window watching the raging storm with curious, brown eyes. The child's hand-me-down tunic, also a muddy brown color, was a bit too large for his slight figure.

A tremendous thunderclap shattered the air, rattling the window pane and startling the boy. Several bright bolts of lightning split the sky, tracing jagged, blue lines across the boy's vision. Kanstanon backed away from the window and joined his master at the table, sliding into a chair across from Gwydnan.

"Master, what is Hál?" he asked. He was enthralled with tales of mysterious places and things, and the Winds of Hál sounded very mysterious to him.

The old man looked at the boy with a brow cocked.

Kanstanon believed his master often enjoyed satisfying his inquisitive mind, but he could never be sure, for Gwydnan always put on a weary frown when asked a question.

As the boy anticipated, Gwydnan grimaced and testily replied, "Come now, Kanstanon, have you learned nothing? Or have you slept through all your lessons?"

"Oh no, Master," Kanstanon quickly replied, thinking his master only playing at being vexed. Still, he had to be careful. "But you haven't never taught me nothing about Hál. I heard Master Roby and Master Tasic mention it a lot, but what they said didn't make any sense."

"You never mind what they were talking about. If either of them said anything about Hál, you can be certain it was well out of context," Gwydnan told the boy. "And, yes, I have taught you about it, though I may not have referred to it by that name. Tell me, what are the Three Spheres?"

"The Three Spheres make Ona Orilal, the Great Sphere of the World," Kanstanon answered with a proud grin . . . which promptly vanished when his master waived his reply.

"Yes, yes, that's very nice, but it is not what I asked you. Perhaps, I should rephrase my question. What are the *Realms* of the Three Spheres?"

Kanstanon knew that his master was truly perturbed now. He bit his lip thoughtfully, drilling through his lessons in his mind. Finally, when he believed he knew the desired answer, he put voice to his thoughts. "The First Sphere is Alaren Orilal, the High Realm, ruled by Elekar, the Dawn King. There, the Alara and other immortals of the Dawn dwell also."

Kanstanon glanced at his master, but Gwydnan's expression had not yet changed. He hoped that he had not left something out. He continued, this time thinking everything out very carefully. "The Second Sphere is En Orilal, the Mortal Realm. Here dwell the Free Kindreds: Men, Dwarves, Elves, and Saereni. The Elves are the only immortals among the Free

Kindreds, and the Saereni have not yet been revealed to the other Kindreds.

"Some beasts of Darkness also dwell here: Kubruki, Trolls, Dragons, Drolar, and Jaf." His brown eyes darted to his master again, and this time the elder was nodding his approval.

Elated by this, Kanstanon went on a bit more enthusiastically. "The Third Sphere is Maelen Orilal, the Under Realm, ruled by Machaelon, who is also called Thanatos, the Deathlord. There, the Dark Alara and other immortals and beasts of Darkness dwell.

"These Spheres combined form Ona Orilal, the Realm Complete," he ended.

Gwydnan gave Kanstanon a proud smile and pointed a finger at him, playfully poking the boy's nose. "The Third Sphere is the answer to your question, lad. 'Tis called Hál in my native tongue, and by most here on the mainland.

"You will need to remember that when you are come of age, lad, for someday En Orilal shall have to face the Winds of Hál, the Storm of Death's Legion, when the Black Gates of Maelen Orilal open and the Deathlord returns to this world."

Kanstanon now understood a little as to what the Winds of Hál were. The Great Prophecies of the Third Age told that Thanatos would come into En Orilal to conquer the Second Sphere, and that his Shadow would be as the winds of a great storm, sweeping over the lands of the Mortal Realm. Only the return of the Heir of Ascon, the lost High King, would hold any hope for the world in that day, for Elekar's prophecies told that only by Ascon's hand would Machaelon be defeated.

The stableboy was awed and more than a little frightened by the thought. But he abandoned his wonder and reached a hand towards his master as Gwydnan's outstretched arm dropped to the table. The old man leaned forward a little, as though under a weighty burden, every breath becoming more difficult. Soon, his breathing became normal again, and total silence fell.

"Are you all right, Master Gwydnan?" Kanstanon asked in alarm.

The man did not answer him, but straightened in his seat. He sat in complete silence, rubbing his chin with a gnarled and sinewy hand. One small lamp spilled a dim glow over the table, glinting in the man's unblinking eyes.

Though his gaze was focused in the direction of his ward, Kanstanon knew that the old man did not see him. Kanstanon was no more to him at that moment than a speck upon a wall.

The child sat there in bewilderment, watching his master. The glow of the lamp softened the man's features, driving the deep lines and shadows from his face. The longer Kanstanon stared, it seemed to him that age drained out of the old man's features. Gwydnan looked neither young nor old to the boy. He appeared the same, yet somehow different.

After a few minutes, Gwydnan's lids relaxed, all signs of his great age returning to him, heavier than before. A deep weariness fell upon him. He looked at Kanstanon and spoke. "Gather some food, lad. We shall have company this night."

The stableboy jumped up from his seat and hurried off to the pantries to do as he was told. He did not question his master, for he knew that Gwydnan had seen the visitor through a vision. He had suspected for many of his short years that there was more to Gwydnan than anyone knew, for he had witnessed many strange things in the presence of his master which to him seemed miraculous—sick horses suddenly becoming well, casks of flour that seemed never to empty—and he had often heard Gwydnan chanting quietly in a strange tongue in the privacy of his room.

Kanstanon nervously fumbled with honey-cakes and small loaves of bread—freshly baked that afternoon—sweet fruits and hunks of white cheese, and stuffed them into a basket. The boy hurried back to the front room, trembling with excitement.

When Kanstanon came back into the room, he saw his master sitting at the table, his right elbow propped on its hard surface, quietly staring at the kitchen's outer entrance as if expecting it to swing open at any moment. The boy's eyes slowly followed Gwydnan's gaze to the front door. A heavy silence, a nervous peace, blanketed the chamber.

All at once, a vortex of wind swept into the room as the door slammed open, and a man hobbled in, his dusty, grey cloak and white robes flapping in the gale. He swiftly shut the door behind himself, without the slightest effort, even with the force of the high wind blowing against him.

The visitor held in his right hand an oaken staff, and under his left arm, he bore a long, tin box. He carefully rested his rune-marked stave against the wall, then filled the seat which Kanstanon had only just vacated a few minutes before, setting the box on the table before the other man. The stranger drew back his travel-worn hood and smoothed out his flowing, white beard.

Kanstanon's eyes glided to the staff propped against the wall. The strange lettering etched around the head of the stick told him that this man was a Wizard, for his master had taught him the rune-letters of Holy Athor, a form used only by Wizards. The boy backed into a dim corner, fearful of coming nearer, his eyes locked onto the long-bearded stranger.

Gwydnan, however, regarded the newcomer in fond recognition. "It has been a long time, my friend, since you last sat in my presence."

The wanderer nodded slowly. "Aye, a long time, indeed."

The kitchenhand held the visitor's gaze in his own, the visionary light briefly returning to his eyes. "You have grown a little, Odyniec. When last we sat together it was as Master and Apprentice. Now, I no longer bear the staff, but you."

Kanstanon grew confused by his master's words. Master and Apprentice? Bearing the staff? The conversation that followed bewildered him all the more.

Gwydnan chuckled, settling back in his chair. "I remember my anger at being appointed such a young pupil. But I was hasty in my judgment. You have kept a pure heart through these last years and have nearly completed your time."

A light smile cracked Odyniec's aged features at the recollection. "Nay, Master, I am still the same rascal that you took under wing those many years ago! But now I am weary; the staff weighs heavily upon my heart. I long to return home to the Temple. I only hope that Zanyben shall call me back to take an apprentice soon."

"Aye, your time will come soon enough," the elder assured his old student. "Have patience, my friend. Even I am forced to wait for my final charge to be delivered."

The smile on Odyniec's lips faded. His grey eyes strayed to the box, then back to Gwydnan. He spoke again, his voice low. "Nay. The time has come, Gwydnan, old master. The time has come for the Bearer of the Flame to be revealed. That is my purpose here, as I am sure you knew before now."

The kitchenhand registered no surprise at his former student's declaration. "I thought as much. In our work, casual visits are few and far between. Very well, Odyniec, where is he? When shall he come?"

"You must give the box to a certain young man named Brendys," the Wizard responded. "He is the son of a local Horsemaster . . . from Shalkan, I believe."

Gwydnan's brow wrinkled in confusion. "Brendys? Of Shalkan? Are you certain of this?"

"Then you know of him?"

"Know of him? I know the boy all too well," Gwydnan replied. "He does not serve our King. He cannot use it. The Flame would destroy him should he try!"

"Brendys of Shalkan," Odyniec repeated evenly. "Fear not for his ignorance, Gwydnan. Fanos Pavo shall see to that. Your only worry is to deliver the Flame safely to its Bearer. The Winds of Hál are stirring!"

He paused before going on. "It has come to me that this Brendys shall be making a journey to Hagan Keep early next summer; you are to pass it on to him then . . . Fanos Pavo has so decreed. Do you know the words to say?"

"Aye," Gwydnan replied with a sigh. "I was the first to speak them long ago, was I not?"

"Good! Then all is in readiness."

Gwydnan slowly nodded, then motioned a hand towards his ward. "Kanstanon."

The boy was startled at the calling of his name, for his confusion had subsided a degree, and he had become deeply interested in the two elder men's conversation. Kanstanon froze when Odyniec glanced towards him and smiled a little.

The Wizard breathed deep the scent of freshly-baked bread and gave a deep sigh. "Ah, me! But I cannot stay for supper," he announced, bringing quick relief to the boy. "I must be fast on my way! Farewell, Gwydnan. May Fanos Pavo keep you and yours."

The bearded man rose to his feet, taking his staff in hand, and shoved open the door, a blast of cold wind gusting into the room once more. When the door was shut and the Wizard gone, Gwydnan arose from his chair and returned to his place at the window to watch the storm-wracked Sea.

"Put the basket on the table, Kanstanon, and come here... the time has come for you to learn who your master is."

Chapter 2

A cold blast of wind blew Brendys's thick, black hair to one side as he came out of the stable. He drew his hood over his head and walked on, heedless of the cold. He was tall and built extremely well for a youth of fifteen. His work had kept him from becoming lank and awkward like most lads his age.

He stopped, his arms crossed over his chest, and waited impatiently. Soon, his father came out of the stable, accompanied by Aden, a young street-urchin found by Brendyk on a trip to Elnisra, a town only a few miles east of Ahz-Kham.

Brendys's father was a man in his late thirties, with the raven-black hair and deep-blue eyes common to most Shalkanes. His worn features were those of a man who had seen many years of hard labor. He was a Horsemaster, and a rather prominent one in the Northwest Quarter. His trade and close friendship with Lord Dell of Racolis helped build him a reputation among the peoples of the Northwest Quarter, Man, Elf, or Dwarf. He was also greatly respected by most of the surrounding community, though many thought some of his habits strange.

Ordinarily, he and his son lived alone on the farmstead, with the exception of an old woman who kept house for them. However, Brendyk was notorious for taking in every tramp and urchin who begged a little money or food from him and teaching them some responsibility by making them earn their keep on the stead. Brendyk later found work in Ahz-Kham for most of them.

Presently, however, the workers' quarters were empty. All of his workhands had left long ago, tired of sharing their quarters with the rabble Brendyk dragged in. Even Aden had found a home and decent employ as a houseboy in Ahz-Kham.

Brendys, like the workhands, was also fast becoming weary of what most considered his father's overdeveloped sense of compassion. Not that he had anything against the poor wretches his father brought in—he had made friends of many, including Aden—but his privacy was constantly stripped away from him. The orphans most commonly taken in by his father never left him alone, no matter how much he grumbled, complained, or shouted at them. But he had been granted relief for a time. There had been no more vagrants or beggars living at the stead since Aden had left the Horsemaster's service two years before.

Brendys continued towards the main house when his father and Aden had caught up to him.

"Are you sure you don't want Brendys to take you home, Aden?" Brendyk asked the boy as they walked.

Aden shook his head with a grateful smile. "No need, Master Bren'yk. 'ee's gots work t' do, an' I've two legs o' me own t' carry me."

The Horsemaster slapped him on the back. "Very well, then. Farewell, boy. Again, you have been a great help to us. Thank your master for me."

Aden nodded in reply. "That I will, sir." He turned his face towards Brendys before leaving and said, "Will ye be comin' t' town t'night, Bren'ys?"

Brendys gave a nervous glance at his father, wishing that Aden had not said anything at that moment. Though he had little hope that his father was unaware of his visits to the *Green*

Meadow Inn, a particularly disreputable hostelry in Ahz-Kham, the subject was never broached. He quickly replied in hopes of belaying any suspicion. "Perhaps. I don't know yet. There's much to be done here, you know."

"If ye say so," Aden said with a shrug and a wink, a bright grin crossing his face. He raised a hand in farewell to Brendys and his father, then ran off down the road.

Brendyk turned to his son, a stern look on his face. "What was he talking about, Brendys? Were you going to meet with that Languedoc again? You know I don't like him. The filthy scoundrel is no good."

Brendys was relieved that his father had not guessed his true purpose for going into town, but he did not like his father's attitude about his friend, and he was not going to let it pass. "Languedoc is my friend, and I am not about to forfeit my friendship with him just because you don't happen to like him. He's not all bad."

"Hah!" Brendyk walked on, his back to Brendys. "Fetch some wood for the hearth. The weather's turning bad. It's going to be cold."

"Yes, Father," Brendys answered resignedly. Grudgingly obeying his father, Brendys trudged to the woodpile stacked beside the house. Once there, he began moving the top fagots, wet from the recent storm, and set them on the ground, then began gathering a few dry ones. He stopped when he heard his father calling to someone at the front porch. He moved to the edge of the house and peered around the corner.

"Hello there! Is there something I can help you with?" his father called, hurrying to the porch where a man was standing, one foot on the bottom step.

The small stranger was garbed in a grungy blue tunic and trousers, hidden to some degree by a threadbare cloak. He had the hood drawn far over his face, shadowing his features. Brendys could see the thin, bare legs of a child behind the man, but nothing more.

The traveler shoved his hood back, revealing a thin, unshaven face and a thick mat of dirty, blonde hair. His narrow eyes regarded the farmstead's owner with a cold gaze that sent shivers through Brendys's spine. Brendys thought the man looked somewhat like a weasel and not at all a pleasant sort.

"M'name's Brugnara," the stranger said in response to the Horsemaster. "Ye must be Master Bren'yk."

Brendyk nodded, and the man stated his business. "A feller in town told me ye 'uz lookin' for summun t' lend an 'elpin 'and wi' your stable. I knows a bit o' 'orses an' am in need o' some work. So . . . 'ere I be."

"Well, I am sorry but. . . ." Brendyk paused, taking in the man's bedraggled appearance. His voice gentled. "You look as though you have been traveling for some time."

Brendys slapped his forehead and hissed under his breath, "*Hál!*"

Brugnara wearily nodded his head. "Five days now, down from Nord'n in Fekamar."

"That long, eh?"

The traveler nodded again.

"Well, I *am* short-handed," Brendyk admitted, but he stopped before going on. Brendys realized that his father had, for the first time, noticed the child, who was now peering anxiously from behind the man.

He knew that his father would not turn away the stranger now, not when the boy was in such a pitiful condition. The child appeared as haggard as any common street-urchin. His wavy, amber locks, dangling to his shoulders in the back, were matted down with grime; his face and body were caked with mud and slime as well; and he was in desperate need of a healthy meal.

The boy shivered uncontrollably, for the cold wind of the coming winter blew strong and hard, and he was not attired for such weather—his feet and legs were bare, and he had as a covering only a ragged, patchwork tunic, for the little warmth it could provide. He was obviously ill as well.

"And who is this?" Brendyk asked. "Your son?"

"Aye, sir," the traveler replied, quickly jerking the child out from behind himself, holding him firmly before the Horsemaster.

Brendyk squatted down, giving the child a friendly smile. "Hello there, lad! And what might your name be?"

The boy did not answer him, but just stood silent, staring into Brendyk's face, shaking fearfully. The child's gaze gave Brendys more chills than the lad's father. Though his face was filled with fear—or terror, rather—his eyes were empty, void of all emotion, reminding Brendys of nothing less than the eyes of a corpse. He had never seen anything like it.

Brendys shook his head, shifting his attention back to the boy's father.

Brugnara gave the Horsemaster a sad look. "'is name be Willerth. Th' poor lad ain't spoke nary a word since 'is mama died six years 'go. 'ee 'uz only a wee tyke then."

Brendyk studied the boy's frightened face and shook his head in sympathy. "And so goes the Curse of Humanity! My own wife perished when my Brendys was but four, taken by the Plague."

The Horsemaster glanced at the boy's father. "I suppose it was the same with yours?"

Brugnara gave the Horsemaster an almost comically grave look. "Plague. Aye, sir, that 'uz it."

Young Willerth began to shake worse at his father's words, nearly losing his balance. Brendys cast a suspicious eye at Brugnara, but what exactly troubled him, he could not say.

Brendyk reached a hand out to steady the child, but Willerth jerked away, terrified. The Horsemaster rose to his feet with another sad shake of his head, then spoke to the boy's father again. "You begin work tomorrow. The wages are ten pence a week, housing and board provided."

"Thank'ee, sir. That be right kind o' ye."

Brendyk nodded in return, then continued speaking. "You will have every Fifthday off—you may then go into town if you feel the need to wet your palate. Just be sure that you are sober before you set foot on my property again. I do not hold to such draughts and will not tolerate their use or misuse on my property. I have had too many difficulties in the past."

Brugnara began working his hands nervously. "O' course, sir! Be there anythin' else, sir?"

The front door to the house suddenly opened, and Farida, Brendyk's houseservant, stepped out and came down the porch steps. She glared at Brugnara and his son for a moment, her fleshy face red, then turned to Brendyk.

"Master Brendyk!" she huffed. "You are taking these people in, aren't you?"

The Horsemaster started to reply, but Farida rambled on. "And with no consideration to me, at that! You put every scamp and rogue you take in to working in your stable, but who's to help me cook and clean for them?"

"We'll be no trouble a'tall, ma'am," Brugnara interjected.

"I do not remember speaking to you," the old woman replied, poking the small man in the chest, pushing him back a couple of steps.

Brendys noticed the corners of Willerth's mouth playing in a slight smile, but that stopped abruptly when the boy saw his father looking at him. The child's face then stiffened as he braced himself for a slap, which did not come at that time.

Farida returned into the house, still raving. "The workers' quarters! What a cleaning it will need. And linens. It will need fresh linens. I should think the old ones are rotted away by now!"

The door slammed shut, and Brendyk spoke to Brugnara. "I think she approves," he said with a slight shrug. He turned and called to Brendys.

Brendys stepped out in the open and called back. "You wanted me, Father?"

"Brendys, show our new stablehand and his son to their quarters."

Brugnara, rather roughly, shoved his son out ahead of himself. "C'mon, Willie, m'boy! We's gots ourselfs an 'ome now."

Willerth and his father met Brendys halfway to the stableyard. The new stablehand gave a quick introduction of himself and the boy. "I'm Brugnara, an' this be m'son, Willerth."

Brendys hesitantly shook the worker's crusted hand and gave his name in reply. "I'm Brendys."

He then reached out to take Willerth's hand, but the lad darted behind his father again.

"Ee's a shy 'un, 'ee is," the tramp spouted brightly.

"Oh! I'm sorry for frightening him," Brendys apologized. He turned and led Brugnara and Willerth to a small cabin near the stable.

The building seemed sturdy on the outside, but its durability was certainly less than it appeared. The entrance was raised almost a yard off the ground, and there were no steps leading up to it—they had broken and collapsed years before and had never been replaced. The roof leaked as well.

Brendys shook his head and sighed. "We haven't had any real help around here for a very long time. I'm afraid it is going to need a bit of work, especially after that rain a couple nights ago."

Brugnara shrugged. "I gots plen'y o' time. I'll fix'er up, a'right."

He pushed the door open. Inside, the cabin was a shambles—several floorboards rotted and sagging, broken furniture scattered about, a window missing. The walls and roof, however, were still extraordinarily strong, despite a small leak or two.

Brugnara reached down to lift Willerth through, but the boy cowered back out of his reach, almost falling down. Brugnara's eye twitched a little, but he kept a smile on his face. "C'mon now, Willie, lad! There ain't nothin' t' be a-feared o'."

Willerth, still shaking, clambered through the open doorway on his own, keeping a watchful eye on his father.

Brugnara quietly muttered something to himself, then said aloud, "Sometimes, I jest can't figger th' boy out."

Brendys dared a nervous chuckle. "Don't worry yourself about it. He will get used to this place sooner or later."

The stablehand only gave the youth a sharp glare.

Brendys nervously shrugged a little under the stare. "Uh, when you have gotten yourself settled in, I'll show you about the stead and what your duties will be."

Brendys took his leave from the man and walked back to the stable. He glanced back over his shoulder just in time to see the door of the workers' cabin slam shut. He shook his head, a doubtful look on his face. This man was going to be trouble.

The sound of approaching hooves brought him to a halt. He looked up and saw a blonde youth riding up to him on a bay stallion. The newcomer was slightly smaller than Brendys, though possibly a little older, and his face seemed fixed in a permanent sneer.

The rider called out as he approached the stable. "Hoy there, Bren! Haven't you finished here yet?"

Brendys waited for the visitor to reach him, then said wearily, "What is it, Languedoc?"

"Adina and the others are waiting for us at the *Green Meadow*. Saddle up or we will be late."

Brendys cursed, then sighed loudly. "I can't. Father just hired a new stablehand, and I have to show him around. Go on without me."

The other youth shook his head. "Adina is going to be very upset, not to mention...."

"I can't help it, Languedoc," Brendys replied with a shrug. Then he smiled. "Besides, I know Adina will forgive me."

"Perhaps right now," Languedoc admitted. "But not when you aren't there tonight."

Brendys placed his fists firmly on his hips. "And who says I'm not going to be there tonight?"

"Your father will find some excuse to keep you at home."

Brendys frowned. "I will think of something. Now get yourself gone before Father comes out and runs you off with a hayfork!"

Languedoc laughed. "Your father wouldn't run a horse-thief off with a hayfork!"

"But I might!" Brendys took a step towards the horse, but Languedoc turned his steed about and rode out of the farmstead, giving Brendys a backhanded wave.

Brendys went back about his work. He did not see Brugnara and Willerth again that day until he delivered their supper to the cabin that evening. Even then, Brugnara appeared at the door only long enough to take the food and say goodbye. The man seemed rather in a hurry to be rid of him, and Brendys returned to the main house wondering why.

Not long after he had his own supper, Brendys rode out to Ahz-Kham to dispel the cold specters of that morning's strange arrivals in the warm embrace of his lovely Adina.

* * * *

The next morning, Brendys arose from a troubled sleep, had a quick breakfast, then started out to the stable to look in on his old grey, Hedelbron, as he did every morning. When he entered the barn, he noticed Willerth standing outside one of the stalls, watching his father's new colt. Brendys paid no heed to the boy and went about his own business, continuing down the aisle of stalls. As he passed Willerth, his cloak brushed the boy.

Willerth suddenly snapped around, freezing for a moment, staring up at Brendys in fear. Just as suddenly, he dashed behind a stack of hay bales, peering around the corner as if to make sure that Brendys came no closer to him.

Brendys shook his head. He found himself pitying the boy. This was the first time he had seen such fear in a child.

"There's nothing to be afraid of, lad," he said, trying to coax the boy out from behind the bales. "I'm not going to hurt you."

Willerth did not move.

The deep fear in the boy's face, and even worse, his dead stare, unnerved Brendys. It was not natural. The youth stared intently at the boy for a moment, then knelt down on one knee.

"You're a strange one," he said. "I don't think I've met anyone quite like you before. What is it, Willerth? What is it that you are afraid of? You can tell me."

The boy bit his lip and lowered his eyes as if considering the youth's words, but then moved entirely out of sight and did not come out of hiding until Brendys had gone.

Brendys returned later in the morning to exercise the colt and again found Willerth watching Ekenes. The colt's head was thrust over the door of the stall, staring back at the boy, nostrils flaring. As Willerth slowly raised his hand towards the horse's head, Brendys quickened his step, thrusting a hand out to the boy. "Watch out! He's not clear broken."

Willerth jerked his hand back with a frightened glance at Brendys. He turned to run to the far end of the stable, but hesitated. His father was there, mucking out one of the far stalls. He spun back to face Brendys, his small chest visibly heaving in panic.

Brendys threw his hands up in front of him, palms outward, and slowly backed to the closer end of the barn, making room for the boy to leave without coming too near. "It's all right, Willerth. I didn't mean to frighten you. Ekenes isn't safe. He could hurt you very badly. You shouldn't try to touch him."

Willerth, still shaking fiercely, cast an uncertain glance at the colt, who had backed into his stall and was pawing at the hay on the floor. He looked again at Brendys, then turned back to the horse, his expression a mixture of fear and indecision, as though he were too afraid to stay, but also did not want to leave the stable.

"*Willie!*"

The boy snapped his head around to stare at his father, jogging towards him from the other end of the stable. The man's thin face was set in a hard scowl. Willerth darted out the open barn door, leaving behind a bewildered Brendys and an angry father.

Brugnara turned his sharp gaze on Brendys. "'ee 'uzn't doin' nothin'."

"I didn't think he was," Brendys replied, shaking his head in confusion. "Ekenes isn't completely broken. I didn't want Willerth getting hurt."

Brugnara's scowl deepened. "I kin look after me own son."

"Aye, I can see that," Brendys replied, his voice heavy with sarcasm. He was becoming quickly annoyed with the vagrant's attitude.

Brugnara held back a harsh reply, but glared darkly at Brendys. The small man threw a glance in the direction Willerth had run, then turned his back on Brendys and returned to his work.

Brendys stared after him for a moment, then went about his own task, shaking his head in disbelief.

He did not see Willerth again until after he had finished exercising the colt. When he brought the colt back to the barn, he noticed Willerth standing outside Hedelbron's stall at the far end of the stable. Brugnara was nowhere to be seen.

Brendys hesitated outside the colt's stall, his eyes on Willerth. He thought he could see the boy's lips moving, but he was not sure at that distance. Slowly, the boy lifted his hand to

Hedelbron's muzzle, but only barely touched the old grey's nose before jerking his hand away and taking a step backwards. Hedelbron stretched his head out towards Willerth, but the boy remained just out of reach.

Just out of reach, Brendys thought to himself. *A fitting description of the boy.*

The youth took Ekenes into his stall and removed the saddle. While brushing down the colt, he heard the barn door open and the sound of Brugnara's rough, tenor voice.

"Willie! What'd I tell 'ee? Stay out o' 'ere, I said."

The boy did not reply, but Brendys could hear the slap of his bare feet against the floorboards of the stable as he ran towards the barn door. The footsteps stopped abruptly as they neared Ekenes' stall. Brendys heard a muffled yelp and the sound of something dropping to the floor.

"Ye stay 'way from 'ere and 'way from them people, or ye'll gets worse 'un that!"

Brendys stepped out of Ekenes' stall in time to see Willerth disappearing from the stable.

Brugnara turned to face him, wearing an expression of mixed fear and anger. The anger quickly melted away, but a hint of fear remained. "I-I di'in't want 'im 'urtin' 'imself."

Brendys clenched his jaw and fixed a harsh glare on the small man, fighting down the urge to give him a piece of his mind. After a moment, he strode out of the stable, past Brugnara, on his way to the main house. When he reached the worker's quarters, he paused, looking towards the shadowed doorway.

The door was open, but the angle of the sun cast a deep shadow upon the entrance. Still, Brendys could see Willerth sitting on the floor just within, his knees pulled up to his chest, arms wrapped around his legs. His chin rested on his bare knees. The child's face was streaked with tears, but though he stared directly at Brendys, the youth was sure Willerth did not see him.

Brendys was again struck by the emptiness of the boy's eyes. This was not the first battered child that had been brought to the farmstead, but none had ever shown the utter terror, the completely broken spirit, that Willerth had in less than twenty-four hours.

He felt a sudden chill run down his spine and glanced back over his shoulder to find Brugnara standing just outside the stable, staring coldly in his direction. Brendys briefly returned the man's glare before continuing on to the house.

Disturbed and a little angry over the miserable progression of the day, he stomped up the porch steps and into the house, closing the door behind him a bit more loudly than he intended. His father was sitting in his favorite chair in the front room, staring sadly at a portrait of Brendys's mother, Danel. Brendyk looked up when his son entered the house.

"Brendys?" the Horsemaster said, slowly rising to his feet, a look of concern in his eyes. "You look upset. What's wrong? You didn't yell at the boy, did you?"

Brendys looked oddly at his father. "Why would I do that?"

Brendyk shrugged. "You hadn't exactly been kind to the last few waifs we took in."

"That's not it," Brendys replied, shaking his head. "If anything, I'm worried about him."

The Horsemaster raised a brow. "Are you well? This doesn't sound at all like you. Brugnara and his son have been here less than two days. You don't even know them, yet you are worried about the boy?"

Brendys avoided his father's gaze. "I don't know. There's something . . . *wrong* . . . about Willerth."

"I know what you mean," Brendyk replied in a quiet voice.

Brendys looked at his father. The man's gaze seemed distant.

Brendyk sat back down. "I tried three times to speak to the boy today, and he ran away each time. Twice, he did something very strange. He. . . ."

The man hesitated, then shook his head. "Nay, it is nothing, I'm sure. The only person he doesn't seem utterly terrified of is Farida. She was able to coax him to the kitchen for a little snack, but as soon as I entered the room, he ran."

"She is not the only one," Brendys replied. "Willerth is not afraid of the horses either. He tried to touch Ekenes this morning."

Brendyk started in alarm, but his son waved him back down.

"I stopped him in time," Brendys said quickly. "But then Brugnara chewed me out for scaring Willerth out of the stable."

He shook his head in confusion. "Then this afternoon, he hit Willerth for coming back and threatened him with worse if he came to the stable again or if he spoke to us."

His father's expression hardened and his blue eyes narrowed. "You saw this?"

Avoiding the man's gaze, Brendys sighed and shook his head. "Nay. I was brushing down the colt. They were out of my sight, but that's what it sounded like to me."

Brendyk frowned. "But you did not see him strike the boy?"

"No, sir," Brendys replied quietly.

"Then you cannot say for certain that is what happened?"

Brendys silently shook his head.

The Horsemaster sighed. "Then there is nothing I can do. You know that without evidence, my hands are tied."

Brendys grimaced. "Would you do anything even if you had evidence?"

A hurt look crossed over his father's face.

Without another word, Brendys turned to go up to his room.

Before he could start up the stairs, his father spoke again. "Brendys, for what it is worth to you, I am proud of you for the care you have shown, but I don't want you getting involved with those two. Let me deal with this in my way."

Brendys continued up the steps without looking back.

That night, Brendys sat at the small table in the library which he used as a desk, his ragged journal open before him. He chewed his lip thoughtfully, staring at the blank page before him. Slowly, he picked up his quill, inked it, then began scribbling down his thoughts.

*I witnessed something today which troubles me, but I don't know why. This isn't the first time I have seen this happen, but for some reason I cannot get it out of my mind. Father is right. It is none of my concern. I don't even know the boy. But there is something unusual, **unnatural**, about Willerth. I don't know. I am just not sure I **can** let it go.*

Brendys put his quill aside and stared at the entry, waiting for the ink to dry. After a few minutes, he closed his journal, blew out the lamp on the desk, then went to his room.

Chapter 3

Brendyk stood on the porch, staring across to the worker's cabin by the stable. Over the last few days, the weather had become colder as winter began to settle in. Small icicles had formed on the eaves of the buildings, and small puddles had frozen over.

The Horsemaster was dressed in a tunic and trousers, with no overcoat or cloak to protect him against the frigid morning air, but he did not notice. His attention was focused elsewhere. He had seen Brugnara head towards the stable several minutes earlier. Shortly thereafter, Willerth sneaked out of the worker's quarters and went to the barn, checking carefully to make sure no one saw him before entering. Despite the freezing temperatures, the boy was still clad in only his makeshift tunic.

He shook his head, frowning. Brugnara had clearly not even begun repairs to the cabin. The windows were still missing, the roof still leaked, and the steps had not been replaced. He was sure the interior was in much the same condition. Brugnara might be outfitted for cold weather, but the boy certainly was not. The repairs had to be done.

He heard the front door open behind him and someone step out onto the porch. After a moment, he turned to face his houseservant. "Farida, would you fetch. . . ?"

He stopped midway through his sentence, his gaze dropping to the basket in the old woman's hands. In it was a bundle of children's clothing suitable for winter weather. He broke into a smile. "Farida, how is it you always know my mind before I do?"

"That is what your father, bless his soul, hired me to do when you were but a wee thing," the maidservant replied brusquely.

It was true. She had been a second mother to him as a child, seeing to his needs as if he were her own. After he married Danel, she took the role of midwife and helped deliver Brendys into the world. And later, when Danel died, she continued to care for father and son. After all those years, it was no wonder that she knew his mind so well.

Brendyk took the basket by the handle, then leaned forward and kissed Farida on the cheek. "Nonetheless, I would be lost without you."

The old woman gave a flattered blush, but replied abruptly, "Oh, begone with you. Such nonsense!"

Brendyk smiled again, then turned and went down the porch steps. He walked across the yard to the barn. As he entered the stable, he found Brugnara cleaning Fines' stall. Brendys had the colt out for his morning exercise. He glanced to his right and noticed Willerth hiding behind the saddle rack.

He cleared his throat, calling Brugnara's attention to himself.

The smaller man turned quickly at the sound. "Oh, Master Bren'yk! What kin I do ye?"

"I thought the boy could use these," Brendyk replied, holding the basket out to Brugnara. "Brendys will certainly never use them again."

Brugnara rejected the gift with a shake of his head. "We nae wants chari'y, Master Bren'yk."

Brendyk kept his unblinking gaze firmly fixed on Brugnara's, a gentle smile coming across his lips. "Think of it as additional compensation for your valued labor. I insist."

The stablehand shifted uncomfortably under his employer's steady gaze, but took the basket. "Uh, o' course . . . I'll gi' 'em t' Willie right 'way."

Brendyk's expression did not change. "Certainly. Why don't you call him here?"

"I-I'm nae sure where 'ee be," Brugnara stammered in reply.

"Why, I believe he's hiding behind the saddle rack," the Horsemaster replied, his blue eyes never leaving Brugnara's face.

Brugnara's startled gaze turned to his son. His face reddened and his eyes narrowed in anger. "Willie, come 'ere . . . now!"

The child slowly came out from behind the rack and inched his way towards the two men, visibly shaking, his face a mask of terror. Tears streamed down his face, but he made no sound. Willerth's unwashed skin held a faintly bluish tint, causing Brendyk's heart to flutter in fear. He may have come too late. It was clear the boy was freezing to death. He calmed a little when he could see no sign of serious frostbite.

"Boy, I warned 'ee not t' come 'ere!" Brugnara snapped, causing his son to cower back. The blood suddenly drained from his face, leaving his skin pallid. He turned back to his employer, fear entering his own eyes. "I-I jes' don't want 'im 'urtin' 'imself, like I told yer son."

The only change in expression Brendyk allowed himself to show was a slight tightening around his eyes. His gentle smile remained. "Aye, Brendys mentioned something about that."

Brugnara's thin face paled another degree.

"I certainly understand your fears," Brendyk continued. He turned his gaze towards Willerth. "It isn't safe for him to be here without a chaperone."

He was not sure whether the boy understood his message or not, but he was certain Brugnara got the point. He turned back towards Willerth's father. "I believe you have something for the boy?"

Brugnara stammered for a moment, then looked down at the basket in his hands. "Oh . . . oh, o' course. 'Ere, Willie, Master Bren'yk brought these 'ere clothes fer ye."

The child cautiously stepped forward and took the basket from his father. He gently ran his fingers across the heavy trousers, quilted tunic, and warm, wool cloak lumped together at the top of the stack. He looked up at the Horsemaster, cocking his head curiously.

Brendyk could see that fear and distrust had not left him, but there was also a sparkle of wonder in his eyes. His smile broadened as he gazed down at the child. "You look cold. Perhaps you should go put those clothes on. I think you will find everything you need in there."

Willerth glanced down at the basket, then at his father, and ran from the stable, protectively hugging the basket to his body.

Brendyk started to follow him, but paused and turned back to Brugnara. "When you are finished here, hitch the wagon and go into town. Pick up anything you will need to finish the repairs on the worker's cabin. Use my name . . . the merchants will give you whatever you need. I will settle the debts when next I go into town."

His voice evened. "I want the repairs done by tomorrow evening. Brendys will see to the horses until then."

"Aye, sir."

As Brendyk turned his back on the man and walked back to the stables, a satisfied grin spread across his face. He was sure he had put enough fear into Brugnara to keep the boy safe for a good while.

When he neared the worker's cabin, he saw Willerth jump down from the doorway, attired in his warm new clothes, boots, and cloak, and run towards the smaller of the pastures where Brendys was riding Ekenes. Brendyk watched in growing curiosity as the boy clambered over the fence and dashed to the old fallen tree to watch Brendys and the colt. With a shrug, he returned to the house.

* * * *

Brendys grinned in triumph as he guided Ekenes around the pasture. This was the first morning he had not had any difficulty with the colt. His work was almost done.

As he circled around to head back to the stable, he saw Willerth sitting on the old fallen tree near the fence. The boy's hair drooped on either side of his face as he stared down at himself, smoothing his fingers across the quilted tunic he wore. Brendys immediately recognized the clothes as those that he had worn at Willerth's age. They were a little large on the boy, but he was sure the warmth they provided was more than enough to delight the child on this morning.

The youth urged the colt towards the log. He stopped a few yards from the tree, not wanting to frighten the boy away. "Good morning, Willerth. I'm guessing my father gave you the clothes."

When Willerth looked up at him, he almost gasped in surprise. There was no fear in the boy's face. Beaming, Willerth responded to his comment with an excited nod. His eyes fell back to the clothes he wore, and he drew the cloak around himself, reveling in the warmth.

Brendys gave the boy an encouraging smile. "A little large perhaps, but they look good on you."

Willerth's head snapped up suddenly, his grin replaced by the fear which Brendys had become accustomed to seeing.

Brendys's own smile vanished, and he slowly dismounted. He squatted on the ground so that he had to look up at the boy, hoping to make himself less intimidating. "What is the matter, Willerth? What are you afraid of? I don't want to hurt you."

A spark of hope rose within Brendys. Though the boy did not answer, he also had not run away as he usually did. He decided to press a little further. "If you tell me what you are afraid of, I might be able to help you."

The fear in Willerth's eyes lessened, but did not leave entirely. After a moment of hesitation, the boy slid off the tree trunk and slowly took a step forward, stopped, then took a second step. He paused again, his gaze steady upon Brendys.

"It's all right, Willerth," Brendys said gently. "Take your time. I'm not going anywhere."

The boy stared for a moment longer, without word or movement, as though an invisible barrier had come between him and the rest of the world. Suddenly bursting into tears, he turned and ran for the fence.

Brendys watched the boy in complete confusion. He had seen Willerth do many odd things in the past few days, but this was by far the strangest. He watched Willerth until the boy had disappeared from view, then remounted. He returned the colt to his stall, then went about the rest of his chores, all the time pondering Willerth's behavior.

Brendys kept an open eye out for Willerth while he worked, but the boy did not show himself again for a long while. When he was finished, Brendys headed back to the house. As he neared the porch, he heard the sound of hoofbeats behind him and a familiar voice calling to him. "Hoy there, Bren!"

Brendys rolled his eyes, then turned around. "What do you want, Languedoc?"

"Are you joining us at the *'Meadow* this afternoon, or not?" Languedoc replied with a casual air.

Brendys sighed. "I can't. I have too much work to do. Really, Languedoc, some of us actually have to work. You know I can't get away at this time of the day, so why do you keep asking me?"

"It never hurts to try," Languedoc said in return, then added with a half-mocking tone, "If you would rather stay home and play with the mutt instead of Adina, I suppose that is your business."

Brendys gave him a questioning look, then realized that his friend's gaze was not directed at him, but rather behind him. He glanced back over his shoulder and saw Willerth standing a few feet behind him, hidden partly by the porch.

"Willerth!" he said in surprise, turning to face the boy.

The boy made a startled noise and opened his mouth as if to say something. Languedoc laughed at the boy's shocked expression, and Willerth dashed off in tears.

Brendys called after Willerth, but the boy did not stop until he was safely inside the workers' quarters.

Brendys angrily spun around to face his friend. "Blast it all, Languedoc! What did you do that for?"

"Calm down, Bren," the other youth said, trying to stifle another laugh. "I am sorry if I hurt the little mongrel's feelings. Now, are you coming or not?"

"I am not," Brendys gritted back.

"Tonight then?"

Brendys stared at his friend, fighting back a bitter reply. After a moment, he turned away and started to the house again, looking back only when he heard the trotting hooves of Languedoc's horse leaving the farmstead. He quietly spit out a curse at the older youth's back, then continued on.

Still angry at Languedoc, Brendys did not leave the house that night.

* * * *

The afternoon sun was high, but the air was becoming colder as Brendyk walked from the house toward the workers' quarters. He knew it would not be long before the first of the winter storms blew in. As he neared the cabin, he could see that the windows had been replaced and crude steps built at the doorway. He sighed. It was not perfect, but better than nothing.

The Horsemaster stepped up to the open door and peered in. Brugnara was cleaning out the chimney and hearth. "Very good, it's coming along nicely."

Brugnara pulled his head out of the fireplace and looked at his employer. Despite the cold, he was sweating, perspiration turning the soot on his face to grime. He coughed once, then responded. "Aye. Be done soon."

Brendyk gave a quick nod. "There is firewood beside the house. Do not hesitate to use it. The winter storms can be rough here."

"Aye, sir." Brugnara went back to work without another word.

Brendyk continued to the stable. He had not seen Willerth yet that day, though he had also not expected the boy to be anywhere near the cabin while his father was working there, despite the apparent gentling of Brugnara's hand. When he was a few paces from the barn door, Brendys stepped out of the stable.

"Brendys, have you seen the boy?" the Horsemaster quietly asked his son.

The youth nodded, then motioned to the stable with his head. "He's inside."

Brendyk sighed. "He should not come here without one of us."

"He isn't hurting anything, Father," Brendys said in the boy's defense. "He touched Hedelbron once, and that scared him so much he hasn't gotten that close since."

"I am not worried about the horses, Brendys," Brendyk replied. "It isn't safe for him to be here."

The Horsemaster's son gave him a surprised look. "Then you believe me?"

Brendyk glanced back towards the workers' quarters. "I never doubted you, Brendys. I have never before regretted the decision to take someone in, but Brugnara disturbs me. I felt something . . . *dark* . . . about him when he first arrived."

"Then why did you hire him in the first place?"

Brendyk's eyes snapped back to his son. "Do you need to ask that?"

The youth's gaze dropped, and he shook his head. "Nay."

"It has been a week," Brendyk continued. "Would you have me send them away now?"

Again, Brendys shook his head. "Nay. It wouldn't be fair to Willerth."

Brendyk allowed a smile. Before his eyes, his son was becoming a man. The thought brought with it a tinge of sadness, but the pride he felt overshadowed all else. He laid his hands on his son's strong shoulders. "As I told you before, your concern is admirable . . . it shows that you are growing. But what I said still stands. Do not get involved."

"I think it is a little too late for that," Brendys replied dryly.

"What do you mean?"

Brendys looked his father in the face. "Yesterday, Willerth came out to the west pasture while I was exercising Ekenes."

"Aye, I saw him," Brendyk replied. "But you have already told me the boy likes to watch the horses."

Brendys nodded. "Aye, that's true. But yesterday, he didn't even look at the colt. He just sat on that old tree, preening. I think he went out there to show off the clothes you gave him."

Brendyk wrinkled his brow. "To *you?* They were your clothes to begin with . . . he knew that."

Brendys shrugged and shook his head. "I don't know. I . . . I spoke to him, tried to find out why he is so afraid."

The Horsemaster's gaze turned disapproving. "Brendys. . . ."

"Wait," the youth interrupted. "He started to come to me, Father! Then he just stopped, like . . . like he *couldn't* come any closer."

"Go on," Brendyk said with a slow nod.

His son shrugged again. "Then he ran away, crying. And this morning, he was already in the stable, outside Hedelbron's stall, when I got here. Only he wasn't looking at Hedelbron . . . he was watching the door, like he was waiting. He didn't run or try to hide.

"When I took Ekenes out, he followed and watched us from the tree as usual. I didn't try to speak to him again. I didn't want to frighten him away. Then, when I brought the colt back, he sneaked in behind and went back to Hedelbron's stall. He has been there for the last couple of hours . . . watching *me!*"

Brendyk rubbed his chin thoughtfully, looking past his son. He wondered whether the boy was, in his own way, warming up to Brendys because Brendys was not much more than a boy himself. He shifted his gaze back to Brendys, placing one hand on his son's shoulder. "You did right by not pressing him today. If you want to help, make yourself available, but let the boy come to *you*. Do not force the issue. Do you understand?"

Brendys nodded in reply.

"Good. Now, go on back to the house."

"Aye, sir."

As his son walked away, Brendyk entered the stable, leaving the barn door open wide. He found Willerth exactly where Brendys said he would, standing outside the Hedelbron's stall. The boy's lips were moving rapidly in a voiceless, one-sided conversation with the old horse.

Brendyk shook his head, then called out to Willerth. "Boy!"

Willerth spun to face the Horsemaster, his sunken eyes wide in fear.

"Your father is nearly done with his work on the cabin," Brendyk said, keeping his gaze fixed on the boy's face. "I don't think he will be pleased to find you here."

Willerth chewed his lip in consideration, then glanced towards the open door.

Brendyk motioned to the door. "Go on, boy. Your father will not learn of this from me."

Willerth threw a quick look at the Horsemaster, then dashed out of the stable.

Brendyk ran a hand through his short, black hair and sighed. It had only been a week since the boy and his father had come to the farmstead, but it was beginning to feel like years.

* * * *

Brendys did as his father told him. Several days passed, but he did not try again to draw Willerth out. Every morning, unless Brugnara was present, he would give the boy a smile and a friendly greeting, but otherwise go about his own business. Willerth reciprocated by following him out to the pasture to watch him exercise the colt.

Brendys started out of the house, heading for the stable, attired in his heavy winter clothing for the day's work around the barn. The night before had seen the first heavy snow of the winter. The morning sun was yet low in the east, glimmering orange on the white snow. The breeze bit, causing the youth to pull his worn cloak closer.

Every morning, he had entered the stable to find Willerth standing one stall nearer to the colt's, waiting for his arrival, but he was still surprised when he opened the door to find the boy standing only a few feet from Ekenes' stall. The boy wore an expression of mixed fear and anticipation.

Brendys paused in the doorway, a plan forming in his mind. He cast a smile in Willerth's direction, then shifted his gaze to the far end of the barn. "Actually, I was going to see to Hedelbron before I take the colt out."

He glanced back at Willerth and saw a hint of disappointment on the boy's face, but the boy moved to the other side of Ekenes' stall, allowing Brendys to walk to the opposite end of the stable without passing too close. Without another moment's hesitation, Brendys went to Hedelbron's stall and brought the old grey out, walking him towards the door. Willerth backed as far away as he could in the tight confines at that end of the barn as Brendys went to the saddle rack to retrieve his old, battered saddle.

Tossing the saddle on Hedelbron's back, Brendys tightened the girth and slipped the bridle over the horse's head. He led the old grey into the stableyard, then shortened the stirrups as far as he could. He gave Hedelbron a pat on the neck and muttered to the horse, "You'll behave, won't you?"

The horse snorted and turned his head back to give Brendys a dull stare.

Carefully keeping his eyes on the horse, Brendys said a little more loudly, "Willerth, I could teach you how to ride, you know—if you want me to, that is."

There was no answer. He began to lose hope in his plan. He had thought that the boy might have been ready to open up a little, but it was beginning to appear that his supposition was premature.

Brendys sighed and rubbed Hedelbron's muzzle. "I guess I was wrong, old boy."

"W-would'ee really, Master Bren'ys?"

Brendys looked down, startled by the small, timid voice. Willerth stood just within hand's reach, staring up at him. Though a small amount of fear remained in the boy's face, Brendys saw something in those grey eyes that he had never seen before . . . the sparkle of life.

"Would'ee really teach me t' ride a 'orse?" the boy asked again.

A surprised smile gradually crossed Brendys's face. "Of course, if that's what you want."

Willerth turned his gaze to Hedelbron. "I likes 'orses. Papa 'ad 'un, but 'ee 'ad t' sell 'er."

"That's too bad. I've had Hedelbron for a long time," Brendys said, rubbing the horse's flank. "You can pet him, if you like. He won't hurt you. He likes it."

The boy wrinkled his brow. "'Ee does?"

"Aye," Brendys replied. "Go ahead."

Willerth slowly stepped towards Hedelbron and reached his hand out, gently pressing his palm against the old grey's side. He left his hand there for a moment, staring strangely at the horse, then slowly stepped back again.

Brendys watched the display in growing bewilderment. "You look like you have never even pet a dog before."

Willerth bowed his head and muttered something that Brendys could not hear.

"What was that?" Brendys asked.

"Ne'er 'ad a dog," Willerth said in a slightly louder voice.

"Oh," Brendys replied. He was sure that was not what the boy had said first, but he did not press the issue. He gave a sympathetic shrug. "I suppose not. Well, I guess we should get started."

He reached down to help Willerth into the saddle, but the boy suddenly fell back out of reach, wrapping his arms tightly around himself, shaking in terror. Brendys sighed and put his hands on his hips. "If you want me to teach you how to ride, Willerth, you are going to have to trust me."

The boy did not move.

Brendys glanced at Hedelbron, then turned his gaze back to the boy. Kneeling down beside the horse, he cupped his hands in front of himself, near the ground. "All right, how about this. You put your foot in my hands, and I'll boost you into the saddle. Will that work?"

Willerth's gaze darted between the youth's cupped hands and the horse. After a moment, he nodded, then slowly rose to his feet. He lifted his right foot, but Brendys stopped him.

"No, the other foot," the youth said with a smile. "You don't want to be riding him backwards, do you?"

Willerth blushed and put his left foot in Brendys's hands.

Brendys could feel the boy trembling at the touch, but Willerth did not back away again. He looked up at the boy. "All right, when I lift you up, swing your other leg over Hedelbron's back. Are you ready?"

The boy gave a quick nod, and Brendys lifted him up.

Brendys led Hedelbron around the stableyard several times to let Willerth get used to the movement of the horse's back as he walked. He glanced up at the boy and received another surprise. The beginnings of a smile were tugging at Willerth's lips, soon blooming into a bright grin.

Brendys patiently showed the boy how to hold the reins, how to tell the horse when to speed up or slow down, how to guide his head. After a couple of hours, Willerth was riding Hedelbron in circles around Brendys as if he had been born in the saddle, though Brendys knew it was partly Hedelbron. The horse had aided in the training of many riders and knew what was expected of him.

Brendys let the boy ride on for a few more minutes, then grabbed Hedelbron's bridle and brought the old horse to a halt.

"I have to work the colt now," he told Willerth. "But you are welcome to come along. I suppose you could use some more practice yourself."

Then he added, patting the grey's shoulder, "And old Hedelbron could do with a bit more exercise, too."

Willerth beamed at the invitation.

Hedelbron swung his head around, looking at Brendys with tired, brown eyes, and snorted, then lowered his head and loped to the pasture fence, where he stood, waiting patiently for Brendys.

Brendys returned to the stable and saddled the colt. He gave Ekenes an uncertain frown. He had not given Brendys any trouble for the last few days, but this was the first time he had been exercised with another horse. He mounted carefully and started out to the field. Willerth rode beside him, an excited grin brightening the boy's dirty, frail features.

Within the fenced pasture, Brendys turned his head towards Willerth. "We'll have to take it slow—the ground is icy and the horses might slip and hurt themselves."

The moment Brendys finished speaking, as though understanding the youth's words and not liking them at all, Ekenes bucked once, tearing the reins from his rider's unprepared hands. The colt swerved away from Hedelbron, sending snow flying from beneath his hooves as he happily crow-hopped straight for the fence at the other side of the field.

Brendys frantically grabbed for the reins—*The bloody idiot is going to jump! Better to make him fall here than at the fence.* In desperation, the youth heaved at the right rein with both hands, but Ekenes recovered, turning until he faced the direction from which he had come. The colt was not discouraged; he bolted back towards Willerth and the surprised grey.

Willerth had his hands full with a snorting Hedelbron, who was now trying to dodge out of the colt's intended path. The boy managed to pull the grey around in a small circle, and then—with Ekenes only a few strides away and wavering, not knowing which way to duck around the obstacle—Willerth shouted and drove his heels as hard as he could into his mount, almost directly at the runaway. The boy squeezed his eyes shut and held on tightly to Hedelbron's mane.

Ekenes skidded on the slick earth and half-reared, finally throwing Brendys from his back. The colt recovered quickly, standing innocently as if nothing had happened, his steaming breath the only sign of his activity.

Hedelbron trotted up to Ekenes, neighing in angered reproach and nipping at the colt. Willerth's face was buried in the grey's mane, his eyes still squeezed tightly shut. Hearing Brendys groan, he lifted his head, then frantically tumbled down off Hedelbron's back, rushing to Brendys's side. "Are you a'right, Master Bren'ys? Are ye 'urt a'tall?"

Brendys shook his head, glaring at the colt. "Nay, just my pride."

Brendys climbed to his feet and turned to the boy, "Come on, let's get you back up. Now, I shall *have* to ride this idiot of a beast some more."

The remainder of the workout contained no more surprises; twenty minutes later, they dismounted. Brendys took hold of Ekenes' reins, and Willerth grabbed Hedelbron's, and they walked the horses to the stable, not returning them to their stalls until they were dry and cool under the old, hairy blankets that Brendys had left ready. Brendys let Willerth brush down Hedelbron, or at least as much as the boy could reach, and only then, Brendys explained to Willerth, should the water and hay be left.

As Brendys finished putting the saddles on the rack, he felt the tips of Willerth's fingers lightly touch his arm. He turned around and looked down at the boy.

Willerth stepped back, startled by the movement.

"Is something wrong, Willerth?" Brendys asked.

The boy shook his head. "N-nay, sir."

"Did you want to tell me something?"

"I-I. . . ." Willerth's voice failed him. Swallowing, the boy slowly reached out and wrapped his fingers around Brendys's hand, his eyes following his own actions, the same strange look on his face as he had worn when he touched Hedelbron, a look of new discovery.

Brendys could feel the boy's hand trembling, and he repeated his first question. "Willerth, is something wrong?"

The boy shook his head again, his confused gaze remaining on his own hand. Releasing his grip on Brendys's fingers, he dropped his arm to his side.

Brendys looked at Willerth thoughtfully for a moment. The boy began to visibly tremble as he raised his grey eyes to meet the youth's.

Brendys gave him a half-smile. "Are you trying to say thank you?"

In response, Willerth nodded his head quickly, then ran out of the stable.

Brendys watched the boy until he was gone, a half-confused smile playing on his lips. He shook his head, then headed for the door. As he neared the entrance, he could hear Brugnara's voice just outside. Breaking into a run, he reached the door in time to see the stablehand sweep the back of his hand across the side of Willerth's head hard enough to send the boy into a daze.

"Damn ye, boy!" the small man bit out, an almost fearful edge to his voice. "I told 'ee t' stay 'way from them people!"

As he raised his hand for a second blow, Brendys leapt forward and grabbed the man's wrist, at the same time pulling back his own fist and letting it fly into Brugnara's jaw. Brugnara's head snapped back as he was thrown to the ground.

Fury welled up within Brendys as he glared down at the man. "Lay another hand on him, and by Elekar, I swear you will lose it!"

Brugnara started to rise, hatred reflected in his own features.

Brendys poised himself for a fight. Though only fifteen, he stood several inches taller and was several muscular pounds heavier than the stablehand.

As Brugnara studied Brendys, his anger melted into fear and then shame. "It won't 'appen again . . . I swear! I-I jes'. . . ."

"See that it doesn't!" Brendys snapped. He turned to steady Willerth, who was coming to his senses. "Are you all right?"

The boy threw a terrified look in his father's direction, then ripped himself from Brendys's grasp and ran from view behind the workers' quarters.

Casting one last glare at Brugnara, Brendys strode away, the cold breeze blowing his cloak out behind him like a roiling storm cloud. As he climbed the porch steps, he removed his cloak and draped it over his shoulder. Once inside the house, he closed the front door and hurried up the staircase to his room. There was a knock at his bedroom door almost as soon as he had closed it.

"Come in," he said in a loud, sharp voice, dropping his cloak on his bed.

The door opened, and his father stepped into the room. "Have you finished with the colt?"

Brendys stared back, his face still flush with anger. "Aye, Father."

The Horsemaster nodded slowly, gazing uncertainly at his son. "Good. I want you to ride into town with me. There are a few debts I need to clear."

After a moment's hesitation, Brendyk turned to leave, but his son stopped him.

"Father," Brendys quickly said, catching his father's attention.

"Yes?"

"It happened," Brendys said, while changing out of his work clothes. "Willerth came to me."

Brendyk slowly sat down on the foot of his son's bed. "Go on."

"When I got to the stable this morning, he was standing close . . . *really* close," Brendys continued. "I offered to teach him to ride, and everything just fell into place. He even *talks* to me."

"Did he tell you anything?"

Brendys shook his head. "Nay. Not really. But I must say, Father, if I thought he was strange before, today proved it to me. I told him he could pet Hedelbron, and I swear he didn't even understand what I meant!"

Brendyk stared at the floor in thought, lips pursed. After a moment, he shifted his gaze back to Brendys. "The fact that the door has been opened is what's important right now. Do you think it will last?"

Brendys felt his cheeks begin to burn again. Avoiding his father's gaze, he replied, "Aye, but . . . not because I taught him how to ride."

"Yes?" There was suspicion in his father's voice.

"Willerth left the stable before me," Brendys replied. "When I got to the door, Brugnara was there. He hit Willerth . . . right there in front of me! Knocked him witless!"

Brendys sheepishly met his father's gaze. "I . . . I sort of lost my temper."

Brendyk's face had become stern. "What did you say?"

"I-I threatened to break his hand if he ever struck Willerth again," the youth replied. "After I tried to break his jaw."

Brendyk closed his eyes and rubbed his forehead. "Brendys, you need to learn restraint. Rather than attack Brugnara, you should have come to me at once. As it is, your actions may make things worse for the boy."

"I know, Father," Brendys said, lowering his gaze. "I just had to do *something*."

Brendyk stood up. "Think before acting."

As the Horsemaster turned to leave, Brendys spoke again, this time with more concern. "Father, there is something else. . . ."

But his words went unheeded. His father had already left the room and was starting down the stairs. The youth quickly pulled on a clean tunic and followed him.

At the foot of the stairs, they found Brugnara and his son standing just inside the front door, the stablehand's hand tightly gripping Willerth's collar. The boy's feet hardly touched the floor.

Willerth! A wave of concern suddenly swept over Brendys.

Brugnara paled at the sight of his employer and released Willerth, giving the boy a soft pat on the back. "Oh, 'scuse me, Master Bren'yk! I-I jest came t' get me Willie."

Brendyk nodded, a stern look couched deep in his azure eyes. "Very well. But, please, do return tonight for supper. I have been thinking . . . we have not been properly acquainted."

Brugnara started to decline on his employer's invitation. "I 'udn't wanna' impose upon yer generosi'y, Master Bren'yk. . . ."

"I shan't take no for an answer, Brugnara," Brendyk insisted.

The stablehand must have seen something in Brendyk's smiling face which Brendys could not, for he quickly changed his mind.

"O' course, Master Bren'yk," Brugnara replied slowly. "But I think Willie ought t' stay 'ome . . . 'ee's frightened easy."

Brendyk's smile froze, and Brendys knew that he would not let Brugnara hide Willerth away anymore. "This morning, I might have agreed with you, but now I cannot. The boy seems to have found a reserve of courage. Besides, I am sure that the child would much rather be here among friends than locked up all alone in an old shack. Be here after the horses are fed at sunset."

Brugnara finally gave in with an obedient nod. "Aye, sir—sundown."

The small man shoved Willerth out the door and followed behind him.

Brendyk shut the door, then glanced at his son. "My debts can wait. I have some thinking to do."

Brendys stifled a grin.

* * * *

As instructed, Brugnara and his son were at the house by dusk. Farida showed them to the front room, where Brendys was seated in a high-backed chair.

Brendys smiled when he saw Willerth.

The boy surveyed the room in awe. Only the faint ticking of the clock on the mantlepiece broke the silence. This was the largest room in the house. There were three chairs, a couch, and a low table scattered about the room. In the far wall was a fireplace and three large windows lined the outside walls. A few paintings decorated the others, most notably the portrait of Danel, Brendys's mother.

Brendys chuckled lightly at the boy's wonder, heedless of Brugnara's presence. "It's small really, but I suppose it is a grander place than you have ever seen. Do you like it?"

Beaming, Willerth started to nod his head, but he stopped, glancing up at his father, his grin disappearing.

Brendys glared at Brugnara. The man's very presence seemed to drop a chill shadow over the room. For several minutes, the three sat in silence, Brendys and Brugnara scowling at each other, Willerth watching them in fearful alertness.

Brendyk soon joined them and led them to the dining hall, where the Horsemaster ordered Farida to bring in the food. As soon as everyone was seated, Brendyk turned to face Brugnara, his expression growing severe. "Before the meal is served, Brugnara, I would like to clear something up. It has come to my understanding that you were giving your boy a bit of a rough going over this morning, for some unclear reason."

Brugnara's small eyes twitched a bit, and he gave a venomous glance towards Brendys. "Uh, aye, sir—I'm sorry. An' as I told Master Bren'ys this mornin', it won't ne'er 'appen again, sir."

"I am glad to hear that," Brendyk replied. "How you wish to raise the child is none of my concern, but abuse is something that I shall not stand for as long as you are in my service and are living on my property."

Brugnara glared, but said nothing.

In a few minutes, Brendyk's maid came in with the food, serving the guests first. There was beef, boiled potatoes, stewed carrots, and bread, freshly-baked that morning and served with sweet honey.

Brendyk waved a hand at his bustling maid. "Sit down, Farida."

"I will when I am of a mind to," the old woman shot back.

"Very well, have it your own way," the Horsemaster quietly replied. "Now sit down."

Farida huffed, then took her place at the table.

There was no exchange of conversation throughout the meal. Everyone ate in silence, occasionally glancing at each other. Brendys and Brugnara frequently exchanged glimpses of mutual hatred, adding to the tension.

Brendys watched Willerth out of the corner of his eye. The boy ate sparingly, mostly just poking at his food with his fork. He seemed to be deep in thought. Out of all who were gathered there, he seemed to be paying the least attention to Brugnara or Brendys, either one. After a short while, Willerth put his fork down and, pushing his chair back a little, rose to his feet. His trembling legs threatened to topple him, so he planted his hands firmly on the table to steady himself.

"M-master Bren'yk," he stammered quietly.

The Horsemaster looked at him with a somewhat surprised smile on his lips. "Yes, boy?"

Willerth swallowed heavily, then answered. "Master Bren'yk, I-I'm goin' t' be Master Bren'ys-s's ser'ant."

Brendyk choked on a bit of meat. Catching his breath, he opened his mouth as if to speak, but only managed to gasp the boy's name. "Willerth. . . ."

A strange worried look passed over Brugnara's scruffy features, which Brendys took quick notice of. Again, his distrust of the stablehand took hold.

"Would you mind repeating that, boy?" Brendyk said, coughing.

Willerth reddened in embarrassment, but cleared his voice and repeated his statement. "I-I'm goin' t' be Master Bren'ys-s's ser'ant."

"That is what I thought you said," the Horsemaster muttered half to himself. He turned to his son. "Did you put him up to this, Brendys?"

Shaking his head, Brendys raised his hands in denial. "I knew nothing of this, Father. I swear!"

Brendyk looked Willerth in the eye, but with a smile on his face. "Now what in the Realms would make you want to go and do something as absurd as that, boy?"

The boy shot a fearful glance at Brugnara, which Brendys was sure his own father had taken note of as well, but he replied in an almost comically resolute tone. "I'm gonna."

Brendyk shook his head. "I have never heard anything more ridiculous! Now finish your supper, boy, and let us have no more of this foolishness."

The child sank back to his chair, tears welling up in his eyes.

Feeling a little betrayed himself, Brendys opened his mouth to defend the boy, but Farida spoke first.

"Now look what you have done, Master Brendyk!" the maid scolded. "You have hurt the poor lad's feelings. You should be ashamed of yourself!"

Brendyk stared at her, a look of disbelief on his face. "Are you saying that I should give in to such an outrageous request?"

Farida primly nodded once.

Brendys knew what his father's response would be. He had never been very good at saying no, especially to Farida.

Finally, as Brendys anticipated, the Horsemaster sighed and turned back to Willerth. "Very well—if your father permits it. But if you are going to be my son's servant, you are going to be paid for your services."

Brendys caught a sideways glance from his father, before the Horsemaster turned his gaze to Brugnara. "Well, how about it? Do we humor the lad? I suppose no harm could come of it."

The stablehand seemed to struggle with the decision, perhaps afraid of what Brendys might discover from Willerth, but he finally gave in. Brendys was certain that it was only because the man's greed was stronger than his fear.

"I can't see no reason why not," Brugnara replied slowly. Then he quickly added, "But 'ee'll 'ave t' come back t' th' cabin after dark. A man oughter 'ave a bit o' time wi' 'is youn'lin's."

Willerth bent his head further, trying hard to hold back his tears.

Brendys met Brugnara's gaze once again, anger building within him.

"Then it is settled!" Brendyk announced, apparently not noticing the boy's tears. "Willerth will, from this day forward, receive a sum of three pence each week in return for his services to my son."

Brendyk then leaned over to Brendys, hissing under his breath, "Don't you even dare take advantage of this!"

Brendys did not respond. His attention was fixed firmly on Brugnara.

A short time later, the stablehand excused himself and his son, and they returned to their quarters.

Brendys turned to his father as the front door closed. "You set Brugnara up, didn't you? You fully intended to give in to Willerth from the beginning, but you wanted to make it look like you disapproved."

His father smiled. "It is called diplomacy, Brendys. Make it look like you are on your enemy's side, then convince him to do what is best for your own."

Brendys considered his father's words for a moment and found they made a certain amount of sense, but he could not help feeling that a compromise had been made. "Still, do you think that was a good idea?"

Brendyk gave his son a puzzled look. "Do I think *what* was a good idea? I thought you would have been in favor of my decision."

Brendys shook his head. "Nay, I mean letting Willerth stay with Brugnara. You know that was the whole reason he came up with this scheme."

Brendyk stared at Brendys for a moment before answering. "The boy is his son, Brendys. There is nothing that I can do about that."

"But the way he treats him. . . ." Brendys persisted.

"Brendys, I will ask you again, would you have me send them away?" his father returned. "You are asking me to take the man's son from him, and that I cannot do. And I can only protect the boy while Brugnara remains under my employ."

An incredulous expression came over Brendys's face. "Father, I am afraid for Willerth. I think Brugnara is capable of killing him!"

Brendyk's gaze turned stony. "Brendys, you know I have never raised a hand in violence against another, and I do not condone it. Years ago, when I was not much older than yourself, I stood by as your grandfather was murdered . . . I will *not* make that mistake again."

The Horsemaster's features softened. "I must ask you to trust me, Brendys. There is a time for everything. The Dawn King will make his will known, then I will act."

"Of course," Brendys replied sourly. "Which means as certain as night follows day, Willerth is going to die. If you wait on the Dawn King, he will take Willerth . . . just like he took mother."

A depth of pain entered his father's eyes that he had not seen in years. Brendys felt a pang of guilt rise within him, but anger erased it, leaving an empty space in his heart. Without waiting for a response, he fled up the stairs to his bedroom.

Surrounded by darkness, he slid into bed, but sleep would not come. In his mind, he could see clearly his mother lying in bed, her golden hair matted with perspiration. Sweat poured in streams down her face, contorted in pain. After a few more agonizing minutes, peace came over her features.

Papa, is Mama going to get better? He could hear his grief-stricken, tiny voice asking.

His father's voice, both sad and gentle, answered him. *She has walked the Road to Elekar. She has gone to see the Dawn King. Do you understand, Son?*

No! He had screamed. *I hate him! I hate the Dawn King!*

Tears rolling freely down his cheeks, Brendys whispered into the night. "Why did you take Mama?"

Still weeping, Brendys finally fell into an uneasy sleep.

Chapter 4

Shrieking demons and monsters of unimaginable terror chased little Brendys throughout a surreal world of intangible walls and open gateways through which he could not pass. The fearsome creatures never came close enough to catch him, for when escape seemed least likely, a new avenue would open to him. He screamed for his mama as he ran, but he could not find her.

The chase ended as Brendys approached a dark opening, blacker than night. The walls on either side suddenly became solid, and Brendys was pushed by an unseen hand into the darkness. An iron gate clanged shut behind him, leaving him trapped, unable to see to find a way out.

He felt strange. No longer was he a child, but a grown man, and yet his childlike fear had not subsided. He could sense something with him in the darkness. He remained absolutely still, hoping the presence would not sense him there.

A few feet before him appeared a large, black stone, illuminated by a dim greyish light, and bound hand and foot *upon that stone was a small boy. The child was unconscious, his body splotched black and blue with bruises and torn by a scourge. Brendys stepped closer to see the boy's face, but a shadow passed over the child's features, blurring them.*

Hissing laughter filled Brendys's ears, and he looked up. A face appeared in the darkness across from him, on the other side of the stone. It, like the child's face, was blurred, but its eyes burned with a crimson light. An arm suddenly extended over the altar from beneath an unseen cloak. At the end of the outstretched arm was a black claw. The claw hovered over the child's heart for several minutes, while the creature chanted in a vile tongue. When the serpentine voice fell silent, the claw plunged downward.

Brendys bolted upright with a yell. "*No!*"

He glanced around the dark room, half-expecting to find the demon standing over him, then settled back to his pillow. Trembling, he wiped the sweat from his brow.

"Just a dream," he whispered to himself, his voice wavering. "Just a dream."

Sleep did not return to him that night.

When the dim rays of the early morning sun began to leak through the shutters, Brendys slid his legs over the side of the bed and rose to a sitting position, rubbing his eyes wearily. Slowly, he stood to his feet and walked across the room to the window and opened the shutters, letting the morning sun filter in. He leaned on the window sill, resting his head against the cold glass, and stared out at the workers' quarters. The cold morning air gave him gooseflesh, but he ignored it.

After a few minutes, he saw Brugnara come out of the cabin and hurry towards the stable. Brendys knit his brows. He was sure this was Brugnara's day off. Why, then, had he gone to the stable? Brugnara quickly reappeared, his head darting from side to side as if searching. After a moment, he started towards the house.

Willerth! Brendys hurriedly grabbed some clothes and began dressing. When he was done, he threw open his bedroom door and launched himself towards the stairs, nearly taking a headlong tumble down the steps. He stopped halfway down the staircase. His father was standing at the front door, talking to someone . . . Brugnara, Brendys assumed.

Brendyk was nodding his head. "Aye. Willerth came to the house a while ago. He asked to begin his duties, and I saw no reason why he shouldn't."

"Could ye call 'im?" Brendys heard the boy's father ask. "I 'uz goin' t' take 'im t' town wi' me."

"Oh dear," Brendyk replied in a concerned tone. "I had forgotten this was your day off. I must say, it would be inconvenient at the moment . . . Farida is giving him a bath."

There was a brief moment of silence. Brendys leaned back against the wall. He was having difficulty imagining Willerth allowing anyone to bathe him, as shy as the boy was.

"A *bath?*" Brugnara said, his voice reflecting Brendys's sentiments.

"Aye," Brendyk replied. "I must say, as filthy as he was, the boy looked more a slave than a gentleman's servant. People would talk if they saw my son in public with him."

Brendys stifled a laugh. People talking behind his father's back was nothing new, and there was not a soul in Ahz-Kham who would consider Brendys a *gentleman.*

Brendyk continued before Brugnara could respond. "I was planning to send Brendys and Willerth into town a little later to take care of some business for me. Is there some place they could meet you, perhaps?"

"Nay," Brugnara replied after a moment of hesitation. "They don't need t' trouble."

Brendyk inclined his head. "As you will."

Brendys watched as his father's gaze followed the stablehand's retreat.

The Horsemaster finally closed the door and looked up at his son, unsmiling. "You look awful."

Brendys curled his lip. He could imagine the dark circles under his eyes, resulting from his sleepless night. "Thank you very much."

As the youth descended the remainder of the stairs, his father started into the front room, speaking back over his shoulder. "I want you to go into town this morning to settle the debts with the glazier and carpenter. You may as well take the boy with you. It would do him good to be out among people."

Brendys noticed that his father was pointedly avoiding the argument of the previous night. He followed the Horsemaster into the front room. "Yes, Father."

Brendyk sat down in his favorite chair, donning a pair of spectacles. As he began to study a parchment note, he glanced up at Brendys. "Speaking of the boy, would you check in with Farida? She has had the boy in the washroom for nearly half an hour."

"I can only imagine," Brendys replied, shaking his head.

He headed down the hall leading to the kitchen and through to the washroom beyond. When he opened the door at the back of the kitchen, steam wafted out around him. He stepped into the washroom and found Farida standing over a washtub containing a pale, terrified Willerth. The old woman, her grey hair a frazzled mess, her apron and frock both soaked from the boy's frantic splashing, was holding a bar of soap in one hand and was trying to hold the boy with the other. Willerth, his thin arms wrapped around his undernourished body, deftly dodged her attempts.

"Sit still!" Farida snapped. "I swear, even your master was never this difficult!"

"Farida," Brendys said from the doorway. "Father wants to know how much longer you will be."

Willerth, seeing his master, disappeared beneath the edge of the tub, sending a spray of soapy water into the air.

Farida straightened with a huff and turned a baleful eye to Brendys. "I have hardly been able to lay a hand on the child! You can tell your father that I will be done when I'm done."

While the houseservant was speaking, Brendys saw Willerth's eyes poke up above the rim of the tub, his sodden hair plastered to his scalp. He cast a sideways glance up at Farida, then leapt to his feet and tried to jump out of the washtub, but the old woman thrust a hand out and shoved him back into the water.

"I am not through with you, yet, boy!" Farida said, taking a firm grip on the back of Willerth's neck. She dropped the soap and reached for a stiff scrub brush.

Brendys winced in sympathy for the boy and backed out of the washroom, closing the door behind himself. He made his way out of the kitchen and back down the hallway. When he came back into the front room, his father looked up.

Concern swept over Brendyk's face. "Brendys, are you all right? You look ill."

"I'm fine," Brendys replied with a half-smile. "Farida is using the brush on him."

Grimacing, his father removed his spectacles and rubbed his eyes, remembering similar experiences as a child. "Poor boy."

"They are likely to be at it a while longer, Father," Brendys said after a moment. "Perhaps I should feed the horses."

Brendyk nodded. "Aye. If they are finished before you are back, I will send the boy out to you."

Brendys went about the morning stable duties which Brugnara had been carrying out for the last three weeks. After another half an hour had passed and Willerth had still not appeared, he returned to the house. As he entered the front room, Farida came through the kitchen door and made her way up the hallway.

The old woman stopped just inside the front room. "It was work, to be sure, but I think you will find it worth the effort."

"Well, where is he?" Brendyk asked, rising to his feet.

Farida looked to either side, then with an exasperated huff, pulled Willerth out from behind her. The boy stumbled forward a step, then came to a standstill, shoulders slumped and head bowed.

Farida nudged him from behind. "Don't slouch!"

The boy straightened his back, but only lifted his head partway. He glanced shyly at the Horsemaster and his son. His tawny hair, cleaned and combed, was a shade brighter than it had appeared originally. Though cut short, its natural waves still rippled back across his head. His well-scrubbed cheeks glowed pink.

He wore a white tunic with a sleeveless, sky-blue jacket and matching trousers and shiny, knee-high, black boots. Unlike the old work clothes Brendyk had given him before, this set fit snugly over his slender form. His dark, sunken eyes were the only reminders of the fearful young vagrant who had come to the farmstead nearly three weeks earlier.

Brendys glanced at his father, then turned his gaze back to the boy, gaping in amazement. The transformation was nothing short of astounding. "What did you do with Willerth?"

Brendyk gave an approving nod. "Indeed. This young man looks a proper gentleman."

Willerth's cheeks brightened noticeably and his lips formed a shy smile.

"Thank you, Farida," Brendyk told his house servant. "A job well done."

He turned to Brendys, handing him two small coin pouches. "Here are the payments for Verak and Nathon. You should leave now, so you can be home by midday."

His expression turned meaningful. "I would rather you avoid any *unnecessary* confrontations."

Brendys nodded in understanding. "Of course, Father."

The youth turned to his new servant. "Come on, Willerth. We're going into town."

The boy took a step backwards, his eyes widening in fear.

Brendys placed his hand on his hips. "Willerth, if you are going to work for me, you are going to have to learn to do what I tell you."

Willerth hesitated, then gave a nervous nod and followed his master to the stable, taking his cloak from a wall peg before leaving the house.

Brendys saddled Hedelbron for Willerth and a bay mare for himself, and soon they were on their way down the eastward road to Ahz-Kham. As they entered the town, Willerth began to lag behind his master, despite the youth's encouragement. The boy grew more apprehensive as they neared the *Green Meadow*, Ahz-Kham's single inn and a place with an unwholesome reputation.

Brendys noticed the look of fearful recognition in his servant's eyes as he tied the horses off at the post. "Willerth, have you been here before?"

The boy turned his pale face toward Brendys and nodded.

Brendys shook his head and sighed. "I can't believe the gall of your father. This is no place for a boy."

Willerth gave him a confused look.

"Well, if it is any consolation, we aren't going in," Brendys went on.

Relaxing a little, Willerth dismounted and went to his master's side.

Brendys glanced around at the nearby buildings and side streets, then pointed to a small avenue to the north. "I think Master Nathon's shop is this way. Let's go."

Brendys headed across the street, Willerth tagging along behind. After a few minutes, they found the glazier's shop. When they had paid Nathon, they walked across town to the carpenter's shop in the eastern quarter. Half an hour later, they returned to the horses at the *Green Meadow*.

"Now, that wasn't so bad, was it?" Brendys said as they neared the inn.

Willerth cocked his head thoughtfully, then shrugged. "Nay, no' really. I ain't ne'er knowed nobo'y 'oo 'uz nice t' me afore. I on'y knowed Papa, an' 'ee ain't ne'er nice t' me. 'Ee...."

The boy stopped suddenly, a visible shudder running through his body.

Brendys followed his gaze and saw Brugnara preparing to enter the inn, a local whore dangling on his elbow. The small man saw Willerth and stopped. He looked the boy up and down a couple of times before his narrow eyes widened in amazement, realizing that he was looking at his own son. What appeared to be an attempt at a fatherly smile crossed his thin lips, but to Brendys he looked more like a half-starved wolf grinning at a piece of fresh meat.

Brendys took Willerth, who for once did not resist, by the arm and pulled the boy behind himself.

Brugnara seemed to notice his employer's son for the first time. His smile vanished abruptly, replaced by an expression of seething anger. The whore at his side said something to the man to which he snapped back a sharp reply, then the pair disappeared into the inn.

Brendys turned to Willerth. "You don't have to be afraid of him anymore, Willerth. If he tries to hurt you again, he'll have me to deal with."

The boy's eyes began to mist. "Don't ye make 'im mad, Master Bren'ys, please! 'Ee'll 'urt ye bad, 'ee will."

"He will do nothing of the kind," Brendys replied firmly. "I promise you that."

Willerth was about to respond, but before he could, someone grabbed Brendys by the shoulder and spun him around. Brendys found himself suddenly drawn into a passionate embrace. After a moment, he took the girl by her shoulders and pulled her away.

"Adina, not out here in the street," he hissed. "People might talk. I don't need Father hearing about it."

Adina's male companion snickered. "There isn't a soul in Ahz-Kham that doesn't know you've shared more than just some ale with Adina, including your father."

Brendys rolled his eyes and turned to face the speaker. "Are you still alive, Languedoc? If so, I would happily remedy the situation."

Pursing his lips, the other youth raised his hands before him in surrender.

Brendys faced the girl again.

Adina smiled seductively at him. Unlike most Shalkanes, she had brilliant, red hair and green eyes, indicating an Ilkatari heritage. Though she was nearly two years older than himself, Brendys found her irresistible. She reached out and stroked his hair. "I've missed you. Are you going to stay for a while?"

Brendys swallowed and looked longingly into her green eyes. "I-I can't. Father is expecting Willerth and me home soon."

"Willerth?" Adina said, stepping back. She looked down and noticed the boy standing halfway hidden behind Brendys. She gave a surprised smile. "Is this the boy Languedoc was telling me about? The way he talked, you would think he was the ugliest thing in the Mortal Realm."

Brendys glared in Languedoc's direction. "I can only imagine."

Languedoc shrugged. "Well, he was a filthy little mutt the last time I saw him. Now he is a clean little mutt."

"Oh, do be quiet, will you?" Adina chided him. "I think he is just adorable."

She reached out to stroke Willerth's hair, but the boy dodged back out of reach. She gave a startled look to Brendys.

Brendys shook his head. "He doesn't like to be touched. His father has been rather beastly to him, I'm afraid."

Adina looked at Willerth with an overly sympathetic frown. "Oh, the poor thing. You really should bring him with you more often. We would see to it he was treated right."

Ashen, Willerth backed farther towards the horses, and Languedoc covered his mouth, stifling a laugh.

"My father would have my hide for it, and you know it," Brendys replied wryly. He glanced back at Willerth, then cast one more lustful eye on Adina. "We really should be going."

A grin slowly spread across his lips as he quietly added, "I will see you tonight."

As he turned to go to his horse, he shot another glare at Languedoc. "And you can drop dead."

The other youth smirked in return.

Brendys boosted Willerth onto Hedelbron's back, then mounted his own horse, and they headed out of town.

Brendys glanced at Willerth every once and awhile as they rode. The boy had not said a word since leaving Ahz-Kham, his gaze distant and thoughtful. Finally, Brendys let his own attention drift away.

As they neared the farmstead, Brendys felt Willerth's gaze on him and turned his face towards the boy. Willerth's head was cocked in a mixture of curiosity and concern as he stared at his master.

"What's wrong, Willerth?" Brendys asked after a moment.

"Tha' girl, th' 'un whats ye were talkin' wit'," the boy started conversationally.

"Adina?"

Willerth nodded. "Aye, 'dina. Does she do thin's t' ye?"

Throwing a shocked look at the boy, Brendys reached out and grabbed Hedelbron's reins, bringing both horses to a halt. "What was that?"

Willerth drew back uncertainly. "D-does she do thin's t' ye?"

Brendys ran a hand across his mouth before saying, "I don't know why I should be shocked . . . knowing your father, you have probably seen the inside of every brothel between here and Fader Keep."

Willerth frowned and shook his head. "Jes' inns."

Brendys sighed. "What Adina does or doesn't do is none of your concern. You just forget whatever you heard back there, do you understand? My father, especially, doesn't need to know about this."

The boy's brow wrinkled in confusion. "But tha' mean 'un, 'ee said 'ee alrea'y knowed."

"My father knows what he *chooses* to know," Brendys replied. "He doesn't approve, so he ignores it."

Willerth looked down at his saddle. "I likes yer papa. 'Ee's a good man."

Brendys drew in a sudden breath. For some reason, the boy's words stung him. His blue eyes drifted to the farmstead. Did his father truly ignore the talk? He shook the thought from his mind and started his horse moving again. "Come on, Willerth."

"Aye, sir."

After stabling the horses, they returned to the house, where Farida had lunch waiting for them. Before they were done eating, Brendyk joined them. The Horsemaster sat down at the kitchen table across from his son. "You were longer than I expected."

Brendys gave Willerth a warning glance, then answered his father. "We ran into Languedoc outside the *Green Meadow*."

Brendyk raised his head. "The *Green Meadow?* You didn't take the boy into *that* place, did you?"

Brendys curled his lip. "Of course not, Father. We simply left the horses there."

"Good," his father replied. "That is no place for a child."

"I nae likes it there," Willerth said quietly, frowning at the plate before him. "It's a bad place."

Brendys looked at him and saw a hint of the emptiness he had seen so many times before creep back into the boy's grey eyes. When no one said anything for a moment, Brendys turned his gaze back to his father.

The Horsemaster stared intensely at Willerth. He gave his son a sideways glance, and Brendys straightened.

"Father, I swear I didn't take him in there," the youth said in response to his father's look. "He and Brugnara must have stayed there when they came to Shalkan."

"I gathered as much," Brendyk replied. He placed his hands palm-down on the table and raised himself to his feet. He looked down at his son. "I have some things to think about, and I think best while working. I will take care of the horses this afternoon. You cut some more wood for the bin, then take the rest of the day off."

Brendys gave his father a startled look. "Thank you, Father!"

Brendyk gave him a vague nod and left the room.

Brendys reached over to Willerth and gave the boy a light slap on the shoulder. "We've work to do, Willerth."

The boy jerked in his seat as if startled from a dream. His eyes focused on his master, a small smile crossing his lips. "Aye, Master Bren'ys."

As they left the house and went around to the wood pile, Brendys told the boy, "I really wish you would leave off with the *Master* Brendys, Willerth. I am *not* your master."

Willerth looked up at Brendys with a panicked expression. "Ye are! Ye gots t' be!"

Brendys sighed. "You aren't going to let this go, are you?"

The boy shook his head adamantly.

His master shrugged, then picked up the axe leaning against the woodpile. As he split logs, Willerth would pick up the smaller pieces and carry them to the wood bin beside the house. After a few minutes, Brendys removed his cloak. Despite the frigid weather, chopping wood was hard, hot work.

Half an hour later, the bin was full. Brendys put the axe down, then leaned back against the woodpile and exhaled, sending a cloud of breath drifting away. He watched as Willerth promptly did the same in imitation, though his manner was stiff and uncertain, as though unaware of the purpose of the exercise.

Brendys grinned and shook his head. "Come on, Willerth. Let's go in the house. I am going into town later, but I've nothing to do until then, so I may as well teach you some games."

Willerth gave him a quizzical look, but followed him into the house.

"Why don't you wait in the front room," Brendys said as they entered the house. "I will be down in a moment."

Without looking back, Brendys climbed the stairs to his bedroom. He closed the door behind him as he entered the room, then removed his belt and slipped off his sweat-soaked tunic. Giving the shirt a quick sniff, he winced and tossed it on the foot of his bed. He grabbed a wet rag from his washbasin and began mopping at his perspiring torso.

When he was finished, he turned to retrieve a clean tunic from his dresser and saw his bedroom door standing open. Willerth stood just inside, staring at his master with the same look of abject horror that Brendys had seen in his eyes the morning he and his father first came to the farmstead.

"Willerth, what's wrong?" Brendys asked cautiously.

The boy's gaze drifted up to meet his own, but there was no recognition in them, only fear.

"Willerth?" Brendys repeated, taking a step towards the boy.

Willerth began to tremble and quickly backed away.

As Brendys advanced, the boy turned and ran from the room and down the stairs. Brendys hurried to the balcony railing, calling after the boy, arriving in time to see Willerth vanish through the front door. Farida came into view, attracted by the noise, and looked up at Brendys in confusion.

Brendys spread his arms and shook his head in equal bewilderment.

After a moment, he returned to his room and finished changing his clothes, then went out to look for Willerth. He went first to the workers' quarters, but the boy was not there. He searched around the house, then went to the stable, but Willerth was nowhere to be found.

As he walked down the row of stalls, he called to Brendyk. "Father, have you seen Willerth? He just ran away from me like I was trying to kill him!"

"What did you do?" Brendyk asked as his son drew closer.

Brendys shrugged in confusion. "That is just it . . . I didn't do anything! I can't find him anywhere, Father."

"Don't worry about the boy," the Horsemaster replied. "He will either come back to the house or to the cabin when he is ready."

Brendys pursed his lips. "Aye, I suppose so. I just can't help but worry about him."

Brendyk's gaze drifted away as he quietly replied, "Neither can I."

Brendys gave his father a surprised look. Rarely did he openly express worry or fear. That knowledge only caused the youth further worry, and he left the stable to search some more. After another unfruitful hour of hunting for Willerth, Brendys finally gave up.

Brendys considered staying home that night, but he had not seen Adina in nearly two and a half weeks. His desire to be with her won out over compassion. To avoid confrontation with his father, Brendys waited until the Horsemaster had left the stable before saddling Hedelbron.

He rode into Ahz-Kham, retracing the snow-packed road into town. When he reached the *Green Meadow*, he dismounted and tethered Hedelbron to the post. The horse stared at Brendys for a moment, then snorted and lowered his head. Brendys hesitated before entering the inn, confused at the sense of guilt he suddenly felt.

Shaking off the feeling, he continued. As he entered the smoke-filled common room, his eyes began to water, and he choked with his first few breaths, but he quickly grew accustomed to the air.

The innkeeper's assistant met the youth at the door, a toothy grin stretched across his scruffy face. "Here you are at last, Master Brendys! You've been missing for quite awhile. We wondered why, and that Languedoc gave us his version, if you know what I mean. 'Course, none of us listen to a word he has to say."

Brendys rolled his eyes and groaned. "Aye, I know exactly what you mean, Allic, and I swear if he starts in tonight, he will be picking his teeth up off the floor."

Allic snickered, then pointed to a table in a corner at the back of the room. "Your friends are over there."

Brendys gave the man a nod and started across the room as Allic hurried off to fetch him a mug. Before he had gone very far, he noticed Brugnara sitting alone at a nearby table. The man's face twisted into a scowl when he saw the youth. Slowly, he rose to his feet and marched to the exit, pausing long enough to glare up into Brendys's face. Brendys watched him leave, jaw clenched, then continued on to the table where his friends were seated.

There were two girls sitting at the table with Languedoc. One of them was unknown to Brendys. He assumed she was new to the local brothel—it was rumored to ply in the slave trade, and the frequent changes in girls served to support the belief. The other was Adina.

Languedoc looked up as Brendys approached. His blurry eyes and slurred speech made it clear that he had already had a few too many mugs of the inn's best ale.

"Well, so here you are at—last!" he said with a short but loud belch before the last word. "We were beginning to wonder. . . ."

"Languedoc," Brendys began. "Not another word, or I promise you will regret it."

"Oh, be still and come here," Adina said, standing up and throwing her arms around Brendys's neck. She gave him a long, passionate kiss into which he gave himself fully, allowing his cares to drift aside. Adina leaned her head back a little. "I thought you were never going to come, Brendys. It would have been lonely tonight without you."

At that, a local man sitting nearby laughed and said, "If there is a man around, Adina, you are never lonely!"

A brief ripple of laughter spread through the common room.

"You shan't have to worry about loneliness tonight!" Brendys said, sweeping the girl up into his arms. "Perhaps we should find someplace a little more private, eh?"

"That, you won't find, Brendys my lad," Languedoc said, taking a swig from his mug. "Aden and Lorella slipped away a few minutes ago . . . I expect he is plying some of those tricks you taught him."

Brendys dropped down onto the bench across from Languedoc, still holding Adina on his lap. "I didn't teach him anything. It's that sister of yours, and I'm sure *you* taught *her* everything she knows."

Languedoc shrugged off the comment with mock indignation, then put down his mug and grabbed the girl beside him and pulled her to himself.

Adina reached up a hand to Brendys's face, turning it towards her own. "I thought you said something about not worrying about loneliness?"

"I always keep my promises," Brendys replied, breaking into a grin. He drew her into another kiss, then moved downward, his lips exploring Adina's neck.

"Better than playing nursemaid to the mutt, eh, Bren?" Languedoc spouted suddenly.

Brendys slowly raised his head. For a reason Brendys could not explain, his friend's words stung. A fresh wave of guilt flooded over him.

Frowning miserably, Adina sat up and moved from his lap to the bench. "Pay no heed to Languedoc, Bren. He is drunk."

"I am, and I am proud of it," Languedoc responded in a snobbish tone. He looked at Brendys again. "I can't understand you, Bren. You never got upset over any of the other whelps your father took in before."

Brendys stood up and turned to face the blonde youth, speaking through clenched teeth. "Willerth is different."

Languedoc nodded. "Maybe so, but something isn't right with the mutt. I swear he has got you bewitched!"

"Well, I think he's cute," Adina interjected, trying to support Brendys.

Languedoc curled his lip. "You think everything that's male is cute."

Adina gave him a venomous look. "And you make love with your horse!"

Another laugh went up from many of the customers.

Brendys put a calming hand on Adina's arm. "Languedoc is right. There *is* something wrong with Willerth. Seriously wrong."

"Let me give you some advice, Bren," Languedoc responded. "To Hál with the mutt and get on with your life."

Brendys stared Languedoc in the eye. "What do you know about life?"

"What do *you* know about life?" the blonde youth countered. "You spend most of yours mucking out stalls and wenching Adina. You and I aren't really all that different."

Brendys stood there, staring down at the table, battling his temper back.

"Aw, I've made poor little Brendys upset," Languedoc sneered. "But perhaps now you will think about what I've said. That brat is no good. He'll destroy your life, to be sure."

Again, Brendys did not answer. He realized at once that Languedoc was right about nearly everything, and it was beginning to make him uncomfortable. He suddenly felt out of place, as if he were no longer among friends, but unwelcome strangers.

He looked Languedoc in the face, his lip curling into a half-grin. Without warning, he shot his arms out, catching the other youth by the front of his tunic, and dragged him across the table. Adina and Languedoc's whore leapt away from the table with a mutual squeal.

Brendys lifted Languedoc to his feet and lashed out with a fist, striking the shocked youth in the jaw. Languedoc struck the wall, then slid to the floor, dazed by the blow.

Allic and the innkeeper, Igin, rushed to the youth's side and tried to bring him around.

Brendys turned and stalked out of the inn, without even a backward glance. Mounting Hedelbron, he rode home.

* * * *

The ride home was lonely and unsettling. The winter darkness had already fallen, but the sky was clear. The moon and stars shone brightly overhead, but their beauty was overshadowed by the bluish glow the moonlight cast upon the snowy fields. There was little wildlife in Shalkan, other than birds and reptiles, for the surrounding wall of Barrier Mountain discouraged the migration of other forms, but the knowledge that there were no wolves did nothing to purge his growing sense of danger.

The nearer he came to the farmstead, the longer and deeper the shadows seemed to become. As he entered the stableyard, he dismounted and led Hedelbron into the dark barn. When he had seen to his horse's needs, he left the stable and started towards the house.

He paused when he came to the workers' cabin. A thin wisp of smoke trailed from the chimney, and through the nearest window he could see the flicker of a low fire. Silhouetted against the light was Brugnara, seated at a table, his back to the window. Brendys could see nothing of Willerth.

Brendys stared at the back of the stablehand's head for a short while, wondering nervously how long Willerth would be protected from his father's anger.

Brugnara's head turned to his right, and Brendys heard him call out. "Willie, come 'ere, boy."

Brendys was surprised that there was no malice or anger in the man's raspy, tenor voice. He could see Willerth's thin silhouette appear in the window, reluctantly approaching the man at the table. Brugnara continued to speak, but his voice was too low for Brendys to distinguish the words, only that the man's tone was almost compassionate. Brugnara reached a hand out to stroke his son's head, but Willerth jerked away, turning his head to face the window.

Brendys quickly turned his face away and walked on towards the house, cursing himself for intruding upon their privacy.

As he entered the house, he hung his cloak on a wall peg and climbed the stairs to the second floor. He hesitated at the door to his bedroom. He felt drained, despite his lack of chores that day, but he had rarely gone to bed without first recording the day's events in his journal.

Brendys glanced down the hall to the library and noticed a gleam of light escape from beneath the closed door. His father only used the library when he was working, and Brendys was not certain he wanted to confront his father that night, but after a moment of consideration, he walked down the hall and opened the door. As he entered, he saw his father sitting behind his desk, leaning forward on his elbows, with his chin propped on clasped hands.

Brendyk glanced up as his son entered the room. "You are home earlier than usual."

Brendys nodded and mumbled in return, not wanting to discuss the evening. He walked to his writing table and picked up a taper, which he kindled in the flame of the lamp on his father's desk.

"You seem a bit upset—is something wrong, Brendys?" Brendyk asked as the youth returned to his table and lit his own lamp.

Sighing, Brendys dropped into his chair. "Languedoc was drunk and making a nuisance of himself."

"So you finally got some sense into that thick head of yours and left his company?"

Brendys shrugged and sheepishly glanced up at his father. "Nay, not exactly. Some of the things he said actually made sense. I left because I didn't want to be there when he woke up."

Brendyk sighed and shook his head. "You struck him?"

Brendys nodded in admission, then rubbed his sore knuckles. "A little too hard, I think. The worst part is I really enjoyed it."

"I have told you many times you need to learn to control your temper, Brendys," his father replied sternly.

Brendys bowed his head. "Aye, sir."

"But it *was* overdue."

Brendys's head snapped up in surprise.

His father avoided his gaze. "But you still shouldn't have done it."

Brendys almost laughed, but a shadow seemed to have fallen over his father's features. A cold feeling slowly crept over him. "Father? Are you ill?"

Brendyk shook his head. "Nay. It's the boy. He came back to the workers' quarters shortly after you left. He wouldn't let me near him, nor Farida. It was as though the last two days had never happened."

"He was fine this morning," Brendys replied in confusion. He knit his brow and turned to face the journal lying on the table.

Nay, he reminded himself. *Not **all** morning.*

He recalled the boy's fear when they approached the inn and later when they had seen Brugnara.

63

"Are you certain that the boy has not said anything about himself or his father?"

Brendys glanced at his father, surprised by the intensity of his question, then shook his head, returning his gaze to the ragged journal before him. He ran his fingers along the frayed edges of the leather cover, something hidden at the back of his mind troubling him. He flipped the book open and thumbed back through the pages, hoping to find an answer to his unknown question.

As he glanced through the entries he had made over the last couple of weeks, memories came back fresh into his mind. One memory stood out above the others: the touch of a little boy's hand on his arm, a touch completely devoid of emotion, and the confused look the boy had worn as he reached his hand out, the look of someone who did not comprehend his own actions. One last image flashed through his mind: a man standing in front of an inn, a predatory grin splitting his scruffy features. Brendys felt the bile rising in his throat and swallowed it back.

"*Gods!*" he burst out, slamming both fists on the table. "Why didn't I see it before?!"

Brendys abruptly stood up, nearly toppling his chair. He stepped towards his father's desk, leaning with his fists on its surface. He looked his father in the eye. "Willerth has never let anyone touch him, Father . . . not even to comfort him. Even a soft hand sends shivers through him. It isn't a *beating* that he's been afraid of!"

Brendyk bowed his head, lowering his gaze. "I know."

Brendys stared down at his father in open-mouthed shock. Anger began to boil up within him once more. "If you knew, why didn't you do something? Why didn't you tell the constable?"

The Horsemaster looked up at him. "And tell him what, Brendys? I have had suspicions for a while now, but no evidence. All I could do would be to have Brugnara dragged off for battering the boy, and I could probably convince the Magistrate to give him the highest penalty for it . . . a public lashing. Then what? He would probably come back and take the boy from Ahz-Kham, leaving him no better off than before."

"The Magistrate would believe you if you told him what you know," Brendys countered.

His father's features hardened. "Aye, that is probably so. But without evidence, I don't *know* anything. I have suspicions. What if they proved wrong, Brendys? Do you know what the penalty for that crime is?"

Brendys silently shook his head.

"They would hang him, Brendys," his father replied. "I have to know for certain. Do you understand now why I gave in to the boy's ridiculous scheme? I hoped he would trust you enough to tell you something I could use to confirm my suspicions to the Magistrate . . . and to myself."

Brendyk pushed his chair back and rose to his feet, coming around the desk. He placed his hands on his son's shoulders. "Brendys. . . ."

He was interrupted by a loud crashing noise.

Brendys and his father both froze. The brief silence was followed by another crash. The commotion came from the direction of the stable. Without another moment's hesitation, they ran to the door and hurried downstairs where they were met by Farida.

Brendyk threw open the front door and stared out, Brendys beside him. The door of the workers' cabin was standing open, though no light could be seen within. They could hear Brugnara wailing some coarse Fekamari drinking-song, his words slurred beyond recognition.

Brendys started to push past his father, but the Horsemaster grabbed his arm and held him back. "Let me deal with this, Brendys. He is drunk, and we don't know how dangerous he could be.

"I want you to stay *right here*. I have to get something, but when I come back, *I* will deal with Brugnara, and *you* will ride into town to fetch the constable. Do you understand?"

Without waiting for Brendys to reply, the Horsemaster hurried back into the house.

Brendys glanced at his father's back, then turned his gaze back to the workers' quarters, muttering, "To Hál with it."

Farida tried to restrain him, but he easily pulled from her grasp and leapt from the porch, landing at a run towards the cabin. He could hear the old woman call after him, but he ignored her. As he neared the cabin, he slowed down.

Brugnara was still singing at the top of his lungs within the dark confines of the building, apparently oblivious to the youth's presence just outside. Small footprints broke the blanket of snow, trailing away from the cabin steps. Brendys followed the trail with his eyes and saw Willerth lying face-down, naked, in a snowdrift. Brendys hurried to the boy, kneeling down beside him and reaching out to turn him over.

At the touch of his hands, Willerth jerked around to face him, cowering back with his arms clasped protectively around himself. He shivered fiercely both against the freezing temperature and from fear of his father. The utter shame and terror reflected in the child's face sickened Brendys.

Brendys quickly unbuckled his belt and pulled off his tunic. Willerth did not resist as Brendys wrapped his shirt around him. The youth rose and turned as Brugnara came stumbling out of the cabin, flask in hand.

"Yoo 'oo! 'ey there, Willie, m'boy, where're ye?" The man caught sight of his son and advanced, apparently not noticing Brendys. "Why'd ye go, Willie? Don't 'ee care 'bout yer ol' Papa?"

As Brugnara came closer, Brendys began to tremble in anger, the blaze of hatred driving away all sense of the cold air around him. He planted himself firmly between Willerth and the stablehand, poising for a fight. "One step nearer and I'll make sure you never hurt him again!"

Brugnara took a startled step backwards. "Eh? I 'uz'n't 'urtin' n'un . . . jes' 'avin' a bit o' fun, that's all. Ye've nae call t' threaten."

Brendys stared at the man in disbelief for only a moment before lunging towards him with an outraged cry. "You sick bastard!"

The youth pulled back his fist and launched it forward, but a pair of strong hands caught him by the wrist and shoulder, yanking him to a halt. Brendys snapped a glance over his shoulder to find his father standing there.

Brendyk pulled his son to the side, away from Brugnara.

Something brushed Brendys's leg as he was moved aside, and he looked down. His anger was instantly forgotten when he saw the sheathed sword hanging from his father's belt. He knew his father owned a weapon, but he had never seen his father wear it, professing a pacifistic philosophy.

He looked up at his father's face and found it grim and hard.

"I warned you that I would not tolerate this, Brugnara." Brendyk's voice was flat, stern, as cold and hard as his grave features. "You will leave at once."

The inebriated man suddenly turned mournful, almost to the point of tears. "Ye're jes' goin' t' sen' us off in th' dead o' winter, wi'out e'en th' week's pay!"

"Nay," Brendyk replied matter-of-factly. "I am sending *you* off. The boy will remain here. Be thankful . . . I was tempted to have Brendys summon the constable. Your life would certainly have been forfeit. But I will not have another man's death on my conscience. Go, and quickly, for even *my* patience wears thin."

Brugnara's mood made another sudden change. His features twisted in livid rage. "Ye ain't gots no right! I'm leavin'—but I'm takin' m'boy wi' me!"

The small man lunged past Brendys and his father and grabbed Willerth by the wrist, dragging the boy to his feet. Willerth tried vainly to pull free from his father, but that only caused Brugnara to tighten his grip on the boy's wrist. Willerth yowled and bit down hard on the man's hand, drawing blood. Brugnara swiftly brought that hand back to his mouth, but struck out with the other. His fist caught Willerth full in the face, driving the boy backwards into the drift.

Shouting a curse, Brendys took a step towards the man.

Brugnara spun around to face the angered youth. With a flick of his right wrist, he thrust a closed hand before him.

Brendys sprang back in surprise as a silvery arc streaked downward between the stablehand and himself. Brugnara's hand sprang upward a few inches with a loud snap as the blade of Brendyk's sword cut through his wrist.

As the hand fell to the ground, spattering blood across the snow, Brugnara screamed, tightly grasping his stump. He turned wild, hate-filled eyes on Brendyk. "By all the powers o' Hál, ye'll pay wi' yer 'ead fer this! Ye'll die! Ye'll all die!"

A sneering grin crossed his lips. A shadow seemed to pass over the man's features, deepening the shadows in his face, filling his dark eyes with a hellish blackness. His shrill voice suddenly calmed, taking on a tone which reminded Brendys of nothing less than the hiss of a serpent. "Oh, but not that wretched whelp o' yours. Nay, not yet. 'is life, while it lasts, shall be plagued wi' death and sorrow. Many'll die afore 'im, an' th' last o' those'll be 'is own son. Then shall 'ee die! This curse do I swear!"

Brendyk took a step towards the man, brandishing his sword before him. "Begone with you!"

"Hál take you all!" Brugnara spat at the Horsemaster, then ran off into the night, laughing wildly, the sound of it echoing on long after he had vanished into the shadows.

Brendys stood in awe, gaping at his father. Not only had he never seen the sword, he would never have dreamed that his father was capable of using it. He was beginning to understand just how much he underestimated his father.

Brendyk stared into the darkness, in the direction Brugnara had taken, his expression disclosing an unbridled hatred for the drunken stablehand.

Perspiration beaded his brow, even in the cold of the night. His expression suddenly changed to one of horror. Ashen, he quickly turned away and went back to the house, sword in hand.

Brendys's eyes fell to the crimsoned snow, where Brugnara's severed hand lay, his stomach turning at the sight of it. A rusty dagger was clutched within the hand's frozen grip—a blade Brugnara had carried, concealed in his sleeve. Swallowing hard, he let his gaze drift back to the retreating form of his father.

A thin moan rose to his ears, and he spun around. "Willerth!"

Brendys dropped down beside the boy. Blood trickled from Willerth's nostrils and stained the melting snow upon his chest. Brendys made a quick examination and was relieved to find no injuries more serious than a bloodied nose.

Brendys carefully lifted the boy in his arms and carried him to the main house. Farida opened the door and led them into the kitchen, where she had a basin of warm water and some soft rags waiting on a table to one side of the room.

Brendys sat Willerth down on the table, the boy remaining somewhat dazed. He picked up a damp rag and proceeded to gently clean the blood from the boy's face and chest. The bleeding had stopped, but Brendys knew the boy would hurt for quite awhile yet.

As Brendys finished cleaning him up, Willerth seemed to focus on the youth's face. His voice weak and tremulous as he spoke. "I'm a-feared, Master Bren'ys!"

Hesitantly, uncertain of Willerth's reaction, Brendys reached out and gently stroked the boy's head with one hand. Willerth stiffened, but did not resist. "I know that, Willerth. But don't you worry yourself—I don't think Brugnara would ever dare to return here again."

"'ee kilt Mama, an' 'ee's gonna kilt Master Bren'yk too!" the boy insisted. 'Ee said so!"

After all he had seen and learned, the revelation that Brugnara had murdered Willerth's mother did not surprise Brendys in the least. Brendys looked at the boy's trembling face, taking in the fear, the pain, the growing hopelessness.

Not again, he thought. *I won't let this happen again!*

He gently pulled the boy to himself. "You are safe here, Willerth. I promise you . . . no one will ever do this to you again."

He could feel Willerth tremble beneath his touch, but he did not sense fear. At last, he understood. "It's all right to cry, Willerth. Farida says it's good sometimes."

Gradually, the child's breaths came more quickly, and sobs began to wrack his small frame. Tears came at last, beginning as a trickle, but transforming quickly into a river.

Brendys hugged the boy close, surprised to find a few tears forming on his own cheeks. He felt a touch on his shoulder and looked up. Farida stood there, a gentle, but proud smile on her lips. Brendys looked away in embarrassment.

"I will see if I can find some more of your old clothes and put them in your room," he heard her say quietly.

Without looking up, he nodded.

He lost track of time as he held the boy. When Willerth had finally cried himself to sleep, Brendys picked him up and carried the boy up to his room. After he put Willerth to bed, he turned to blow out the lamp.

The door cracked open, and Brendyk poked his head in. "Is everything all right now?"

"Aye," Brendys replied over his shoulder. "He's asleep."

Brendyk nodded and turned his gaze towards the sleeping boy's face. After a short time, he spoke again. "I will be away tomorrow morning, I expect for several hours. I want you to tear down the workers' cabin—and I want it down before I return, every timber."

Too tired to argue, Brendys just nodded and replied, "Aye, Father."

"Good night, Brendys."

"Good night, Father."

Brendyk closed the door, and Brendys blew out the lamp.

Chapter 5

Old Goffin huddled in the ruins of one of the old guardposts nestled in the walls of the Western Pass. Despite the shelter of the stone chamber, the winter night seemed colder than usual and the shadows deeper. When he wanted to be alone, he came here, for few travelers passed through Shalkan, especially in the winter.

But for some reason, he felt unsettled, as though he were being carefully watched. He knew the sensation was ridiculous. The entrance was partially collapsed, hiding him from the view of any who might travel through the Pass. Even the passage into the old fortress tunnels within Barrier Mountain was blocked by debris. But he could not rid himself of the feeling, no matter how silly it seemed.

A sound outside the guardpost startled him. No one had tripped the alarm trap he had set, but he had definitely heard something. He cautiously edged towards the entrance and peered through the rubble.

A man stumbled into the Western Pass, his right hand pressed under his left arm. A second assessment brought Goffin to the realization that the man had lost his right hand. Clearly, he had also lost a lot of blood, but the frigid night air had now frozen the stump and stopped the bleeding.

The stranger fell to his knees in the packed snow. Goffin considered bringing him into the guardpost. He had a feeling the poor fellow was not going to last through the night, and it did not seem appropriate to let him die alone in the Pass. Before he could move, an icy chill ran down his spine, freezing him in place.

A cloaked figure, a giant of a man, appeared from the shadows of the guardpost in the opposite wall. The cloaked man reached a strong hand out towards the wounded man. His muscular arm was bare, which Goffin found curious, given the weather. A deep, soft voice issued forth from within the man's black hood. "Do you know who I am, Brugnara?"

The dying man tried to choke out a reply, but could not muster the strength.

"You are soon to enter my Realm," the giant continued. "But I am a fair master . . . for a price. You have tasted of my power—shall you accept your part of it?"

The man named Brugnara mouthed an answer, but no sound came forth.

"Yes," the voice continued. "You are already mine."

The giant reached out his hand and touched Brugnara's forehead. Darkness, like a black flame, sprang from his hand and engulfed the dying vagrant. Brugnara screamed in agony, his shrill voice echoing in the Pass, then he collapsed, unmoving.

Goffin would have screamed himself, but for fear the cloaked man might notice him. But it did not matter. The giant slowly turned towards his hiding place. Within the depths of the hood, he could see a pair of burning red eyes glaring back at him.

The giant began to advance.

* * * *

Willerth shivered. An uncanny chill had come over him in the night. He opened his eyes and found himself standing in a doorway, staring into a darkened chamber. It was Brendyk's room, but what he was doing there, he could not imagine. He had never walked in his sleep before, and this felt strange to him. He was numb all over—or rather, he had no sensation in his body whatsoever.

Knowing he should not be there, Willerth was about to return to his master's bedroom when suddenly the shutters flew open, and a wind blasted through the curtains. Brendyk stirred, but did not awaken. Willerth felt a chill, like icy fingers wrapped around his heart . . . the first sensation he had felt.

A dull, red light leaked through the open window, forming a faint column beside the bed. It began as a flicker, but soon started to grow and expand. Willerth's lips formed words of warning, but no sound came forth.

The light faded away, leaving a strange creature in its place. It was a slender beast with sleek, black fur and lithe muscles, and its head was like that of a wild panther. Its left hand was large and boasted long, sharp claws, but its right was the size of a man's and was covered with a black gauntlet. The fingers on that hand were stiff and splayed out, curving at the tips as if the beast were reaching out for something. The creature's red eyes blazed bright as it looked upon the sleeping Horsemaster, its gloved hand stretching towards Brendyk's neck.

Willerth again tried to cry a warning, but still could make no sound.

Just as the beast's hidden claw came over Brendyk's throat, the creature stopped, turning its catlike head towards a table on the opposite side of the room, baring its xanthic fangs in an evil grin. Its glaring eyes had brushed over Willerth, but it did not seem to have seen him.

Moving away from the bed, it walked over to the table and laid both hands, palms down, on a long object which was lying there. Its blood-red eyes began to glow brighter and brighter, until their scarlet aura completely surrounded the beast. It turned its gaze back towards the bed and exposed its fangs once more.

When the creature glanced back at Brendyk the second time, Willerth made an attempt to charge the beast, but he was restrained by the grip of a strong arm around his waist, which slowly pulled him back.

Willerth jerked his eyes open and glanced fearfully around the room. His young body was soaked with perspiration, and he was panting heavily. The arm around his waist, holding him still, belonged to his master.

"Calm down, Willerth," Brendys yawned. "You were only having a nightmare."

Willerth yielded to the protective strength which held him down. Sobbing, he settled back and lay his head on his master's shoulder.

Brendys pulled the blankets up over the boy's shoulders, keeping a comforting arm around him the entire time. "Everything is going to be all right now, Willerth. Brugnara is gone. Go back to sleep."

* * * *

At breakfast, Willerth related his dream of the previous night to Brendyk and his master, fearing that it was a foretelling of some dire event.

"'at do it mean, Master Bren'yk? I'm a-feared," the boy said when he was finished with his tale.

Smiling gently, the Horsemaster reached out and patted him on the shoulder. "And without cause. It was a nightmare, boy, nothing more...doubtless brought on by last night's troubles. I promise you, nothing will come of it."

Willerth glanced towards Brendys, receiving an accordant nod in return. He sat back, sighing with a slight amount of relief.

Brendyk rose to his feet. "Brendys, I am heading out to Meyler Roam. I shan't be back until late this afternoon. You have that cabin down! No dawdling. Farewell now."

"Farewell, Father," Brendys returned with a sluggish nod.

"Good-bye, Master Bren'yk."

The Horsemaster turned and left the room.

Brendys finished his breakfast in exhausted silence. When he was through, he leaned forward on his elbows, trying unsuccessfully to rub the sleep from his face with both hands. He ventured a glance at Willerth, who was cheerfully forking food into his mouth.

Brendys grimaced in disbelief. Unlike himself, Willerth showed no sign of weariness from the very short night. Indeed, only a pair of black eyes that he had developed hinted at the events of the previous night. As well, he had almost instantly put aside the memory of his nightmare upon Brendyk's assurances.

When Willerth was done, he put down his fork and looked up at his master, smiling.

Brendys sighed and pushed himself to his feet, using the table for support. "I suppose we ought to see what we can do about that cabin."

Willerth hesitated, looking up at the youth in uncertainty, then slid out of his chair.

With the boy trailing closely behind him, Brendys made his way through the house to the front door. He took his cloak down from its wall peg and flung it around his shoulders, fastening the broach at his neck. Before opening the door, he heard Farida's voice and turned to face her.

"You are *not* taking the boy out in the cold without a cloak," she said firmly as she approached them. A small green cloak was draped over her arm.

Brendys glanced at Willerth. The boy was wearing a new tunic and trousers, but nothing heavy enough to protect him from the winter chill. "I forgot. The cloak Father gave him must still be in the cabin."

"Never mind," the old houseservant replied, draping the new cloak over Willerth's shoulders. "I found this one last night. It's a much better fit, if I may say so."

Willerth's pink cheeks brightened further as Farida fastened the clasp at his throat, then straightened his tunic and smoothed out his tawny hair.

"Farida, don't make such a fuss over him," Brendys chided her. "His hair and clothes will be a mess again by the time we're finished anyway."

"Don't you make a fuss, young man," the old woman returned. "You are not so old that I wouldn't do the same to you, if I were of the mind."

Brendys snorted and opened the door. He ushered Willerth outside, then followed, closing the door behind himself. When he came to the bottom of the porch steps, he stopped and turned around. He had not heard the sound of Willerth's footsteps behind him. The boy stood at the head of the steps, gazing across to the workers' quarters, a haunted look in his grey eyes.

Brendys frowned. He understood now why his father wanted the building torn down. As long as it stood, it would serve as a reminder to Willerth of all he had endured at Brugnara's hands.

He decided not to press the boy for what meager assistance he might be able to lend with the task at hand and went on. He walked around the house to the woodpile to retrieve his axe, then turned for the workers' quarters. As he neared the cabin, he slowed, a curious chill running down his spine.

Brendys stopped at the place where he and his father had confronted Brugnara. He looked down with a shudder of trepidation. The snow had melted away from the spot where Brugnara's severed hand had lain. The ground there was blackened as though scorched by fire, and there was no sign of the hand or knife.

The youth took a tighter grip on his axe and glanced around fearfully. After a moment, he felt his face flush in embarrassment. *Get a hold of yourself, Brendys! Brugnara is gone . . . likely dead.*

Nevertheless, he shoved snow over the black spot with his foot, before continuing to the cabin.

He ruefully surveyed the building. The walls and foundation of the cabin were incredibly durable, despite the wear the rest of the building had suffered over the years. Tearing it down would not be a simple task.

His first thought had been to burn it down, but he quickly dismissed that idea. Even if he had enough dry kindling of the sort that would burn in this weather, the cabin was too close to the stable to risk a fire.

Exhaling heavily, he drew back his axe, then brought it down on the makeshift steps Brugnara had built onto the entrance. The steps splintered quickly with each successive stroke, but Brendys knew they were the weakest part of the building.

When the steps were destroyed, he started hacking into the bottom edge of the raised entry. He spent nearly two full hours at it, succeeding only in splintering a small pile of chips from the heavy plank and dulling the bit of his axe. He stopped and leaned on the axe, shaking his head. At this rate, it would take him a year and more axes than could be found in Ahz-Kham to bring down the workers' quarters.

He was left with no other choice. He would have to risk a fire. He was only glad his father was nowhere near Ahz-Kham at that moment. Brendys took the axe back to the woodpile, then jogged to the foot of the porch steps. Willerth was still standing on the porch, gaze fixed firmly on the cabin.

"Willerth?" Brendys said cautiously.

The boy jumped a little at the sound of his voice, but turned his attention fully to his master. "Aye, sir?"

"I need to run a quick errand," Brendys told him. "Why don't you go see if Farida needs help with anything until I get back?"

Willerth nodded and disappeared into the house, glad to be sent into the relative warmth of the house.

Brendys trotted to the stable and saddled Hedelbron. Down the road a little way lived a brewer, an old friend of his father's. Brendys knew Kotsybar would provide him with enough kindling to burn down every building in Shalkan if he asked. Brendys had never understood the brewer's fierce loyalty to Brendyk, nor the unwavering friendship they shared. It was a strange relationship, considering Kotsybar's occupation and Brendyk's extreme disapproval of strong drink. Whenever Brendys brought up the subject, no one ever seemed willing to talk about it.

As Brendys rode out of the farmstead, he fretted over his father's inevitable reaction over his decision to burn the workers' quarters, but he had no choice. He had been given a task, and that task could not be completed any other way.

As Brendys had expected, it had not taken much effort to convince Kotsybar to assist him in the matter of kindling. He soon returned with the brewer close behind him. The man appeared to be a few years older than Brendyk, though Brendys was sure the fact that his black hair was mostly absent on top accounted for the difference. Like most Shalkanes, Kotsybar's eyes were a deep blue and his skin was well-tanned. He wore a coarse brown tunic and trousers and heavy leather boots and was driving a small wagon loaded high with kindling.

They stopped in front of the workers' cabin, and Brendys and the brewer began emptying the wagon, stacking the kindling beside the building. When the bed of the wagon was empty, Kotsybar climbed back up, taking the leads in hand.

"'Tis your work now, lad," the brewer said. He added in a warning tone, "And not a word of this to your father!"

Brendys laughed in return. "You shan't have to worry about that, Master Kotsybar. If I told him I had asked you for kindling, I would be mucking out stalls for a month—with no relief!"

Without another word, Kotsybar waved in farewell to the youth and urged his horses on with a flick of the reins. Brendys waved in return, then set about the chore of spreading the kindling around the foundation of the building. Finally, he picked up a small bundle of the fast burning wood and climbed inside the cabin.

He dropped his bundle on the table at the center of the single-room building and looked around. The interior of the cabin was a mess. Chairs and night stands were toppled—the probable cause of the crashing noises that had drawn the attention of himself and his father the night before. Also scattered about the room were the various articles of clothing Brendyk and Farida had given to Willerth.

Brendys picked up the child's sky-blue jacket and held it up. He considered gathering the clothes and taking them back to the house, but looking at the jacket conjured the memory of Brugnara's leering face. He dropped the jacket and began piling whatever loose items he could find under and around the table, finally scattering the remaining kindling over the pile.

He smashed a leg off one of the chairs and wrapped the jacket around one end. Kneeling down, he placed his makeshift torch on the floor, then withdrew a small tinderbox from a pocket inside his cloak. A short time later, the jacket was burning.

Brendys jumped down out of the cabin's entrance, torch in hand. He lit the kindling outside in several places, then tossed the torch back into the building. He backed away from the cabin as the flames soared higher.

When the entire building was finally engulfed in flame, he felt a touch at his arm. He looked down as Willerth took his hand. Fear melted from the boy's eyes as he watched the last vestiges of his old life burn away.

As Brendys and Willerth watched the blaze, Brendyk returned. The Horsemaster quickly dismounted and rushed to his son's side. "Brendys, are you mad! What were you thinking?"

Startled, Brendys turned to face his father. "You're home early!"

"Answer the question!" Brendyk snapped.

Brendys squirmed under his father's angry gaze. "Father, I had no choice. You've said yourself that Great-Grandfather told you this place used to be part of a garrison. It was built to stand up to the axes of an army . . . ours did nothing!"

Garnering a little courage, he added, "Besides, I've been keeping an eye on the stable."

The Horsemaster glared for a moment longer, then his gaze softened, and he sighed. "Aye, I should have known what kind of chore it would be. How did you manage the fire?"

Without thinking, Brendys started to reply, "I got some kindling. . . ." then stopped before he revealed where, mentally kicking himself for his slip.

"How much did it cost us?" his father asked.

Brendys hesitated, trying to think of a viable excuse.

Brendyk tersely repeated his question. "How much?"

"Well. . . ." Brendys looked down at Willerth, who was staring at him with a puzzled expression. Sighing, he replied to his father, "I went to Master Kotsybar."

Brendyk motioned his son towards the house. "Come with me."

Brendys followed his father into the house and upstairs to the library.

The Horsemaster produced a sack of coins from one of his desk drawers, which he handed over to Brendys. "Take this to Kotsybar. It must have cost him more than he could afford, surely."

"Father, I don't understand it!" Brendys responded. "You will do favors for others, but you will not accept them! Why?"

Brendyk turned and looked out the library window, but did not reply.

Brendys knew better than to force the issue.

He took the money to the brewer as his father had told him to do, but Kotsybar would not accept it. In that way, Brendyk and the brewer were much alike. Instead, Kotsybar dropped several more gold pieces into the bag and handed it back to Brendys.

"Call it a birthday gift for the boy," the man told Brendys.

"But, Master Kotsybar," Brendys pleaded. "Father will have my head. . . ."

Kotsybar held up a palm, silencing his protests. "Be on your way, lad. Brendyk will be much angrier should you get back after dark."

Dejectedly, Brendys left as ordered. His heart was not in returning home. He knew his father would be angry, and he was not sure he was up to facing him. He considered riding into Ahz-Kham, but after a few minutes decided against it. He knew his actions the day before had most likely severed what ties he had to his friends at the *Green Meadow*.

As Brendys expected, his father was in the stableyard, waiting, when he returned. Brendys dismounted and handed the sack of coins to his father.

"Master Kotsybar wouldn't take it, Father," he declared before Brendyk could utter a word. "He gave it back to me, told me it was a birthday gift for Willerth, and sent me home. I tried to change his mind, but he wouldn't listen!"

Brendyk looked long at the bag, and Brendys knew his anger had been diverted. But he thought that his father would surely take the money back to Kotsybar himself. Instead, the Horsemaster gave him an odd smile and returned to the house. Brendys watched him leave, brow wrinkled in puzzlement.

Willerth appeared from the stable and joined his master.

"Father has been acting stranger than usual today, wouldn't you say?" Brendys said to the boy.

Willerth said nothing in return, but took his master's hand as they walked to the house.

* * * *

A traveler walked his horse down the road from the Western Pass through Barrier Mountain into Shalkan. He was a rugged fellow, toughened by years of wandering. His hair was red and curly, but greying heavily around the edges, and his greyish-green eyes were dark, nearly as dark as his drab, travel-worn clothing. His mount walked with a slight limp, having come up lame on the way through the Western Pass.

The man stopped to give his injured horse a rest. From his vantage point upon the hill leading into the valley of Shalkan, he could barely make out the farmstead belonging to his old friend Brendyk in the distance, partially hidden in the wintery landscape. He reached a hand into his pocket and drew out a tarnished silver ring—or at least it seemed silver. He had noticed when he placed it next to a silver coin, the ring appeared more golden in hue. The ring seemed to pulse with a warmth of its own, but that did not surprise him, for the ring was made of Gloriod, the rarest of all Elvinmetals.

The warmth, however, did not hold his attention. His eyes were fixed on the signet: a bird of prey—a falcon or a hawk, he could not tell which—blazoned on a sun, grasping a sword in one talon and a heart in the other. Blood stained the emblem, almost bringing a sort of life to it.

Wearing a grim frown, the man replaced the ring in his pocket and went on.

* * * *

Brendyk hunched over his desk in the library, pouring over his records, a pair of spectacles resting on his nose. Willerth sat on the floor beside the Horsemaster's chair, a large, leather-bound book lying open before him, staring at the letters in frustration.

Brendyk glanced down at the boy through the corner of his eye, then leaned against the back of his chair and removed his spectacles, tucking them in the pocket of his open waistcoat. "I should have known you could not read. Your father certainly had no knowledge of letters. I suppose if you are going to remain with us, I shall have to teach you. Would you like that, boy?"

Willerth returned his gaze to the unfamiliar marks on the pages of the book, then slowly nodded his head in affirmation.

"All right then, up you come," he said, beckoning the boy to him with his hand.

Willerth, slouching down, stared up at the Horsemaster, frowning.

Brendyk shook his finger at Willerth in gentle reproach. "I'll have none of that now, boy. You are going to have to learn to trust me as you would your master. You want to learn your letters and make Brendys proud, don't you?"

Willerth again slowly nodded.

"Then come here."

The boy stood up, leaving the leather-bound tome on the floor, for it was too heavy for him to lift, then stood up and went to his master's writing table. He dragged the chair around the desk and placed it beside Brendyk's, then sat down.

Brendyk's stare briefly saddened as he looked down at the boy. Withdrawing his gaze from Willerth, he reached into a drawer and drew out a few pieces of a yellowish parchment and placed them on the desktop, then withdrew his spectacles from his pocket and brought them to his face again. "I think we will start with the names of the letters and what they look like. . . ."

There was a quiet knock at the door and Farida entered the room. "Master Rister is here, Master Brendyk. He is waiting in the front room."

Brendyk's face brightened slightly. "Thank you, Farida. I will be right down."

The old woman nodded and left.

Brendyk rose from his chair and headed for the door. "I'm afraid your lessons shall have to wait a little while longer. Come along now."

Sighing, Willerth followed the Horsemaster out of the room and down the hall to the staircase. Brendyk started down the stairs with Willerth on his heels, but the boy hung back when he saw the rough-looking stranger.

A delighted smile crossed Brendyk's face as he came into the front room. "Rister! It has been too long! What will you be needing this time? Supplies? Horses? Or just a bed for the night? I will have Farida bring us some tea and we can talk about it."

"I haven't the time, I'm afraid," the man replied gruffly. "Champa went lame on me; he can't make the travels. I wanted to make a trade. Champa is good stud; surely, he must be worth something to you."

"He certainly is!" Brendyk replied. "I've been waiting to get that old fleabag from you for four years!"

"I'm sorry to part with Champa though," the trader started a little mournfully. "But I need a working horse more than I do a stud. I knew that you liked Champa, so I thought I would give you the first chance at him. Besides, you have enough riding stock that old Champa can take it easy until his leg heals up. Aye, I imagine that he will be much better off here."

The tone of regret in the man's voice was greatly exaggerated, and Brendyk knew that he was trying to get a better bargain than would be reasonable for an injured horse. But for his old friend, Brendyk was more than happy to oblige.

"I have a three-year-old chestnut colt that might do for you," Brendyk told the trader. "He is spirited—quite spirited—and built beautifully! He's the best of my stock! Unfortunately, Ekenes is all that I have to offer at the moment—Dell bought nearly every horse I had this summer."

The Horsemaster pretended to mull over his own offer for a minute, then continued. "For anyone else and for any other horse, Ekenes would not be for sale, but for you, and especially Champa, well—I am getting a good bit of horseflesh in return.

"Ekenes will work out exceptionally well as either a working horse or a stud. Brendys has been working with him, and he is not just fast, but more important, he is agile. He has steadied down a great deal since last year and filled out; this spring, he will be ready for anything you want to do with him."

The trader gave Brendyk a satisfied nod. "Aye, I remember that colt from last summer. I am sure he will do very well . . . after all the sire and dam were quite good."

Rister's voice slowed. "Aye, I'm sure he will do just fine. . . ."

Brendyk started to the door, elated at the addition of as fine a stallion as Champa to his stable, as well as being rid of the devilish Ekenes. "Good. I will tell Brendys to get him ready for you."

Rister spoke before Brendyk was to the door. "Brendyk, sit down."

Brendyk turned back to face the man. The trader's features told of grim tidings. Brendyk knew the look. He had seen it before when Rister had told him of his father's murder. He shrugged and complied with the man's order.

Rister reached into his pocket and withdrew a ring, which he tossed to Brendyk. The Horsemaster did not have to study it long. It was a signet ring—his own, an old heirloom of his family. The bloodstains worried him a little. He had not noticed them before.

Brendyk looked up at his trader friend. "Where did you get this?"

"From the hand of a dead man that I found up in the Western Pass. This was on the ground beside him. . . ." Rister drew a sword from his own sheath and tossed it hilt-first to Brendyk.

Brendyk caught the weapon in his right hand. It, too, belonged to the Horsemaster, and it too was bloodstained.

Rister continued. "This fellow was missing a hand, and his head as well. He was rather well frozen, but I would say that he had only been dead for a day or two at the most."

Brendyk grew pale as his old friend spoke. He knew the implications. Brugnara was dead, murdered by his sword.

Rister's voice became sharper. "Brendyk, I know you are not capable of taking up arms against another man, much less killing him! Even when you received that sword, you refused to draw it. I should know: *I* gave it to you!

"I remember what you told me when I forced it into your hands. You told me, '*Tis not mine to take a man's life, nor to draw his blood. That is given for others. My charge is to save lives.*"

Brendyk stared at the sword, his expression saddening. "You are wrong, Rister. We were both wrong. I do confess to cutting off the man's hand—he attacked Brendys with a knife—but I did *not* kill him! I don't even know how my sword could have gotten up in the Pass, nor the ring."

The trader leaned back in his seat, rubbing his chin. "I think that you had best tell me the whole tale, Brendyk."

Brendyk again complied, starting with Brugnara's arrival at the farmstead. Rister quietly listened while Brendyk told his story. When the Horsemaster had finished, Rister stood up and moved over to a window, leaning with his hands on the sill. His roving eyes fastened on Brendys as the youth went about his chores, his gaze becoming thoughtful, then stern. "By what you tell me, Brendyk, your son perhaps had the most. . . ."

Brendyk started to his feet, shocked by the thoughts he knew were going through the trader's mind. "Now you look here, Rister! Bren. . . ."

The Horsemaster's words were halted by a small voice. He had forgotten Willerth. "Master Bren'ys di'n't kilt no 'un."

The two men looked up at the boy, and Rister said, "What was that?"

Willerth cowered down behind the stair railing and said nothing in return.

"Come on now, boy," Brendyk said. "Answer him."

Willerth timidly did as told. "That thin' kilt 'im."

Rister gave the boy a curious look. "What *thing?*"

Willerth hesitated, then replied, his words spilling out suddenly at an amazing speed. "It was black, an' it 'ad a cat's 'ead, an'-an' claws, an' red eyes, an' big fangs, an'-an'. . . ."

Brendyk cut him off with a sigh. "That was only a nightmare, boy."

Protests sprang to Willerth's lips, but a sharp glare from Brendyk hushed them before they were put to voice.

Rister turned his eyes from the boy back to Brendyk. "It is quite obvious that whoever did this was trying to place the blame on you, perhaps hoping that the constable would imprison, perhaps even hang you as the law demands . . . which, of course, I know Brendys would never do."

"But that is impossible!" Brendyk responded. "No one but myself had access to either the ring or the sword."

The Horsemaster paused in thought. "No, I left the sword out that night, and I did find the window open in the morning—but whoever stole it had to have walked right past me!"

"That thin' did it!" Willerth put in, but the men ignored the boy . . . at least Rister ignored him.

85

Brendyk cast a quick glance at the boy. He was beginning to wonder exactly how much of Willerth's dream was truly a dream.

Rister cleared his voice, drawing Brendyk's attention back to him. There was a twinkle in the trader's grey-green eye as he shrugged and said, "Then we have run into a slight obstacle, haven't we? I am certain that you will solve this riddle, sooner or later, on your own.

"Though I do love a good mystery, I am afraid that I cannot stay to help you. I must be in Meyler Roam by sundown, or I lose my deal."

Relief flooded over Brendyk. He knew Rister was convinced of his innocence and would say nothing of this incident to anyone.

Rister continued to speak. "I should be back in a few months, though. I am traveling east to Gos to have a look at old Selph's stock. He claims that he has developed the perfect breed, but with Selph, one never knows.

"Farewell, Brendyk." Rister turned on his heels and started for the door.

"Don't forget your horse," Brendyk said quietly. "Tell Brendys . . . he will know which one."

Brendyk paused, then added, "And, Rister . . . thank you. Once again, I owe you. Farewell."

The other man paused a moment and spoke without looking back. "I may take you up on that some day," he said, then continued out the door.

Brendyk, still staring at the door, spoke to his son's servant. "There goes a true friend, lad. Anyone else would have gone straight to the constable. Thank Elekar it was he that found the body and not someone else."

Willerth shrugged with a frown.

Brendyk looked up at the boy. "Perhaps someday—when you are older—I will tell you how we met."

Chapter 6

Gwydnan slept uneasily. He had felt all day that something was amiss in the land, but the Dawn King had given him no sign, so he dismissed the feeling as a trick of his imagination. But the excuse did not satisfy him, for his imagination had never been a fertile one, and even his dreams were troubled by a sense of foreboding.

Crimson lightning rent the clear night sky, and Gwydnan suddenly jerked upright in bed, sweat beading his brow. The old kitchenhand's aged features were stiffened in agony, a child's terrified screams echoing in his mind.

Kanstanon!

Gwydnan scrambled out of his bed and hurried to his ward's room, but found the stableboy sleeping soundly.

A storm is brewing, he thought. *It must have only been the wind howling.*

Gwydnan looked out the window, expecting to see billowing thunderheads rolling overhead, but instead found the stars shining brightly in an otherwise empty, winter sky and the wind was calmer than usual. Scarlet bolts slashed through the sky again, glaring red against the glass of the window, and a great clap of thunder shook the pane. In a few minutes, the lightning ceased and all was silent.

Gwydnan dropped into a chair beside Kanstanon's bed. He slouched forward in his chair. A heavy weight fell upon him, as it always did when a vision was thrust upon him. A dim mist enshrouded his sight, reality melting away into a dark smoke, as he was pulled into Reanna Orilal, the Vision Realm.

The wall of fog opened before Gwydnan, revealing to his mind's eyes the long stair of a tower, dark in the night shadows. A giant of a man slowly traced his way up the spiral staircase, up to the open parapet at the top, bearing a young child in his muscular arms. His long, grey hair fell down past his shoulders, draped over black robes. His grey eyes were cold as the stone of the fortress, and his skin had the pallor of a corpse. His pale face was set with a grimness that would freeze the heart of the boldest warrior.

In the huge man's arms, the small boy cried in terror, knowing what was to be his fate. He had been bred solely for this purpose. But there was no one there to come to his aid, no one even to comfort him in his time of dread. But his cries were not unheard, nor unheeded. Gwydnan uttered a few words in his native tongue, and the child drifted into a deep and peaceful sleep, heedless of his surroundings.

The giant paused. Gwydnan knew he had felt his presence, despite the leagues that separated them. The giant's lip curled slightly as he continued up the stairway.

Gwydnan watched in growing horror as the giant brought the child out of the tower and onto the balcony where he was stripped and placed upon an altar of black stone, his wrists and ankles bound to the stone with black thongs. The Sorcerer pulled a large, two-handed axe from a harness on his back, slowly passing the twisted weapon over the boy in a circular motion. Chanting filled the air as the ritual began. Six times, the giant passed the sacrificial axe over the child, at first in small circles, then gradually in larger ones, raising the axe higher with each pass.

Gwydnan uttered every word of power that he knew, but in vain. He was powerless to stop the dark ritual.

The ground shook as the Black Shadow, a darkness deeper than the darkest night, sprang up from the base of Chi Thanatos, the Tower of Death, slowly winding up around the battlement until it surrounded the altar. As the Darkness closed in about the black stone, the Sorcerer plunged his axe downwards. . . .

Gwydnan turned his head away, shielding his mortal eyes with his hand, but unable to hide his mind from the vision. "No more!"

The Sorcerer's laughter thundered loud in his ears. Gwydnan looked upon the gruesome vision, rage replacing his horror. In that moment, he heard—or rather, felt—a familiar voice speaking to him the words of prophecy. The Dawn King, had passed judgment.

"Fanos Pavo shall have his vengeance, Iysh Mawvath!" Gwydnan hissed angrily. His voice turned sepulchral as he uttered the prophecy. "You who have slain by the axe, so shall you die by the axe. Vengeance shall be borne by the Free Kindreds—Man, Elf, Dwarf. Even the smallest shall have his due."

The giant started down the winding stairs, laughing in amusement and ridicule at the words of condemnation flooding his mind, undaunted by them.

Gwydnan watched until the Sorcerer had passed from view.

The mist swallowed up the vision, then reopened, revealing a childlike face. This being, too, was a seer of sorts, Gwydnan knew. The path to his destiny had been illuminated.

"You have heard the words?" Gwydnan said to his brother prophet, his voice hollow in the mists of the vision.

The other's sapphirine eyes blazed in his childlike face with a cobalt light. "I have."

"Then your time shall soon come, my friend," Gwydnan responded, his voice grim. "Be ready for that day."

The small being inclined his head. "Elekar's will shall be done!"

When the being had spoken his last word, the mists faded away, and Gwydnan's mind was returned to the Shipyard of Ilkatar.

Kanstanon's eyelids flickered open, and he sat up, looking upon his elder with frightened eyes. The boy's tired voice trembled as he spoke. "Master, I'm afraid."

Gwydnan raised an understanding hand to the boy's head, gently rubbing it. He was afraid, too. In a short moment, he gave answer to the boy. "There's nothing to fear, lad. Nothing to fear."

Gwydnan slid onto the bed, atop the covers, putting a comforting arm around his ward. He did not sleep. He waited through the night for another sign, but that sign never came.

His part was almost finished. He would soon need to make arrangements for Kanstanon's future . . . but no, he could not think of that now. There would be time for that later. There was more to be done before he could cross to Alaren Orilal. Much more to be done.

* * * *

Iysh Mawvath relaxed upon his twisted throne in the great hall of Chi Thanatos, fingering the bloodied edge of the sacrificial axe laid out across his lap, a comfortable smirk on his face. He could already taste the sweet savor of victory; it was only a matter of time before it would actually be his to claim. He had waited centuries for the opportunity to lead the legions of Thanatos against the Free Lands, and now that time had come.

Centuries—Iysh Mawvath's faint smile vanished completely. Centuries before, he had been a *Nerad*—apprentice to a Wizard—in the holy city of Athor, but he had quickly grown tired of his life of servitude. There was greater power to be had.

That was when he began dabbling in the Black Arts. At first, he practiced minor incantations that he had learned from the priests of the gods—spells of healing, for the most part, for his heart was still gentle at that time. Then his brother discovered his secret interest in the Black Arts and warned him of the consequences it would bring, the heavy price it would exact from him.

Lenharthen, as he was known then, ignored his brother's warnings and continued to delve into his arcane studies. His brother's words proved true—Lenharthen betrayed his people and turned to the service of Thanatos. He became the Deathlord's greatest pupil and was later transformed by the Black Hand into the hulking monster he now was—Iysh Mawvath, Warlord of Thanatos.

All semblance of his former humanity was torn from him, his compassion and desire to help others twisted into a seething hatred for all things human, indeed all things living. Few now could call him friend, save the devils he kept around him—fellow Sorcerers and creatures of Darkness—and even they were more his servants than friends, trembling in his presence.

A bitter chill pierced his heart, a burning agony coursed through his body, a life worse than death—but such was the price of power and immortality, he had learned. Iysh Mawvath's heartless smile returned to his lips. The terrible pain that he was forced to endure seemed to strengthen him. In that, he reveled.

Around the Sorcerer stood four of his agents. One was a member of the renegade Dark Elves. He was a lithe being and stood a hand or two shorter than the average Man. Like all Elves, he was strangely fair to look upon, despite his snow-white skin and hair, but his immortal youth and beauty were marred by a deep, grey scar hooking from below his left eye down his jaw.

Beside the Elf stood a human warrior adorned in full mail. He was a younger man with long, black hair and patches of black whiskers on his cheeks and chin, marking a failed attempt at a beard. His surcoat was black, red, and gold, arranged in a saltire, the same badge emblazoned upon the shield strapped to his back. His left hand gripped the diamond-shaped pommel of his sword.

Nearer to the throne were Iysh Mawvath's closer allies. On the Sorcerer's right hand, sitting on its haunches, was a great beast likened to a three-headed timberwolf. Two of its heads drooped forward, their eyes closed, but the middle one was held high, its blazing red eyes glaring upon Man and Elf, its great jaws gnawing upon the raw flesh of an unfortunate, slowly savoring the fresh meat.

At the Sorcerer's left, one of the reptilian Kubruki, a War-Chief, awaited his Warlord's command. Like all Kubruki, the beast stood at a height of around seven feet, fortified with great bulking thews and tough, black scales. Leather bands embedded with small, steel spikes crossed the Kubruk's chest, fastened to the rough fur worn at the beast's waist. A row of horns protruded down the middle of the creature's skull, starting between its slitted, yellow eyes and proceeding into a column of bony plates running down its back.

Iysh Mawvath's allies seemed impatient—all save the wolf-beast who was busily tearing at the bloody remains set before him—and rightly so, for when all was ready, the armies of Kubruki gathered at the base of Chi Thanatos would march forth from the barrens of Machaelon to begin their long-awaited conquest. Death's Legion had nearly been destroyed in the last war. It had taken almost fourteen-hundred years to rebuild their strength. In the last few centuries, Iysh Mawvath had managed to sway nine nearby nations—dubbed the Dark Lands by the Alliance of the Free Kindreds—to the service of Machaelon, but many were still hesitant to join this venture. Soon, all the allies of Thanatos would join together, of that he was sure.

The conquest would begin with the smaller nations of the Southeastern Quarter. When that was done, they would join with their fellow Kubruki in the Silver Mountains and the Blue Mountains, and with the Men of the Dark Lands and their other allies, and revive the Death's Legion of old. But not all of Iysh Mawvath's war-commanders had assembled—the council lacked one.

The young human finally put words to his agitation. "What do we wait for? Why do we not march?"

"Aye," the Elf chimed in. "We do not need Krifka and his Dagramon horde. Our numbers are strong enough now to make the attack."

Iysh Mawvath raised his cold, grey eyes to meet the Elf's gaze, his voice rumbling low. "You are wrong, Lord Chol. My armies are half what I shall need. The Dragon Riders will compensate for my shortage of Kubruki."

"Nay, they shall not," a thin, hissing voice said, echoing out of nowhere. At that moment, a dim red glow, like a mist, began to gather in the center of the room, swirling into a column, growing brighter. The form of a strange beast appeared within the glow, a fur-covered creature with the figure of a man and a head like that of a panther. As the glow dissipated, the creature was transformed into a man in grey robes and a black cloak. The hood was drawn over his face, covering all but his grey-bearded chin.

"Just what we need—another shapeshifter," Lord Chol sneered, then added, turning his head to the wolf-beast, "Eh, Kerebros?"

The creature lifted its third head, and yawning, replied in a growling voice, "The fool's powers do not concern me, Chol. But his gall in coming here, unsummoned, does, indeed, interest me."

"Enough," Iysh Mawvath rumbled. The giant sat like a statue in his throne. He had been in the service of Thanatos long enough to know another touched by his master's Black Hand. Only his eyes moved, shifting to look upon the hooded stranger. "Name yourself, Brother of Darkness, and what your words mean."

The cloaked intruder drew back his hood, his narrow eyes searching Iysh Mawvath's own. "My servants call me the Great Father. My word to you is this, Iysh Mawvath: your demon friend, Krifka, has not found his eggs, and the Dagramon cannot hatch until their keeper returns."

The human warrior spat on the floor. "I knew this was a useless enterprise the moment my Lord Klees sent me to this bloody waste land!"

Grotan, the Kubruk War-Chief at Iysh Mawvath's left hand, snarled and stepped towards the young knight. "It is not useless! My Kubruki will destroy the Free Men and gnaw their bones to dust!"

Iysh Mawvath raised a hand and the Man and Kubruk stumbled back away from each other, drawn apart by an unseen force. "Grotan is right. Our plans are delayed, but only until spring when his people's young have become strong enough to join my legions."

The Great Father shook his head in mock sadness. "You will not take this world by brute force, Iysh Mawvath. You must be more subtle."

Kerebros now raised his first head. "Brute force has always worked for me. Perhaps you feel the way you do because you lack the power yourself?"

Iysh Mawvath again raised his large hand. "Nay, Kerebros, the words of our uninvited guest bear some truth. We must know our enemies' strengths and weaknesses before we can engage them."

"Now you speak wisely, Iysh Mawvath," the stranger said. "But I am still skeptical of your plans."

"Who are you that we should care what you think of our decisions?" Kerebros growled out, all three heads now poised threateningly at the robed Sorcerer.

"I grow tired of your wagging tongues, dog," the stranger said. His eyes glowed red for a brief moment as he stared upon the wolf-beast.

Kerebros yelped as the gaping jaws of his three heads snapped closed. He pawed at one mouth in a frantic attempt to pry it open. This persisted for only a few minutes before Kerebros rose to his feet, a malevolent glare in his red eyes. Suddenly, there was a loud *crack!*, and waves of power emanated outward from the beast. Kerebros bared his fangs and leapt, snarling, at the stranger, his massive jaws freed from the Sorcerer's spell.

The stranger raised a hand towards the beast, and Kerebros collapsed to the floor, instantly transformed into a shapeless, fur-covered mass, writhing helplessly on the flagstones. "What say you now of my power, beast?"

Iysh Mawvath nodded slowly, impressed by the show of power, but inwardly angered by the defeat of his valued companion. "Indeed, you are strong in the Black Arts, Nameless One. But not strong enough. Your insolence has brought you destruction."

Iysh Mawvath raised his hand a third time. Streaks of crimson lightning burst out at the unnamed Sorcerer, but were deflected in several directions before they could strike the stranger.

"Your power may be stronger, Iysh Mawvath," the Great Father hissed in laughter. "But you cannot touch me! I have been granted immortality by the Black Hand of Thanatos, as only you can also claim. In me, life is no more, but shall go on forever!"

Iysh Mawvath rose to his full eight foot height, dwarfing even the mighty Grotan. His deathly features twisted in rage as he thundered forth, "Begone from my presence, or I will bring the very power of Hál down upon your accursed head!"

His fellow Sorcerer casually bowed and replied, "As you wish."

The red light again engulfed the small man, and in but a moment he was gone.

Iysh Mawvath strode to the balcony overlooking the barrens of Machaelon. "Our first conquest shall be Gildea. I have a plan to undermine its defenses. The Gildeans will be helpless against us."

He turned back to his allies. "There is a Trostain Lord named Quellin, the last of his ill-begotten House. As the blood of Trost runs strong in the veins of the peasantry, they will join us and revolt against the Gildean nobility—*if* we can turn their Lord to our cause."

Iysh Mawvath's dead, grey eyes searched out the human knight. "It will be your task, Balgor, to see that Lord Quellin does indeed turn. I will arrange for your King to send you as his emissary to negotiate a treaty between your nation and Gildea. We shall learn all we need to bring the Gildeans to their knees!"

Chapter 7

The afternoon sun had been shining brightly only a short time before, but now the small town of Gerdes was blanketed in an unearthly darkness. The townspeople did not panic, nor were they even really afraid. More than anything, they were confused by the strange murk. What had been a warm, cloudless day had become like a cold night illuminated by invisible stars. Although color could not be discerned in the Shadow—everything held a more or less greyish hue—the people could see quite clearly, up to a certain distance, beyond which all vision was gone. A turbulent wind had preceded the Shadow, which fell upon the village like a great wave, and many wondered that Gerdes still stood.

Horsemen thundered into the town—one to begin with, then three, and another one after that—all riding to the home of the Township Governor. All five of these men were warriors, arrayed in the fashion of the Royal House of Gildea—silver and green surcoats dimmed to grey and darker grey by the murk. This heightened the curiosity of the townspeople, and they, too, assembled at their Governor's door, hoping to receive answers to their questions.

The last of the riders halted before the Governor's abode, leaping down from the back of his lathered steed, leaving the horse untethered at the entrance of the house. He knocked loudly at the door and was promptly admitted by Deciechi, the Governor's guardsman.

Henfling, the Governor of Gerdes, a bald man, well-dressed and rather fat in the stomach, greeted him. "Hail, warrior. No doubt you bring the same tidings as the others. Death and Darkness have come already upon their villages. Where do you hail from, good sir?"

"Algire, Your Grace," the last of the messengers replied. "The enemy has overrun us and is now marching in this direction."

Henfling shook his head. Gerdes—with the exception of the obscure, fishing village of Tarlas—was the nearest town to Gildea Keep, and the Governor knew that for an enemy to come this close to their capital city, nearly the whole of Gildea would had to have already been defeated. Gerdes would fall, as well. There could be no deterring that. He had but one choice open to him.

Henfling beckoned to his guardsman. "Deciechi, my good man, ride to Gildea Keep. Tell them this: Gildea has fallen! Remember that. Now hurry, my friend, before it is too late!"

"But Guv'ner!" Deciechi protested. "'oo'll pertect ye?"

Henfling waved a hand in the air. "Time has run out. There is no more protection, Deciechi. You must go at once!"

Deciechi bowed low, clearly distressed. "Aye, sir."

The guardsman dashed from the house and out to the stable where he mounted up. The herald rode like the wind out of Gerdes, soaring westward across the open grasslands.

Governor Henfling turned to those assembled in his house. "If the enemy marches upon us, we must prepare for battle. Perhaps we will give King Treiber time to gather his strength."

The township's small Royal Guard and militia swarmed in the village square, awaiting final words from their Governor. There were no more than two hundred warriors, and a few of the village men—not nearly enough to protect the town from the expected onslaught. But the Gildeans were known to be a hardened people.

Governor Henfling stood on a platform at the center of the square. His heavy features looked pale in the odd luminescence of the Shadow. He cleared his throat and started speaking, loudly, so that all could hear. "According to some of these heralds, this Darkness arose within the Blackstone Mountains, in Machaelon . . . around Year's Death, it seems. From there, it began a westward march, and now has all but encircled its apparent objective: Gildea Keep. Within this Shadow, not far from our town, marches a mighty legion of Blackstone Kubruki. They are led by a Sorcerer of Thanatos."

Distressed murmurs ran through the ranks of the warriors.

Henfling frowned deeply. "I do not expect that we shall survive their onslaught. I doubt that, even if my herald makes it safely to Gildea Keep, help could arrive in time to save us. But for the glory of Gildea and the Lord Elekar, let us fight! The shedding of our blood shall but serve to strengthen the might and resolve of Gildea."

He struck a clenched fist to his chest and cried out, "*Kindone Getheirne un hason!*"

Those gathered in the square answered the war-cry of Gildea with a single voice, though without spirit. "*Kindone Getheirne un hason!*"

Henfling watched as the nervous, untrained warriors armed themselves with what weapons they could muster and dispersed around the outer boundaries of the village. About a quarter of the men remained within the town to protect the noncombatants, and many because they wished to remain where they could more easily protect their families.

Henfling and his people did not have to wait long. Within that very hour, their enemies came—only in small raiding parties of two or three dozen to start with—and the two hundred determined warriors held them at bay. But Henfling knew they could not hold out for long. He knew well that the Kubruki's main force numbered in the tens of thousands. His warriors' valiant effort would be to no avail. Even now, they were being overrun by the raiders, their life's blood being spilled for a hopeless cause.

Not too long after the first parties attacked, a larger force of the reptilians swept through Gerdes. Henfling watched, with his final contingent of knights, as the Kubruki burned and pillaged houses, slaughtering man, woman, and child alike, taking few prisoners.

As the Kubruki neared the center of the town, Henfling ordered his men to attack. He drew his own sword, a light, narrow-bladed weapon, and joined the fray. He thrust and slashed at the advancing enemy, but to no avail. His light weapon just skittered off the Kubruki's hard scales. It was all that he could do to keep himself alive, for a short time at least.

A Kubruk fell dead beside Henfling, where one of the Governor's warriors had struck it down. Henfling snatched up the dead beast's axe with both hands and swept it in a wide arc, slashing its bit across the massive chest of one Kubruk, then thrust the beak of the weapon into a second.

Sweat ran from his forehead, stinging his eyes. His vision impaired, Henfling began wildly swinging his Kubruk axe, his sole intent to slay as many of the creatures as he could before he himself was slain. The Kubruki suddenly parted and moved away from Henfling.

The Governor stood ready, his few remaining warriors around him, axe poised to strike. But his hand was stayed. One of the knights cried out as a ghostly-white form rose up before them, towering over even the Kubruki.

* * * *

The sun was just peeking up from behind a hill, its orange and golden rays glistening on the low hillocks and dew-covered fields along the eastern reaches of Gildea. Four horsemen crested the hill, one at the fore, two riding side-by-side in the middle, and the fourth guarding the rear. The two riding before and behind were warriors; the pair at the center were clearly nobles, or at least persons of some wealth.

The sun magnified the brilliant blue and green surcoats worn by the warriors over their mail coats. The youthful and handsome faces of these men were grim and alert. Each knight rode with one hand resting upon the pommel of his sword, and their azure and green shields were slung on their shoulders, ready to be put in place at need. Though they were traveling well within their own borders, Qatani raiders were not uncommon, even this far within Gildean borders, and they knew that they must be ready to defend their noble charges at any cost.

The warriors' boots and gloves were of leather, bound about with steel bands. Their helms were of common steel, and rather dull in comparison to their colorful surcoats, but the bright green stars painted on the sides of the headgear gave them a new light. The stars represented the token of the noble House of Trost— Stajouhar, green Elvinstone. The knights' emerald-green eyes, staring out around the steel noseguards matched almost exactly the hue of that token.

One of the riders under their protection appeared to be a youth of around fifteen summers. He was extremely—indeed, *strangely*—fair for a youth of his age, almost as though he were of Elvin blood and not a Man at all. His eyes, like his guardsmen's, were a deep, sparkling, emerald-green, and his hair was of a dusty, reddish-brown color.

The youth's rich attire consisted of a pale green tunic, bound at the waist with a black, leather belt, clasped by a gold buckle, and brilliant red hose. On his feet, he wore soft, leather riding boots, which reached nearly to his knees. A beige cloak, embroidered with the same azure and green coat-of-arms borne by his escort, was slung about his shoulders. At his belt was girt a sheathed long-knife, its gleaming silver hilt intricately-fashioned in the manner of the Elves.

The youth's traveling companion and personal guardsman was not of the same House as he. This man had dark hair and brown eyes, common to the House of Horack-Gildea, and he was not nearly as fair. His garments were not as extravagant as his companion's either, for such was rare among the Gildeans as they preferred a comparatively simple lifestyle.

The youth looked back over his shoulder, thinking he heard the sound of thunder in the distance. Sure enough, a dark band could be seen rising on the horizon.

"It looks as if a storm is brewing in the East, Erwin," the youth, Quellin, told his guardsman.

Erwin grunted in reply. "Aye, My Lord. But we should reach the Keep long before it strikes."

Quellin curled his lip. "I wasn't worried about that. I was only making an observation."

"Aye, My Lord."

The Trostain Lord rode in silence for a while, occasionally glancing over his shoulder at the quickening storm front. In a few minutes, he spoke again. "Did His Majesty send word as to what this council is about?"

Erwin shook his head. "Nay, My Lord. The herald said only that it was urgent."

Quellin sighed. "I see. Then I do hope we shan't be late. Radnor always has fits when I arrive late."

"Aye, My Lord."

* * * *

The final leg of their journey was a dull and uneventful one. They arrived at Gildea Keep by midmorning. Quellin left his mount and belongings to the care of his guardsman and hurried across the courtyard to the Keep. He jogged down the spacious corridor leading to the heart of the Keep. Already, he was late.

Quellin slowed his pace as he approached the giant, oak doors of the Great Hall. There, he paused briefly to make himself presentable to the Council of Lords. He nodded to Mikva, the chief door-warder, and the doormen slowly drew open the great portal.

The young Lord stepped into the chamber.

The bright rays of the sun streamed in through the many open windows of the Great Hall of Gildea Keep, illuminating three huge banners suspended from the ceiling of the chamber: the shimmering argent standard of the House of Gildea, emblazoned with a pale-green gona, the Gildean G; the rust-colored banner of Horack-Gildea, also charged with a green gona; and the banner of Trost, azure and green, divided in a bend dexter.

The golden light also beamed down upon the council table set below the standards at the opposite end of the chamber. Quellin bit his lower lip. Apparently, his peers had been awaiting his arrival for a longer time than he expected. A few of the men leaned forward, their elbows propped on the table, their heads resting in their hands. Even King Treiber was propped against the side panel of his large chair, with his crown tilted down over his eyes, snoring.

The last of the seven men sat straight in his seat, impatiently tapping the arm of his chair. He was a young man—in his early twenties—with long, black hair, cropped at his shoulders, and dark eyes. Under his sable, gold, and crimson tunic, he wore a mail shirt and sable hose. As Quellin started across the Great Hall, the knight in black came to the end of his patience.

"We can wait no longer!" he burst, pounding a gloved fist to the table. "We must start this council without your Lord Quellin!"

Yawning, King Treiber shoved his tarnished, silver crown back and muttered, "Be still, Balgor. He will come soon."

Another of the men—a rugged, dark-haired fellow with a perpetual frown—then straightened his back. Quellin paused as the man spoke in a weary voice. "Sire, I am forced to agree with Lord Balgor. This happens every time! That Trostain scamp is an incompetent and blasted nuisance. Besides that, he is a Trostain! We are wasting time. I say let us get started with the negotiations while we yet have daylight."

His words aroused a ragged chorus of agreement from the other Lords.

King Treiber whipped off his battered crown and rapped it on the table, calling for order, his face dark with anger. "Quiet! I shall not have that kind of speech made in my presence again!

"Though Quellin is descended from Trost, he is not Trost, who enslaved our fathers those centuries ago. Nor is he his father whom you accused of treason before the Plague took him. Who should know better than I? Your Queen and I raised him and his sister with our very own hands since they were children.

"Though Quellin is not of Gildean blood, he is Gildean in spirit. He is still a Lord in this kingdom and shall henceforth be treated as such! Is that understood, Radnor?"

Treiber replaced the crown on his head and glanced towards one of the windows, then added, "Besides, it is not yet the noon hour—I should think that we have plenty of daylight remaining."

Reining back harsh words, Lord Radnor rose to his feet and bowed to his King, "My apologies, Sire," then returned to his seat.

Quellin started forward again, his footsteps falling loudly on the stone floor. All eyes turned to him as he approached the council table. His emerald-green eyes sparkled as he bowed to Treiber.

"*Mondone, Treibeirne Delorin!*" he said in the old Gildean Tongue.

The Gildean King heartily returned the greeting. "*Mondone, Kiloni Velarin!*"

Quellin quickly moved to the vacant chair across from Balgor, his apologetic gaze sweeping across the faces of his fellow noblemen. "I am truly sorry for being so late. It shan't happen again."

Radnor muttered the apology under his breath in tandem with the youth, but a sharp look from King Treiber silenced him.

Balgor became incredulous at the sight of the newcomer, for he had clearly not expected one so young. "*This* is the Lord Quellin! Do you mean to say that we have been waiting all of this time for a mere child!"

Lord Balgor cast quizzical glances around the table as great gales of laughter arose from the Council.

King Treiber was the first of the Gildeans to regain his composure. "Nay, My Lord, not a child, for in but a week from this day, His Lordship shall have reached his twenty-eighth year! 'Tis true, Quellin is the youngest member of our Council of Lords... but then, you are younger yet, are you not, Balgor?"

Lord Balgor stared across the table at Quellin, his eyes wide in wonder.

Quellin returned the Qatani's look with a smile. There were mysteries surrounding the House of Trost of which few knew the answers, including the Trostains themselves. Many believed that Quellin was the living image of the ancient founder of his noble House, but the old tales of Trost were forgotten, and so also were the causes of the Trostains' prolonged youth.

Treiber spoke again, this time addressing the Trostain Lord. "Quellin, may I present Balgor, Lord of the House of Robel-Rigus of Qatan."

The Qatani rose to his feet and bowed to Quellin. But he was not received with the same dignity.

Quellin's smile vanished immediately at his King's words. "Sire, since when have we ever allowed our adversaries to sit at our councils?"

Balgor reddened at the Trostain's remark, but held his tongue.

"He is here to negotiate a peace treaty, Quellin," Treiber replied sternly. "You will treat him with due respect."

"As you wish, Sire," Quellin answered resignedly. "But that shan't be easy."

Balgor took his seat again, still openly upset at the Trostain's hostile attitude.

Satisfied, King Treiber settled back in his own chair and looked at each nobleman gathered there. His brown eyes passed over Lords Aragon, Quellin, and Ubriaco on his right, Radnor at the opposite end, then Bernath, Balgor, and Derslag, the oldest member of the Council, on his left hand.

Clearing his throat to gain the full attention of the Council, Treiber spoke again. "Now, My Lords, ere we begin our bickering, I have an important announcement to make. . . ."

"Your Majesty," Balgor interrupted. "We all know the importance of this treaty."

Treiber continued, pardoning the interruption. "I am sure we do, Lord Balgor. It is not of the treaty that I speak, but rather something of a much more immediate significance to my people."

His eyes then re-examined each of the Gildean council members with an expression of cruel delight.

"Being childless," he began in a slightly cynical tone. "And having no heirs fit to rule a pigsty—much less a kingdom—I now name my ward, Quellin, Lord of the House of Trost, Heir to the Throne of Gildea!"

The Gildean Lords moaned their disapproval and muttered between themselves.

"A Trostain to be King?"

"Intolerable!"

Quellin, equally shocked by the announcement, looked around the table, his eyes falling upon Radnor last. Lord Radnor said not a word, but his frown deepened. Quellin's attention was averted from the Horackane Lord when Radnor's gaze shifted from him to Balgor, his look of frustration turning to suspicion.

Quellin glanced towards Balgor, who gave the newly-named Prince an odd smile and eased back in his chair, rubbing his bristly chin thoughtfully.

Treiber's voice again averted his attention. "Prince Quellin, have you aught to say?"

Lord Radnor put on a mocking smile. "Aye, *Your Highness*, a speech!"

Taking a deep breath, Quellin slowly rose from his seat. "I-I am not sure where to begin. I-I. . . ."

The King motioned for Quellin to return to his place, "That will be enough, my son. 'Tis not surprising that words are stolen from you. It is not every day that a man becomes Crown Prince, whether he will it or not."

Quellin returned to his seat as commanded.

Treiber returned his focus to the council at hand. "I shall make the official, public announcement of Quellin's inheritance tomorrow morning. Now that you have had the opportunity to express your overwhelming enthusiasm over my selection, we may begin the Council. I am eager to hear what Gramlich has to say."

He faced the Qatani Lord. "We shall begin with you. I would hear what terms your King puts forth, Lord Balgor."

"First and foremost, Your Majesty," the Qatani replied. "King Gramlich demands that you cede Lake Xolsha and the lands immediately surrounding it to the control of the Qatani monarchy. . . ."

A murmur broke out among the Gildeans.

Radnor rose to his feet, leaning with his palms held flat on the table, his already strained temper breaking. "Gramlich demands that we turn Lake Xolsha over to him? It seems to me that it was a similar *demand* that started this whole affair!"

Treiber clapped his crown to the table a second time, this time scarring the surface of the polished wood and adding a few new dings to the crown. "*Sit down*, Radnor!"

Scowling, the Horackane Lord dropped back into his seat. No apology was forthcoming this time.

Quellin stared at Balgor. He knew, as he guessed Radnor did, that there was more to the Qatani's visit than the treaty negotiations, and the terms presented could as well be tools for accomplishing that other purpose. He wanted to hear the Qatani out, then perhaps he would learn Balgor's true intent.

King Treiber turned his gaze upon the Qatani ambassador. "However, I agree with Lord Radnor. For what reason should we give in to such a demand? Why should we give Gramlich Lake Xolsha? What would he give us in exchange for the land?"

"Den Xolsha is the only outlet to the river commerce in Qatan's locality, and Lake Xolsha is the only accessible harbor to that river," Balgor replied. "Your folk, even before the war began, refused the Qatani people access to that trade.

"However, in exchange for that land, King Gramlich has authorized me to relinquish to Gildea the southern corner of Qatan to the point of ten miles west of Zirges Keep—a piece of land a great deal larger than that which we require. Of course, Gildea shall retain sufficient trading rights in the Xolsha region."

Lord Radnor burst out in disbelief, "That would put us nearer to the northwestern wilderness of Machaelon . . . a truly desperate position, Sire. It would not be wise to take such a chance. 'Tis likely a ruse to drag us deeper into the clutches of Machaelon!"

"I would not be so hasty to make such a judgment, Radnor," Quellin interjected, his deceptively youthful voice tinged with doubt—a simple ruse to draw Balgor into revealing some of his intent. "The offer does have some advantages. The lands and fortifications in that region of Qatan would be a great asset to our defense."

Radnor scowled. "If I did not know your hatred of the Qatani, I should say you are in league with them."

Quellin sighed and shook his head. Inwardly, it saddened him to bring more distrust upon himself from his fellow Lords, particularly Radnor.

"That will be enough," King Treiber said, glaring hard at Radnor. The old King rubbed his grey beard thoughtfully. Finally, resting his hand on the table, he gave answer to Lord Balgor. "Again, though, I must agree with Lord Radnor. This term is unacceptable. It would put my nation at a greater risk than it already is. Gramlich must do without."

"But, Your Majesty, Qatan cannot survive with its outside trade cut off!" Balgor protested. "Surely, you can understand our position!"

Lord Ubriaco, Treiber's trade counselor, countered the Qatani's objection. "My Lord Balgor, Den Xolsha could only serve as a shipping lane to the Free Lands, who have a mutual embargo against the Dark Lands, which of course includes your own Qatan. King Gramlich's primary trade is with Charneco and Bulkyree, not to mention his unwholesome dealings with Machaelon, all bordering Qatan. The lack of the river trade will hardly affect Qatan's survival."

Balgor flushed a little at the mention of Machaelon, and Quellin could again see suspicion rise to Lord Radnor's face. Indeed, Balgor's persistence in the matter only strengthened Quellin's own suspicions. Lake Xolsha could not serve as a trade center for Qatan, but it would serve well as a military outpost.

Balgor, aware of the eyes upon him, composed himself and answered Ubriaco. "If there is to be peace, Qatan must have a route to the Free Lands!"

And so for three long hours, the Council of Lords argued and debated, relying on volume when tempers flared and logic fled, with no significant results. All the while, Quellin watched the Qatani, as did Radnor, who kept his eye on Quellin as well.

At the end of the third hour, King Treiber called an adjournment for the noonday meal. Quellin rose from his seat and gave a slight bow in Treiber's direction. "If I may have your leave, Sire. . . ."

Treiber looked up at him. "What? Are you not hungry? Nay, I suppose you wouldn't be. Very well, you have my leave. Perhaps your appetite will return when you have gathered your wits together."

Again, Quellin bowed. "Thank you, Sire. But my wits are not what I wish to gather." His sparkling eyes briefly met Balgor's gaze. An intentional smirk playing on his lips invited the Qatani to join him.

The Trostain left the table and retreated to a more secluded corner of the Great Hall to await Balgor. Indeed, not long after Quellin had found a seat, Balgor also left the table and approached him.

"My Lord, might I join you?" the Qatani said, showing his white teeth in a smile.

Quellin gave a friendly nod in return. "Of course, Lord Balgor. I must beg your pardon for my earlier behavior. I was not told why the Council was being called together, and it was a surprise to find one of our longtime enemies sitting at our own council table."

"I quite understand, My Lord."

"Quellin—please, call me Quellin. Now that I understand your purpose here, of course I will do all I can to help in this situation."

Quellin felt a cold sensation run through his body. There were eyes other than Balgor's upon him. He shrugged off the feeling and continued his deception of the Qatani. "I believe that the interests of both our countries are the same. We both want peace—but we must both give something to prove it. Your King's plan is not without merit. I would know more of it."

A strange conspiratorial grin came over Balgor's face as though Quellin had given him a signal—a signal telling that he knew the Qatani's true purpose and that he was ready to collaborate. Though Quellin did not know, nevertheless he continued to play his part.

Quellin looked back towards the council table. Radnor was nervously watching Quellin and Balgor as they quietly conversed, signs of worry tracing his rugged features. But Radnor, upon seeing Quellin's gaze upon him, suddenly smiled and nodded, and Quellin knew that any doubts that had occupied the Horackane's mind were ended. Quellin did not know what message his own expression had sent to Radnor; he could only hope that it was not visible to Balgor.

The doors of the Great Hall burst open before Quellin could resume his speech with the Qatani Lord. Mikva, the doorwarder, stepped into the Great Hall, lending support to an injured warrior.

The Gildean noblemen marveled that the man yet lived considering the wounds that he had taken. The knight's argent and green surcoat was stained crimson from the blood oozing from his slash-riddled body. Blood had been cleansed from his eyes, but the streaks where it had run down into them could still be seen on his forehead, trailing from a nasty gash.

Quellin made his way back to the council table when he saw the man, careful not to exhibit any outward signs of losing interest in Balgor's plans.

The wounded man raised his scarred and blood-crusted face to his King and forced words from his raw throat. His voice was strained, hardly audible. "Sire, *Gildea 'as fallen!*"

At a glance from King Treiber, Lord Ubriaco got up from his chair, beckoning to the doorman. "Bring him here, then fetch a healer!"

After the wounded soldier was seated and Mikva had gone, the knight spoke again, his words heavy with urgency. "Sire, I'm Deciechi, 'erald o' 'enfling, Guv'ner o' Gerdes. I come wi' evil tidin's: Gildea 'as fallen. . . ."

"What is the meaning of this?" Radnor interjected, rising to his feet. "What has happened? Has Qatan attacked?"

"M'Lord, let me finish," Deciechi replied.

Treiber gave a slight wave of his hand, and Radnor returned to his seat.

"You may continue, good sir," Treiber told the wounded herald.

Deciechi dared to incline his head to the King. "Yestereve, we fell under attack, an' I 'uz sent t' call fer aid. But afore I got t' th' city, I met five other 'eralds, an' they all told th' same tale as me."

The herald's voice cracked, forcing him to stop for a moment and take a deep breath before going on. "A Warlord—a Sorc'rer—'oo goes by th' name o' Iysh Mawvath 'as raised th' Kubruki! They've taken all but Gildea Keep, an' e'en now they march upon us, un'er th' protection o' a Shadow o' Evil! Th' Shadow stopped its march long 'nough fer me t' gain some time, but I fear it won't be long now afore it o'ertakes th' ci'y."

The color drained from the King's face at this news. "What of the other heralds?"

"We 'uz set upon by a band o' Kubruki, Sire," Deciechi replied. "I 'uz th' only 'un t' 'scape, an' that but barely."

Quellin suddenly realized that he had ridden on the wings of that storm on his return to Gildea Keep. He stepped forward and laid a hand on the knight's shoulder. "Rest now, good Deciechi. You have served your King well."

The herald moved his head and closed his eyes. "Thank'ee, M'Lord."

When the healer came, the king commanded him to take Deciechi to the Lower Halls, then turned back to the council. "If the herald is correct—and his very appearance gives us every reason to believe that he is—we must set our defenses immediately. Go now and prepare yourselves, then return for the council: the war-council!"

At his word, the Lords of Gildea withdrew from the Great Hall.

As Quellin left the chamber, he could hear Treiber say to his personal guardsman, who stood ready at his side, "Turan, my friend, see the women and children to the Lower Halls, then warn the villagers. After you have finished there, ride on to Matadol—we shall have need of aid!"

The guardsman bowed and exited the chamber, passing Quellin on his way to the Keep's stables. Turan was the king's most trusted and devoted servant, and Quellin was certain that if anyone were to get word to Matadol, he would.

Quellin hurried to his quarters, more rushed than need be, for he finally understood Balgor's true purpose at Gildea Keep. The appearance of the herald from Gerdes and the message he bore were the final pieces that solved the puzzle.

Quellin's guardsman met him as he came into his private chambers. "My Lord, Turan just informed me of what happened at the council. I will get your sword."

Quellin shook his head. "Nay. I will see to my own gear. I have a more urgent task for you. I want you to go at once to the Great Hall and stay with King Treiber. Detain the Qatani ambassador. I believe he is in league with this Iysh Mawvath. It is time his ruse is revealed. Warn King Treiber and make certain that Balgor does not escape."

Erwin snapped his fist to his chest and rushed out of the chamber.

Quellin entered his bedchamber and strode to a large closet in the far wall. He drew a key from a pouch at his belt and slipped it into a lock set in one of the silver-trimmed doors. He swung open the doors, revealing the last remnant of the inheritance granted him by his late father, Quiron, Lord of the House of Trost.

Hanging high in the middle of the back wall of the closet was Quellin's shield, bearing the blue and green ensign of his noble House. Below that, resting on a pair of brackets, was his sword, Kalter, a mighty blade of Elvin make, like his long-knife, handed down father to son from Trost himself. But unlike the smaller weapon, it had a hilt and blade fashioned of Elvingold, which glimmered brightly even in the shadows of the closet. Kalter's sheath, trimmed with Elvingold as well, hung below the sword on a second pair of brackets.

The shield was the only piece of armor that he would wear, for he preferred, as the Elves, the freedom of movement that the lack of heavy chain afforded. He fastened the sheath's belt to his own, then drew forth Kalter from the closet and ceremoniously slid it into its scabbard, first saluting his family's coat-of-arms. Then he took down his shield and slung it on his shoulder, over his beige cloak.

Quellin was startled by the sudden ringing of the alarm bell and the clamor of the Castle-Guard hurrying throughout the

Keep in answer. He ran out of his chambers and made for the Great Hall, fearing that Balgor had already made his move.

Quellin's fellow noblemen joined him at the open doors of the Great Hall. Treiber immediately sat the Lords down as they entered the Hall. It was just as Quellin had feared. Balgor had made his move, but a stronger action than Quellin had anticipated.

"Only a few moments ago, Lord Balgor attempted to . . . to *relieve* me of my crown," the King began. Oaths and curses rumbled through the chamber, until Treiber spoke again. "Thanks to Prince Quellin's quick wits, Erwin and Mikva foiled that attempt. However, Balgor escaped. The Castle Guard searches for him even now. Erwin informed me of Balgor's true purpose here—as a spy—which Quellin cleverly ferreted out. We must assume, therefore, that Qatan is in league with Iysh Mawvath!"

Quellin felt undeserving of his King's praise, for he had not truly ferreted out anything.

"Lord Balgor has been with us for three days now," Ubriaco said, grimacing. "Enough time to have studied every weakness that this Keep has, and time enough to have reported these somehow to their Warlord."

His observation was met with agreement from the Council.

"It is, then, my suggestion that we set forth a plan of defense immediately," Lord Aragon, Treiber's chief aide, said in answer.

"And what do you suggest, My Lord?" Treiber asked.

"This is my plan: we should separate our warriors into three forces. One force will stand the Walls—each fortified with a complete company of archers—one will stand ready as reinforcements should a Wall Guard require it, and the last shall act as a reserve and as the inner defense should the enemy manage to break through. To meet this enemy on the open field would be to our disadvantage. We should make full use of what fortifications we have here."

Treiber looked around the table. "Are there any other suggestions?"

Quellin spoke, but only to lend support to Aragon's strategy. "It is a sound plan, Sire, that Aragon has put forth. Given the situation, I can see nothing else that we can do."

Radnor voiced his approval as well. "For once, I must agree with Lord Quellin. Our options are few, and Lord Aragon's plan gives us *some* hope—at least to delay the enemy long enough for Turan to return with King Taskalos."

Treiber nodded, convinced of his chief aide's suggestion. "Unless there are any questions or objections, we shall put this plan into execution immediately."

None of the Lords gave reply.

"Very well then. Ubriaco, you shall have command of the Keep Guard. Derslag, you have command of the North Wall, and Bernath, you shall head the replacement guard for him. Quellin, you shall command the South Wall, and Radnor shall act as your replacement commander.

"I shall personally lead the East Wall, with Lord Aragon as my secondary. If my memory serves me correctly, Kubruki fear water—Den Jostalen shall then be our Western sentinel. As a safety measure, fortify the river with a company or two of archers."

"But, Sire!" Quellin burst out, rising to his feet in protest. "That would put you in the thick of it all!"

"I know," Treiber replied. He continued before any further objections could me made. "This is not up for discussion."

The King stood to his feet, crying in the old Gildean, "*Kindone Getheirne un hason!*"

The war commanders rose from their chairs, their clenched fists striking the arms emblazoned on their surcoats, then left their King's company to make ready the Keep's defenses.

Chapter 8

King Treiber made his way through the labyrinth of Gildea Keep to the passage leading down to the deepest chambers of the castle. At the entrance to the Lower Halls, he was met by his Royal Marshal—Grintam, a man of great stature—who had come to make a final inspection of the ordering of the Halls.

The Gildean warlord pounded his fist to his chest, his voice booming in greeting. "*Mondone, Treibeirne Delorin!* How may I serve?"

"I seek your Queen, Marshal Grintam," Treiber replied. "I wish to speak with her, while I am still able."

Marshal Grintam drew a large key from his belt and unlocked the door, then stepped to the side to make way for his King. "Then I will show you to her quarters, Sire."

Treiber followed his military advisor down the long, winding staircase into the Lower Halls. They passed through many crisscrossing passages and chambers, crowded with minor nobles and servants alike. All of the Keep's noncombatant occupants had been evacuated to these halls. Treiber halted occasionally to speak words of encouragement to his people, but his stops were brief.

At last, they came to a grouping of chambers at the heart of the Lower Halls. These chambers were reserved for the Gildean royalty in times such as these. Treiber could not recall ever journeying this far into the Lower Halls, nor had he ever dreamed it would become necessary. The room next to the living quarters was a council chamber, from where, in other days, Treiber might have guided his armies. But this time, Treiber understood the probable outcome of the battle, and he would lead his knights with sword in hand.

Marshal Grintam motioned one of the two guards standing at either side of the archway to open the door to the Queen's chamber. Dismissing the Royal Marshal and the guardsmen, King Treiber stepped into the room.

Queen Sherren rose from her seat and went to her husband's side. Her long, silver hair fell straight and smooth across her shoulders, but for a single braid encircling the base of her tiara. Her face was lean and smooth, though the lines around her brown eyes spoke of the decades she had seen pass by. She was a beautiful woman, despite her age, and strong of spirit. Early in her life, she was considered one of the fairest women in Gildea—save for the ladies of the House of Trost who, like Prince Quellin, were unusually youthful and radiant—but now in age, her beauty was become a noble and regal one, unchallenged by the Queens of many courts.

Lady Arella and Lady Mattina, the sisters of Radnor and Quellin, were there at the Queen's command. Also with them was a small boy—Berephon, the young son of Runyan the Bard, one of the most renowned minstrels in all the lands—who was remanded to Mattina's charge while his father wandered the courts of Milhavior.

Arella was in her mid-twenties, many years younger than her brother. Unlike Radnor, she had long, golden hair, but her eyes were the same dark brown. She also differed with her brother in her attitudes concerning Quellin. The Trostain Lord had been openly courting her for the last few years . . . an attraction she shared. Her brother complained and argued with her against the relationship, but to no avail.

Quellin's younger sister, Mattina, was a young lady of fifteen summers. Like her brother, she was gifted with the same Elvin comeliness. Mattina was known to be unpredictable in her behaviors—one moment she might be as shy as a lamb, the next haughty and proud.

Treiber smiled as he looked upon her. His little girl was no longer little. She had become quite a young woman. Quellin had been playing the matchmaker for her since her entrance into womanhood two years before, but she would have none of it, never giving any youth a second glance—not that she was ungrateful for her brother's concern or for the boys' attention, but she had determined that when she wed, it would be to the man of *her* choosing.

Treiber respectfully inclined his head to each of the women, greeting them as was proper. "My Ladies."

Treiber lowered his gaze to young Berephon, forcing a smile that did not come willingly in that dark hour, and patted the boy on the head. "And greetings to you, Master Berephon!"

The child quickly returned the king's smile with a little giggle.

"Sire," Lady Arella said. "Turan spoke to us of war—of Kubruki. What transpires? Do legends walk the fields?"

The Gildean King's smile died. An odd feeling stirred in him at the question. His eyes scanned the stone walls of the dimly lit chamber—the only sources of light being a pair of small lamps.

"Turan speaks true, My Lady," he said in reply. "Gildea is besieged. This Keep is the last bastion of hope for our kingdom. We must defend this city until Turan can return with aid from Matadol.

"That is why I have come. I have chosen to take up the sword of my fathers and lead my people in the defense of our city. Should I be slain before the battle's end, it falls to you to lend courage to Quellin, for he shall be King in my stead."

"King?" Mattina said with a start.

"Aye," Treiber replied with an affirming nod. "It had been my intention to make the announcement on the morrow, but now that may be too late. I have dispatched messengers throughout the city to proclaim the selection of my heir."

Treiber glanced at Arella, then back to Mattina. "Please, leave us."

"As you wish, Sire," Arella answered. Mattina took her ward's hand, and the three of them left their rulers alone as their King had commanded.

Sherren held her husband's hand and looked full into his face. "Treiber, your heart is deeply troubled by this turn. It is written upon your face."

"Aye," Treiber admitted, knowing that it was futile to hide anything from her. "I am old, Sherren. My very strength is gone from me."

"You speak nonsense," his wife chided him. "Your true strength grows ever stronger—the strength of your spirit."

Treiber sighed wearily. "I am not certain of that, either."

"A kingdom cannot stand without its King," Sherren responded. "And that King must be strong in spirit in the face of any adversity. Elekar shall guide you and strengthen you. You must not break faith, elsewise Gildea will crumble in spirit, in hope, and in courage—and eventually as a kingdom."

Treiber managed to smile. "Ah, patient ears and a wise tongue. You are ever a shield for my weakness, dear Sherren."

"Again, you speak nonsense."

"Nay, I do not!" Treiber drew his wife close and embraced her. "You are my sole foundation. Without you, I would surely falter."

* * * *

Mattina and Arella waited silently in the small room adjoining the Queen's antechamber, seated in adjoining chairs. Berephon sat cross-legged near the door. Though neither of the women desired to intrude upon the privacy of their rulers, they were unable to ignore the voices that drifted through the wooden door.

Mattina had felt a tremor of fear when King Treiber had verified his guardsman's words. The Kubruki were subject to the Curse of Darkness placed upon all creatures of the Death Realm by the Dawn King, a ban from the light of the mortal sun on pain of eternal death. For a legion of Kubruki to have passed this far into Gildea, they would have to had found a way to dispel the curse.

Indeed, as her foster parents continued to discuss the coming trials, she began to understand. Treiber spoke of a Black Shadow, which blotted out the light of the sun, blanketing the land. His words also confirmed rumors that had been spreading throughout Gildea for the last several years: a new force had risen in Machaelon and had taken the seat of power in the rebuilt Chi Thanatos. This same Warlord was now rumored to lead the legions marching upon Gildea Keep.

Mattina's ward rose to his feet and came to stand before her, looking up at her with a puzzled frown. "What are King Treiber and Queen Sherren talking about? Is there going to be fighting?"

Throwing a worried look in Arella's direction, Mattina reached down and lifted the five-year-old into her lap.

"Yes, Bipin," she replied, using the pet name the court servants had given him. "There is."

"Is that why we have to stay down here?" the boy asked.

"It is safer down here," Arella replied, smiling gently at the boy. "That way, if the enemy enters the castle, they will not find us."

Mattina could tell that, despite her reassuring words, Arella was just as anxious herself.

Bipin pondered the answer for a moment, then said, "What if the enemy finds the stairs?"

"Do you remember the other door in the Queen's chamber?" Arella asked him. When Bipin nodded, she said, "That door leads to a tunnel that comes out well beyond the city walls. If the enemy finds the Lower Halls, we will escape that way."

"Oh." The boy rested his head against Mattina's breast, a frown of uncertainty maintained on his lips.

A short while later they could hear their rulers' voices fall silent and the outer door of the antechamber open and close. The women stood up, Mattina still holding Bipin, and returned to the Queen's chamber. As they entered, they found Queen Sherren sitting in a chair, facing the door, a single quiet tear running down one cheek.

Mattina stepped closer, concern sweeping over her. "Your Majesty?"

Sherren lifted her grief-stricken face to her. "Oh, Daughter, I fear I have seen the last of your King."

"Your Majesty, do not speak so," Mattina replied. "Our numbers are few, but we are strong. We shall withstand until Turan returns with aid."

Sherren shook her head, wiping the tear from her cheek, regaining some of her composure. "Nay, Daughter. I believe as Treiber. Gildea Keep shall fall ere this day is finished. This city was not built as it should have been. We do not have enough protection here. We can only pray that a remnant survives to flee."

With her reply, she slid from her chair, carefully lowering herself to her knees. For nearly an hour, Mattina and Arella watched their Queen pray, her hands and face raised in supplication, her lips moving silently. After that time, Sherren's eyes flew open in alarm. Arella hurried to her side as she struggled to rise to her feet. She turned to face the door leading to the postern exit. From beyond it, they could hear the sounds of battle echoing in the tunnel.

After a few moments, the door flew open and a single warrior stumbled in. He slammed the door and threw the bolt, then leaned back against the door, his chest heaving as he gasped for air. The man's helm was missing and one side of his head was covered in blood. His argent surcoat was torn in several places, revealing bloody wounds, and in his hand he held a broken sword.

"Your Majesty," he gasped painfully, eyes wide in panic. "The Lower Halls are no longer safe. Rock Trolls found the postern gate. We held them back as long as we could, but our weapons are no use against them. . . ."

His words ended in a terrible shriek as shards of wood from the door burst through his torso. A huge claw erupted through the door, grasping the warrior's body and ripping him backwards into the tunnel. The remains of the door exploded into the room.

Sherren and her ladies-in-waiting huddled into a corner, Bipin clinging to Mattina, screaming. The massive form of a Rock Troll squeezed into the room, hunched nearly double beneath the ceiling of the chamber. Its huge claws were spread at either side and its fanged jaws gaped wide in fury and hunger as it glared down at the humans with stony, yellow eyes.

A loud rumble sounded above their heads as a series of cracks began to form in the stone ceiling. In fear, the Troll tried to back into the tunnel, but did so too late. The ceiling came crashing down upon its head, mountains of rubble tumbling into the room.

* * * *

A heavy silence blanketed the defensive wall around the city of Gildea Keep. The warriors who stood there, battle-ready, watched the oncoming Shadow in mounting tension. Quellin stood beside his secondary in silent vigil upon the parapet of the South Wall. His lack of mail accentuated his boyish appearance. If the men under his command had not known him on sight, they might have laughed him off the wall.

Beside him, Lord Radnor glared out at the Shadow in agitation. The Horackane wore full mail, with the brown and green surcoat of his House and a plain helm. The sword at his side was likewise plain and unadorned. The earth tones of his House's arms were dull in comparison to the garishly bright colors of Quellin's garb.

The expression on Radnor's face was not the patient anticipation of the coming storm worn by his newly-named Prince, but was red and contorted in frustration. After several minutes, he finally turned to his commander, his voice expressing his chagrin. "Blast it all! Why did His Majesty have to pair me with you!"

Quellin gave him a puzzled look. "What do you mean?"

"You know full well what I mean," Radnor growled in return. "You are a Trostain!"

"I am afraid that is not of my choosing," Quellin responded with a helpless shrug.

Radnor's anger and disdain did not abate. "Whether your will or no, the blood of Trost runs in your veins. Your kind should have been banished from Gildea when they betrayed us."

"Radnor, I am not responsible for the errors of my ancestors," Quellin replied calmly. "A full Age has passed since then. Even my father, avaricious as he was, was not the traitor that he was accused of being."

"Indeed?" Radnor shot back. "I do not recall that ever being decided."

Quellin gave a sad sigh. "I will not argue the point, Radnor. You desire to see my House destroyed, and I have decided to give in to the inevitable."

Radnor raised a brow in suspicion. "What do you mean?"

"Mattina and I are the last of pure Trostain blood," Quellin replied quietly. "Any offspring that either of us bring forth will be of mixed heritage. The line has ended. When this is over, I will ask Arella for her hand in marriage and seal its fate."

Radnor gawked at his Prince in stunned disbelief. "You wouldn't *dare*. . . !"

"Yes, I would," Quellin replied with a nod. "I had meant to announce it a few days ago, but I never got around to it—first, I was sent to Yasgin, and now this."

"*You never got around to it!* You assume to wed my sister, and you *never got around to it?*" Radnor snapped in return. The Horackane Lord stalked away from Quellin, leaving the South Wall and returning to his own command, angrily fuming over the gall of "that Trostain scamp." But ere the man passed from view, Quellin caught the glimmer of a smile on Radnor's lips.

Quellin stared after him in confusion. This was the second time that day that such a smile had appeared on Radnor's face. If he had not known the Horackane's intense hatred for his people, he might have thought Radnor was actually *pleased* by the news.

Unable to comprehend Radnor's thoughts, Quellin turned his gaze back to the grasslands surrounding Gildea Keep, fixing his stare upon the Black Shadow. He was known to have a greater range and depth of vision, even at night, than most Gildeans, but even his eyes were unable to pierce the murk. He had never in his life seen anything darker than this. A presence of evil emanated from the black wall, causing a chill in Quellin's spine. Even the heavens felt the presence, for the sky had turned blood-red at the Shadow's approach.

The Trostain Lord allowed a worried sigh to escape his lips. The view was the same from all the Walls. The Shadow had completely encircled the city and was fast closing in upon Gildea Keep . . . a vast, evil flood threatening to drown all that lived.

Quellin's attention was attracted by the voice of his guardsman. "I pity the poor wretches who venture into that devil's shadow, My Lord—I mean, Your Highness."

Quellin nodded in silent agreement. Scouts had been dispatched to learn the precise location of the enemy forces within the wall of Darkness, and they had not yet returned. Quellin did not hold out much hope for them. The Shadow was alive with evil . . . an evil which no man of his own might or will could triumph over.

The Trostain turned and looked across the fields between the South Wall and the city, past the few scattered dwellings, to Keep Hill, which rose high above the village. Upon it sat the fortress of Gildea Keep, looming pale against the Shadow. From his vantage point, the more thickly-populated northwestern edge of the city was hidden from his sight.

If the Walls fell to the Kubruki, the villagers and remaining warriors would retreat into the Keep, and there make their last stand. Quellin expected the withdrawal to be quick. Here at the city wall, their forces were spread too thinly. Their strongest defense would be at the Keep.

Even as he stared out towards the castle, alarm bells began to ring within the towers of the Keep. He stepped forward, near the edge of the parapet, a worried frown crossing his features. He turned to ask Erwin his opinion of the alarm, but the words never left his mouth. In just the few minutes he had turned his attention away from the Shadow, it had crossed the remaining mile to the city wall.

As the Darkness struck, a terrible wind buffeted the walls, blasting many warriors backwards off the wall-walk to the ground below. Quellin, himself, was blown to the parapet, his breath wrenched from him. He felt himself sliding towards the edge, but Erwin, clinging to another warrior who had braced himself behind the wall, grasped his leg and struggled to pull him back. The wind lasted only a few seconds, then passed on, leaving the walls darkened by the strange, light-consuming shroud of the stygian Shadow.

Quellin rolled onto his stomach, drawing himself onto his knees, and watched in growing horror as the devastating winds converged on Keep Hill. With a deafening *crack!*, the castle twisted in on itself as though the hand of a god had reached out to crush it, exploding in a cloud of stone and dust. The remains of the Keep collapsed into the hill itself, filling the Lower Halls.

Quellin could only watch in shock as all he loved was destroyed in one blow. When the ruins of the Keep collapsed into the Lower Halls, he felt his very spirit ripped from him. A scream of anguish erupted from his lips. His head drooping forward into his hands, he wept bitterly as the hellish Shadow whispered words of despair to his heart.

But he was not permitted time for grief. Quellin felt a hand on his shoulder and heard a voice calling him amidst the turmoil on the wall. "Your Highness! Your Highness. . . !"

Quellin jerked his head up to face Erwin.

His guardsman wore an urgent expression. "Your Highness, should I dispatch some men to search the ruins for survivors?"

Survivors? Dazed, Quellin turned his gaze back to the rubble. Could anyone have survived that? Nevertheless, if there were even the slightest chance that Arella and Mattina could have lived through the destruction of the Keep, he had to know. Before he could answer Erwin, he saw a small contingent of warriors break away from Radnor's forces at the base of the wall and start towards Keep Hill.

Before they had gone very far, they halted again. A voice boomed from the east, like a roll of thunder, its words clear even from a distance. "*Treiber, King of Gildea, come forth!*"

The enemy had come.

* * * *

King Treiber stared in horror at the ruin brought to his beloved city, even before the ravages of war had taken their toll. The loss of his beloved Sherren was the worst of all, but he could not let grief dominate him yet. He had no doubt that he would be joining her in the High Realm before the day—or what passed for day in the murk of this strange Shadow—was ended.

He turned his attention to the ordering of the walls. His gaze swept across the walls and city. Chaos had ensued with the destruction of the Keep; an attack now would prove fatal to Gildea. He considered going himself to spread courage to his people, but he could not leave his post now.

Royal Marshal Grintam called Treiber's attention to himself. "Sire, look!"

Treiber followed the man's outstretched hand.

Three horsemen rode with great speed towards the main gate of Gildea Keep: the remnants of the scouting party, which had originally numbered seven. Treiber was prepared to give the order to open the gate, but stopped and shook his head. His heart sickened within him.

Upon a small hillock before the wall, standing between a pair of tall banners, was a man clad in a strange form of armor, consisting of plates rather than the familiar linked rings. The white metal gleamed with a pale, ghostly light, undaunted by the Darkness. The man's helm was fashioned in the likeness of a skull, and upon the great black standard at his left hand was the symbol of Death: a white skull pierced through, top to bottom, by a sword. The banner on his right was black as night, devoid of any marking—the standard of Machaelon. The man leaned heavily against a long, double-bitted pole-axe, its silver head gleaming against its black shaft.

The gates could not be opened now, for the enemy was nigh. Three men would be slain without a chance. Treiber watched in anguish as both riders and mounts fell dead, struck from behind by black arrows.

Grintam turned back to his King. "Sire, this man is, no doubt, the enemy for which we have been waiting, but if his armies are likewise populated by giants, we shall surely perish!"

Treiber smiled grimly to the man as he replied, "Nay, Grintam. The Kubruki are not of his stature—not quite. I have never seen the like of this man before. But do not lose all hope. We still have the Fire of the Dawn as our ally! Elekar shall not fail us."

One of Treiber's captains suddenly called out. "Sire, he stirs!"

The man upon the hill straightened to his full eight-foot height, seeming to grow in stature against the backdrop of the Shadow. When he spoke, it was like thunder rumbling throughout the sky, though the words were spoken calmly. "*Treiber, King of Gildea, come forth!*"

Treiber called down from the East Wall in answer, his voice sounding frail in comparison to the giant's. "I am the King of Gildea. Say what you have to say and be done with it."

"I have come to offer you and your people a chance to live," the giant boomed back. "Surrender to me and swear fealty to Machaelon or perish!"

A shadow gripped Treiber's heart, but he did not waver. His voice became stern and resolute in the face of his enemy. "Hear me, Sorcerer: I fear you not, for I am a servant of the Dawn King. Gildea shall not be overcome!"

The giant raised his left hand, and bolts of red lightning—the only color Treiber had seen since the Shadow had swept over his city—streaked through the sky, illuminating the earth below. The fields teemed with Kubruki for as far as the eye could see in the murk of the Shadow.

Death and defeat were now certain for the Gildeans. There would be no hope. Treiber felt the desire to weep, his despair intensified by the choking power of the Darkness, but he withstood.

"I am Iysh Mawvath, Warlord of Hál!" the Sorcerer roared. "In the name of my master, the Deathlord Thanatos, I command you to choose now—*surrender or die!*"

Treiber watched as his warriors ducked behind the wall in terror, unable to overcome the fear conjured by the Shadow. Though fear scourged the King's heart as well, he recognized it for what it was: the product of sorcery. Instead, he stood straight and proud, his voice unwavering. "I care not who your master is,

Iysh Mawvath. If freedom means death, then so be it. In the name of Elekar, we shall *fight!*"

The Gildean knights marveled at their King's boldness and stout words, but were also encouraged by them. They took their positions at the wall once more, standing firm.

"Very well, old fool," Iysh Mawvath returned, lowering his voice. "Then you have chosen your *death!*" The last word echoed loudly in the Darkness.

Iysh Mawvath raised his hand once more. A web of crimson lightning flashed out from his armored palm, lashing across the East Wall at several points, striking everyone who was not fast enough to duck behind the protection of the wall. Treiber, King of Gildea, was the first to perish, his body, like many after him, set ablaze by the Sorcerer's power.

The Kubruk army charged forward, but before they could scale the wall, another line of men replaced those slain—Lord Aragon had not stood idle. The battle for Gildea was joined. Gildean archers rained arrows down upon the heads of their unprepared foe, causing the Kubruki to fall back from the wall, but the Kubruki's retreat was only temporary. At Iysh Mawvath's thunderous command, they swarmed forward again, great siege towers trundling behind them, pulled along by entire companies of Kubruki.

The Kubruki overwhelmed the Gildeans in numbers and swarmed over the city walls like ants. But not so upon the South Wall. Quellin, upon seeing the great siege engines, commanded his archers to set their shafts aflame and aim for the towers. The first volley fell short, but the second flight struck true as the towers came within range. One by one, the towers went up in flames, blazing brightly even in the light-dampening Shadow. The Kubruki were forced to use clumsy scaling ladders to climb the wall, providing easy prey for Quellin's well-trained archers.

Quellin drew Kalter from its sheath. The Elvinsword blazed forth with a golden light, unaffected by the power of the Shadow, for Kalter was a token of greater power. "They are coming over the wall! Hold them back, men!"

The Trostain leapt towards a crenel and slashed his Elvinsword at the first beast. In an arc of golden flame, the blade ripped through the Shadow and the Kubruk's neck. The Kubruk grabbed at its scaly throat, black gore leaking between its thick claws, then toppled backwards, knocking a few of its comrades off the shabby ladder, as well.

The warriors under Quellin's charge drove the Kubruki back and held them at bay. The Trostain shouted commands to his knights and called for more archers to help repel the invaders. Young errand-runners hurried to and fro bringing more arrows and other supplies to the warriors on the South Wall.

Quellin turned to face Keep Hill. Grief whelmed his heart once more as thoughts of his loved ones sprang up in his mind, but his sorrow was soon put aside. Through the light of the Elvinsword, Quellin could see shadows moving about in the ruins of the Keep. At first, he thought that the Darkness was playing tricks on his sight, for the distance was far too great for Kalter to illuminate the ruins or for his eyes to pierce.

Unwilling to let go, Quellin called to the nearest of his warriors. "Captain Gerren! Erwin! The Kubruki have broken through and are in the ruins."

"If anyone perchance survived the devastation of the Keep, their lives are in grave danger," Captain Gerren shouted back.

"My thought exactly," Quellin responded. The Trostain stopped one of the errand-boys, a dark-haired lad of twelve summers with much the same bearing as Lord Radnor. "Shanor, tell your father to take command here—some Kubruki have broken through, and I am taking some men after them."

"I don't know where Father is, My Lord," the boy answered.

"Then tell Captain Umbrick." Quellin slapped the lad on the shoulder, shoving him towards the nearest ladder. With the other two knights close behind him, he abandoned the South Wall and made his way across the wide fields to Keep Hill.

At many places, the city walls had been breached, and the battle had entered the confines of Gildea Keep, but the stout Gildean warriors kept them from entering the city itself. The death-screams of Man and Kubruk, the clatter of shields and bucklers, the clanging of sword and axe and scimitar as they met in the fury of battle filled the air. The ground was turned to mire with the blood of the fallen, and fires burned throughout the battlefield as the war raged.

In the confusion of the battle, no one noticed Quellin and his companions as they crept up Keep Hill, small and dark against its ascending slopes. Slowly and silently, they climbed the mound to the ruins above, passing through the four wards ascending the slopes of the hill, only to be met by large stones and boulders when they reached the summit. Sword held ready, Quellin carefully scanned the grounds as they walked through the broken stones, ignoring the carnage which lay half-buried beneath the rubble. From the corner of his eye, he noticed something hidden behind a nearby boulder, a shape which moved slightly as he passed.

Careful not to turn around, Quellin motioned with his head for the other two men to hang back. They would trap the enemy between them. When he was far enough away, he dived behind a rock, his shield slipping from his arm as he landed. He winced as the shield clattered against a stone.

Cautiously, he made his way back to the boulder, using rubble as cover, and came up behind the figure. Like a prowling cat, he pounced on the struggling form and brought it to its feet, tearing his captive's hood back. His gaze met that of a woman. Her hair shimmered pale in Kalter's blazing light, her eyes showing dark in once smooth features, now bruised and smudged from the destruction of the Keep. All thoughts of the war and of his men waiting at the rim of the hill escaped his mind.

"Arella!" he said, embracing her with his free arm. He pressed his lips to hers and held her close, then pulled away again, staring into her face. "I feared you were dead."

"I nearly was," she replied with a wavering smile.

Releasing his hold on Arella, Quellin sheathed his sword, its light dying the moment the blade entered the scabbard. He sat down upon a stone, head bowed in sorrow. "I have terrible news. King Treiber is. . . ." But his voice failed him.

"Is dead," Arella finished for him. "Aye, I know. But now is not the time for grief."

The Trostain raised his head. "Do you know of any other survivors? Mattina?" He grew anxious as he spoke his sister's name.

Arella smiled again. "Aye, Mattina is alive and well. . . ."

Quellin breathed relief.

"As are Queen Sherren and Bipin. If there are others, we have not found them. We were huddled together when the Keep collapsed—it is only by the hand of Elekar and the corpse of a Rock Troll that we lived. We managed to find an open passage through the rubble to the surface."

At the mention of his Queen, Quellin started to his feet. "Queen Sherren—does she know about. . . ?"

Arella answered before he could finish, her gaze becoming stern. "Aye. But as I have already said, now is not the time for grief! She knows that the people have a new King. That is enough to bear her up."

Quellin's youthful features became sullen, and he turned away. "Some King! I should be down there fighting—leading my people—not standing up here, out of harm's way, groaning over Treiber's death! Every minute that passes, our armies fall into greater disarray. Already the Kubruki press deeper into our city."

Quellin faced Radnor's sister again, the sullen look replaced with a defeated one. "I am not ready, Arella. Radnor has the right of it there. I am not a King."

"Bravo! Bravo!" a sarcastic voice cheered loudly. "I have a passion for shoddy drama. Is this the part where you fall on your sword in despair?"

Quellin swung around to face the speaker. Lord Balgor sneered back. The Qatani wore a shield on his left arm, bearing the same saltire ensign as displayed on his tunic, and a sword was belted at his waist. His tunic was torn in several places and his face showed signs of the ruin of the Keep.

Quellin glanced to either side—there was no sign of either Erwin or Captain Gerren. "Where are my men, Qatani?"

"Would you happen to mean those two unfortunate fellows down on the hillside?" Balgor answered with an unconcerned smile. "I assure you that they are quite dead. But such is the price of war, Your Majesty, as you have undoubtedly learned already."

Quellin's hand slid down to the hilt of his sword, his fist tightening around the Elvingold grip. He could feel hatred stirring within and fought to harness it, lest he lose control of himself and the situation.

Balgor continued in a half-mocking tone. "Don't be a fool, Quellin—it would be very unprofitable. Join us, and Gildea shall be yours!"

Quellin's quiet anger grew hot. He drew Kalter, and a golden flame ran down its blade. "You speak of fools, Balgor? You are the worst fool of all. I have no need of you, nor your demon master, to *give* me Gildea. The crown has been passed on to its heir. By right, Gildea is already mine."

"Your right matters little, Your Majesty," the Qatani returned, his smile gone. "But it is just as well that you have declined my offer—I would have had you slain anyhow. At least now, you have given me cause that even Iysh Mawvath would accept."

Balgor raised his hand, and a pair of black Kubruki lumbered into view.

The slow-witted beasts raised their great iron maces to attack, but Quellin hewed them both down with two flashing strokes of his Elvinsword before either could make another move. Facing the Qatani Lord again, Quellin reached down with his left hand and drew his long-knife. Its blade, crafted from a single Stajouhar gem, also burned with an inner fire, casting flickering shadows on nearby rocks.

Balgor was startled for only a moment, but soon regained his balance. He laughed in ridicule. "I fear no sliver of Elvin tin, nor a harmless piece of green glass! There is naught like good, strong steel to teach manners!"

Baring his own sword, he charged. He swung his sword downwards in an attempt to power through Quellin's defenses, but the Trostain dodged aside. The clash of steel rang loudly and sparks flew as blade met stone.

Quellin recovered quickly and slashed at Balgor, but the Qatani was too swift for him, fending Quellin's blade away with his own. At the same time, Balgor opened his right side to an attack. Quellin took advantage of the opportunity, thrusting down with his Elvinknife, which easily sliced through Balgor's mail, gashing his side.

The reek of charred flesh filled Quellin's nostrils as the Qatani shrieked in agony, for though Balgor's wound was not otherwise a serious one, the power of the green Elvinstone was to cause wounds it inflicted to burn with an unseen flame. Quellin backed away as his opponent arose from the ground. The black fire of hatred burned deep in Balgor's eyes.

Driven mad by the burning agony of his wound—a pain which would have slain a weaker man—Balgor began swinging wildly at the Gildean King, forcing Quellin to stumble backwards. Once more, Balgor drove away the golden sword of Trost, but this time he succeeded also in blocking a thrust of the long-knife. The glowing, green blade bit through the top of Balgor's shield, sticking to the hilt. The Qatani tossed his shield aside, wrenching the shorter weapon from Quellin's hand. He roared out a cry of victory, plunging his blade towards his enemy's head.

Quellin threw up his left arm to protect himself. His features contorted in pain as his enemy's sword pierced through his forearm, but the wound did not hinder him. With one final effort, he thrust Kalter forward, driving its razor edge deep into the Qatani's abdomen.

Balgor released his grip on his own sword and stumbled backwards, his eyes gaping in horror as he watched Quellin's blade slide from his body. He looked up at the Gildean King, his eyes rolling white in madness, and made a move as if to spring. But Quellin was faster—Balgor's body fell headless to the ground.

Quellin clenched his teeth and retched as he jerked Balgor's sword from his arm, throwing it aside. He then dropped to his knees, while Arella ran to tend to his injury. Arella tore away his sleeve and used it to bind the wound, tying it as tight as she could in an attempt to stop the bleeding. When she was finished, Quellin took her hand in his.

"The herald from Gerdes spoke true. Gildea has truly fallen. There is no hope left. I shall meet my end here, beside you."

Arella squeezed his hand and spoke, her voice gentle. "Nay, all is not yet lost! Qu. . . ." But Quellin hushed her before she could finish.

The Trostain took up his sword once more; warriors were coming up the hill—about five or six. His vision blurred by the Shadow and tears of pain, he could not make out whether they were friend or foe. Quellin relaxed his grip on Kalter's hilt as Radnor and a band of Gildean knights came into full view.

The Horackane Lord glanced down at Balgor's body, then at his sister, and finally turned to Quellin. He struck his right fist to his heart in salute. "I am glad to see you still among us. The Kubruki have breached our lines, and we cannot hold them back. What are we to do, Sire?"

Quellin stared sullenly at the ground for a long moment. The pressure was too great, and the agonizing pain in his arm muddled his thoughts. He could think of nothing, except that he had failed his people. Shaking his head, he replied, "I don't know."

Radnor nodded. "I knew *that* even before I asked you. But I have a plan that might just succeed!"

Quellin looked up.

"I know an old woman named Etzel, who would take you in and give you peasant attire. Iysh Mawvath will probably leave the villagers alone for the most part, as they pose no threat to him and would make dandy slaves. With that disguise, you should be able to avoid the Kubruki long enough for help to arrive!"

"And just what, exactly, are *you* going to be doing in that time, might I ask?" Quellin demanded, his mind clearing a little.

"My men and I have gathered enough steeds to make the ride to Matadol," Radnor replied. "We are going to attempt to break through Iysh Mawvath's forces and hopefully return with aid from King Taskalos."

Quellin felt the heat of anger rise. "I'm sure you are—while the rest of us are slowly being roasted over a nice, hot fire!"

Radnor grabbed his King's shoulders. "Blast it, Quellin, trust me! Would I leave my own sister, and in such a desperate situation, if there were no hope? Much less, Queen Sherren?"

Quellin wrinkled his brow. "How do you know about the Queen?"

Radnor sighed, releasing his grip on Quellin. "I came here long before you. Queen Sherren and the others are already safely hidden away at the house of the witch-woman—and my dear sister is supposed to be. When I returned to the South Wall, you were gone."

Quellin rubbed his forehead, then glanced towards Arella. "Why didn't you tell me this to begin with? It certainly would have saved us a lot of time!"

"I was about to," the woman returned. "But you did not let me finish."

The cacophony of the Kubruki's harsh voices and the retreating cries of the remaining Gildeans thundered as the pursuing enemy streamed up the northern and eastern slopes, bringing a renewed sense of dread to the group.

Radnor quickly turned back to his King. "Head down the west slope—Etzel's house is the largest one nearest the river. Hurry now, before the Kubruki find you! I do not know why, but I have an uncanny feeling that your youth shall be your salvation this day. Go!"

Quellin retrieved his Elvinknife before he and Arella retreated to the town.

Radnor watched them with worried eyes as they stumbled down Keep Hill toward the village. When they had passed into the Shadow beyond the limits of his sight, he turned back to his men. "Come along. We have no more time to waste here!"

They hurried down the southern slope just as the Kubruki came pouring over the hill, slaying the few remaining Gildeans and giving chase to Radnor and his band.

* * * *

The battle was over. The Gildeans were routed, their city destroyed. Kubruki wandered among the bodies of their foes, slaying any wounded they found.

Two great, grey-scaled Kubruki strode up to the top of Keep Hill, carrying a throne fit for a Giant King. Behind them came their Warlord, Iysh Mawvath, his pale armor radiant with a deadly light, and Grotan, his captain. As he topped the hill, the

Sorcerer's cold, grey eyes caught sight of a small hairy object on the ground beside him. He stooped down, and grasping a tuft of dark fuzz, drew it up to his faceplate.

"You failed, Balgor," he said darkly, then tossed the head of the vanquished Qatani to the nearest Kubruk, who squealed in delight and scampered away, hugging the severed head close to its scaly hide.

Iysh Mawvath turned to his captain. "Bring the prisoner to me, Grotan . . . *alive*."

The creature scuttled back down Keep Hill.

The Sorcerer lowered himself into his throne. His victory was swifter than he had anticipated; he had been sure that the Gildeans would have put up a much stronger fight. But all the better for him that they did not—it meant that their will was broken. It would make his work here easier. They would not revolt against him. But first he would have to find Queen Sherren and the Trostain Lord, Quellin. As long as they were still alive, he could make use of them.

Iysh Mawvath smiled to himself. Full victory would soon be his. But now he needed to choose a place to build the Black Temple—a temple for his master and a palace for himself. His pride and arrogance chose a likely location: he would build the temple upon the rubble of the Keep and seal it with his black sorcery so that it would stand firm upon the stones filling the pit of the Lower Halls. The sight would drive the Gildeans deeper into despair.

The Gildeans—now his slaves—were another problem that he would have to deal with. Den Jostalen would need to be reinforced. The river might terrify his Kubruki, but Men would cross it without fear—slaves might escape or armies might invade. Building a western wall would take more time than he could afford. He would have to find other means of guarding the perimeter.

Grotan returned, interrupting his master's plans, prodding a ragged and beaten warrior before him. The Gildean knight slowly lifted his bruised head to glare upon the Warlord of Thanatos.

Iysh Mawvath, rising to his feet, greeted him. He motioned the prisoner to the throne. "Lord Radnor, my dear friend! Please sit down."

Radnor gave the giant a disgusted scowl. "I am no friend of yours, Iysh Mawvath. Nor have I any intention of sitting on a throne defiled by refuse such as yourself."

"Such kind words could only come from a tongue such as yours," the Sorcerer wearily replied. "But now I am not asking you—I am *telling* you! *Sit down!*"

The Gildean Lord only stared back.

Iysh Mawvath grabbed him by the shoulder and threw him into the chair. Radnor landed with a loud grunt, but quickly recovered his haughty glare.

"Already, I grow weary of your company," Iysh Mawvath gritted through the faceplate of his skull-helm. "You will answer my questions, directly, or so help me I shall tear you in two!"

Radnor appeared unimpressed with the threat.

"Where is your Queen?" demanded the giant.

The Gildean Lord gave a tired sigh. "Dead. What do you think?—if anything."

Iysh Mawvath growled. "Do not lie to me, Radnor. It is very unwise. Now tell me where she is, or I will turn you over to my Kubruki, here and now!"

Radnor gave the Sorcerer a wan smile. "Tell me, Iysh Mawvath, what is the difference between here and now or there and later? Frankly, I enjoy the knowledge that Quellin and the Queen have slipped through your grubby, little fingers."

"I assure you that your Lord Quellin is quite dead, or if not, he soon will be," Iysh Mawvath guaranteed him.

"Now you are the fool, Iysh Mawvath," Radnor laughed. "He is the one that you want alive! And you are a fool for thinking that you could turn him.

"It is common knowledge that most of the peasantry in this region have dedicated Trostain blood flowing through their wretched veins—Elekar knows, the Trostains got around enough. If you could turn Quellin, they would turn also, making it a great deal easier for you to gain complete control of the people, and crush any thought of resistance.

"What a fool! No matter what else he may be, I know that Quellin is no traitor. He would die before he would betray his Queen and his country!"

Malice gleamed in Iysh-Mawvath's steel-grey eyes beneath his evil helm. "We shall see, Lord Radnor."

Radnor shook his head, chuckling grimly. "Why don't you go squirm under a rock like the worm you are—you shall get no more from me."

"As you wish. I have quite finished with you." Iysh Mawvath turned as if to leave, but instead slowly came to face the Horackane Lord again. "Oh yes, I nearly forgot! We caught one of your errand-runners hiding in an armory at the southern wall. A rather young lad—it is a shame he has to die."

Radnor's mind went reeling. His own son was one of the errand-runners for the South Wall! But no, Shanor had escaped—he had made certain of it! Hadn't he?

"Shanor, forgive me," he whispered in his final despair. Crying out in anguish, he lunged at the giant, pulling a hidden dagger from his boot, aiming for an open spot in the Warlord's armor.

As Radnor charged, Iysh Mawvath reached out and caught him by the throat. There was a loud snap, and Radnor's body hung limp in the Sorcerer's hand. Iysh Mawvath dropped the man's carcass to the ground.

"You did have to make it difficult, didn't you?" he growled in distaste. He called to his captain. "The boy is yours, Grotan. Go now! I want Lord Quellin. I will find him if I have to tear this city apart! Assemble every male above the age of sixteen and bring them before me . . . *alive*."

* * * *

Two Kubruki tromped to a black pavilion erected at the base of Keep Hill. One of the black-scaled beasts started through the entrance, trudging to the back of the tent, while the other remained outside.

The Kubruk inside hunched over a large bundle lying on the ground. It was a mass of greyish cloth with a thick patch of dark fur at one end. The creature snatched at the fur and jerked it up, revealing the face of a young boy. The boy was more in pain than he was frightened.

"Let go of my hair—it hurts!" the boy snapped.

The Kubruk pulled again, and the boy uncurled himself, rising to his feet. Only then did the Kubruk release him. The creature shoved him forward with a snarl. "*Shilnuk!*"

Young Shanor had no idea what the creature said, but he guessed that he had better walk. As the boy came out of the pavilion, the second Kubruk grabbed him and bound him, hand and foot, between a pair of short posts, a few inches off the ground. The boy struggled uselessly for a moment, then gave up.

It took only a few brief minutes in that splayed position before he felt as though he would be torn in two. He felt a burning fire in his thighs that spread up through his body and arms. The cords securing him to the posts tore at his wrists and ankles. Soon the pain became too much for him to bear, and he began to whimper a little, tears trickling down his cheeks.

The Kubruki waited for a while, gleefully watching the boy suffer. After a few minutes, the first one nudged his comrade and unslung his axe. The second took his weapon in hand as well and both advanced on the lad.

Shanor looked up as the Kubruki approached. He quickly forgot his pain, seeing the double-bitted weapons in their clawed hands. He started jerking at his cords again as the Kubruki lifted their axes, until blood began to trickle down his arms.

A golden light suddenly blazed to life, blinding the boy, forcing him to close his eyes and turn his head away. When he opened them again, the Kubruki were lying on the ground, black gore leaking from their corpses.

The cords around his ankles snapped free, and then those at his wrists. He felt an arm wrap around his waist, and he was swept off his feet. Rescue had come for him; there was still a resistance at Gildea Keep.

Shanor held on tightly, until they reached the safety of old Etzel's house—he knew it well. He had been there many times with his father. He knew he would be safe there until his father could return with help from Matadol.

Chapter 9

Winter finally passed, and so too did spring, bringing the warmth of summer to Shalkan. The trees and fields were green and lush, summer flowers in bloom. The bleating of sheep as drovers led them on their yearly pilgrimage through Shalkan to marketplaces far and wide, where they would be sheared for wool and sold for meat, and the gleeful sounds of children playing in the afternoon sun filled nearly every corner of the valley.

As life sprang up anew, memories of death were buried deep beneath the shadows of Barrier Mountain. Young Willerth's old wounds were beginning to heal, replaced with new joys. Thanks to Brendyk's horse-trader friend, Rister, the knowledge of Brugnara's death had remained silent, and like other memories better forgotten, gradually faded away with the turning of the new year.

The arrival of summer also heralded Brendys's sixteenth birthday. A day for which Brendys had long been waiting, had finally come. His closest friend, Kradon, whom he had not seen in almost five years, would arrive from his home at Hagan Keep in Racolis for this occasion.

Brendys had first met Kradon nearly eleven years earlier when he accompanied his father on a trip to Hagan Keep. They were small children then—Brendys was only five—but they had become fast friends.

Brendys and Kradon had much in common at that time. Their fathers had grown up the best of friends; they were both motherless—both Brendys's mother, Danel, and Kradon's mother had fallen victim to the Plague—and they were both little imps at heart, though that changed shortly after their first meeting. Rather, Kradon changed; Brendys did not.

Though similar in some respects, Brendys and his Hagane friend were truly as different as a knight's charger and a swaybacked pack-mule. Brendys was the mule. Kradon was a little more than a month older than the Shalkane youth and had dusty-blonde hair and brown eyes, as opposed to Brendys's raven-black mane and blue eyes. But the greater differences lay in their heritages: Kradon's father, Dell, was Lord of the House of Hagan—a title far greater than that of Horsemaster of Shalkan. But just as their fathers, neither of them had let the difference in class bar their friendship.

Brendys could hardly hold back his excitement when the long-awaited day arrived. He felt a childlike giddiness such as he had not felt in years. Arrangements had been made the summer of the previous year, before Willerth had come, for Brendys to return with Kradon on his voyage home.

This news greatly upset Willerth, for the following month he would turn ten, and his master would not be there for that day. But when Brendyk announced that they would celebrate Willerth's birthday as well, the boy seemed a little satisfied.

Kradon rode into the farmstead early in the afternoon of Brendys's birthday, accompanied by a messenger from the Shipyard of Ilkatar. As he arrived, he was met by Brendyk and Brendys. Kradon dismounted in front of the house. He removed his pack from the saddle, then gave his reins over to the Shipyard's messenger, who without a word started back up the old road to the Western Pass.

A broad grin livened the visitor's features as he embraced his Shalkane friend. There was no hesitance in their greeting, for though their only contact with each other since they were young lads was through written correspondence—a luxury provided for by Kradon's father—they still remained close as brothers at heart.

The two youths pulled apart to size each other up.

Kradon gave Brendys a good-natured chuckle. "You are still too big for your trousers, Brendys, old chap!"

"And you are still too small for yours," Brendys returned, a grin brightening his sun-darkened features. Brendys's sturdy build and Kradon's trim figure formed yet another stark contrast between the two.

Brendyk gave his guest a quick handshake and a light slap on the shoulder. "You have had a long journey, lad. You will probably want to freshen up a bit and get some rest."

"Thank you, Master Brendyk. Indeed, I would," Kradon gratefully acknowledged.

The Horsemaster nodded and looked at his son. "Well, don't just stand there dawdling like a fool, Brendys—though I know you can't help it. Show Kradon to your room! I have an engagement with Kotsybar in Ahz-Kham, but I should be home before the evening meal."

Brendyk briefly turned back to Kradon. "I must apologize for vanishing so quickly, but it really is important. This obviously is not Hagan Keep . . . I hope you find everything to your liking here."

"I am sure that I will, Master Brendyk," Kradon replied with a smile.

Brendyk nodded. "Very well. Good-bye."

"Farewell, Master Brendyk."

With a brief wave of his hand, the Horsemaster continued on to the stable.

Brendys took his friend's pack and led him into the house, climbing the stairs to his room. The Shalkane youth opened his bedroom door and waited for Kradon to enter before following behind.

Willerth stood at the window, his green-grey eyes scanning the stableyard, not realizing that his master and the visitor had already entered the house and were in the room with him.

Kradon nudged Brendys's arm and started to speak. "Who. . . ?"

Startled at the sound of Kradon's voice, Willerth spun around and took an anxious step back against the window sill, eyeing the stranger in nervous curiosity.

Kradon raised a brow in mutual curiosity and looked at Brendys.

Brendys pursed his lips and went to the boy's side, pulling him forward. He playfully rubbed the boy's head. "This is Willerth—he is easily frightened."

"That, I can see," Kradon said with a slight nod. "A neighbor-lad, I suppose? Or perhaps another of your father's *boarders?*"

Willerth partially hid himself behind his master, a half-fearful, half-uncertain look on his face, and muttered, "I'm Master Breny's-s-s ser'ant."

Kradon looked at the boy's master with a look of mock surprise. "*Your* servant? I never knew low-class, Shalkane stableboys like you had their own servants!"

Glaring at Kradon with distrust in his eyes, Willerth grasped Brendys's arm protectively and tugged him backwards.

Brendys looked down at him. "What are you doing, Willerth?"

"I don't like 'im," the boy replied, still watching Kradon in suspicion and fear. "I don' wan' 'im 'ere."

Kradon registered surprise at Willerth's response, as did the boy's master. "Apparently, the lad misunderstood my intentions."

The Hagane youth spoke gently to Willerth. "I didn't really mean what I said to your master, Willerth. I was only jesting."

"Get 'way from us!" the boy quietly and fearfully responded. He gave another tug on his master's arm.

Brendys jerked his arm away from Willerth. "Willerth!"

"What's 'ee want?" the boy hissed, with a worried glance at his master. Kradon stepped forward, smiling gently, extending a hand in greeting. "Don't worry so, lad. I'm. . . ."

Willerth quickly backed away. "Go 'way!"

"Willerth!" Brendys barked. "Come here and apologize to him immediately!"

Willerth did not move, his gaze remaining steady on Kradon.

Kradon glanced at Willerth, then at Brendys, and slipped out of the room.

Brendys did not seem to notice his friend leave. His attention was focused on Willerth. "I don't know what's come over you, Willerth! You have been acting awfully strange for the past month, and sooner or later you're going to get me into trouble with Father! What's more, you have caused me a great deal of embarrassment, behaving like that in front of Kradon. He's my best friend, for goodness sake!"

Willerth cowered at the sharp tone of his master's voice. He swallowed hard and fought to keep back tears, but failed in the end. "I'm sorry, Master Bren'ys. I di'n't know 'oo it 'uz. I'll make it up, I will!"

Farida appeared in the doorway of the room. Brendys stepped aside as she came in. The maid looked firmly at Willerth, but her voice was gentle. "Lord Kradon told me what happened, Willerth. You are fortunate that Master Brendyk is not home and that Lord Kradon is a forgiving soul. I think you and I ought to have a little talk."

Willerth sniffed and wiped the tears from his eyes, then followed Farida from the room.

Brendys dropped to his bed, chin in hands, his elbows propped on his knees. He felt like a bully. He had been too hard on Willerth. The boy had meant no harm. Willerth was intimidated by Kradon, that was all. Strangers still frightened him.

Brendys left his room in a sullen mood and went downstairs to join Kradon, but found his friend fast asleep in a high-backed chair in the front room.

* * * *

That night the celebration began. In some cases, Shalkane celebrations lasted for two to three days, occasionally longer, particularly when the host was as renowned and wealthy as Brendyk. After a long and festive meal, Brendys, his father, and his friends gathered in the front room, where there was the usual giving of gifts.

Brendyk sat in his favorite chair, while Brendys and Kradon sat on the couch. Willerth sat cross-legged on the floor at his master's feet. Farida had retired for the evening. She had seen more birthdays in her years than she had patience for.

There were several packages piled around the couch, some wrapped in brown paper and others in fine cloth. The more elegant gifts were delivered to the farmstead just before sundown by messengers from the Shipyard of Ilkatar. Kradon brought them with him from Racolis, but had not waited for them to be unloaded at the Shipyard, instead instructing the Dockmaster to send them on later.

Brendys quickly opened several of the brown-wrapped packages addressed to him in his father's careful script, showing polite enthusiasm over gifts that he found less than exciting. However, the last of those gifts impressed him greatly, more than it would have another common youth of his age.

Brendys lifted a small, leather-bound book out of the torn, brown paper on his lap. On the cover, inscribed in gold and in three languages, was his name. The pages inside were blank, except for a colorful entanglement of vines and twisting Dragons around the borders.

"Do you like it?"

Brendys looked down at the beautiful cover of the journal, then up at his father. He blinked back the tears that threatened to come. "I haven't words to describe it. But it's too expensive, Father, even for you. The decoration alone is worth a normal month's profits in gold!"

"Indeed, it is," Brendyk replied, his dark-blue eyes gleaming. "And it was gold well spent. That old scrap of a book you have been using is not fit for *my* son's journal.

"I asked Lord Faroan—the Elvinlord from Dun Rial that I dealt with last summer—to have this made for me. I had your name crafted in the Common Tongue, Caletri, and Kjerekil—the tongues of the Free Kindreds: Men, Elves, and Dwarves."

"But, Father, you were going to use that money to purchase horses from Rister when he returns from Gos!" Brendys objected.

The Horsemaster waved away his son's objection. "Your concern is appreciated, Brendys, but I will hear no more on it. I wanted to give you something that would please you, something special, and so I did."

Brendys smiled and lightly traced the gold lettering on the cover of the journal once more.

"Ain't ye goin' t'open th' rest o' yer presents, Master Bren'ys?" Willerth piped up.

Brendys placed his new journal on the low table before him. "Yes, of course."

He picked up the largest of the finely-wrapped gifts and pulled away the brilliant red cloth. Brendys nearly gasped with delight. Sliding both arms under his burden, he slowly lifted up a saddle made of dark leather with silver trappings. "Sedik's beard! Again, I don't know what to say, save that I could never want more than I have received today."

Kradon took the saddle from Brendys and set it aside, then placed a small bundle, wrapped in a white cloth bordered in gold, into his friend's hands. "My father sent you this."

Brendys pulled back the folds of the cloth and withdrew a thin gold chain. At the end of the chain dangled a large ring. It was a curious piece, for Brendys could not discern its true color. Next to the silver on his new saddle, the ring appeared a rich gold, but against the golden lettering upon his journal, it appeared to be of the brightest silver. The metal felt strangely warm to his touch.

Brendys examined the signet upon the ring for only a moment, for it was one he knew well. Emblazoned upon a sun was a hawk. In one talon, the bird clutched a sword of fire, and in the other a heart.

"This looks like your ring, Father," Brendys said, his voice tinged with wonder.

Brendyk leaned forward in his chair and held a hand out to his son. Brendys gave him the ring, and the Horsemaster held it up to look at it. "Aye, indeed it does. In fact, it's identical. It is even made of the same metal . . . Gloriod."

"My father said he found it while on a journey to Ascon," Kradon said as Brendys took the ring back from his father. "In a bazaar at Ascon Keep, of all places. We knew it was your family crest, though how it came to be at Ascon Keep was beyond us."

Brendyk leaned back, frowning thoughtfully. "I don't recall my father ever traveling as far as Ascon, though my grandfather may have. Either way, if that ring was ever in my immediate family, it has been lost for a long time."

Brendys turned the ring over in his hand to look at the signet again. He often wondered why a common family from a country where nobility did not exist had their own crest, and what did the crest stand for? These were questions he had asked before as a child, but his father was always too busy to answer.

Brendys looked up from his study of the ring. "Father, what do the charges mean?"

"My grandfather, Evin, told me once, long ago," Brendyk said, knitting his brow in concentration. He was silent for a moment as he dredged through the deeper regions of his memory. Finally, he nodded. "Ah, yes. There was a legend that Shalkan was once ruled by nobility—our ancestry—though there is no record of such a time. The hawk signifies our House, though its name is forgotten. The sun is the Glory of the Rising Dawn, the Lightlord Elekar, the King whom our family has served for as far back as our history tells. The heart stands for the compassion we live by, and the sword. . . ."

Brendyk stopped in mid-sentence, the light of understanding entering his expression.

"Father?" Brendys pressed. "What about the sword?"

Brendyk replied with a start, as though waking out of a dream. "Eh? Oh—we have spent too much time with you. We have not given any consideration to the boy. I am sure he is eager to open his gifts."

"Ne'er mind me, Master Bren'yk," Willerth replied quickly. "Master Bren'ys ain't finished."

The Horsemaster shook his head. "Brendys can finish tomorrow. It is getting late, and you have not opened one present yet."

Willerth shrugged and began opening his gifts, though with none of the enthusiasm that Brendys would have expected. Most of the packages contained clothing and other necessities which he had been lacking, certainly very little of interest to a boy of ten summers. Nevertheless, Willerth seemed happy enough with what he received, though he expressed his gratitude only in the form of a simple "Thank'ee" to the giver.

Brendys watched his servant in curiosity. Even at his age, he would have been disappointed if he had not received *anything* special. The boy's behavior was not normal. But then, Brendys reminded himself, Willerth is not a normal boy.

Kradon, sharing his thoughts, leaned forward to look down at Willerth. "Willerth, if I had known about you before I left Racolis, I would have brought you something. Is there anything you want?"

Willerth looked up at Kradon, at first in uncertainty, but slowly a smile cracked his lips. "Don't need nothin' else. A'ready gots all I want."

His unexpected answer caused the others to stare back in silence.

The boy glanced at the others, his smile vanishing, replaced by the fear that he had said something wrong. Brendys placed a hand on Willerth's small shoulder, giving him a reassuring smile.

Brendyk stood up and motioned his son's young servant to the stairway. "It is getting late. Already it is well past the boy's bedtime."

"Jes' a li'l bit longer, Master Bren'yk!" Willerth begged.

The Horsemaster shook his head firmly and pointed to the staircase.

Willerth sighed in disappointment, but climbed to his feet and padded across the room to the stairs leading to the second floor.

As the boy passed him, Brendyk reached beneath his chair and withdrew a small bag, then sat down again. "Oh—come here, boy, I forgot something."

Brendys's stared in disbelief. "Father. . . !"

His father cut him short with a sharp glance.

Head hanging low, Willerth turned around and marched back to stand before Brendyk.

The Horsemaster held the bag out to the boy. "It's a gift from Master Kotsybar."

Willerth regarded the sack with suspicion. Slowly, he reached a hand out to take the gift. As soon as he had his hand around the top of the sack, Brendyk let go. The boy nearly dropped it, misjudging the weight. He carefully opened the bag and peered inside. Willerth's eyes grew wider and wider and wider as he stared down into the sack.

Slowly, Willerth raised his eyes to the Horsemaster, gaping in wonder. "I ain't ne'er seen that much money afore!"

The others laughed at the boy's astonishment. Brendyk stood up, turning Willerth back towards the stairs with one hand.

"Well, you can decide what you are going to do with it in the morning," he said. "But right now, it's off to bed with you!"

"Aye, sir," Willerth replied, a doleful grimace on his face.

The Horsemaster turned to face his son. "You may want to go to bed yourself. You still have an early morning ahead. The horses don't care whether you are a year older or not."

Brendys rolled his eyes, but obediently rose to his feet. "Aye, Father."

He and Kradon retreated to his bedroom. Brendys closed the door behind them, then sat down on the small pallet next to the door, allowing his friend the use of his bed. He and Farida had made the pallet for Willerth a few days after Brugnara had been run off.

Brendys looked up at Kradon. "I suppose I should thank you."

"Thank me?" his friend replied with a puzzled look. "For what?"

"For not mentioning Willerth's behavior earlier," Brendys responded. "Father may be lax in discipline, but it doesn't take much to get to Willerth."

Kradon shrugged. "The boy made a mistake—an honest mistake, based on what Farida told me about him. And, besides,

I saw no reason for him to be lectured to tears three times in one day for the same confounded incident."

Yawning, the blonde youth sat down on the edge of the bed and began undressing. "I don't know about you, but if we are to be up with the sun, I am going to bed."

Brendys chuckled. "Are you ever up with the sun?"

Without waiting for a response, he undressed and slid under his blanket, rolling onto his side to face the wall. The pallet was a little cramped for his tall frame, but he made do by curling up.

The room went dark as Kradon blew out the lamp.

"One thing still puzzles me," the Hagane youth said as he climbed into bed. "Do you have any idea what Willerth meant when he said he already had what he wanted? I mean, as far as I can tell, he hasn't much more than a pallet on the floor and a life of servitude to a stableboy."

Brendys ignored his friend's teasing jibe, but not the question. Quietly, he replied, "That *is* what he was talking about."

* * * *

Brendyk waited until he was sure everyone was asleep, then climbed the stairs to the second floor, carrying a small candle to light the way. He carefully opened the library door so as not to wake anyone and stepped inside, partially closing the door behind him. A quiet moan drew his attention to the floor on his right.

Willerth lay there on his stomach, his head and most of his torso stretched across a pillow, a blanket haphazardly thrown over him. Brendyk had forgotten the boy was sleeping in the library while Kradon was visiting. Instinctively, he bent down and straightened the blanket, careful not to waken the boy.

He crossed the room to a reading stand in the far corner, upon which sat a large tome. Its ancient cover was dulled, but the title was still visible. The *Annals of the Ancients*, the tenets of the Dawn King and the histories of Mingenland and Milhavior as recorded by the Elves and the Wizards of Athor.

Brendyk gently opened the book and carefully began turning through the pages, until he found what he had been searching for. On the right-hand page, bordered by Athorian runes was a coat-of-arms, beneath which was written an inscription in the

Common Tongue. The Horsemaster reached into his pocket and withdrew his signet ring, raising it before him to examine it in the candlelight and compare it with the crest in the *Annals*.

His grandfather's words echoed in his mind as he read the inscription in the book. Finally, he returned his ring to his pocket. A chill came over him, and with it, a sense of impending doom. *I was right.*

He turned around to look at Willerth, fear rising within him. *It wasn't a dream, was it, boy?*

His anxious gaze shifted to the library door. *Oh, my son. Elekar, protect him.*

* * * *

Brendyk's funds and patience were tested to their limits. The celebration of Brendys's birthday lasted a full two weeks, with various obscure relations from other parts of Shalkan coming for a visit. The Horsemaster would have ended it sooner, but as the most prominent citizen of Shalkan, he could not cut short the celebration of his son's sixteenth birthday, his coming of age by the reckoning of Shalkan.

Brendys, himself, had been hoping his father would not give in to social expectations, but as it seemed to bring Willerth a modicum of joy and pride, he did not pressure his father to end it. He knew that at the end of those two weeks, he and Kradon would leave for the Shipyard of Ilkatar, where a ship was waiting to return them to Kradon's home in Racolis, and that disappointment would overshadow Willerth's fleeting moment of joy.

When the day came, Brendys was surprised—and a little hurt—that the boy was not as put out as he had expected. It meant Willerth had become confident enough that he no longer had to rely solely on his master for support.

Brendys came out of the stable, with Willerth close on his heels, leading Hedelbron. The morning sun was low and red on the horizon, and the air was cool. It would be a good day for traveling.

Brendys was still numb with weariness. He had slept little the night before. He dropped his old saddle on the ground—he did not wish to leave his new one at the Shipyard—and stood there for a moment, trying to rub the sleep from his eyes.

Willerth looked up at him eagerly. "D'ye want me t' saddle 'edelbron, Master Bren'ys?"

Brendys shook his head. "Nay. I'll do it myself, Willerth."

He hefted his saddle and tossed it onto the old grey's back. Hedelbron pranced a little, then settled down, allowing Brendys to tighten the cinch.

Willerth looked at the ground thoughtfully for a moment, then pulled on his master's sleeve. When his master looked down, he said, "D'ye want me t' gather yer packs, Master Bren'ys?"

"Kradon is doing that."

Willerth frowned and kicked at a nearby stone.

Brendys, understanding his self-styled servant's disappointment, quickly thought of something for the boy to do. "Willerth, lad, why don't you go fetch a suitable steed for Kradon? One with a little—*flare*."

He slapped Willerth on the back, and the boy ran off to the stable. As he watched the boy run to the barn, Brendys realized that even though he would be gone no longer than two months, he would miss Willerth. In so short a time, he had grown to love the boy almost as a little brother—there had even been a few times when he forgot that he truly was not.

Brendys suddenly felt as if he would be missing a part of himself until he returned and began to regret a little his decision to go to Hagan Keep.

Willerth soon came across the stableyard, leading an old bay mare. The poor animal was not in much better shape than Hedelbron and was nearly as old, but the beast was one of Willerth's favorites. He cared for the animal nearly as much as Brendys did for Hedelbron.

Brendys imagined *Lord* Kradon astride the sway-backed old mare and had to struggle to keep from laughing. He could envision the expression on Kradon's face—it would make a grand jest—but then he decided to have Willerth fetch another horse. He did not wish to risk his friend's anger over a silly beast.

Brendys started towards Willerth with a light chuckle, motioning him to take the animal back to the stable. "That is not quite what I had in mind. . . ."

Brendyk and Kradon came out of the house before Brendys could send his servant back for a different horse. The Hagane's travel dress was quite a contrast with Brendys's, light, clean, and richly decorated with colored trim, whereas Brendys's garb was white, stained grey from its age, with faded splotches of brown and green, and worn through in spots. The Shalkane youth could have afforded better, but he did not like to stand out among the townspeople of Ahz-Kham.

Before Brendys could stop his servant, Willerth took the mare directly to Kradon.

"I picked 'er out meself, M'Lord," he proudly informed the blonde youth.

The boy's master choked in surprise when Kradon gave the animal an admiring smile and replied graciously, "Why thank you, Willerth—quite a noble beast, indeed."

Brendys took his pack from his father and tied it to the back of his saddle, then turned to say his farewells before mounting.

Brendyk put a hand on his son's shoulder. "Mind your manners, Brendys, and don't you go getting yourself into any trouble."

Brendys gave him a mischievous grin. "I shan't. At least not too much!"

The Horsemaster clicked his tongue. "Uh-huh. Perhaps I should rephrase that. Don't you go making any trouble for Dell—and keep your wanton hands off the young ladies!"

"Of course, Father," Brendys laughed. "Would I do anything like that?"

Brendyk held his son's gaze.

Brendys nervously shrugged his shoulders a little at the unspoken answer.

Frowning and head bowed, Willerth stepped up to his master. "I wish I 'uz goin' wi' ye, Master Bren'ys."

Brendys lifted the boy's chin and looked him in the eye. "Hey there, lad, I'll be back before you know it."

When Kradon was finished attaching his pack to his saddle, he turned and bowed formally to his host. "I thank you for your hospitality, Master Brendyk. This has been a most pleasant holiday for me."

Then turning to Willerth, Kradon said, "And also to you, Master Willerth. And have no worries, the next time your master decides to get off his lazy haunches and take a little trip, you can be sure that you will be with him. If what I have witnessed these past days is any testimony, I think he would be hopelessly lost if it were not for you!"

Brendys nodded in affirmation, bringing a hopeful smile to the boy's lips.

When the two youths had said their final farewells, they mounted and started down the road which led to the Western Pass.

Brendyk yelled after them as they rode on. "Kradon, you keep a close eye on that boy of mine. Don't you leave him alone for one second!"

Kradon and Brendys waved in reply.

In a few hours, the two youths started up the hill leading towards the gap in the western edge of Barrier Mountain known as the Western Pass. As they rode through the pass, Brendys took note of the great hinges on either side of the gap upon which there had once been set the massive iron portals of a fortress gate. In the sides of the shadowy passage, he could see the dark entrances of the ancient guardposts and the remains of the old winches used to open the gate. The guardpost on his left was almost completely blocked by rubble. There were three more passages like this out of Shalkan—one in each cardinal direction.

Finally, Brendys and Kradon were through the Western Pass and outside the bounds of Shalkan. They traveled long over the rolling, green fields of Ilkatar, stopping occasionally for brief rests and to take meals. It had been a pleasant journey with no incident, but after several hours, they and their mounts had become exhausted.

The sun was setting in the west, and the first stars of the evening were beginning to glitter in the darkening sky. It would soon be time to set camp for the night. They had passed by many an Ilkatari farmstead on that day's journey, which put an idea in Brendys's mind. He did not feel inclined to sleep on the ground.

As they approached another farmstead, Brendys put voice to his thoughts. "Perhaps we could convince this farmer to lend us the use of his hayloft."

Kradon shook his head as they neared the small stone house. "I really would rather not trouble these people, Brendys. Two strangers knocking on their door after dark—especially one of your bearing—might cause them concern."

"Don't worry," Brendys replied, ignoring his friend's latter comment. "I am sure that it will be no trouble at all. Just let me do the talking."

Kradon curled his lip. "That is precisely what I *am* worried about."

As they approached, the front door of the house opened, illuminating the ground with a yellowish light. A tall man stepped outside and surveyed the youths with a cautious gaze. He was a fair man with thick, golden hair and a heavy, drooping mustache.

"Can I help you?" he said warily, his voice deep and rich.

Brendys and Kradon both dismounted and stepped into the light.

"Aye, sir," Brendys answered. "I am Brendys of Shalkan, and my companion is the Lord Kradon of Racolis. We wondered if you might permit us the use of your hayloft for the night."

Kradon frowned at Brendys and muttered disapprovingly under his breath.

The man did not seem to notice the Hagane youth's reaction. Smiling, he shook his head. "Then my answer is nay. You lads shall rest in the comfort of my home.

"My name is Elgern. I have done business with your father in the past, Master Brendys. Brendyk of Shalkan is a good man. I would not have his son, nor the heir of Hagan, sleeping in my barn when I have a bed to offer."

"And we would not have you sleep in a barn on our account, Master Elgern," Kradon responded. He eyed the man suspiciously, wondering how he knew his House.

Elgern laughed. "Nonsense! 'Tis my barn, is it not? And I may sleep in it when I wish. Now come in. Come in! I have roasted chicken and boiled potatoes on the table—enough for all! Come, let us eat!"

Before either Brendys or Kradon could say another word, they were ushered into the farmer's house. They stopped just inside the door and looked around.

The one-room dwelling was kept extremely neat and tidy. There was a large bed set at one side of the room, and a table and some chairs at the other. In the back wall was a large fireplace. The dark, wood floor and stone walls fairly glistened in the light of the hearth.

Elgern followed the youths inside and shut the door. Placing one hand on Brendys's shoulder, he motioned to the table. "Come, sit down. Rest your feet and fill your bellies!"

To the surprise of the travelers, there were three places set at the table.

"Were you expecting company this evening, Master Elgern?" Kradon asked.

"Indeed, you might say that." There was a twinkle in the man's eye that made Kradon a little nervous. "Now sit down. Sit down!"

The two youths did as told, and Elgern served them. The farmer filled his own plate, then took a seat and began eating. Brendys was quick to taste the meal before him, but his Hagane friend hesitated. Kradon cast a wary eye on Elgern, who simply responded with a jovial grin, then slowly took a bite of the meat. At first he was not sure what it was, but it tasted like chicken. After two more bites, he was convinced that it really was and ate more freely.

"The food is quite good, Master Elgern," Kradon said after a few minutes.

"And you are fortunate to be enjoying it, My Lord," the farmer replied, his demeanor darkening somewhat. "There has been a strange beast about for days, killing livestock and stealing chickens . . . and children, I fear. There have even been rumors that entire families have been slaughtered by the beast. But I suppose you haven't had such misfortune in Shalkan, eh, Master Brendys?"

Brendys shook his head and swallowed his food. "Nay. At least not around Ahz-Kham."

"And a good thing, too," Elgern continued. His voice lowered and his visage became even grimmer. "'Tis a devilish beast—a small part of a greater evil, to be sure."

"Why do you say that, Master Elgern?" Kradon asked.

"There have been strange goings-on all across Milhavior of late," the man answered. "Especially in the region of Machaelon. Some say a black wind is stirring there."

Brendys gave a disbelieving grunt. "A black wind is always stirring in Machaelon, and nothing ever comes of it. The Kubruki are gone, what few Trolls remain—if any—hide in the hills, Dark Elves have not been seen in Milhavior for centuries, and the Dragons are asleep in the wilderlands of the north. Save for the few Dark Lands away in the Southeast Quarter, there is no one left to cause any trouble."

Elgern cast a dark eye on the youth. "I would not be too sure of that, Master Brendys. There is that devil what's been killing my animals, and more. I received ominous tidings late last autumn from a traveler—a strange, old man. He spoke of the Bearer of the Flame of Elekar. The time of Ascon's Heir is nigh!"

Brendys rolled his eyes and gave a dismayed groan. He heard enough talk about Elekar from his father. He did not need it here, too. "Please excuse me, I have grown suddenly tired."

Elgern rose to his feet. "Of course, Master Brendys."

Brendys stood up and walked to the bed. He lowered himself onto the goose down mattress—a strange luxury for a farmer, he thought—then rolled to the far side, facing the wall.

He did not sleep, but listened long into the night as Elgern told Kradon tales of the Early Ages. The farmer seemed well-learned in the history and legends of Milhavior. Brendys had heard these same stories many times before: tales of the great wars between the servants of Elekar and the minions of the Deathlord—the Dawn Wars, as they were called—of the rise of the gods, and of the prophecies of the Third Age. The stories fascinated him, but that was all they were to him. He could not ally himself to a King he could not see and whose name had brought sorrow to him at every turn.

The last words Brendys heard before falling asleep were "Release not the Fire till Death is nigh," the words of a prophecy, a cryptic command to the future Bearer of the Flame. These words echoed in his mind as he drifted into darkness.

Brendys did not notice when Elgern went to the barn and Kradon came to bed. He was fast asleep, every dream ravaged by streams of fire—a cold, pitch-black flame and a shimmering, argent flame—twisting around and lashing at each other in a never-ending struggle. Behind the black flame Brendys could see the faint image of a skull, grinning in malicious delight. The empty stare caused shivers to run down the youth's back and freeze his heart.

Brendys's mind scanned the scape of his dream and saw beyond the silvery-white flame a kind face, the face of a man with snow-white hair and a beard, a face strangely handsome and youthful like an Elf, yet at the same time older than the land and the sea. The vision of this face warmed him and promised to drive away the images of darkness. Then, as if retaliation, shadows fell across his dream, and he found himself once more at his mother's deathbed, watching her final agonizing moments of life. Through shear force of will, he awakened himself.

Hearing a noise outside, Brendys sat up and peeked out the window beside him. An odd-looking dog trotted past the window, heading away from the farm. The large animal was tall and muscular, with bright golden fur; every part showed exceptional breeding—except for its face. The dog's muzzle was flat and had a heavy upper lip. The animal had such a comical look that Brendys nearly laughed.

The dog paused for a moment and looked at the youth with mournful eyes, an almost human look of pity, then continued on its way, jogging away from the house until it disappeared into the night. Brendys lay back down, puzzled. Never had he seen such an animal. He shook his head, trying to clear his mind of the vision, but could not. He went back to sleep, haunted by the animal's stare.

Brendys and his companion awoke the next morning to the aroma of lightly-spiced eggs. Elgern was setting the table.

"Good morning, Master Elgern," Kradon said cheerfully.

The farmer turned around at the sound of the youth's voice, his white teeth showing in a big grin. "And a good morning to you, My Lord. I trust you slept well?"

"Aye, indeed I did."

Brendys moaned and nearly fell asleep again, but Kradon dragged him out of bed.

"Master Brendys, it does not appear that you had as restful a night as did your friend," Elgern mused.

Brendys shook his head. "Nay. I had the strangest dream."

"Tell us about it," Kradon said.

Brendys paused with some uncertainty. He knew that Kradon would have some ridiculous interpretation for his dream, and he was not sure that he wanted to hear it. Finally, he replied. "I'm afraid I can't remember it."

Kradon gave him a dour look. "Of course."

Brendys ignored him. "I do remember waking up in the middle of the night and looking out the window, though. I saw a dog, or at least I think it was a dog. I can't say that I have ever seen anything like it before."

His Hagane friend nodded. "It was probably just another dream."

Half-smiling, Elgern shook his head in response to Kradon's statement. "Nay, 'twas no dream. The dog is mine. And you are right, Master Brendys, you have never seen such an animal. To my knowledge, he is the only dog of his kind."

The farmer motioned his guests to the table.

After a long and welcome breakfast, Brendys and Kradon mounted up and continued on their journey to the Shipyard of Ilkatar. Elgern called to them as they rode away. "May Elekar grant you his protection on your journey. I fear you may need it ere long!"

Kradon looked back at Elgern, who turned and disappeared into his house. "I wonder what he meant by that?"

"There is nothing to worry about," Brendys replied. "Elgern is just a superstitious farmer. There are a lot of those around here."

Kradon did not respond.

As time passed, both youths put Elgern's parting words behind them. Brendys and Kradon traveled hard that day, skipping lunch so as to reach the Shipyard faster. This was Brendys's first real trip in nearly five years, and he was eager to be along.

Kradon, on the other hand, was less than enthusiastic about returning to Hagan Keep. He found life as the son of a nobleman secluded, often lonely, with only a boring chamberlain for company. Sometimes he felt that Hagan Keep was more a prison to him than a home.

"'Tis sad that we had to leave so soon," the blonde youth said as they rode along.

Brendys grunted in response. "I, for one, am glad to be leaving that dusty, old house behind. Shalkan is such a dull place. Nothing to do there but work, and I hardly call that fun."

"My dear Brendys," Kradon replied sadly. "You will be bored to tears after a week at Hagan Keep. No one will let you go anywhere or do anything without a nursemaid along to make sure you do not hurt yourself."

"Will she be young and pretty?" Brendys asked with a grin.

Kradon smiled wanly, but said nothing.

The two started up a long, green slope, quickening their pace a little. When they reached the top of the hill, the youths gazed out towards the Western Sea, now opening before them like the expanses of a vast, blue prairie. There was a group of buildings lying in a small harbor, and beyond that, a number of ships lying in port, their great masts rising into the air.

White swells rolled in from the sea to break upon the shoreline. Flocks of squawking gulls hovered over the northern beaches and dove into the surf, searching for fish. A strong, chill breeze swept over Brendys, exhilarating his senses. He seemed to notice for the first time the stinging smell of brine carried on the wind. Brendys realized that he had almost forgotten what the sea was like.

"There's the Shipyard, Kradon," he said, pointing towards the buildings. "I'll race you!"

Kradon shook his head and yawned. "I don't want to race."

"What?" Brendys taunted. "Are you afraid that I would win?"

Kradon laughed in response. "*You* beat *me* in a race? I doubt that old nag of yours could go a furlong without stopping to catch his breath!"

"You are riding an *old nag* of mine as well, you know," Brendys reminded his friend.

"I happen to be very proud of this old nag," Kradon responded in mock indignation. "Oh, very well then. If you are really so eager for disappointment—*Now!*"

Kradon was already down the hill and racing across the fields before Brendys could move. The Shalkane youth knew he could waste no more time in getting started if he were to catch up, so he spurred Hedelbron forward and gave him his head.

After a few furlongs, Hedelbron slowed down to a light jog and then a walk, despite Brendys's urging to the contrary. Brendys reined his mount to a halt and dismounted. He sat down on the ground while Hedelbron, lathered and panting, bent his head and nipped at the lush grass.

Scowling miserably, Brendys picked up a nearby rock and gave it a strong heave. It landed a few yards away with a heavy thud. Brendys knew that Kradon would gloat over his victory for the rest of the day.

He glared at Hedelbron. "Blasted animal!"

The old grey lifted its head and returned its master's stare, then snorted and started chopping the thick, green blades of grass, occasionally finding a bit of sweet clover.

After a few minutes, Brendys stood up and mounted Hedelbron. "Come on, Worthless."

* * * *

Brendys found Kradon leaning against one of the outbuildings as he approached the Shipyard.

The blonde youth looked up as Brendys approached. "So, where have you been?"

Brendys avoided his friend's gaze. "I had to rest Hedelbron about halfway across."

Kradon shrugged casually. "I shan't say that I told you so, because I said he could not make a furlong without a rest. Well, you proved me wrong."

Brendys grunted and glared at Hedelbron.

Kradon paused for a moment before going on. "Why don't you go have a little visit with old Gwydnan; we still have a while to wait before the *Mariner* casts off, and he wouldn't mind seeing you, I'm sure."

"I suppose I should, if just to be polite," replied Brendys. "If my memory serves me right, he should be up at the North Docks."

"You shan't find him there," his friend informed him. "They have him working in the kitchens now."

Brendys gave the Hagane a puzzled look. "Gwydnan? In the *kitchens?*"

Kradon nodded. "That's where I spoke to him last."

"Are you sure?" Brendys still was not convinced. He remembered Gwydnan as a strong and willful old man, friendly but easily provoked, with too much pride to accept a demotion from Dockmaster's Assistant to a menial kitchenhand.

"I tell you I spoke to him there," Kradon insisted. "What do you think I am? Deaf, dumb, and blind?"

Brendys grinned in return, unable to resist the opening his friend had provided him. "Well, I don't know about deaf and blind, but I have always known that you were dumb!"

"I shall take that as a compliment, thank you." Kradon took the horses' reins. "I'll meet you aboard the *Mariner*."

Then he gave his friend a warning look. "Don't be late! Her captain is a rough fellow and easily roused." With that, he led the horses off to the Shipyard's stables.

Brendys hesitated a moment before entering the cluster of buildings. His father had left him in Gwydnan's care many a time, while he checked in with the Dockmaster. His memories of those experiences were not always pleasant. With a reluctant sigh, he went on.

When he reached the kitchens, he found the door standing wide open and entered with a shrug. There was an old man sitting at a small table in the center of the room, studying some equally aged scrolls, the yellowing rolls of parchment cracked and torn at the edges. Without looking up, the man spoke.

"Didn't hear you knock," he grumbled. "What do you want?"

Grinning, Brendys replied with false pomposity. "Is that how kitchenhands speak to their betters?"

The old man's dark eyes darted up to glare at the youth. Brendys backed towards the open door as Gwydnan rose from his chair and walked towards him, jaw set, fists clenched. The former dockhand stood over six feet tall and was easily in better shape than Brendys, despite his extraordinary age.

Brendys backed into the door and it slammed shut. He jerked his head and shoulders around to see the closed door, then turned to face the kitchenhand again, his eyes showing white all around. With no means of escape, he crouched, raising his fists in defense.

Gwydnan stopped a couple feet away from Brendys and reached out a strong hand, turning the youth's head to either side, examining his profile. He knit his white brows. "Brendys of Shalkan, is that you?"

Brendys gave a deep sigh and relaxed, lowering his fists. With a half-smile, he replied, "Aye, sir."

"Ach, I should have guessed. Only you could be so witless," the old man grumbled. Gwydnan embraced the dark-haired youth, then held him back to get a better view of him. "It's been a long time since you were here last. You were naught but a scrawny, little thing then."

"It's been nigh on five years," Brendys replied. "And Kradon was the scrawny one, not I."

Brendys shifted uncomfortably as Gwydnan looked him over a couple of times. The old man shook his head with a deep look of pity, bringing an insulted look to the youth's face. "What?"

"Sit down," Gwydnan replied curtly, motioning to his own chair. Scooping up the scrolls, he went to the pantries to gather some food.

"What?" Brendys repeated as the old man walked away. Sighing, Brendys did as he was told. His memories of Gwydnan had not been far wrong, though to him the man did seem a bit more eccentric than he remembered. He waited quietly for a short time, but soon became restless in the close confines of the room. He was about to get up and walk over to a window when Gwydnan returned.

The old man was carrying a basket in one hand, and a clay vessel in the other. Setting these down on the table, he drew two mugs out of a cupboard and proceeded to pour a golden-brown liquid into them. Putting the jug down on the table, he reached into the basket and produced two hunks of cheese and two small loaves of bread, just large enough to span Brendys's open hand. Gwydnan handed one of each to Brendys, then pulled a chair over from the near wall and seated himself.

"Kradon is going to be furious with me," Brendys said, taking the food from the kitchenhand. "Neither of us had any lunch."

Gwydnan grunted. "*Hmph!* That's his own fault."

"Quite right!" Brendys agreed with a grin. He nibbled at his cheese. "Where is Kanstanon? Is he still in your charge?"

"Aye, he is, and that's one reason why I am in the kitchens now," Gwydnan replied. "The boy's about his work in the stables. He has had to take more responsibility since the Stablemaster quit. The storms of late have this lot of superstitious idiots in a panic."

"I'm sure Father could recommend someone to fill the position," Brendys replied hopefully. "Perhaps even me."

Gwydnan snorted and sipped at his drink. "I doubt that, lad. Not many, including you, know as much about those confounded animals than Kanstanon. Besides, your father can't work that stud-farm alone."

Brendys frowned dismally. "Maybe so. But it's worth a try—anything to get away from that wretched place!"

The look of pity again crossed the old man's features.

"I think you are going to learn that Shalkan is not as wretched as you think, lad," he said, staring at his mug, his voice quiet as though speaking to himself. He looked up at Brendys with a surprised expression as if suddenly remembering the youth was there, and spoke more casually. "So, where are you headed off to this time?"

"Hagan Keep, as usual," Brendys replied between bites, his eyes never leaving Gwydnan's face, a mixture of curiosity and suspicion on his own. "Father made arrangements last year for me to return with Kradon and spend the rest of the summer there. It's a good thing, too—I could do with some excitement."

Gwydnan cast a sharp glance at the youth. "Excitement? You're a young fool. Those mountains are Kubruk territory!" To reach Hagan Keep, Brendys would pass through the Silver Mountains, an ancient Dwarvinholt conquered by the Kubruki long ago.

Brendys scoffed at the old man's remark. "*Kubruk territory*, indeed! The Kubruki have been extinct for nearly an entire Age!"

"Aye, so it's been said," admitted the old kitchenhand. "But word has it that a Shadow has arisen in Machaelon and is spreading westward—and that a Sorcerer in the service of Thanatos has revived the Kubruki."

"Sorcerers and Thanatos!" Brendys snorted derisively. "Myths and old wives' tales, I say!"

Gwydnan shook his head and sighed. "Did your father never teach you anything?"

"Certainly," Brendys replied. "But who could believe any of that nonsense about some kind of *Dawn King*, and all that other rubbish?"

The kitchenhand's dark eyes flashed, but he held his composure. "I can, your father can, Kradon can...."

"You can believe what you will," Brendys said quietly. "I'll have none of it."

Gwydnan leaned back, staring intently at the youth. "Then what *do* you believe?"

Brendys met his gaze. "I will tell you what I believe: I believe in Brendys of Shalkan. At least that way I can't be disappointed by false hopes and promises."

"Aye," Gwydnan agreed, his eyes still studying the youth. "Only yourself. The Dawn King didn't cause your mother's death, Brendys, and it is time that you accept that."

Brendys felt a sudden, irrational surge of anger swell up within himself. "He may not have caused it, but he didn't stop it, either! He could have done that one thing, but he didn't!"

Brendys lowered his eyes from Gwydnan's now gentle gaze and slumped back in his chair, feeling very foolish for his outburst.

"Very well, Brendys, have it your own way for now, but there shall come a day when you will see," Gwydnan said quietly, a foreboding tone to his voice. Before Brendys could respond, he changed the subject. "I nearly forgot to ask—how is young Willerth? The poor lad must have been through some terribly hard times."

Fingering the last bit of his cheese, he started to mumble in reply, "Aye, he. . . ." but suddenly stopped. His eyes flashed up to meet Gwydnan's. "How do you know about Willerth?"

The old man's features went blank. A quick reply stumbled from his lips. "Oh, rumors get around. . . ."

Brendys knit his brows in suspicion. "What rumors?"

"Uh, yes—well," Gwydnan stammered. Suddenly, he straightened. "What ship are you on?"

Brendys sighed, knowing the old man was avoiding his question. Nevertheless, he answered. "The *Scarlet Mariner*."

"Then I had best get you moving! She'll be casting off soon!" Gwydnan climbed to his feet and grabbed Brendys's arm, jerking the youth out of his chair, then dragged him out the door. The old man led Brendys past several small buildings until they reached the stable. Gwydnan called to his young ward, who had just come out of the barn. "Kanstanon, bring me that box from up in the hayloft!"

The boy disappeared into the building, soon returning again, bearing a long tin box in his arms. Gwydnan took the container from the lad, then proceeded with Brendys to the docks.

The *Scarlet Mariner* was not hard to find. It was by far the largest vessel in port, nearly twice the size of the other ships anchored in the Shipyard, built from the red wood of the voss tree—found only in the captain's home country of Ovieto—to withstand the roughest seas and the attacks of the northern rovers. The *Mariner's* brilliant red sails were just being unfurled when Brendys and Gwydnan arrived at the docks.

Gwydnan shoved Brendys up the gangplank and onto the ship, thrusting the long box into the youth's hands. "A traveler gave this to me last autumn. He told me to pass it on to you when next you came. There was also a message for you—it said: *Release not the Fire till Death is nigh*."

The words struck Brendys. He remembered them from his stay at the house of the farmer Elgern—a warning to the prophesied Bearer of the Flame—but could not fathom what they had to do with him.

Gwydnan's face held deep concern. "Lad, heed my counsel—do not open that box unless absolutely necessary! It could be dangerous. Remember that. Farewell, my boy, and may the Dawn King protect you."

Brendys opened his mouth to reply, but the old man had already gone.

Almost immediately, the ship was cast loose and the anchor weighed. The water slapped against the sides of the ship as she warped away from the docks, causing her to roll.

Brendys realized at once that not only had he forgotten what the sea was like, but also what sea voyages were like, and how his stomach suffered them. He shifted the box in his arms, then went below deck to find Kradon.

He had just come to the bottom of the stairwell when a bear of a man lumbered right into him, knocking him flat on his buttocks. The man wore a scowl that could have curdled fresh milk. His thick, brown beard bristled angrily as he reached down and caught Brendys by the collar, lifting him to his feet, all in one motion.

"Why don't you watch where you're going, oaf!" he growled, violently shaking the Shalkane. "What are you doing blundering about, anyway?"

Brendys froze, eyes wide. If he had been intimidated by Gwydnan, this hulk terrified him.

"Speak up, boy!" the big Ovietan bellowed.

"L-looking for m-my cabin, sir,' Brendys finally stammered in reply. "Y-you see, I-I-I was late boarding, and-and. . . ."

The big man quieted down. "Looking for your cabin, eh?"

Brendys gave a relieved sigh. "Aye, sir!"

The sailor started searching his pockets. "Well let's see. I've got that list of landlubbers around here somewhere. Ah, here it is! Now then, what's your name."

"Brendys, sir," the youth replied.

The man ran his finger down the short list, muttering to himself as he read. "Count Agidon, Tonys, Omusok, Delvecaptain Asghar, Nibys, Dinugom, Lord Kradon, Captain Nisbud, Tinsor. . . ." The man's face grew fiery again. "There's no Brendys on my list! You're a blasted stowaway! Do you know what I do to stowaways?"

Brendys backed up, shaking his head. "Nay! You don't understand! I'm sharing a cabin with my friend, Kradon!"

The man seemed startled for a second at the youth's response, but then began howling with laughter. "This is the first time in all of my sailing days that I have ever had some common stowaway make such a ridiculous claim. A friend of the Lord Dell's son!"

Brendys's temper flared at the ridicule. "And what is wrong with that? What right have you to detain me here, you oversized tub of horse. . . ."

The sailor interrupted him before he could finish his last remark. The big man lowered his voice menacingly. "This is also the first time that *anyone* has ever dared yell back to me."

But as the man spoke, a strange look came over his features. He began mumbling to himself. "Blast my memory!"

The sailor studied Brendys's face one more time. "Where do you hail from, boy?"

Brendys glared at his inquisitor, but answered, despite his anger. "Shalkan. What is it to you?"

The huge man suddenly raised his hand, causing Brendys to take a surprised step backwards. His hand came down to slap the youth on the back with such force that it knocked the very wind out of him.

"Well met, Bren!" he boomed. "I'm Captain Folkor!"

Brendys looked up in amazement, gasping for air. Folkor had captained the ship which had taken him and his father to Racolis five years past. The beard and mustache greatly changed his appearance. "But I thought you captained the *Sea Cutter!*"

"So I did," replied the Captain. "Until one of my crewmen accidentally set fire to the hold and sunk her. Master Ramsin, the *Cutter's* owner, nearly had my head, and he would have, too . .

. that is, if he could have reached it. Instead, he thought it best just to send me on my way.

"That's how I came to captain the *Mariner*," The big man gave the wall off the corridor a loving pat. "I *own* her!"

Brendys finally regained his breath. "What happened to the crewman who set the fire?"

"He was sent to Zoti," replied Folkor grimly.

Brendys swallowed nervously. Zoti was the god of death.

The Captain motioned down the hallway, his mood perking up once more. "Here, let me show you to your quarters."

Brendys followed the Captain down the passageway. There were fourteen doors along the corridor—seven on each side—and one at the end, which opened into the ship's galley. Beyond that was a small cabin that served as the kitchen. The *Scarlet Mariner* was built to carry up to sixteen passengers—mostly persons of some wealth or military position—and forty crewmen, as well as the standard load of cargo.

Twelve of the cabins lining the corridor were for the passengers. Each contained a bed and a table, which were fastened to the walls and floor, and a wash basin that was secured to the table and could be removed to change the water. Four of these cabins had two beds for pairs traveling together. The other two cabins accommodated the off-duty crewmen, ten men housed in each cramped room.

Folkor turned to Brendys when they reached the cabin, the third from the last on the port side. "I've a good deal of work to attend to right now. But should you need anything, just ask for me. Good-bye, for now."

He glanced back at Brendys before going on. "By the way, Bren . . . you are to leave the cook's daughter alone."

Rolling his eyes in exasperation, Brendys let himself into the room, finding Kradon sprawled out on one of the beds. The blonde youth opened his eyes and looked up when Brendys entered.

"Well, I have learned one thing about you—you certainly take your time," he said yawning. "So what is your excuse this time?"

"I ran into Captain Folkor," Brendys replied. "Or at least he ran into me. Couldn't you hear? Or are you really deaf?"

Kradon shook his head. "I am afraid I was asleep. Now, why don't we take a walk down to the galley and see if we can bribe the cook into feeding us?"

Brendys nervously rubbed the back of his neck. "Uh, you go ahead—I'm not very hungry."

The Hagane cocked a brow. "Here now, do you mean to tell me that you are not about to shrivel of starvation after all this time?"

"Uh, well, I ate back at the Shipyard," Brendys admitted sheepishly, leaving off Folkor's parting command.

Kradon shrugged. "Oh. All right."

Brendys looked quizzically at his friend. "Don't you ever get angry? I thought you would be furious with me!"

Kradon shook his head apologetically. "I am sorry if I disappoint you, Brendys, but I am just not capable of it."

The Hagane youth quickly changed the subject, pointing to the container in his friend's arms. "What is in the box?"

"I don't know," Brendys replied, pulling the box in front of him. It had some weight, but not as much as he would have expected for a container that size. Something rattled inside when he shifted his grip.

Kradon wrinkled his brow. "What do you mean, 'I don't know?'"

"Exactly what I said! *I don't know!*" Brendys returned, a little frustrated. He suddenly wanted very much to open the box and see what worried the kitchenhand so much. "Gwydnan gave it to me. He just stuffed it in my arms, gave me some silly message, then told me not to open it. He was gone before I could ask him why!"

"What was the message?" his friend returned.

Brendys shrugged nervously. "Something like, 'Release not the Fire till Death is nigh' or some such gibberish."

Kradon stared at the tin case, a distant look entering his brown eyes.

Brendys knew he had said too much, but it was too late to change anything. Finally, he broke the silence. "What's wrong, Kradon?"

The young Lord shook his head. "I don't know exactly. That bit about the Fire is from a prophecy about the Bearer of the Flame, but I cannot imagine what it has to do with you. If I were you, I would listen to Gwydnan and wait until we reach Hagan Keep to open that box. There is a Wizard there right now who might be able to tell us a little something about it."

"*Wizards!*" Brendys muttered under his breath. "All right, I think it's silly, but if you believe there is actually something behind all of this nonsense, I'll wait until Hagan Keep."

Kradon then stood up. "Good! Now I am going to run down to the galley."

When Kradon had gone, Brendys put the box on the table fastened into one corner of the cabin, then dropped to his bunk, gazing at the container. As he stared at it, he again felt strangely compelled to open it, but he resisted the temptation, and soon it was forgotten.

That night, his sleep was again plunged into chaos. He dreamed that a mountain began to move, and that great boulders rolled from its peak, striking the ship as they fell, until the ship splintered apart. The crew and passengers screamed in terror, until they had all drowned. Then all went black, and he heard a cry for help and hideous laughter. Monstrous shadows danced through his mind.

The voices ceased, and the shadows faded, replaced by the image of a man. His strong body bulged with grotesquely-knotted muscles, and when Brendys looked into the man's face, he found a skull grinning back at him. The creature reached out to grab him, and Brendys awoke with a cry.

Kradon jerked up as well. "Brendys, what is it?"

Brendys shivered, his brow drenched with perspiration. "Nothing. Go back to sleep."

"Are you sure?" Kradon replied, a touch of concern in his voice.

Brendys did not answer. Yes, he was sure. There was nothing to talk about. It was just a silly dream, that was all. But dream or not, dread had crept over him, chilling him to his bones, and he did not close his eyes again that night. All night, he lay awake, staring into the dark. His imagination brought images of his dream flickering before his eyes. When the beast would arise, he would swipe at it, trying to drive the picture away.

The same nightmare persisted for two more nights, often accompanied by his dreams from the night at Elgern's house. And a new element had appeared: a sword, a terrible sword, black-hilted and black-bladed. He was sure that he would go mad if the dreams did not stop.

Kradon, just as persistently, tried to find out what it was that his friend was dreaming, but Brendys would only tell him the same thing night after night—that it was nothing and to go back to sleep.

On the fourth day of the voyage, Captain Folkor called a feast for his passengers, or as much of a feast as could be contrived on a sailing vessel. It was a trivial custom of his—he believed it brought him the favor of the sea god—and had earned him a favorable reputation among his wealthier passengers, including some nobility, such as Count Agidon of Fekamar who was a passenger on that very voyage. The crewmen, of course, were banned from the galley when the passengers were enjoying their meal.

Kradon quickly prepared himself and went to join the Captain and the other passengers, leaving Brendys alone in their cabin. Exhausted, Brendys had dozed off, but he awoke when Kradon slipped out of the room. Cursing, he hurriedly washed up and threw on his best clothes and his cloak.

As Brendys was about to walk out the door, his eyes brushed over the box. A thrilled shiver ran through his body, a tingling sensation borne of both fear and desire. Sweat beaded his brow as he turned away from the box and reached for the handle of the door, but he stopped before his hand touched the brass lever.

Unable to resist the sudden urge, Brendys returned to the table where the box sat and, hands trembling, broke the seal. With a mixed feeling of expectancy and forboding he slowly lifted the lid and peeked inside. Within lay a sword, complete with scabbard and belt. It was a short weapon—no more than three feet from pommel to point. Its hilt and wire-wrapped grip, like the ragged scabbard, were a dull black. Runes were etched around the round pommel and decorated the cross-guard.

He swallowed as he drew the sword out of the box. It looked like the weapon in his dreams, but seemed smaller, less menacing. A warmth radiated from the hilt, drifting through his arm while he held it. He attempted to pull the sword free from its sheath, but it would not budge, no matter how hard he tried.

Muttering curses, Brendys sat down on his bunk. Sighing, he shook his head. "This is ridiculous. What danger could this thing be? It won't even come out of the sheath."

He stood up again, intending to return the weapon to its box, but instead affixed the sword belt to his own and left the cabin.

Brendys did not immediately join the others in the galley, but instead went up on the deck to get a breath of fresh air. He leaned on the guard rail and inhaled deeply. His eyes came to rest on the mighty forms of the Silver Mountains, which rose up in the east like an army of massive, stone giants. In the moonlight, he could see the first great Dwarvinarch of the Silver Pass, like a bridge between two mountains, high above the river Anatar.

The sense of foreboding returned to Brendys as he stared at the dark mountains, and his hands began to tremble. He could almost imagine the stone giants moving as they had in his dreams. He quickly turned away and went to join the feast.

When he came into the dining hall, Brendys found the other passengers standing around or sitting at the long table in the center of the large room, cheerfully conversing with one another—with the exception of one. A dark-eyed Dwarf stood alone in a shadowy corner, staring at Brendys. He was about four-and-a half-feet tall, but his shoulder breadth was half again that of the Shalkane youth's, thickly muscled. He was bald-headed, but he had great bushy eyebrows and an extremely long, red beard which flowed over his immense chest.

The Dwarf's stare was making Brendys nervous, and he began to hope that the stranger would either come right out and say what he wanted or just go trouble someone else. As if in answer to his thoughts, the Dwarf moved out of the shadows towards Brendys.

"Lad," he started in a deep, throaty voice. "For the sake of these people, get rid of that sword! 'Tis cursed!"

"Get rid of it? I can't do that—it was given to me by a friend," Brendys said in return. He paused as the Dwarf's words seized hold. "What do you mean by *cursed?*"

Before the Dwarf could reply, Kradon joined them. "So, there you are at last! Brendys, I have been waiting. . . ."

Kradon's eyes narrowed when he saw the weapon at his friend's side. "Where did you get the sword?"

Brendys nervously glanced around the room. "Uh, well, you see, I got it out of that box. . . ."

"You *what!*" Kradon burst out, his demeanor taking on an uncharacteristic turn for the worse. "What in Hál do you think you are doing! Are you trying to kill us all!"

Silence immediately blanketed the room. The other passengers each turned their gazes upon the two youths and the Dwarf. Captain Folkor hurried to draw his guests' attention back to the feast, but met without much success.

Brendys stared in astonishment at his friend. He had never seen Kradon angry before, and it frightened him. Before he could give a reply, the ship lurched with a wrenching shock and the sound of snapping timbers. The floorboards cracked and gave way beneath Brendys's feet. As the youth fell through, something sharp struck him on the side of the head, and all went dark.

Chapter 10

Brendys slowly came to his senses. The first thing he noticed was the cool, wet grittiness of sand beneath him and a chill breeze blowing across his body. Soon, he could hear the soft lapping of water at the shore, and cold water rushed over his head and shoulders, causing him to choke and lift his head up, just to drop it back to the wet sand again, a stabbing pain passing from his right temple through his head.

After a moment, Brendys was able to open his eyes. Everything was dark, hazy. His vision was filled with small pinpoints of light, but as his eyes focused more, he found that the pinpoints actually *were* stars. Brendys placed a hand on his throbbing head; it felt sticky. He quickly drew his hand away again, covered with blood.

He tried to get up, but his body felt heavy, as though a wagon-load of stone had been dumped on him. Every muscle in his body ached as he forced himself onto his knees. Finally, he managed to stand and limp around for a few minutes, unsuccessfully trying to clear his mind and loosen his joints.

Brendys looked down at himself. His tunic and trousers were in shreds and his belt was gone—and with it, the sword that had hung at his side.

"*Skud!*" he breathed, putting a hand on his forehead. "What happened?"

Brendys stood silent, half-expecting a reply, until he looked around and realized that there was no one there but himself. Jetsam littered the shore, and more driftage was being washed up from the river every minute. The scattered wreckage was the only sign remaining of the *Scarlet Mariner*. Either the ship had been utterly destroyed, or the bulk of the vessel had sunk below the river's surface. Which of these was true, Brendys did not know, nor did he at the moment care.

Neither did he know what could have caused the disaster. All he knew right then was that he had to find Kradon.

Brendys looked back. Not far behind him, the base of one of the great Dwarvinarches rose up from a mountainside. Before him, the beach stretched on for several yards. He could see where the sandbelt ended, blocked by a low ridge formed of rubble from another mountainside. Beyond the rubble, he could see the second Dwarvinarch rising up. The area to the south was a maze of dank, mossy stone leading back into the mountains. It looked fairly traversable, but Brendys had no desire to wander through that place.

Had he the voice to call out—and the patience to wait for an answer—he would have done so, but he was short of both, and that left him no choice but to search the banks himself. Brendys stumbled towards the eastern end of the beach, his eyes scanning the rocks on his right and the river's edge on his left for signs of Kradon or other survivors. Though the stretch of sand was not very long, it took Brendys nearly half an hour to search its length, dragging himself along, constantly tripping over small rocks or his own feet.

Reluctantly, Brendys plunged deeper into the labyrinth of rocks that led into the Silver Mountains. His vision became foggy again as he scavenged the stony terrain for his friend. After a short time, he became too dizzy to search any longer.

Brendys stumbled into a clearing in the rocks and fell to his knees. Slowly, he raised his head and looked around. There were several long, carefully-stacked piles of stone scattered about the clearing. Etched in the sand around each pile were strange symbols, each mark glittering blue in the moonlight as if the sand within the grooves was made of pure crystal.

Brendys crawled towards one of the piles, careful not to disturb the symbols in the sand, and reached out to remove a stone from the top of the mound. Several rocks fell away as he touched the mound, exposing a hollow space. Brendys cautiously peered into the opening, then fell back, horrified. He looked away for a brief moment, then turned his eyes back upon the pile of stones, to the ghastly image of the corpse which lay within the rocks, the badly mauled body of one of his fellow passengers—which one, he could not tell.

Brendys drooped his head. His spirit crumbled at the thought that Kradon might lay beneath one of the many barrows around him. Tears formed in his eyes and slowly made their way down his cheeks to drip into the sand at his feet. Hope dwindled away, leaving Brendys with a hollow feeling in the pit of his stomach. For once in his life, he was truly afraid.

He was trapped within the Silver Pass. There was nowhere for him to go, no way of escaping this terrible place. He would surely starve to death, if he was not killed by some mountain animal first. He began to shiver as if noticing for the first time the cool wind which stirred through the rocky pass. Never had he thought that he would be cast, alone, into such a desolate place, with no means of survival.

Brendys took in several slow breaths in an effort to calm himself.

"Come on now, Brendys, this is no time to go losing your wits!" he said aloud to break the monotony of the silence. Gradually, he came to the realization that he was not alone. Someone had built the burial mounds, and that someone was still trapped with Brendys in the Silver Pass.

Brendys started to get up, but a sharp pain suddenly pulsed through his wounded temple, and he collapsed to the ground. The landscape around him melted into shadows, but his hearing seemed to sharpen. He could hear a familiar laughing—a croaking, nightmarish cackle. Then a cry split the air, a deep, but pleading cry that he had heard every night for the last three nights.

"*Kuntok ê, Kolis Bazân!*"

Brendys pulled himself to his feet, startled by the wailing voice. The gruff plea was followed by more shrieks of croaking laughter and wicked cheers. Brendys, dazed by the sudden, painful attack, made off in the direction of the cry. His mind began to spin, and he tripped over a stone, crashing to the ground behind a larger rock. His hand landed upon something metallic. He grabbed the object beneath his palm and crawled up onto the boulder.

As he rose to his feet, he could barely make out a ring of huge shapes encircling a shorter, broader one. Without thinking, Brendys brought the object in his hands down upon the nearest shadow. His weapon landed with a sickening crunch, and the shadow gave way beneath the blow.

The action drew the attention of the other shadows. The light of the full moon was directly behind the youth, making him a silhouette in the sight of the creatures. The remains of his tattered cloak and tunic streamed in the wind like the graveclothes of some long-dead corpse come from its tomb. The beasts scattered in fear and ran shrieking into their mountain halls.

Brendys took one step forward, slipping from the rock, and fell unconscious.

* * * *

Kradon drifted to the shore as quietly as he could, half-swimming, half-floating amid the flotsam of the Scarlet Mariner, to avoid being noticed by the Kubruki and Rock Trolls standing high above upon the ancient Dwarvinarch of the Silver Pass. The Trolls had rained great boulders from their perch a hundred feet above the river down upon the Scarlet Mariner. He had been fortunate to escape the wreck without injury, but he knew his fortune would change if he were seen by the monsters above.

As he slid onto the southern shore of the Great River, Kradon was grappled by a pair of large hands. One muscular arm wrapped around him, holding his own sore limbs close to his body, while the other hand was clamped firmly over his mouth. Panicking, he tried to free himself from the strangling grasp, but his attacker's heavy body pressed him into the sand, immobilizing him.

A voice breathed in his ear. "*Shh!* 'Tis I, Captain Folkor!"

Kradon stopped his struggling, and the big man released him. The young Lord rolled over and sat up, breathing a sigh of relief. "You cannot know how glad I am to see you!"

The sea-captain waved away his comment. "That is well, but there is no time to tarry here. We must be away at once."

Kradon whipped his head around to look at the river. "But what about Brendys? He is still out there!"

"That may be, but I have my doubts," Folkor replied. "He was probably killed when that plank struck him in the head. It was no light tap."

Kradon slowly turned his face away from the water. "But. . ."

Folkor's voice gentled. "Watch for him if you must, while I look for a way to escape. But when I have found that path, we must go."

Kradon nodded silently and looked around. The beach was actually a small, sandy cove set in the mountainside, with no noticeable passages leading from it. Off to his right, rising above the edge of the mountains' roots, a second Dwarvinarch mounted into the sky and crossed over the river to join the branches of the Silver Mountains. Several yards to his left, the grasping feet of the mountains formed a low ledge, tall enough that neither he nor Folkor could see over it.

While Folkor searched for a way out of the cove, Kradon turned his attention to the river, scanning for a sign of Brendys among the floating wreckage and the bodies of those who had been less fortunate than the Captain and himself. He watched for several minutes, praying that Brendys would appear, what little hope he had of his friend's survival dwindling with each second.

When he could not find any evidence of Brendys near the cove, he turned his attention to helping Folkor find a route of escape.

Folkor moved along the edge of the mountain, sliding his hands along the stony wall. The mountain face was too smooth and sheer, and it would have been an impossible climb for them to make even if there had been holds for their hands and feet. Throwing aside the idea of climbing to safety, he walked back to the edge of the river. But that, too, proved fruitless.

Kradon slumped to the ground with his back to the wall of stone. "This is hopeless. We cannot escape by eating through stone."

Folkor looked grim. "I do not suggest we do."

"Then what do you suggest, Captain?"

"That we seek to escape by way of the river."

Kradon stared at him in surprise. "What? And how are we to manage that? I haven't the strength to battle the river again. Perhaps if I rested for a day and a night . . . but to do that would be inviting death as well. The Kubruki shall find us sooner or later if we remain here much longer."

"I don't see as we have any choice," Folkor replied flatly. He picked up a large rock from the sandy bank. "We shall wait and rest. And should the Kubruki become too inquisitive, they shall not find me easy prey."

* * * *

When next Brendys opened his eyes, the sun was shining, and a Dwarf was kneeling over him, tending the wound on the side of his head. Fireballs burst in his mind every time the Dwarf dabbed at the gash. Aside from his head injury, Brendys was hale, though he was terribly numb. He worked his hands until he regained the feeling in them, then tried to move his legs.

The Dwarf backed away, allowing Brendys to stand up.

"There will be a scar, My Lord," he said as the youth arose.

Brendys recognized his healer almost immediately. "You are the Dwarf from the Mariner. You're alive!"

"Aye, My Lord," he replied, picking up a dark object—a familiar weapon. He knelt down on one knee, head bowed, and offered the sword to Brendys, cradling it with both hands. "I am Asghar, son of Asghol, Delvecaptain of the Crystal Mountains.

You have saved my life—I am eternally at your service, My Lord."

Brendys nearly laughed at the absurd sight before him.

"I am no Lord," he politely informed the Dwarf. "Just a simple Horsemaster's son!"

The red-bearded Dwarf climbed back to his feet, but still offered the weapon out to Brendys in deference. "Then I offer you my service out of friendship, Lord Horsemaster."

Brendys shrugged and took the weapon from Captain Asghar's hands, not fully realizing the honor that had just been bestowed upon him. "If you insist. I am named Brendys, son of Brendyk, of Shalkan, and I, too, am at your service."

The Dwarvin warrior straightened his muscular shoulders, beaming with pride.

Brendys looked at the sword in his hands. Though he had worn it only briefly, he recognized the weapon, with its black hilt and scabbard and the warmth of its touch, as his own. He turned his gaze upon Asghar, agape. "Where did you find it?"

The Dwarf shook his head. "I did not find it at all. You were carrying it in your hand when you saved me last night."

Brendys sat down on the ground, rubbing his head. "I don't remember anything about last night."

"Indeed? Then I will tell you." Asghar pointed towards a group of rocks. "You came out of nowhere and brought Denasdervien, sheath and all, down upon the head of the Kubruk War-Chief. The rest of the Kubruki were so frightened by the sight of you that they ran off into the mountains."

Brendys was now even more amazed. "Kubruki! But. . . ."

Asghar sighed deeply. "Surely you did not believe, as so many dim-witted fools do, that the Kubruki were slaughtered into extinction by the High Steward Ailon during the Third Age when he freed your very own land from their control?"

"What else should I believe?" Brendys replied. "The Kubruki have not been seen in Milhavior for almost two thousand years!"

"The Kubruki had been greatly reduced in numbers, 'tis true," Asghar replied. "But a race as strong as theirs cannot be annihilated with one blow. They drove my people out of the halls of the Silver Mountains and have remained hidden there until now. I fear their numbers have swollen to their former greatness. These are the days of prophecy!"

The word *prophecy* brought a frown to Brendys's face. It was a word he had heard far too often recently and did not care to hear again. He replaced the sword at his belt, which Asghar had repaired while the youth was unconscious, and turned the conversation to the weapon. "I thought you said that this thing was cursed."

"So I did," Asghar replied lightly. "And so the letters on the pommel and cross-guard say."

Brendys winced at the pain in his head. "Then why did you risk handling it?"

"Because we Kjerek—we Dwarves—are ourselves already cursed," Asghar answered bluntly. "But I was wrong. This weapon bears no evil. Rather, it is the key to my people's salvation. 'Tis Denasdervien you wear at your side, the Living Flame of Elekar."

Brendys groaned. Dazed as he was, he could see where this was leading, and had the situation been less serious, he would have scoffed. "No more. I have had enough of children's stories."

"You do not serve Kolis Bazân—the Dawn King?" Asghar responded, raising a brow in confusion.

"Nay, I don't," Brendys replied flatly.

The Dwarf's puzzled expression deepened. "But you are the Bearer of the Flame . . . how can this be?"

Brendys sighed. "That is just it! I'm *not* the Bearer of the Flame, any more than this sword is Denasdervien!"

"Nay," the Dwarf countered. "You have come from the heart of a mountain, bearing the key of redemption, as my people have been taught throughout the centuries. And as to the sword, there is no doubt . . . this weapon *is* Denasdervien.

"This sword is of Dwarvin make, and we Kjerek have forged no other weapons of Crorkin—black Elvinmetal—since the last Dawn War. It is an evil metal with the power of death. And no sword of ordinary steel, nor of Crorkin, in the hands of a youth, no matter how large, would have smashed that Kubruk's skull as did this one! Only a blade of Gloriod could have accomplished a feat such as that—and still encased in its sheath!"

Brendys averted his gaze from the Dwarf. "There has to be a logical explanation. You are wrong."

"I shall not argue with you, Kjerken," Asghar said, sighing deeply. "For such have I named you, and among my people, Kjerkena do not quarrel, lest evil come of it."

"Kjerkena?" Brendys asked, returning his gaze to the Dwarf. "What is that?"

"To be named a Kjerek's Kjerken is to be given a special place in his family, a place recognized and honored by all Kjerek—all Dwarves," Asghar answered. "And when one accepts that position, he does the Dwarf an even greater honor. Mockery of that gift bears a grim penalty, though this is unknown to most *Jontn*— Men— so it can be pardoned in the ignorant."

Brendys said nothing in return. He was beginning to feel very foolish for arguing with the Dwarf. He had not realized the honor placed upon him by this stranger, and he was shamed by the thought that he might have scorned that honor by acting as rudely as he did towards Asghar.

"Rest, Brendys," the Dwarf said at last, his voice gentle and understanding. "You are hurt and should rest."

Brendys noticed that his head was beginning to ache worse, especially where he had been struck by the broken timber. He laid back, but try as he might, he could not sleep.

"Asghar," he said. "How are we going to escape?"

There was a long pause before he heard the Dwarf reply in a low voice, "It is a quandry which I must think upon. Rest."

Brendys lay still, wondering if he would ever see his home again, if he would even escape the Silver Pass. He cursed himself for leaving Shalkan and for opening the box when both Gwydnan and Kradon had warned against it. In contradiction to his own better judgment, he remained unconvinced of Asghar's tale of Denasdervien, the Living Flame. Neither was he entirely convinced that the weapon was cursed as Asghar had originally said.

Such powers do not exist, Brendys reminded himself. *There must be a logical explanation to it all.* But what that explanation could be, he had no idea.

When next he awoke, night had fallen. He sat up and looked around. Asghar was sitting cross-legged on the ground a few feet to his right, staring into the empty air. The moonlight glittered in the Dwarf's dark eyes. His mood seemed darker yet.

Brendys suddenly realized that they were sitting in the midst of the cairns he had stumbled upon the night before. All around them were the piles of stones and glittering runes. Asghar must have carried him there while he was sleeping, he realized. But why? He looked towards the Dwarf again. "Asghar, what are we doing here?"

The Dwarf raised his head and looked away in the direction they had been that morning.

Brendys looked and saw the dim yellow glow of Kubruk eyes glaring back from among the rocks several yards away. His heart began to race. He turned back to Asghar, but the Dwarf wore an expression of assurance.

"They will not come nearer," he said. "I have set words of protection here so that they will not defile the graves. I am no Wizard, but what craft I have will suffice against the likes of them—at least for now. I am not sure how many more nights their fear shall last."

Asghar turned away again, staring up at the great Dwarvinarches. A confused mixture of fear and desire entered his gaze.

Brendys watched in bewilderment for a little while, then lay back down. It was long before he could fall asleep again, but eventually injury and weariness won out over fear.

In the morning, Asghar awakened him. The Dwarf tended as well as he could to Brendys's wound, then helped the youth to his feet. "I have come to a decision. We must go east."

Brendys looked down the beach. "East? There is no east, Asghar. Or have you forgotten—the mountains block the way."

Asghar looked towards the rough outcropping of which Brendys spoke. "Nay. What you see is but a ledge which runs for several feet. Beyond that is. . . ." The Dwarf paused, that strange look of fear and yearning coming across his features once more. "There is a way out."

At first, Brendys was filled with a sudden rush of hope, but Asghar's expression worried him. "Asghar, is there something you haven't told me?"

The Dwarf did not answer the question, but said, "Come," and started away towards the rocky wall of the mountain.

As they neared the east end of the beach, Brendys saw that the outcropping was exactly what Asghar had told him—a ledge, no higher than seven or eight feet. As well, it appeared to be a manmade construction, worn by the years, rather the remains of a rockslide as he had first thought.

Asghar knelt down at the base of the stony outcropping. "Climb onto my shoulders, and I will lift you onto the ledge."

Brendys did as told, not doubting the strength of the Dwarf's powerful shoulders. As Asghar raised him up, he could see over the edge of the ledge. Indeed, it was as Asghar had told him—it was a ledge. How far it ran, he could not tell. When he was high enough, he pulled himself onto the wide ledge. He paused for a moment, becoming suddenly lightheaded.

"Are you all right, my Brother?" Asghar asked.

"Aye," Brendys replied. "Just a little dizzy."

Asghar climbed up behind him, though what he used for hand holds, Brendys could not see. No sooner had the Dwarf crested the ridge, than he lifted Brendys to his feet. "We must press on. Can you walk?"

Brendys gave a slight nod, and they started eastward along the ledge. Ten minutes later, Brendys could see the end of their path. The ledge dropped off again to another smaller cove. Beyond that was another, higher outcropping at the base of the second Dwarvinarch. He looked down at Asghar. "We have come all this way for nothing?"

Asghar glared darkly at him. "Be silent."

Brendys shut his mouth, feeling quite foolish.

Asghar suddenly flattened himself against the rock wall, hauling Brendys back with him. He raised a finger to his lips and motioned towards the cove ahead of them.

Brendys understood. There was someone—or something—awaiting them below.

Asghar motioned for Brendys to take Denasdervien in hand.

Brendys stared uncertainly at the sheathed weapon, but at Asghar's prompting, he removed it from his belt. He started to hand the sword to Asghar, but the Dwarf swung him around nearer to the clearing. Brendys pointed at himself, a look of astonishment on his face.

Asghar nodded grimly and motioned him onward.

Brendys became dizzy again, but he turned and started towards the lip of the ledge. As he came nearer to the edge, he raised Denasdervien in both hands and proceeded forward in an attack posture. He did not notice Asghar clamber down the side of the ledge facing the river.

Brendys took a running leap off the ledge, landing flat on his face in the sand six feet below. He gasped for breath, taking in a gulp of sand, causing him to choke. Curses ran through his mind, expecting a crushing blow and sudden death as a reward for his stupidity. He rolled over onto his back, and indeed there were two figures waiting there with large rocks in hand.

He heard Asghar's voice bark out, "Captain Folkor!"

Brendys's head started to clear, and he saw that indeed one of the two figures standing over him was the Captain of the *Scarlet Mariner*. The other was Kradon.

Kradon dropped to his knees beside Brendys. "I thought you were dead. Where did you come from?"

Brendys started to breathe easier. "There's a larger cove beyond that ledge. Asghar and I both drifted ashore over there."

"Aye," Folkor said. "I had forgotten it. Perhaps we shall find a way out there."

"Nay," Asghar said, joining them. "There is but one way for us to escape the Silver Pass . . . and you are standing at its very threshold."

"There is nothing here," Folkor said. "I have made a thorough search of the cove. There is no path to find."

"That is because you do not have the eyes to see it," Asghar responded. His voice quieted almost to a murmur. "Long has it been since my folk were driven from the Silver Mountains, but its ways have been passed down from generation to generation."

Brendys saw Kradon and Folkor start in surprise, but why he could not say.

The Dwarf turned and faced the smooth face of the mountain and raised his arms to either side, touching the stone wall. "Behold! *Neza Bokân*, the Gate of the Arches!"

Before their eyes, a shadow moved across the face of the wall in the shape of an arched doorway. At the top of the shadowed area, an image like that of one of the great Dwarvinarches appeared, traced in silver. The silver roots of the arch ran down either side of the shadow. The image of a smith's hammer appeared in the very center. Dwarvin runes of crystal sparkled in the stone, running along the inside edges of the arch.

"This is but one of many minor portals used by my people in the old days to receive goods from river merchants," Asghar said. "Through it we may find our escape."

Brendys's head began to ache worse, and he nearly swooned. Now he understood the reason for his friends' shock.

"*Escape!*" Folkor exclaimed. "Death is more likely. Are you actually suggesting that we enter the Silver Mountains? Perhaps we should just ask the Kubruki for directions along the way!"

Asghar started to snap back a reply, his face nearly as red as his beard, but was interrupted by Kradon's quiet voice.

"Asghar is right, you know. If we stay here much longer, the Kubruki will come to us. This is our only chance, Folkor. The worst that could happen is what we know *will* happen if we remain here."

Brendys found his voice. "What? You can't be serious! You heard Asghar—he has never been in there before. How would we find our way out, once we've gotten in?"

"I told you," Asghar rumbled. "The knowledge of the Silver Mountains has been passed on to its descendants—of which my father is the Crown Heir. I *know* the way."

His voice softened. "It is not far. If we can manage to avoid the Kubruki, it should only take us a few hours to cross to the northern gate."

Kradon looked at each of his companions. "We must decide now—shall we take Captain Asghar's path or remain here and wait for the Kubruki to find us?"

Though he clearly disliked the idea of entering the mightiest stronghold of the Kubruki, Folkor finally admitted he could see no other way, and Brendys did not have the strength left to put up an argument. The prospect of entering the Silver Mountains left him drained, his head throbbing painfully.

It was decided. They would enter the Silver Mountains. If the way was still open, they would seek out the stair which led out onto the eastern Dwarvinarch and across the Great River to the northern tip of the Silver Mountains. There, they would begin their descent to the northern gate, *Neza Edvêjga*, the Gate of the Golden Trove.

Asghar knelt beside Brendys. "First, I must see to my Kjerken. His wound has begun to bleed again."

Brendys raised his fingers to the makeshift bandage around his head and did indeed draw them away blood-stained.

The Dwarf pulled the bandage away, mopping the excess blood away from Brendys's temple. He shook his head. "I know not why the wound does not begin to heal. There should be at least some scabbing by now."

"It is a nasty wound, Captain," Kradon suggested. "Perhaps worse that you thought?"

Asghar shook his head again. "Nay. That Brendys has had his head broken is beyond doubt, but the surface wound should be at least scabbing. Whatever ails Brendys is beyond my feeble skill."

"I am all right," the Shalkane youth asserted, though his head disagreed. "I'm lucid enough, aren't I?"

"At the moment, aye," Asghar replied. "But what is to say a fit will not come upon you again? Nay, we must keep an eye on that wound."

The Dwarf tore another strip of cloth from his tunic and bound it around Brendys's head, then rose to his feet. "It is time to go."

Asghar turned back to the Dwarvingate and raised his muscular arms again. He began to read the Dwarvin runes aloud beginning at the base of the left column, up across the silver arch, and down the right column. The crystal letters began to shimmer with an iridescent light. The shadowed area split in the middle and swung inward, groaning and scraping, into a dark tunnel. The tunnel was wide enough for two Dwarves to walk abreast—three Men—but the ceiling was low, forcing Folkor and Brendys to hunch over as they walked.

"Come," Asghar said. "We are committed now. It will not be long before the Kubruki are alerted to our presence."

He went first through the gate, but waited just inside as the others entered. Then he spoke a sharp word, and the gates grated shut again, leaving the four companions in utter darkness.

"Why did you close the gate?" Folkor hissed. His voice echoed in the shadows. "Now how are we to find our way out of here?"

"Do not fear," Asghar whispered in response. "Join hands, and I will lead you. In the mountains, a Kjerek does not need his eyes. We must travel in darkness for a distance—and in silence as well."

Asghar reached out and grasped Brendys by the hand, then waited for the others to find each other. In another minute, they were on their way, moving slowly down the lightless corridor. To Brendys, the journey through the darkness seemed to take Ages. More than once, he heard a muffled grunt of pain behind him as Folkor cracked his head on the low ceiling. Asghar did not seem concerned about warning the sea-captain of lower tunnel entrances, or perhaps he was too deep in concentration to think of it.

Brendys did not know. He was only concerned with keeping his own footing. He was so disoriented by the darkness and his wound that he was not sure how much longer he could keep from falling. Nevertheless, he staggered on behind Asghar, Kradon just behind him. Kradon's firm grip on his forearm gave him a little reassurance.

I can't give up now, he thought. *Just have to keep going.*

But despite his self-encouragement, the pitch black of the tunnel was maddening. Just as Brendys thought he could go no further, Asghar stopped.

"Something is wrong," the Dwarf said in a hushed voice. "Stay here—I must learn where we are."

Brendys felt Asghar release his hand. His throat tightened, but he resisted the desire to cry out. Instead, he tightened his grip on Kradon's hand.

Kradon flinched and hissed, "Not so hard, Brendys."

Brendys did not reply, but did loosen his grip a little.

Asghar was gone for several minutes, but the darkness and silence made it feel more like several hours. The companions began to stir in agitation.

"Where is the Dwarf?" Folkor muttered. "Left us for dead, I wouldn't doubt."

"Patience, Captain Folkor," Kradon replied, his own whispered words uncertain. "We do not know how far he must go to find the correct path. Mayhaps, he was mistaken about the corridor we should follow."

"Heh," Folkor grunted. "You forget: Dwarves don't lose direction in the mountains. We should move on . . . I would rather risk finding a lighted Kubruk-hole, than remain trapped in this damn cave."

"I don't think we should move, Captain," Kradon replied a little more firmly. "I believe you are wrong. If we leave here, we are just as likely to get ourselves into worse straits, and Asghar may not be able to find us again."

Brendys listened in silence to his companions' discussion, debating in his own mind the possibility that Asghar had abandoned them in the tunnel. It made no sense, when he thought about it. The Dwarf seemed to view his new acquaintance with Brendys as a matter of deepest honor, an honor deeper than the tunnels of the Silver Mountains and stronger than their roots. But that did not exclude the possibility that Asghar had been discovered by the Dwarvinholt's Kubruk occupants.

Brendys felt panic welling up within him. Suddenly, a surge of pain ripped through his head, starting at his wounded temple. His fingers clamped down hard on Kradon's arm, then fell away completely as he collapsed to the stone floor of the tunnel. He could barely hear Kradon yell out before he lost consciousness.

A light flared up in the darkness before him—more like the corpse-light of fireside stories than the light of a true flame. The eerie glow gradually spread until Brendys could see the area around himself. Folkor and Kradon were gone. In fact, the tunnel was gone.

Brendys came to the conclusion that he was outside from the light, chill breeze that occasionally brushed across his face. In the greenish-white corpse-light before him, he could see a large black stone, and upon the stone a child was bound, naked and bleeding. Slowly and cautiously, he moved closer to the stone.

When he was standing over the stone, he looked down at the child. His heart lurched as he looked down upon the boy. He realized quickly that he was staring down at himself as a small child. He glanced up suddenly and saw a black knife plunging down towards the child.

Brendys threw himself between the ebony blade and the little boy that was also him. The knife plunged into his temple, and he screamed in agony. . . .

The last echoes of his voice disappeared into the darkness of the tunnel as he opened his eyes. He was breathing hard and his head still ached, but otherwise he was unharmed. It took him a moment to realize where he was, but Asghar's voice cleared his mind.

"His wound has begun to bleed again," the Dwarf said to the others. Brendys noticed that he was not whispering as he had been earlier. "Blast it! Even as it seems to stop, it begins again. We must quicken our pace. I fear I will need to sear the wound, and that requires fire."

"W-what happened?" he asked weakly.

Kradon's voice responded to him out of the blackness. "You passed out shortly after Asghar went to scout out the way ahead. You have been unconscious for hours."

"Hours?" Brendys raised his hand to rub his head, but quickly drew it away again when he felt the stickiness of his blood. "I-I suppose I. . . ."

He let his voice drift off, unsure of what he was going to say.

"Asghar found the end of the tunnel," Kradon went on. "The entrance had collapsed. He's been digging away at it. . . ."

"I think I am almost through," Asghar said. "Once or twice I thought I saw a speck of light just before the stones settled again. I must keep at it."

Brendys heard the Dwarf stand up and take a few steps away. Then the sound of falling stone came to his ears.

"What was that?" he said, trying to stand. Lacking sufficient strength, he laid still.

"That is Asghar digging," Kradon replied. "After he found the end of the tunnel, he came back and led the rest of us here. He carried *you* the entire distance."

Brendys closed his eyes and tried to rest, while Asghar tried to break through the rubble blocking the tunnel. Images of his dream entered his mind and could not be shaken away. *What can it mean. . . ?*

Nothing, idiot! another thought said. *It was probably just a fever dream.*

Still, the image tugged at him. Somewhere in the back of his mind, he knew he had seen it before—or something similar. He pondered the dream a little while longer, until his thoughts were interrupted by a shout from Asghar.

There was a loud crash, and light poured into the tunnel, blinding Brendys and his companions. The Shalkane struggled to his feet. He stood there, wavering and blinking, until his eyes adjusted to the light. It took a few more minutes before he had regained his equilibrium.

Brendys squinted in the direction of the light. Asghar was standing before a large spot of brilliant silver-white, staring in awe at the glowing blotch. Brendys and his other companions moved closer. The spot of light turned out to be a hole in the rubble blocking the entrance.

"It is no wonder the Kubruki have not found us by now," Asghar said, his voice reflecting the awe in his face. "This corridor is completely overlaid in Elvinsilver . . . the Kubruki would not enter here for fear of the Elvinmetal's power."

The Dwarf glanced back over his shoulder. "Come, Folkor. Help me to widen the breach."

Captain Folkor and the Dwarf worked for a few more minutes clearing more stone away from the hole, until it was wide enough for the companions to pass through it—though it was a tight squeeze for both Folkor and Asghar. When Brendys entered the corridor, he felt a wave of power rush over him. He would have collapsed, but Folkor reached out and caught him, holding him up.

Brendys dazedly examined the hall. The entire corridor looked as though it were made of mirrored silver, reflecting light from an unseen source. After a moment Brendys realized that the light was coming from the metal itself.

"I do not understand how I could have forgotten this," he heard Asghar say. The Dwarf's voice sounded more dismayed, than awed.

"True enough," Folkor replied, still staring in wonder at the Elvinsilver walls. "This is marvelous."

Asghar shook his head. "That is not what I meant. There is only one corridor like this in all of the Silver Mountains—the Delvelord's Threshold. I thought it was further south. I was obviously mistaken. Now the question is, am I mistaken about the rest of the path? I am not sure where to go from here. East . . . but how far? I cannot say."

"You mean we may be trapped here?" Brendys said weakly. He no longer had either the strength, nor the will to go on. If it were not for Folkor's strong arms holding him up, he would have sat down right there.

"Nonsense," Kradon said. "It may take us longer than Captain Asghar thought, but we will find a way out."

After a moment, Asghar nodded. "Aye. Lord Kradon is right. I would be a fool to give up this soon. Let us move eastward—we will decide what to do as need arises."

"Agreed," Folkor echoed. "But which way is east?"

Brendys said nothing. He no longer cared. He would go with his friends, simply because he knew they would not allow him to remain behind.

"Follow my lead, Captain," Asghar replied. "I may have been mistaken about the path, but I am still in my domain. Direction is a sense we Kjerek do not lose."

The Dwarf motioned for Folkor to lower Brendys to the ground. "I must see to my Kjerken's wound once more. He must be strong, for we still have a long journey ahead of us."

Asghar did what little he could for Brendys without the benefits of healing herbs and medicines, then bound the youth's head with another strip of cloth torn from his own tunic. They rested for a few minutes longer, then started off again.

Brendys did not know how long they had been traveling. They had passed several doors and arches, but they all led to enclosed rooms. Asghar explained that these rooms were the living quarters of a famous Dwarvinlord—Asghar's ancestor—who perished during the Kubruk invasion. Finally, they came to the end of the corridor.

At least, it was the end for them. Part of the tunnel had collapsed, barring their way. After a long examination, Asghar told them that the tunnel could not be cleared without the aid of more Dwarves with the proper tools. Kradon, Folkor, and Asghar set about searching for another way through, while Brendys rested against the rubble blocking the corridor.

Brendys touched the hilt of the sword at his side, but swiftly drew his hand back. The warmth of the metal had intensified. He could feel waves of power throbbing from the weapon. In fear, he started to remove the swordbelt, but stopped as his hand touched the buckle. He did not understand why, but somehow he could not bring himself to part with the sword.

Taking a deep breath, he raised himself to his feet. Using the wall of rubble as a brace, he moved towards the northern wall of the corridor. As he neared the other side of the corridor, he tripped. He thrust his hand against the wall to balance himself, but the stone crumbled to dust beneath his touch and his arm slipped into a crack up to his shoulder. Brendys tried to pull his arm free, but the wall shifted, jamming his arm in place.

"*Skud!*" he muttered. He tried to turn his arm, searching for a position which might make it easier for him to get it out of the crack, but it was no use. Then he realized that in all of his twisting, he had bent his elbow. Excitement welled up in him. He moved his arm again and found that he could bend his elbow almost at a ninety-degree angle.

He felt downwards, grasping at nothing but empty air. He tried to jerk his arm free again, but was unable to budge it. Brendys started yelling for the others. Kradon, Folkor, and Asghar all appeared from different corridors.

Kradon folded his arms and curled his lip. "How did you manage *that?*"

"I found it! I found the corridor!" Brendys said excitedly. His expression turned sheepish. "Only I got my arm stuck."

Asghar came closer and peered through the gap the youth had found. He looked back towards the others. "Brendys has indeed found the corridor. The dirt and stone here should not be too difficult to clear away—at least enough to pass through to the other side."

He bowed his head briefly. "I am ashamed. Once more I failed to see what my eyes, out of all here, should have seen."

He inhaled deeply. "What's done is done. From here on, we must proceed with all caution. The corridor beyond has been ruined—the Elvinsilver is not strong enough to protect us from the Kubruki there."

The Dwarf reached a hand into the crevice as far as he could and grabbed hold of Brendys's arm. Bracing one foot against the wall of rubble, he gave the youth's arm a hard yank.

Brendys's arm came free and he was thrown backwards, landing hard on the stone floor. He groaned and sat up, rubbing his sore arm. When he tried to stand, he found the effort even more painful, so he opted to remain where he was.

Asghar motioned to Folkor, and the two of them began to work on widening the crevice. The closer they came to clearing the gap, the more power Brendys felt pulsing through the sword at his belt. It almost seemed to sense the presence of the Kubruki inhabiting the halls of the Silver Mountains.

Brendys slowly reached down and touched the hilt. The black, wire-wrapped hilt was vibrating ever so slightly, trembling—Brendys imagined—in anticipation of the opportunity to drink the blood of the infernal creatures lurking in the shadows. Part of him scolded himself for a wild imagination, but another, smaller part could not deny the presence of the weapon. Such power at his hand—it awed Brendys, but even more, caused him to fear.

Why me, blast it? Why did this thing come to me? I don't want it!

Once more, he was tempted to unbelt the sword and cast it away from him, but again found his own hand unwilling to obey his thoughts.

Finally, the tunnel was opened. Kradon helped Brendys to his feet, and the four companions began their journey once again. As he came through the gap, Brendys was briefly disoriented by the transition from the bright light into a far dimmer corridor, though it was not the pitch black of the tunnel leading from the gate. Glimmering faintly in the darkness, he could see twisted shards of Elvinsilver buried within the rubble and ruin of the collapsed walls. The shards provided enough light to see by, once his eyes became accustomed to the dimness, but the increasing shadows were disconcerting.

The corridor suddenly twisted to the left and plunged down a steep flight of steps. Brendys steadied himself against the rock wall with one hand, then carefully followed Asghar down the crumbling stairs. "Asghar, why are we headed downwards? Shouldn't we be going up?"

Asghar hissed sharply for him to be silent and went on.

Brendys spent more time concentrating on his footing and less on the reason for the descent. As they neared the bottom of the staircase, Brendys could see that the arch at the foot had collapsed as well, creating a wall about four feet high, but still passable. Beyond that, he could see the flicker of torchlight.

Asghar slowed his descent, creeping down along the wall. Brendys followed behind, trying to be as quiet as he could. As they reached the bottom of the stairs, they could hear the approach of two or three Kubruki, preceded by their muttering and snarling voices. Though he could not understand their guttural language, Brendys was sure they were discussing something dreadfully unpleasant. Brendys and Asghar quickly ducked behind the wall of rubble, while Kradon and Folkor flattened themselves up against the wall farther up the stairs, trying to stay as far in the shadows as they could.

As the creatures came around the corner, the red torchlight cast their shadows over the top of the companions' hiding place, projecting them onto the stairs. Brendys's eyes widened in fear. The last time he had been this close to Kubruki, that was how he had seen them—monstrous shadows set against a dismal background of stone. The Shalkane youth instinctively grasped the hilt of his black sword, once more feeling the increasingly intense power running up through his arm.

The Kubruki stopped and grew silent. For a moment, Brendys was sure that they, too, could feel the presence of the sword.

"*Shilnuk!*" he heard one growl. "*Shilnuk kubu mok!*"

There was a snuffling sound, then the second snarled, "*Shilnuk nik Pragu!*"

Brendys looked up the stairway and saw Kradon and Folkor shrink back farther. A green, scaly, clawed hand grasped the top of the rock wall, knocking dust and small bits of stone onto the youth's head. Brendys barely stifled a cry of terror. In his mind's eye, he could imagine the hideous, reptilian visage of the Kubruk staring down at him from over the wall.

The creature grunted out something to its companion, then the two continued down the corridor at a much quicker pace. When the sound of their footsteps vanished into the distance, Asghar stood up and hauled Brendys to his feet. "We must go—now. They could smell us . . . thank Kolis Bazân that they did not see us."

Kradon and Folkor stumbled down the fragile steps, and one-by-one they all climbed over the wall of rubble at the foot. Asghar paused a moment, considering both ends of the tunnel. Much to the dismay of his three companions, he turned and headed in the direction the Kubruki had gone. They did not follow the corridor very far before the Dwarf made a sharp left turn. They followed the new tunnel for several minutes, until Asghar turned once more at a left-hand passage.

This tunnel was long, but straight, narrowing towards another arched entry. Asghar pointed towards the opening. "There it is! That stair will lead us to freedom!"

As they neared the arch, Asghar and Brendys still leading the way, two Kubruki appeared in the opening. One carried a heavy cudgel, the other a large, grotesque, single-bitted axe. Brendys halted suddenly, his heart thudding in his chest. A moment later, he found himself slammed against the wall of the corridor as Folkor charged past him. The sea-captain grappled one of the Kubruki, while Asghar dove towards the other.

Though Folkor's opponent was a few inches taller than him and outweighed him by several pounds, he managed to heft the creature into the air and toss it back into the stairwell. The cudgel dropped from the stunned Kubruk's grasp, clattering down the stairs to land at the man's feet. Without hesitation, Folkor swept up the club and smashed it down upon the Kubruk's skull.

The second Kubruk fell beneath Asghar's strong hands, distracted by the defeat of its comrade. Asghar bent down to pick up the Kubruk's axe, but even as his hand grasped the haft, a loud, roaring cry arose from the other end of the hall.

Brendys jerked his head around to see Kubruki start to flood into the corridor. He felt Asghar's strong hand grip his tunic and drag him around to face the winding stairway.

"Up the stairs!" the Dwarf cried. "It is our only way now!"

Head reeling, Brendys started up the narrow, winding stair as fast as his weary limbs could take him. Behind him, he could hear Kradon urging him on. In a few seconds, he heard an odd *fwooshing* sound, and a red glare began to lick against the walls of the staircase. Asghar and Folkor appeared from around a bend in the stairwell, joining the two youths in their flight up the steps.

"The fire should delay them for a few minutes," Asghar said as they pushed on. "Perhaps long enough for us to put some distance between them and us."

"What did you use to start the fire?" Brendys asked, panting from exhaustion.

"We piled the dead Kubruki in the archway and put them to the torch," Folkor answered. "Captain Asghar added something from a pouch on his belt. I have never seen such flame from dead flesh."

"Stonefire," the Dwarf replied over his shoulder as he led them up the stairs. "We Kjerek use it to keep fires burning steady under difficult conditions.

The harsh cries of the angry Kubruki echoed up the staircase after them, but faded as the companions went higher. The climb was excruciating—both physically and mentally. Brendys wondered how much farther he could go without a rest. Only the Dwarf did not seem to lag in strength.

After an hour of climbing the steep, winding stair, they came within sight of the exit. The stone door had been ripped off its great hinge and the decorative archway was broken, but it was clear enough to pass. Stars shone in the night sky beyond the doorway.

"We shall rest here for a moment," Asghar said, settling himself down on the top step. "But only for a moment. The fire would only have delayed the Kubruki for a brief time."

Brendys collapsed a couple steps below the Dwarf. He was weary beyond comprehension, and his wounded head throbbed painfully. He glanced back down the steep, twisting stairway past Kradon and Folkor and suddenly became dizzy again. His stomach twisted and his throat burned. Closing his eyes, he swallowed back bile.

When he opened his eyes again, he did not look down. "Asghar, why is the stairway so narrow? And why weren't there any other doors on the way up?"

"These stairwells were used only for the maintenance of the arch," the Dwarf replied. "The Dwarvinarches were not meant to be bridges, as we are using them, but gateways. In the early days of Milhavior, my forefathers sought to restrict the river traffic by building massive tollgates across Anatar, but Beelek and Hagan convinced them of the negative consequences of such an act."

If Brendys's head were not aching so badly, he would have nodded his comprehension. As it was, he, like his companions, remained silent. For a short while, all that could be heard was the gasping breath of the four survivors of the *Scarlet Mariner*.

"Why now?" Folkor suddenly muttered, breaking the stillness. "That's what I want to know. After centuries of hiding in this damnable hole, why do the Kubruki choose to trouble us now?"

Asghar glared at the sea-captain. "First of all, Captain, this is not a *hole*. It was once the greatest kingdom of my people."

His expression saddened as he continued. "If it has become a domain of evil, my people are more than a little to blame for it.

"The Kubruki have not arisen before this because they were not yet strong enough. When High Steward Ailon drove the Kubruki away from their siege of Zhâyil-Kan, the ancient fortress that became Brendys's homeland of Shalkan, they fled here to the Silver Mountains. The Kjerek were not able to withstand such a concentrated force of desperate Kubruki and were forced to retreat—but the Kubruki took even greater losses in the battle that ensued.

"The Kubruki sealed themselves inside the northernmost reaches of the Silver Mountains—where we now are—and began once more to swell their numbers. Because they appeared satisfied with the small corner of the Dwarvinholt which they had taken— and perhaps because my people took pity on them and could not bring themselves to destroy an entire race of living creatures, no matter how twisted—the Kjerek left them in peace. May we be triply cursed for our stupidity!"

Asghar glowered in silence for a moment, then spoke again. "The Kubruki increased in number over the years and began to push deeper into the Silver Mountains until they drove my people from our home entirely. Those who were able escaped to other Dwarvinholts. My own forefathers were from these mountains, as were those of Rodi, my cousin one-hundred times removed, who dwells now in the Podan Peaks."

The Dwarf looked down at Captain Folkor. "The Kubruki have grown strong indeed if they now dare to raid the Free Lands."

Before Folkor could respond, the enraged cries of the Kubruki drifted up the stairwell, approaching quickly.

Asghar leapt to his feet, dragging Brendys up with him. "Fly now! We have stayed too long!"

The companions came out of the stairway onto the expanse of the eastern Dwarvinarch. Asghar took the lead, undaunted by the great height of the arch. Kradon and Folkor jogged behind, careful to stay towards the middle, but Brendys went only a few steps before collapsing, his head dangling off the edge of the arch. He glanced down, his stomach tightening within him.

"*Brendys!*"

Brendys looked up to see his friends almost all the way across the Dwarvinarch, calling for him to hurry. He tried to raise himself up, but could not steel himself against the fear which already gripped him. He started to crawl forward on his hands and knees, as quickly as he could, but it was not enough. Soon, he could hear the voices of the Kubruki nearing the ruined doorway.

Asghar started running back towards him, but Brendys waved him off. "I will be all right! Go on!"

The Dwarf paused in uncertainty.

Brendys was almost a third of the way across the Dwarvinarch when the Kubruki began to pour out of the doorway. He stopped crawling and looked over his shoulder. The Kubruki were clearly unaffected by the height of the arch and were quickly closing the gap between them. His heart began to pound. He knew he could not reach the other side of the arch before they were upon him.

He slowly rose to his feet, swaying unsteadily. A warm shock jolted through his arm as his hand landed upon the hilt of Denasdervien. The hilt trembled under his touch, yearning to be freed against its ancient enemies. Suddenly, he knew what he had to do.

Looking back towards his companions, he saw that Asghar had started towards him again. He held out his hand and yelled, "No! Go on!"

Brendys spun around to face the Kubruki, who were now within feet of him. Tightly grasping the sword's hilt, he jerked with all his strength. The weapon resisted, but came free, briefly showing a sliver of the gleaming Silver-gold blade. Almost immediately, there was a bright flash of white fire and a thundering *crack!* Brendys was flung through the air by the force of the explosion, clothed in brilliant, white flame.

He could feel himself plummeting downward. The air around him blazed a dazzling white. The fire did not seem to burn him, or if it did, he was beyond the comprehension of the pain. The only pains he felt were in his right hand and temple, both excruciating beyond description. The white blaze dimmed before his eyes as he slowly lost consciousness, until finally darkness swallowed him up once again.

Chapter 11

Kradon cried out as Brendys tried to draw Denasdervien. A loud thundercrack echoed through the night air, and a ring of white fire blasted outward from near the crossguard of the sword, lifting Brendys off his feet and throwing him over the edge of the Dwarvinarch. Kradon saw Asghar fall flat on his face, just barely ducking under the wave of fire, then felt himself dragged to the stone arch by Folkor's strong arms. Screams of agony filled his ears, then were silenced, replaced by the roar of flames as the Kubruki on the 'Arch were blasted by Denasdervien's fire.

Kradon crawled to the edge of the Dwarvinarch in time to see Brendys as a ball of fire disappear with a flash of light into the river Anatar. His heart lurched suddenly within him as he realized that Brendys was truly gone. This time, he would not magically reappear. Tears sprang up in his eyes and ran in streams down his cheeks.

"Blasted fool! May the Dawn King have mercy on you, Brendys of Shalkan," he whispered.

He felt Folkor's large hand on his shoulder and looked up. Asghar stood a few feet away, staring over the edge of the Dwarvinarch, his hood drawn over his face in a gesture of mourning. Behind the Dwarf, a great fire blazed, fed by the corpses of the Kubruki which had followed them. The door from which they had just escaped could not be seen through the flames.

"Come, My Lord," Folkor said gently. "The Kubruki are sure to be waiting for us in the halls—we must hurry."

Kradon looked back down at the shadow of the river below, then nodded and allowed Folkor to help him to his feet. Asghar intoned something in the Dwarvin Tongue, then strode past Folkor and Kradon, disappearing into the darkness of the entrance at the northern end of the Dwarvinarch. The two Men silently followed him.

Except for a brief skirmish with a handful of Kubruki at the base of the stairs, the journey to the postern gate leading out of the mountains was uneventful. The Kubruki did not consider the small northern tip of the ancient Dwarvinholt worth guarding in full strength—or else the forces normally stationed there were busy elsewhere—for the halls appeared empty at nearly every turn. Asghar warned his human companions that the Kubruki were not apt to let them go so easily, so they continued to travel without rest until dawn.

The three remaining companions rested at the edge of the foothills, near the banks of Anatar. It did not take long for Kradon to succumb to the strangling grip of grief and weariness. Within moments, he had fallen into a deep slumber. His dreams were strangely pleasant, filled with images of peace and light, yet something still troubled him.

He stood in a field, swirling with flowers of all hues and colors. A sweet-scented breeze kissed at his cheek, revitalizing him. The weariness left his limbs, and he began to wonder if everything that had just happened was all a dream. From behind him, the sudden bleating of sheep drew his attention.

He turned and saw a large flock grazing in the pasture land. Amid them stood an elderly man, a shepherd's crook gripped in his hand. A strange light seemed to shine through his features.

In some inexplicable way, he seemed both young and old, fair and full of wisdom. His bearing was regal, though his garb was tattered and worn. The shepherd beckoned to Kradon.

"Do you see my flock?" The man's indescribable voice matched his bearing perfectly. It was not the speech of a common shepherd.

Kradon looked at the hundreds of sheep milling about the field and nodded.

"They are many, but they are mine." The shepherd motioned to the side, and Kradon looked.

A cliff, where none had been before, rose up from the ground. Upon a high ledge, cowered a single lamb. Around the base of the cliff and on either side of the lamb, wolves stood ready to leap upon the poor creature. On another ledge above the lamb, a great black wolf with eyes and fangs of fire perched, glaring in hatred at the small animal.

Kradon cried out in horror. "You must do something!"

"He is not mine."

Kradon turned back to the shepherd. The man's expression had become one of great sorrow.

"He must desire my help," the shepherd continued. "He must become mine."

Abruptly, the sky darkened and a great wind arose. More wolves boiled into the field, great savage creatures with burning eyes. Kradon watched in growing horror as they ran among the flock, ravaging the sheep, until the field turned crimson with blood. The wolves left the torn carcasses of their victims strewn about the field, gathering their numbers together to the right of the shepherd.

To the shepherd's left, a single ram, battered and beaten had gathered what remained of the flock and stood before them, fiercely watching the wolves. The wolves tried to attack, but the ram drove them back. As it did, it saw the lamb upon the cliff and plowed through the midst of the wolf pack.

Kradon looked at the shepherd. "What can one ram do against so many wolves?"

The shepherd gave him a sad smile. "One ram has done so much already."

The shepherd raised his hands into the air in the manner of a priest. "Engen kellim Arzola, dellis el boradis! Remember this, son of Hagan, for it is the only answer."

The ground around Kradon began to quake....

Kradon awoke with a start. Asghar was gently, but firmly shaking him.

"Arise, My Lord. 'Tis midday, and we must yet travel by daylight."

Asghar stared into the youth's eyes for a moment, then cocked a brow. "Are you all right, My Lord?"

Kradon hesitated before replying, the final images of his dream lingering. "I . . . Yes, I'm fine."

Asghar did not press for more. The Dwarf helped Kradon to his feet, then the companions started off once more, skirting the southern edge of the Golden Hills. The Golden Hills were a craggy extension of the foothills along the northern tip of the Silver Mountains. They were a haven for Trolls, but journeying in the hills would at least provide some cover for the travelers until they could put greater distance between the Silver Mountains and themselves.

For two days, the companions traveled during the daylight hours and camped in silence at night within the deepest crannies they could find, taking turns at watch. On the second night, they found a place to rest that could only be accessed through two small gorges, easily-defended against intruders.

Kradon had the first two-hour watch. He spent most of that time, as he had the rest of the journey, contemplating the meaning of the strange dream which had visited him shortly after they escaped the halls of the Silver Mountains. He tried to dismiss the whole thing as a nightmare brought on by the equally strange voyage from the Shipyard of Ilkatar and trek through the Silver Mountain Dwarvinholt, but deep within he knew better. Though it had ended darkly, it did not carry with it the dread that nightmares bring.

Several times, he considered revealing the vision to his friends, but could not bring himself to it. Asghar finally relieved him, and he found a heavily-shadowed corner in which to sleep.

The Dwarf's watch was equally disturbed by evil memories. Brendys of Shalkan, a youth whom he had known for only a day or so, yet one who was a brother in his heart, had given his life to save his three companions. It was the second time Brendys had rescued Asghar. The first time, within the cove in the Silver Pass, had earned the young son of a simple Horsemaster a place as Asghar's Kjerken, an honored rank which no *Jontn*—no Man—had held in centuries.

But the grief which Brendys's death brought to Asghar was also for his own people. The sword which Brendys had borne symbolized the redemption of the Kjerek—the key which would release them from the Curse of Unending Night which Kolis Bazân, the Dawn King, had lain upon the Dwarves. Denasdervien was also lost, dooming his people to live within the mountains until the Final Day.

Asghar endured the light of the sun for his companions' sake, but continually wore his hood drawn far over his face to hide the shameful terror written there. In the darkness, he wept—for Brendys, for his people, and for himself. In two hours, Folkor took his place at the watch.

Folkor did not grieve for Brendys. He had considered the youth a friend, but like Asghar, he barely knew him. He did grieve for the loss of his ship and his crew. Many of the men who sailed under him were friends and comrades of long standing.

Still more, he was puzzled. He had long thought that the success he enjoyed was a blessing granted him by Heil, the patron god of the sea, in whose honor the feast on the night of the attack was dedicated. Such payment for his service was not something he could understand.

While he sat there, contemplating the curse of the gods, he stared up into a dark patch of sky devoid of stars. As he watched, a speck of light in the darkness caught his attention. Suddenly, the speck became a bright red star streaking across the sky within the black patch. Before it vanished again, a second star appeared—this one golden—crossing the tail of the first. The first star vanished and then the second, leaving the sky black once more.

Folkor's heart fluttered. He knew this was more than just a natural phenomenon. This was a sign.

"Awake!" he cried. "We must hurry!"

Kradon and Asghar groaned wearily as they were dragged from their sleep.

"What is it, Captain Folkor?" Kradon asked.

"I have seen an omen from Great Oran," the sea-captain replied. "We must go at once to the temple of the sky-god—it is only another day's journey east of here. If we hurry, we may be able to reach it before sunset today!"

Asghar's gaze darkened as he grumbled. "I will not step foot in a heathen temple."

Folkor's return glare matched the Dwarf's.

Kradon stepped between them. "We have come this far together—let us not start fighting among ourselves."

The youth looked at Folkor. "Do you truly believe what you saw was an omen?"

Folkor nodded. "Aye—I have no doubt."

"The Dawn King sometimes uses signs in the sky," Kradon replied. "If it was such, your priests will not be able to divine its meaning."

"It may be as you say, My Lord," Folkor replied. "The gods are a mystery to me, but I know what I saw and what I believe. I have been given a sign from the sky-god."

Kradon paused, then nodded. "If you will not be turned from journeying to the temple of Oran, we will accompany you."

Asghar started to protest, but Kradon cut him off. "Captain Asghar, you need not enter the temple. You may wait at the gate until Folkor is satisfied that his questions have been answered."

The Dwarf glowered darkly, but grudgingly agreed.

"Then let us be off!" Folkor said. He trudged off in an eastward direction.

Asghar glared at Kradon. "I hope you know what you are doing, My Lord."

Kradon wore a distant expression as he replied, "So do I."

* * * *

The three companions journeyed hard the entire day, passing the final reaches of the Golden Hills and the Silver Mountains.

Shortly before sunset, they arrived at the temple of Oran, the sky-god, just as Folkor expected they would. It was a grand monument to its god—one of the largest temples in Milhavior, third only to those of the earth-god Sedik and his daughter Braya, the goddess of life—and was built wholly of bricks made of a light shale, pale as the sky itself. Five towers of varied height projected upward from the domed building, four at the corners of the main structure and one from the center of the dome. The tower in the center was the highest and mightiest of all, lancing up into the sky. This Great Pinnacle is where the High Priest resided with the idol of the sky-god.

Folkor, Kradon, and Asghar approached the gates protecting the entrance to the temple's courtyard. On either side of the portal stood a large, squat watchtower where the sect of priests who served as the Holy Guard of the temple of Oran and their wives made their quarters. Smaller towers like these were spread all along the protective wall of the temple, each housing the families of two or three of the Temple Guard.

Asghar stood behind his two Human companions, hood drawn, shadowing his grim features.

Kradon glanced back at him, then at Folkor, and nodded.

Folkor jerked on the heavy rope of the summons bell, and a gong resonated through the air. The sea-captain gave Kradon a warning glance, but it was an unnecessary gesture. Kradon knew well the hatred borne by the priests of the gods for the servants of the Dawn King, but he had no fear. The temple of Oran was within the borders of Racolis, so as the son of a Racoline Lord he had made many an unwilling pilgrimage there with his father. Indeed, there was a brief time when he had been an acolyte in the temple.

In a few brief moments, one gate cracked open. A tall man robed in pale blue appeared in the entranceway. He had the hood of his robe pulled over his head, shadowing his features. In his right hand, he held a spear, slightly taller than himself in length, with a star-shaped head, the top point longer than the other four.

Captain Folkor bowed forward, his eyes to the ground. Kradon remained erect, but smiled diplomatically at the guard-priest. Asghar openly glared at the man, curling his lip in disgust.

The guard-priest glowered at the strangers. "What is your business at the Holy Temple of Oran?" His voice was flat and emotionless.

Folkor hesitated uncertainly before replying, keeping his head lowered. "My name is Folkor, a sailor out of Ovieto." He reached a hand towards his companions. "And these are Delvecaptain Asghar of the Crystal Mountain Dwarvinholt and Lord Kradon, son of your Lord Dell of Hagan Keep. We desire to speak with the High Priest."

The guard-priest glanced at Kradon, clearly recognizing him, despite his filthy and disheveled appearance. He was also clearly intrigued by the arrival of the strange threesome, but not enough to disregard the tenets of his sect.

"We serve no Lord, but Oran," he stated flatly. "You must wait until tomorrow. It is too late tonight, and no one sees the High Priest until the noon hour when Oran's star is at zenith."

Folkor straightened and looked down into the face of the gate-warder. The muscles in his face stiffened in annoyance, causing the guard to take a tighter grip on his spear, but the Captain's voice remained low and reverential. "Master, only yestereve I saw a great omen from the sky-god! I knew I must come immediately, for surely Oran's High Priest would desire to learn of it."

The guard-priest thought quietly on the problem, then motioned for the companions to enter. He held out his hand for Folkor's mace. "All weapons must be left at the gate."

Folkor presented the weapon to the guard-priest, but Asghar laid hold of it before the man could touch it.

"I will remain here with the weapons," the Dwarf said gruffly.

Folkor willingly relinquished the Kubruk mace to Asghar, then nodded to the guard-priest.

The man frowned at Asghar, but did not refuse him. He turned and strode towards the temple. Folkor and Kradon followed him.

On either side of the massive temple were several small buildings for storage, stables, and other practical uses. The four lower towers on the main structure of the temple contained the living quarters of the higher priests and the acolytes. The tallest of those, the eastern tower, belonged to the servants of the High Priest, the second in height, the southern tower, to the Temple Priest and his servants, the western tower to the Low Priests, and the northern tower, the lowest, to the young acolytes.

The guard-priest led Kradon and Folkor across the temple courtyard to a great stair ascending into the temple itself. The flight was one hundred steps high, and close to forty feet in width. The entrance into the dome was as wide as the flight of stairs, and the highest point of the arch was just a little over forty feet. At the center of the temple was the Great Pinnacle of Oran, rising up through the roof of the dome.

The guard-priest brought Folkor and Kradon before a man garbed in dark-blue robes—the Temple Priest. The Temple Priest acknowledged them by scribing an S-shaped rune in the air with his hand. The guard bowed before the greater priest, as did Folkor. Kradon again remained erect.

The Temple Priest was just as brisk as the warder had been, and his voice as flat when he addressed his junior priest. "What is the meaning of this, Brother Molden? Why have you admitted these people after Great Oran's star has fallen from the sky?"

Molden lifted a hand towards Folkor and spoke, his voice rising a little in pitch out of fear of the Temple Priest. "Our servant, Folkor, claims to have seen an omen from Great Oran only last night, Brother Venloo, and desired to speak with the High Priest concerning its meaning. I did not know what I should do, so I thought to bring them to you."

Venloo looked upon Folkor and Kradon with great criticism. But as he gazed at Kradon, his frown turned confused, then recognition flooded over him. His features lost their hardness and so, too, did his speech. "Brother Molden, why did you not announce the Lord Kradon? Our greeting might have been more hospitable! My humblest apologies, Lord Kradon."

Kradon inclined his head to the Temple Priest, still smiling politely. "Apology accepted—though after what I have been through these past few days, I doubt anything you say could offend me."

"Thank you, My Lord." Venloo turned to Folkor. "Tell me your omen, Son Folkor, and I will take it to Father Deran so that he may intercede with Oran on your behalf and divine the meaning of the sign."

Molden, the guard-priest, immediately turned to leave, for priests of his low status were not permitted to hear the telling of dreams and omens.

Folkor waited until Molden was beyond hearing, then began describing his omen to the Temple Priest. "We were traveling out of the Silver Mountains when I saw a star flying to its death across the sky. But just before it found its grave, a second star crossed its death-trail. The first star died and then the second."

Kradon noticed an odd glint in Venloo's eye when Folkor spoke of the Silver Mountains, but the Temple Priest made no mention of it.

"Certainly, you have spoken true. This is indeed an omen that you have seen, Son Folkor," Brother Venloo replied. "I will speak of it to Father Deran and return with his divination."

When the Temple Priest had vanished into the Great Pinnacle, Folkor raised his head and stretched the stiffness out of his arms. "I swear these priests and their tenets can be trying."

Kradon ventured a lighthearted chuckle at the remark. "Is this supposed to be something new to me? I served a year in this very temple."

"*You*, My Lord?" Folkor said with a look of astonishment. "But you are a. . . ."

"A servant of the Dawn King?" Kradon finished for him. "Aye, now I am, thanks to Brendys's father. I was only four summers when I served here. The Plague had recently taken my mother, and my father decided to send me here to learn discipline."

"And. . . ?"

Kradon grunted. "I learned that these priests, Venloo and Deran above all, are heretics and liars, who prey off the coinage of the less fortunate to fill their own coffers."

Folkor gave a fearful glance around the dome. "My Lord, those are dangerous words in these halls."

"I have no fear of them, Captain," Kradon replied. "They know my feelings and return them in kind."

Kradon attempted to lower his voice, but the echo in the domed chamber made the effort futile. "I may not fear them, but I do have my suspicions. Did you notice the look Venloo gave us when you mentioned that we had come through the Silver Mountains?"

"I am sure you were imagining things, My Lord," Folkor replied, though his tone was without conviction. "As for myself, my eyes were not upon the priest."

Before Kradon could respond, the door to the Great Pinnacle opened, and a youth in the garb of a Temple Servant appeared. The boy cast a nervous look in the direction of the pilgrims, then hurried across the chamber to the Tower of the Temple Priest. Though Folkor paid him no heed, Kradon watched him carefully.

The youth knocked at the entrance to the tower and waited. In a moment, the door opened, but the shadows within the entrance hid any occupants from view. As the youth spoke into the darkened doorway, Kradon saw the glint of yellow eyes in the shadows.

Kradon grabbed his companion's arm and breathed, "Captain, look!"

Folkor turned his gaze towards the Tower of the Temple Priest. When he did, the yellow eyes shifted to stare directly at them. There was no doubt in either of their minds . . . the eyes belonged to a Kubruk.

The eyes vanished almost immediately, and a man stepped out of the shadows to speak with the Temple Servant. He wore the garb of a priest, but they were not the garments of a servant of Oran. His robes were the black associated with the priests of Zoti, the god of death.

Folkor cursed under his breath, and Kradon quietly said, "I think we are about to receive your divination. Perhaps we should leave?"

Folkor nodded in agreement, and they hurried back to temple entrance and down the steps. When they entered the courtyard, they broke into a run towards the outer gate. They found Asghar and Brother Molden glaring at each other through the open gate, but otherwise silent.

Kradon quickly darted past the guard-priest, but Folkor hung back. The big man came up behind Brother Molden and ripped the spear from the man's hands, throwing him to the ground. He spun the spear over in his hands, bringing the point to the guard-priest's throat. "I would like to know when the servants of Oran started dealing with Kubruki and Zotists?"

"We have no dealings with the Kubruki," Molden nervously replied.

Folkor pressed the spearhead closer. "Indeed? Then why is there a Kubruk in the Tower of the Temple Priest, and what of the Zotist? The gods banished Zoti from their presence and forbade their servants from consorting with the followers of Zoti. What is the Zotist doing here?"

The guard-priest licked his lips, his eyes widening at the pressure of the point against his throat. "The Kubruk was in the company of the Zotist. The Zotist is here at the invitation of Father Deran, but I swear I know nothing more!"

Folkor cast a disgusted grimace at the man, then raised the spear above his head. He swept the weapon down over his thick knee, snapping it in two, then stepped beyond the confines of the courtyard walls. He closed the gates and slipped both shards of the broken weapon through the exterior gate-handles.

"What was that about?" Asghar said in confusion.

Kradon shook his head. "There is not enough time to explain. We must leave, *now!*"

Without any more delay, they continued on their way, their destination not too distant. After leaving the temple of Oran, they traveled south, reaching the Kahadrali town of Ecavan upon the banks of Anatar by sunrise. There, they arranged for a ship to take them the rest of the way to Hagan Keep.

Upon the sixth night after leaving the Silver Pass, a few hours before the first light of dawn, the ship dropped anchor outside the walls of Hagan Keep. The companions rested for a few minutes on the dock before going on.

Folkor looked up at the sky and sighed before breaking the silence. "I can't understand it. I thought I saw an omen . . . I was sure of it. I still feel as though what I saw was a sign of some kind."

"It may have been," Asghar answered him. "As Lord Kradon said before, Kolis Bazân often uses signs to warn his people in times of danger—or so the *Annals* tell."

"A Wizard of Elekar is here at Hagan Keep right now," Kradon added. "Or he was when I left there. If Father hasn't had him thrown out yet for blasphemy against the gods, he might be able to answer your riddle."

Folkor approached Kradon, his face set in grim determination. "My Lord, I must apologize for dragging you to Oran's temple. I was a pompous fool to believe that a god would give a common man like me an omen in the first place, but to learn that the gods have turned on us . . . that is beyond my comprehension.

"There is too much that I do not understand in this world, but I have lost my fear of the unknown. If your Wizard can unravel my omen, I will take my chances against the gods."

Kradon rubbed his shoulders and the back of his neck, yawning. "There is no *unknown*, Captain. What you call the unknown are simply things beyond the full reckoning of mortals. The Elves and the Wizards are perhaps the only ones who can fully comprehend the immortal Realms.

"But you are fortunate, Captain. Though I have been a servant of Elekar for nigh on ten years, I still fear those things. You will speak to the Wizard and you will learn the truth."

"Then I shall keep my troubles to myself until we reach Hagan Keep," Folkor replied. As he stared off at the castle at the center of the city, he raised a brow. He turned his gaze to examine his companions, then burst out laughing. "We look like a band of common ruffians! However are we going to explain this to your father?"

Kradon shrugged without replying. At that moment, he was not worried about explaining anything to anyone. He only wanted to get home, where he could rest peacefully.

But no, he would not have peace. Not yet. The Deathlord had claimed Brendys . . . he would not have peace until the Deathlord had repaid his debt.

When they had recovered their strength, he and his companions entered the city and ascended the road towards the Keep, passing through the gates of the four defensive walls rising up the face of Iler Hill. At the Keep gate, they were halted, for none but those of noble or military rank could enter the castle without the permission of Kradon or his father.

The gatewarders crossed their spears as they approached.

"Hold," the warrior to the left barked out tersely. "State your business here."

At first, Kradon was taken aback by the guard's demand, but then remembered anew his pathetic state. "I am Kradon, son of Dell, your Lord and Master."

The guardsman examined him with a critical eye, but recognition finally came. "My Lord! What happened?"

"There is no time to explain," Kradon replied brusquely. "My companions and I must speak with my father immediately."

The guards moved aside, bowing their heads in homage, and the first one said, "He is with the Council in the Great Hall, discussing the Midsummer celebration."

Kradon led his companions into the Keep. Once inside, they proceeded unhindered to the Great Hall of Hagan, though they did receive a number of strange looks in passing. Folkor and Asghar shoved past the doormen, who had taken position to bar their entry, and pushed open the great oak doors, ignoring the guards' protests.

The Dwarf and sea-captain fell in behind Kradon, in the manner of honor-guard, as the young heir of Hagan entered the Great Hall. Despite his tattered garments and beggarly appearance, Kradon carried himself with the full nobility of his rank.

As the gate guardsman had told them, Lord Dell and a few of the other nobles of Hagan Keep were gathered in council, making final preparations for the coming Midsummer celebration, which was scheduled to begin in two days' time. Among the noblemen was seated an old man in white robes, whom Kradon recognized as the Wizard, Odyniec.

The Council was startled from their discussion by the three intruders. Lord Dell, a handsome man of medium build with the same features as his son, rose to his feet in anger. "What is the meaning of this?"

Recognizing his son, anger drained from his face, replaced by shock. "Kradon! What has happened to you? Where is Brendys? And who are these people?" He gestured towards Folkor and Asghar with his last question. "You are late, my son. At first, I thought it a deliberate delay in leaving Shalkan, but I was obviously wrong by the look of you. What happened?"

"I am sorry, Father," Kradon answered. "My companions are Folkor, Captain of the *Scarlet Mariner*, and Delvecaptain Asghar of the Crystal Mountains."

His voice broke some as he continued. "The *Mariner* was attacked and destroyed, Father. As far as we know, everyone else perished."

Dell started towards his son, confusion and amazement evident on his features. "Attacked and destroyed? But how? By whom?"

Captain Folkor now spoke. "Kubruki, My Lord. They rolled great boulders from one of the Dwarvinarches in the Silver Pass; a crude and primitive weapon, but effective nonetheless."

"Kubruki, you say?" Dell responded in disbelief. "But none have been seen for an entire Age! High Steward Ailon destroyed them when he slew the sorcerer Michuda almost two thousand years ago!"

The Wizard arose from his seat at the council table and came to stand beside the Lord of Hagan. His face belied no emotion. "My Lord, the good Captain speaks true. The Kubruki have arisen again, for their master prepares to return to En Orilal."

A sense of fear rippled throughout the Great Hall, accompanied by quiet murmurs. Whether servant of the gods or servant of Elekar, everyone present knew that the Wizard spoke of the Deathlord.

"Master Odyniec," Dell said, his own features paling. "How can this be? There have been no omens! If you knew this already, Wizard, why did you not reveal it to us before?"

"There is a time for everything, My Lord, and the time was not right for me to speak," the Wizard replied calmly. "I am aware of many things of which I may not speak. But fear not. As I have told you, there is a time for everything, and this is not the Deathlord's time. The Lord Elekar will not allow for his return until the time appointed. For this task has Denasdervien been unveiled."

Lord Dell stared at him in wonder. "Denasdervien?"

"Aye, Denasdervien," Asghar's gruff voice answered. "That which was borne by my Kjerken, Brendys of Shalkan. . . ."

All turned and looked upon the hooded Dwarf.

"Borne with him into the depths of the Great River," the Dwarf rumbled in closure.

Dell gaped in disbelief. "Brendys is dead?"

"Aye, Father," Kradon replied, tears escaping from his eyes. "He sacrificed himself to save us in the Silver Pass."

Another man left his chair. His sharply-featured face bore a sense of urgency. "My Lord, if you wish, I shall send a rider to Shalkan to inform Master Brendyk of his son's fate."

Lord Dell shook his head, a shadow of grief crossing his own features. "Nay, Wargon. Brendyk has been my friend for too long. I will go myself. This will hurt him greatly, but perhaps not so much if it is I who tells him."

Odyniec's long, white beard wagged as he shook his head, suddenly declaring, "Nay, there is no time!"

"What do you mean, Wizard?" Dell returned, his brow beetling. "More riddles?"

"Trust my words—there are greater matters at hand," Odyniec responded.

"A man's son has died," Asghar growled deeply. "Among my folk there are fewer matters greater than that!"

The Wizard appeared unconcerned. His gaze shifted to the chamber's entrance.

A loud crash resounded through the chamber as the door flew open again and yet another man entered the room followed by the guardsmen. His dark hair was matted with perspiration, and he was straining for breath as he bowed, falling to his knees in the process. He was almost without voice when he spoke. His once-bright argent and green surcoat was dull and stained with mud and sweat. "My Lord, I am Turan, former Guardsman and

Herald of Treiber, King of Gildea, now Herald of all Milhavior. I have come in search of the Wizard, Odyniec!"

Dell stepped forward himself to help the man to a chair. "Gildea is a month's ride from here, man! Your errand must indeed be important."

"Aye, My Lord," Turan replied, choking. "Gildea has fallen, and so also shall Matadol and the remainder of our lands if my errand is not completed soon."

"I am Odyniec," the Wizard announced, moving towards the man. "What do you require of me?"

"A great legion of Kubruki under the command of a Sorcerer has taken Gildea," the herald started. "I was sent to Matadol for aid, but when I came there, I found that they, too, had been long in battle with the Kubruki and could not spare any warriors for our struggle.

"I made my way north, but the news was the same at every Keep along the way. The Kubruki of the Silver Mountains have come out of their holes to invade the Free Lands. At Bascio Keep in Delcan, I was told that there was a Wizard of the Dawn King here who might be able to help us. I journeyed hard from there, stopping only to change steeds—my last one perished at the doors of this very Keep. Master Odyniec, can you help us?"

Odyniec turned to Lord Dell, first casting a piercing eye at Asghar. "As I told you, there are greater matters at hand. We must prepare to ride at the first light of dawn—every man and able lad must ride with us."

"But that will leave Hagan Keep without defenses!" Count Wargon objected.

"It must be done!" Odyniec snapped back. "Iysh Mawvath is the Warlord of Thanatos and the most powerful of his Sorcerers—I shall have need of what strength I have. Someone must be present to contend the Kubruki!"

Count Wargon started to protest again, but Dell silenced him with a wave of his hand. "He is right, Wargon. Hagan Keep is hardly in any immediate danger of being invaded.

"Spread the word of our ride. Then, if you so desire, send a messenger to Racolis Keep to inform King Kosarek; he will send a guard. Send a herald to Lind Keep in Kahadral as well. It is on our path to Gildea. We shall acquire fresh horses there, and perhaps more warriors."

"That I doubt, My Lord," Turan coughed as Count Wargon rushed from the chamber. "I think you will find it difficult to recruit warriors from other Keeps. As I have said, the Kubruki of the Silver Mountains have been stirring up trouble in the Southlands."

"Then we must settle with the few men who serve in my guard," Dell replied. "I will send word to Ascon and to the eastern lands. Perhaps we will receive aid from them."

Odyniec shook his head. "They would come too late. But there are others."

Kradon's father waited for the Wizard to finish, but when no further answer was forthcoming, he turned away. He spoke now to Folkor and Asghar, as well as the Gildean herald. "My friends, chambers shall be provided for you all. There, you may refresh yourselves and get some rest. On the morrow, if you wish to ride with us, my chamberlain will lead you to the North Armory where you may choose arms for yourselves."

Without another word, he dismissed everyone.

Kradon remained behind to speak with his father.

Lord Dell drew his son to the council table, where they sat down. Dell leaned forward putting a hand on Kradon's shoulder. "I am sorry, my son. I know how close you and Brendys were. But now Zoti has claimed him, and there is nothing more we can do."

Kradon uttered a disgusted grunt. "*Zoti.*"

His father settled back, withdrawing his hand from Kradon's shoulder. "You make it hard for me, Kradon. You are everything I have left, and I want no enmity between us, but when two people do not serve the same master, it makes things very difficult."

"Then perhaps you should learn what your master is like, Father," Kradon said, crossing his arms.

"What do you mean?"

Kradon stood up and started pacing the floor. "After we escaped the Silver Mountains, we made a little visit to the temple of Oran. Folkor thought he saw an omen. . . ."

Dell also came to his feet, shocked anew at his son's words. "Kradon! You could have been killed!"

"Aye, so I could have," Kradon replied, his voice taking on an uncharacteristically cynical tone. "And such is the master you serve."

He turned away from his father, ashamed at his tone, then continued with his tale. "At first, I did not wish to go there, but now I am glad that we did. . . ."

And so he told his father of the betrayal of Oran.

* * * *

In the morning, every man and able lad were gathered, just as Odyniec had ordered. They were all armed and mounted and ready for the long journey and the inevitable battle which lay ahead of them. Folkor and Asghar were there as well, each mounted and armed—they both chose to retain their Kubruk trophies, rather than obtain new armament.

Dell rode to the head of the great column, turning his dun steed about to face them.

"My people," he said, raising his voice so that all could hear. "En Orilal is in grave danger. Our friends and allies in Gildea have been conquered by a Sorcerer of Zoti."

Murmurs ran throughout the host.

"I shall force none to ride if it is not their wish to do so, for it shall be a long, difficult, and treacherous journey. We shall have to make a hard-ride, resting only when our steeds—and ourselves—have come to the utter ends of our capacities.

"I do not know what will come of this, but I do know that we have friends in need—indeed, Queen Sherren of Gildea is my kinswoman—and it is my duty to bring them aid. Captain Folkor of Ovieto and Delvecaptain Asghar, Dwarf of the Crystal Mountains, shall ride with us. Odyniec, a Wizard and prophet of the Dawn King Elekar, will share in this venture as well. Who else shall ride?"

The entire host replied with a single voice, and the clap of their fists striking their hearts thundered throughout the walls of the city. The people of Hagan Keep loved their Lord and would face the Winds of Hál if he asked them.

Dell nodded his approval. He gave the signal and the column rode out through the gates of Hagan Keep.

Chapter 12

Balls of fire burst in Brendys's mind. Something moist touched his head, and he awakened once more . . . this time, to the comfort of a warm bed beneath his body and a soft pillow under his head, rather than the sticky grittiness of the beach sand. His eyes still perceived nothing but shadows and his head still felt as though it had been used for an anvil, but he gained some comfort with the knowledge that he was now in a civilized place.

He jerked again at the touch of something wet to his brow, the motion sending a burning pain through his body. Someone was leaning over him, mopping the cut on the side of his head with a damp cloth, but because of his blurred vision, he could not make out the person's face.

The stranger jumped back with a start at his movement.

When his sight finally came into focus, Brendys found himself staring at a young maiden no older than himself, if that. He could not tell the color of her hair or eyes—or anything else around him for that matter, even in the light of the candle on the table beside him. He felt like he was looking through murky water at a shining diamond, but he attributed that to his unsteady vision.

Brendys knew that this was not a girl accustomed to hard labor, for her fingers were soft and delicate—not the rough hands of an average peasant girl. Beneath the dirt and filth, her visage was also that of a noble, or at least someone of a wealthier class. This girl did not belong in these surroundings. She should have been wearing an elegant gown, and the background should have been a palace.

Brendys decided that it was only a dream, but a beautiful and welcome one.

"*Oh!* You're awake!" the girl said, surprised, but quietly. Her voice fell like music on the Shalkane's ears. He was filled with a strange feeling, not at all unpleasant.

Brendys could do nothing but shake his head slowly—a painful enough action—his eyes fixed upon hers, and mumble in reply, "Nay, I'm dreaming!"

The girl blushed. "Don't do that."

Brendys gave her a dazed look. "Huh?"

"Quit sta—shaking your head," she replied with a stammer. "You should not be moving—you shouldn't even be talking. The burns are healing, but that gash in your head is not. If it were not for Etzel's medicines, you might not have lived."

Brendys suddenly realized that he was swathed head to toe in bandages, with only his face and the side of his head the girl had been tending exposed. A slightly pungent scent surrounded him—*The medicines*, he thought. Everything started to come back to him—the wreck of the *Scarlet Mariner*, the journey through the Silver Mountains, plummeting from the Dwarvinarch in flames.

Brendys fell silent, satisfied for the moment to lie still. He kept his gaze steady upon the girl. He could not help himself. Adina was pretty, but this girl—he had no words fitting to describe her beauty.

The girl waited several minutes before she broke the silence again. "My name is Mattina. May I ask yours?"

"Huh? Oh, I'm sorry," Brendys replied, still dazed by the pain which wracked his body. "My name is Brendys."

"Brendys?" she repeated. "I do not know that name. It is certainly not Gildean."

"I should hope not," Brendys replied with a slight chuckle, which sent him into a painful, coughing fit. When he regained his breath, he spoke again. "Why would you think I am Gildean this far north?"

Mattina gave him a startled look. "North? But. . . ."

She stopped abruptly and called towards the door. "*Quellin!*"

After a few tense seconds, the door opened and another youth stepped into the room. At first, Brendys thought the boy was Mattina's twin.

"Did you call, Sister?" he started. His gaze met Brendys's. "Oh! You're awake!"

Brendys nodded carefully. "Somehow, I feel that I have been through this before! You must be Quellin."

The second youth nodded. "Aye. And you are. . . ?"

"Brendys—Brendys of Shalkan."

"*Shalkan?*" Quellin was clearly as surprised as his sister.

"Aye," Brendys replied, more confused than ever at their reactions.

Quellin glanced at his sister, who only shrugged and shook her head in response. He turned his eyes back to Brendys. "Well, Brendys of Shalkan, you have wandered quite some ways from home. Would you mind telling me just what happened to you and how you managed to find your way here?"

"I don't know," Brendys coughed in reply. "I don't even know where *here* is!"

"Then I will tell you," Quellin responded slowly. "You are an unfortunate guest in the city of Gildea Keep. I happen to be its Ki—well, that can wait until later. You are tired, I am sure."

Brendys stared at Quellin in disbelief. "*Gildea!* How the blazes did I get here! The last thing I remember was falling from the Dwarvinarch in the Silver Pass."

Mattina and her brother looked at each other in astonishment, then Quellin turned back to Brendys. "When was this?"

"I-I don't know," Brendys replied, his head swimming.

"What month?" Quellin pressed. "Surely, you know that much."

The Shalkane youth knit his brow. "Golven—what else?"

"And Golven it still is," Quellin said, grimacing thoughtfully. "One of our village lads pulled you out of Den Jostalen not more than a half an hour ago."

Quellin paused before going on in a whisper to his sister. "We asked for a deliverer, and the Dawn King has given us one—though a rather young one, I must admit."

Brendys groaned. "*Dawn King!* Must I listen to that skud here, too! I will tell you now: I do not believe any of that nonsense about Dawn Kings, Thanatoses, or Sorcerers, or Wizards, and the gods be hanged!"

Quellin wrinkled his brow. "Indeed? Then tell me, how do you explain surviving a fall which you surely should not have, then suddenly awakening in the capital city of one of the southernmost nations in all of Milhavior—more than a month's journey south by horse from where you claim to have been—in less than a month, if not a day?"

A barrage of pain was renewed within Brendys's body and mind. This was too much for him to comprehend in his present condition. "I don't know, but there has to be a logical explanation!"

"*Logical explanation?*" Quellin shot back in astonishment. "I have never heard a more logical explanation than the one that I have given you. Elekar has his hand on you. I know this. The sword you were wearing. . . ."

Brendys lifted a hand to his aching head. "I know! I know! It is Denasdervien. Asghar, my Dwarf friend, told me. But I don't believe it!"

Quellin looked stunned. "Denasdervien? This is grand news indeed!"

Brendys gave him a blank stare. "What? But wasn't that what you were going to say?"

Quellin walked over to a table and picked up the sword. "Nay. I was only going to mention this blazon on the scabbard. . . ."

Brendys snatched the sword away from Quellin, wincing at the pain as he did so, and examined the sheath. There was a coat-of- arms emblazoned on one side of the scabbard, near the top. It was a golden hawk perched on a black-hilted sword, with a gold crown above it and a gold star in the base, all upon a field of white. "How did this get there? I swear it wasn't there before!"

"Don't you recognize it?" Quellin asked.

Brendys started to shake his head in response, but stopped. "It looks a bit like the emblem on my father's ring, but not exactly—no, not at all really. The bird just reminds me a little of it."

"It is the emblem of the Royal House of Ascon, Brendys," Quellin said. "Perhaps I should start calling you Sire."

"Nay!" Brendys cried. "I am only a Horsemaster's son, and nothing more. I don't want to be a King!"

"I did not say that you were—that I rather doubt. I was but jesting, nothing more." Quellin went on in a more serious tone of voice. "But I do know that you were sent here for a purpose."

"Why?" Brendys asked. "What possible reason could there be?"

"Not now," Quellin replied. "Your wounds need tending, and you need rest. I have some chores to attend to right at this moment, but I will look in on you again tomorrow.

"Mattina will see to your care. When she decides that you are well enough for a speech, I will try to explain our situation to you."

Without another word, he left.

Mattina remained behind with Brendys. She sat down beside him and resumed washing the cut. "Sleep now, Master Brendys."

Things were going much too fast for Brendys. He found himself wanting very much to wake up from his dream.

Without his own knowledge, he took Mattina's hand in his own and fell into a dark slumber.

* * * *

Brendys lay still as Mattina dabbed a sweet-smelling unguent concocted by Etzel, the old woman in whose home Brendys was now an unwilling guest, upon his temple. His eyes were fixed on the girl's radiant face, his own face drenched with perspiration.

The burns upon his body had healed well, but his head wound had infected shortly after he had been found in the river Jostalen, throwing him into a feverish delirium.

Mattina sat on the edge of the bed and looked down at her left hand, gripped firmly in her patient's. She wiped her right hand on a rag, then placed it on top of the Shalkane youth's. Ever since the fever had come upon him, Brendys would clutch her hand in his and stare at her, never saying a word. At first, his stare and his touch made Mattina uncomfortable, but as the days passed, she became accustomed to them—and soon, in a way, pleased with it.

Mattina wondered often what Brendys was thinking when he stared at her, but as time passed it became easier to read the expressions upon his face. Early on, it was both grim and frightened, the despairing look of one contemplating death; then, after a while, it became thoughtful, meditative, as though her face brought some long forgotten memory to the surface of his mind; now, it was peaceful, yet his gaze upon her had become more intense.

She knew his thoughts. His face spoke to her with silent words, and she understood. It was a bond that could only begin in the heart.

At last, Brendys closed his eyes and fell asleep.

Mattina reached out and tenderly stroked his cheek, then picked up her rag and continued to mop the sweat from his face. A quiet knock at the door startled her. She looked up as her brother slipped into the room.

"How is our young patient?" Quellin asked.

"Better," Mattina replied. "His fever, I think, is abating, but I am not sure."

"A good sign, nonetheless," her brother said with a nod. His gaze shifted to Brendys. "Poor lad. I do not understand why he was sent to us. Etzel tells me he is the Bearer of the Flame, but what use is the Bearer if he cannot use the Flame?"

Quellin shook his head in pity. "Nevertheless, he deserves to know what he has been thrown into. When you believe him well enough, I think I will let you explain his situation to him."

"If you think I should," Mattina replied, a little surprised by her brother's instruction.

Quellin glanced down at Brendys and Mattina's joined hands and smiled a little. "I do."

He cracked the door open and started to back out of the room. "Inform me immediately if his fever breaks. Good night, Sister."

"Good night, Quellin."

* * * *

A few more days passed, and Brendys became more coherent. He would sometimes speak to Mattina, but only for brief periods before he would fall silent again. Deeming Brendys well enough to comprehend her words, Mattina chose that time to tell Brendys of Iysh Mawvath and the Fall of Gildea.

Thus did Brendys learn of her brother's true status as the deposed King of Gildea. Brendys was perplexed by her tale—he found it more than just a little hard to believe—but he relied upon her word. That a lie could pass her lips was unimaginable to him.

In a little over a week and a half, the infection had passed and the fever broke.

* * * *

Brendys sat up in bed as Mattina brought in a tray of food.

"Why won't you let me get up?" he said as he took the tray from Mattina. "I feel fine."

Mattina frowned at him.

Brendys shrugged. "Well, almost. I'm a little tired, that's all."

"You are *not* to get up until I say," the young Princess returned. "Quellin has put you in my charge, and you will do as I say."

Brendys gave her a dour grimace. "Aye, Your Highness, I hear and obey."

The door opened, and Quellin entered the room. He stopped behind Mattina, putting his hands on her shoulders.

"I see you are doing well," he said to Brendys. "My dear sister is quite the healer, is she not?"

Brendys held Mattina's gaze in his own. "Aye, that she is."

"Ah . . . yes," Quellin said slowly, raising a brow. He gently moved his sister to the door. "If you would excuse us for a moment, I need to speak with Mattina alone."

Brendys nodded and watched as Quellin and his sister disappeared through the doorway. He ate the porridge which had been brought to him, while he waited for Mattina to return. The mush was extremely gritty and not at all pleasant to the tongue, but he was too hungry to care. He had eaten very little while he was ill.

He was just finishing when Mattina returned. Brendys swallowed his last spoonful and wiped his mouth, then spoke. "Quellin certainly kept you a while. What did he want?"

"Oh, nothing much," Mattina replied casually. "He was needed elsewhere in the city, and he wanted to give me a few instructions before he left."

"Oh." Brendys settled back a little and yawned. "It is positively dull sitting here. Why won't you let me up?"

Before Mattina could reply, the door swung open again, and a youngster, no older than six summers, stalked into the room. The boy trudged over to stand beside Mattina, his round face bearing a deep frown as he looked up at Brendys.

"That is my bed, you know!" he sniffed. "'Tis Shanor's, too. We have to sleep in the front room on the couches."

"Well, if I had my way, you could have your bed back right this minute," Brendys replied. Then he glanced at Mattina. "But I am afraid your Princess would hurt me if I got up!"

"Well, you can stay there," the boy returned graciously. "For a little longer anyway."

He turned his face up to Mattina and thrust his jaw out. "But not for *much* longer!"

Mattina rested her hands on the child's shoulders and gave him a half-chiding look. "Shush now! Where are your manners? And what are you doing in here anyway? You know Quellin does not want you in here."

The boy pursed his lips in a pout. "I just wanted to see him, that's all."

Mattina smiled and introduced the boy. "Brendys, this is Berephon, son of the bard Runyan. We call him Bipin"

"Hello, Bipin." Brendys extended his hand to the lad in greeting, but the boy just stood there glowering at him.

Brendys shot his hand out and began tickling the unsuspecting youngster. With a squeal, Bipin fell to the floor, giggling, and stayed there until Mattina picked him up and shooed him out of the room.

Brendys grinned as he watched the lad leave. "It works every time!"

Mattina sat down beside him, casting a puzzled eye on him. "Every time?"

Brendys nodded with a yawn. "Aye. You see my father has this dreadful habit of taking in strays. . . ."

He stopped in mid-speech. His gaze grew distant, a knot forming suddenly deep within his heart.

Mattina touched his arm. "Brendys, is something wrong?"

Brendys looked up at her, his eyes misting. "I . . . I can't go home, can I?"

Mattina sat on the edge of the bed and took up his hand, rubbing it sympathetically. She gave him a sad smile and shook her head.

The Shalkane youth blinked back his tears as he looked up into the girl's eyes. Though he could not distinguish their color in the grey Dusklight which illuminated the Shadow, their depth swallowed his gaze. He could see nothing else but the glitter of her eyes. He could almost feel them drawing him deeper into their mysterious embrace.

The door opened again, abruptly breaking the spell. Brendys fell back in surprise against the pillow propped up behind him, while Mattina straightened up, blushing fiercely.

Another boy entered the room. He was perhaps eleven or twelve years of age and had curly hair. Grinning broadly, he gave his Princess a quick wink to which she responded with an indignant huff, turning away to face the wall.

"Oh, 'scuse me, sir," the boy said to Brendys, giving him a slight bow. "I jes' fergot me crook in 'ere. I'll b'out o' yer way in no time, sir!"

Brendys regained his composure and his voice. "You must be Shanor."

"Nay, sir," the boy quickly replied. "I'd be honored if I 'uz, but I ain't. M'name is Kovar, sir!"

"Oh," was the only response Brendys could manage.

Kovar inclined his head towards Brendys again, then stepped across the room. He shuffled through some things in a closet, then hurried back out of the room carrying a shepherd's crook. Mattina's glare followed him until the door closed.

Before either Brendys or Mattina were able to say another word to each other, yet another pair of boys burst through the door and dashed across the room to the table, giving Brendys a quick glance as they passed by. Both of the boys were around Kovar's age, but had straight, dark hair, almost black in the Dusklight. They snatched up whatever oddments they had apparently come for, then headed back towards the door.

Mattina stood up and took a step towards the door, pushing it shut just as the boys reached it. Unable to stop their momentum, the boys ran headlong into the door, falling back hard on their haunches.

Mattina stood over them, hands on her hips. "What is going on here? This is not a parade ground! Brendys is supposed to be resting."

The lads stood up, rubbing their hind ends.

"Sorry, Your Highness," one lad replied.

"Aye, sorry," the other followed.

Mattina turned to Brendys and said, "These two scalawags are Shanor and Brumagin."

The first boy bowed to Brendys with practiced grace. "Shanor, son of Radnor, Lord of the House of Horack-Gildea, at your service."

Brendys leaned back and laughed. "Why don't you just send them all in?"

Mattina gave him a nervous look. "Are you sure?"

Brendys's laughter faded, realizing she was serious. He smiled weakly. "Aye. I fear I am in this mess until the end. I might as well meet those I am to live it out with."

Mattina stared at him for a moment, frowning uncertainly, then turned back to Shanor and Brumagin. "Tell the others that Brendys has asked to meet them all."

After the boys had gone, she turned her gaze back to Brendys. "Quellin will not be pleased."

"Then I will take full responsibility," Brendys assured her.

Mattina hesitated, then sighed. "Very well. But if you become too weary, I will send them away."

Brendys agreed.

The four boys he had already met stepped back into the room, with a youth a little older than themselves, two elderly women, and a younger woman.

Mattina motioned a hand towards the latter. "Brendys, this is the Lady Arella, Shanor's aunt and Quellin's betrothed."

"You may call me Arella. At the moment, I hardly feel like a Lady," the pale-haired woman said with a laugh, brushing her hands across her peasant garments and besmirched cheeks.

"Aye, My Lady," one of the elderly women agreed. She was by far the oldest of those present. She seemed small and frail, and her features were riddled with tiny wrinkles. Her eyes, however, drew Brendys's attention, for they appeared young and vibrant, though at the same time filled with an ancient wisdom, not unlike the man he had seen in his dreams aboard the *Scarlet Mariner*.

"But that is why you still live," the old woman continued. "That is why you all still live. The Gildean nobility shall be reduced to rags until the Throne can be reclaimed."

She turned her gaze on Mattina. The girl shifted nervously under the old woman's eye.

"This is Etzel," she quietly told Brendys. "This is her house."

Her voice sounded awed, and Brendys understood why when Etzel turned her eyes on him. He suddenly felt a strange, throbbing warmth beating upon him, penetrating deep into his very being. Instantly, he felt as though she could see straight into his heart, that even his deepest secrets were open to her. He felt an odd sense of guilt fall upon him. It was clear that Etzel was more than just an old peasant woman, but he did not dare to even guess her nature.

Brendys started to shiver. An iciness spread through his body and penetrated his limbs. The cold did not result from Etzel's stare, but came rather from within. The old woman's gaze became curious for a moment, then she turned her eyes away from Brendys. Gradually, he could feel the coldness being drawn inward until it had vanished entirely.

A youthful voice startled Brendys out of his thoughts.

"'ey there, when're ye gonna' get 'round t' me?" the oldest boy spouted. He was about thirteen or fourteen years of age, with shaggy, dark hair which sagged into his eyes. Not bothering to wait for a reply, he introduced himself to Brendys. "I'm Gowan. I 'uz th' 'un what fished ye outta' th' river. When I tried draggin' in me net, I thoughts I 'ad meself th' biggest fish in all o' Den Jos'len. But then I dragged ye in. . . ."

Gowan started rambling on about fish, and Brendys just stared blankly at him. The other four boys tackled him, slapping their hands over his mouth.

Mattina pursed her lips. "Gowan is rather proud of his skill with the net."

Brendys gave her a vague acknowledgment. He had noticed the last unnamed occupant of the room, watching him intently. He knew that she was a woman of highest breeding—there was an air of nobility about her that even her common garb could not hide. Though she had clearly seen many years in her life, she retained a dignified beauty of a sort. There was a hint of puzzlement in her gaze that caught Brendys's attention.

Finally, the woman spoke, her voice as dignified as her bearing. "Your face is familiar, boy. Have we met before?"

Brendys shook his head. "Not that I can remember, ma'am."

"Strange. . . ." The woman thought for a moment, then smiled. "Ah, yes, I remember now! You remind me of a young man that I once met in my homeland of Racolis, but that was many years ago—before I married Treiber and became Queen of Gildea. His name was . . . Evinrad, I believe. A young horse-trader."

"Evinrad!" Brendys exclaimed. "That was my grandfather's name! Father said he did a lot of trading in Racolis when King Korek was on the throne."

Queen Sherren nodded slowly. "Yes, I thought as much. You have your grandfather's bearing."

"Truth be told," she added with a twinkle in her eye. "If he had not been married already and my class did not forbid it, I may have claimed him for my own."

She cast a meaningful glance in Mattina's direction, eliciting a look of shock from the girl.

Quellin's voice came from the open doorway. "Mattina does not need the encouragement."

The Gildean King entered the room. His angry glare moved from Sherren to his sister. "I told you not to let anyone in. Brendys is not well yet."

"But, Quellin, he told me to send them in," Mattina returned.

Brendys shot a sheepish glance towards Quellin and nodded. "I'm afraid I did. I was dreadfully bored."

Quellin's expression softened as he turned to the others gathered there. "Very well. But the parade is over now. Let the lad get some rest."

Chapter 13

Three days after leaving Hagan Keep, Lord Dell's host had arrived at Lind Keep in Kahadral. There they had exchanged mounts, but as Turan had warned, the Lindens were unwilling to spare any warriors for their venture. They had already sent a large portion of their garrison to Wills Keep at the edge of the Silver Mountains. While new steeds and supplies were being readied for the Haganes, Dell sent a herald on to Lewek Keep in Delcan to prepare the Leweki for the arrival of his army.

The host passed the borders of Delcan in seven days, finally coming to Lewek Keep—normally, a nine-day journey by horse from Lind Keep—however, they found their arrival unexpected by the Leweki. Dell's herald had never come to Lewek Keep. Despite the sudden appearance of the Hagane army at his gate, the Keep's Lord provided a change in mounts and supplies, wishing Dell's host Braya's fortune—but once again, as Turan had foretold, they could spare no warriors.

The Haganes continued from Lewek Keep, traveling on for three more days, bypassing Erutti Keep on the second and crossing Den Inkanar on the third. On that day, they halted at the temple of Manton, the god of justice, located on the southern bank of Inkanar.

The warriors set camp outside the protective wall of Manton's temple, while Dell and his captains and fellow noblemen—those who served the gods—entered the temple to make a sacrifice to Manton and to plead the god's intervention on their behalf in the battles to come. Kradon remained at the camp with Odyniec, Folkor, Asghar, and Turan the guardsman, for none of them would have stepped past the gates of that temple had their lives depended upon it.

Kradon and his companions quietly conversed around a fire outside his father's pavilion near the gate of the temple, waiting for Lord Dell's return. The Temple Guards stood outside the gate, spears in hand, glaring in open hatred and suspicion at the Wizard, Odyniec.

Odyniec patiently abided the unfriendly stares of the Mantonite guard-priests for a long while, but eventually his patience wore thin. The Wizard rose to his feet, taking his staff in hand, and stepped towards the Temple Guards.

"What are you going to do, Master Odyniec?" Kradon asked, casting a worried look in Odyniec's direction.

"Rid ourselves of these bothersome priests!" the Wizard replied tersely. Raising his staff in the air, he cried out, "*Omdi kosumni udinor uktur!*"

The scarlet-robed Temple Guards fled before the wizard, securing the gate behind them. Kradon could see them peering through the barred windows of the gate-towers, their hatred turned to abject fear.

"What did you say?" he asked as Odyniec returned to his place by the fire.

"Absolutely nothing," the Wizard replied as he lowered himself onto the log he used as a seat. "But those superstitious fools don't know that!"

Odyniec glanced at the terrified Temple Guards and nodded his head in approval of his handiwork.

"Master Odyniec," Kradon said, drawing the Wizard's attention back. "Before Folkor, Asghar, and I reached Oran's temple, Folkor thought he saw an omen. And, indeed, what he described to me did seem out of the ordinary."

"Aye," Folkor burst out, suddenly sitting up. "I had all but forgotten!"

"Tell me your omen, Captain," Odyniec said, resting his staff across his knees, his curiosity piqued. "These are harried days and no sign should be considered lightly."

"We had stopped to rest on the outskirts of the Golden Hills, and I took the last watch," Folkor began. "While I sat there, staring at a dark patch of the sky—a place where there were no stars—trying to put my thoughts in order, I saw a star suddenly appear, red as a dragon's breath. It soared to its death across that black patch, but before it was gone, a second star—this one golden in hue—crossed its death-trail. Then they both died, the red, followed by the gold. I was convinced that Oran had given me an omen."

Staring intently into the fire, Odyniec tugged on his beard. "Indeed, this is a sign, but you sought your answer in the wrong place. It was not from the Skylord."

Folkor glowered. "I learned that soon enough, Master Odyniec."

Odyniec turned his gaze to the sea-captain, his own mood darkening. "Your omen was a sign from Elekar—and a strong portent it is. The first star represents the Bearer of the Flame. . ."

Kradon noticed Asghar draw his hood over his face and move back into the shadows. Kradon wondered why, but refrained from asking.

"The second star represents the appointed Heir of Ascon," the Wizard continued. "Your sign retells the prophecies of old; the Bearer shall come, and then the Heir of Ascon. But your sign tells more. It tells when that time shall be. The dark patch of sky symbolizes the darkest hour, upon which Thanatos will return to the Mortal Realm, and such is the hour of the High King's return."

The darkest hour? To Kradon, the Wizard's words were empty. When would the darkest hour be? For that matter, what did it even mean—this *darkest hour?*

Odyniec saw the confusion on Kradon's face and gave an answer to the youth's unvoiced questions, though his answer was a riddle in itself. "Darkness does not always mean a lack of light, My Lord. It can also be a state of mind, a condition of the heart. Thanatos shall come upon the darkest hour, and such is the hour of the High King's return."

"It shall not happen," Asghar grumbled, stepping back into the firelight. "The Bearer of the Flame is dead."

"How do you know this?" Odyniec said without a great deal of concern.

The Dwarf glared at him, angered by the Wizard's apparent disregard for the life of his Kjerken. "Brendys of Shalkan was the Bearer of the Flame, and he is dead."

"Then perhaps the cycle has already begun," Odyniec replied. "Perhaps, Brendys of Shalkan was meant to die. Captain Folkor's sign could indeed indicate that."

"But if that is the case, then the High King shall die also!" Kradon said, disturbed by the thought that the Heir of Ascon might perish before he could reclaim his throne.

"There is that chance," Odyniec admitted. "Sooner or later, every mortal must die in body."

The Wizard then smiled. "But let your fears be laid to rest. Brendys of Shalkan did not perish in the Silver Pass . . . even now, he dwells in the fastness of Gildea Keep."

Kradon started at the Wizard's words. "What? But how? I saw him fall. . . !"

"Indeed, My Lord," Folkor interrupted, glaring at Odyniec. "As did Captain Asghar and myself. You ask us to believe that Brendys was somehow magically transported to Gildea, Wizard? What evidence do you give us?"

Odyniec's grey eyes shone like cold steel from beneath the hood of his cloak. "I need not answer you, Folkor of Ovieto—I need answer to no mortal. Yet I will say what I may. Know you not the prophecies of the Third Age?"

"I must confess that my learning is limited," Folkor replied stiffly.

"*From out of the Darkness, the Flame is kindled. Through the forge of sorrow it is tempered, till the Darkness cannot stay its Light.*"

All eyes turned to Asghar. The Dwarf had thrown back his hood. A fierce gleam was in his eyes.

"Of course!" Kradon cried out. "The lamb amidst the wolves! The wolves must be the Kubruki . . . but who is the ram?"

Folkor and Asghar looked at him as though he had gone mad, but Odyniec suddenly became quiet, lowering his gaze to the fire.

"I can answer no more of your questions," he finally said.

Kradon looked hard at him. "*Cannot* or *will not?*"

Odyniec smiled mysteriously. "Sometimes, My Lord, they are one and the same."

"You know more than you say," Kradon said with a sigh. "I believe you know something of my dream."

Odyniec's smile remained, but he said no more.

Kradon stared at him for a moment, then turned to Asghar and Folkor and related to them the dream which he had dreamt the morning they escaped from the Silver Mountains.

Not long after, Lord Dell and his captains returned from the temple of Manton. Soon, the host had taken to their blankets.

* * * *

After another uneventful day, the host stopped at Estes Keep, where they changed steeds once more. The Hagane army then turned southeast, passing Phelan Keep in Caladin, at last nearing the long stretch of river where the waters of Den Jostalen and Den Smih flowed together.

Now the host could see the Black Shadow, which Turan had described to them, as they neared the Gildean border. They had made better time than any army in the history of Milhavior, for they had made a journey which should have taken a full month in just over three weeks, but even that did not raise their hopes. They knew that they might still arrive at Gildea Keep only to suffer the same fate as the armies of Gildea.

Lord Dell and Odyniec rode at the head of the column, Kradon, Asghar, and Folkor following directly behind them—all dwelling, in one way or another, on the events to come. Folkor brooded, certain that Brendys had perished in the Silver Pass. He dwelt upon that knowledge, building within himself an unfathomable rage to release upon the forces of Iysh Mawvath.

Asghar, satisfied with the Wizard's word that Brendys yet lived, concentrated on fighting down a great fear which threatened to consume him—fear of the mighty beast upon which he rode.

Kradon spent his time pondering the details of his strange vision, since it was clear that Odyniec would say no more on the subject. Some things he could guess at, but not all were clear. The matter would require much thought.

Lord Dell stared ahead, trying to reason out what he was doing leading his people into such a hopeless cause. Thus far, the gods had been with them, he thought, for he had only lost a handful of men to illness during this hard-ride. His gaze fell upon Odyniec. "Why are we here, Wizard? What madness came upon me to issue forth from the gates of my city with every man behind me to ride at a death's pace into certain doom? Why did we not wait until the Host of the Free Lands could be mustered?"

"It was ordained, My Lord," Odyniec replied darkly. "The prophecies will be fulfilled . . . even if we are destroyed in the process."

"Then the gods—or your Dawn King," Dell added. "Are playing games, and we are but the pawns."

Odyniec's beard wagged as he shook his head. "Nay. The choice was yours. But Elekar knows the hearts of Men . . . indeed, it was no accident that Turan arrived at Hagan Keep, for the words he spoke were meant for your ears.

"I am not a fool, Lord Dell. Do you believe that I would throw myself into the fire, if I did not have hope that together we might smother it? We have a mightier ally than you might imagine. And who knows what others we may meet before we reach our goal."

"Others?" Dell said, an incredulous expression on his face. "I am not sure what to think of you anymore. I am beginning to wonder whether I should not have done as King Kosarek bid and banned you from my halls. If it were not for my son, I might have done just that!"

"That, of course, would have been your prerogative," the Wizard replied stiffly. "But I would have ignored your ban as readily as I bid you to ride."

Dell suddenly laughed, a strange sound to break such a dismal silence. "I believe you would have indeed! Ah, Wizard, I pray that you are not wrong."

Odyniec lowered his head until his hood shadowed his face. "So do I."

Lord Dell's smile vanished. He glanced one last time at the Wizard, then turned his eyes forward again, wondering once more what brought him hither.

They rode on in silence for a few hours more. The Shadow over Gildea loomed larger and more sinister, like a gaping rend in the fabric of reality. Even as the Hagane host looked on, it appeared that the Darkness itself was beginning to move towards them. Just the sight of the Shadow cast a gloom upon the hearts of Dell's stout warriors.

A merry voice laughed and called out to Lord Dell from the ranks of warriors behind him. The Hagane Lord wheeled his steed about in surprise, and the column gradually came to a halt.

A hooded man suddenly appeared before him, as though sprouting up from the land. A hunter, he appeared. A sheathed long-knife hung at his belt, and he bore a bow of yew and a quiver of silver arrows upon his back. His garments and hooded cloak were of a strange fabric, seeming to blend with every detail of his environment as though they were made of the combined hues of the earth itself and of the spectrum.

The man hailed Lord Dell once more. "Your thoughts must indeed be bent upon your quest, for it seems your whole host would have passed me by!"

"Hail, Friend, if friend you be," Dell said cautiously.

The stranger drew back his hood, unveiling his shimmering, gold hair and sky-blue eyes. His countenance was wondrous fair to look upon, and a light seemed to shine within him. All who could see him knew that they looked upon one of the Elvinfolk.

"Aye, My Lord," the Elf replied in a voice as fair as his visage, striking his heart with his fist in salute, after the manner of Men. "Indeed, I am a friend. I am Guthwine of the Caletri of Dun Ghalil—Greyleaf Forest in your tongue. Many days have I awaited you here."

Dell knit his brow in confusion. "Many days?"

"Aye," the Elf answered. "News of your brave ride has gone far before you. I desire to join your venture."

"You are welcome among us, My Lord," Dell gratefully responded, surprised by the Elf's request, for the Caletri seldom dealt with mortals. "Indeed, my army could use a hundred Elvin archers, for we ride to a desperate fate."

Lord Guthwine laughed again, and the sound was refreshing to those who could hear. "Then your wish is granted! A company of my kin wait yonder, near the border of the Shadow. The tide has turned in our lands, but the Shadow has begun to spread—it bears down quickly upon Matadol. King Taskalos has dispatched armies from his eastern Keeps to your aid: four-hundreds each from Dahl, Wegant, and Bale Keeps and eight-hundred more from Matadol Keep."

"Two thousand!" Count Wargon exclaimed from Dell's left hand.

"Do not think, however, that this assures victory," the Elf replied. "Iysh Mawvath's legions number in the tens of thousands. Five thousand at least reside at Gildea Keep, and I believe more will gather as they prepare to march."

"Perhaps," Lord Dell responded. "But this does give us hope that we did not have before."

The Elf pointed his hand towards the Shadow. "Then ride, My Lord—for time is short."

"We have a few horses to spare," Dell said in return. "Will you ride with us?"

"You will not need to burden your mounts." The Elf turned and whistled. A strong, bay horse, much like the Hagane steeds in appearance, but bereft of harness, sprang out of a thicket of trees and galloped to meet Guthwine. The Elvinlord leapt effortlessly to the horse's back.

Lord Dell appraised the horse with a look of surprise. "Unless my eyes deceive me, this beast is surely from the stock of Brendyk of Shalkan."

Lord Guthwine shook his head. "Nay. Enerion was foaled in Dun Ghalil. But he is indeed descended from the Horsemaster's stock. My brethren in Dun Rial have traded often with him, and I with them.

"Do not be surprised, My Lord. The stock of Brendyk of Shalkan is most famous. I see you and your warriors also ride steeds of the same breeding."

Dell nodded. "Aye. Brendyk is a dear friend."

Lord Guthwine smiled, a merry twinkle in his sky-blue eyes.

Dell knit his brow at the Elf's expression, but before he could say anything, Guthwine urged his horse forward at a gallop towards the Darkness before them.

The Hagane army started forward once more. In less than an hour, they approached the camps of the Matadane host.

As they neared, they gaped in awe at the ebon maw of the Black Shadow. Like a great gaping hole it was, immeasurably high and deep and wide. Mortal eyes could not pierce the Darkness from without, for it seemed almost solid. Dell ordered his forces to set camp, while he, Kradon, Odyniec, Lord Guthwine, and the Hagane Captains went to meet with the commanders of the Matadane armies. A pavilion in the colors of the House of Matadol—green on sky blue—was prepared for a war council.

Royal Marshal Spiridon, representing his King, was the first to greet the arrival of the Haganes. He struck his right fist to his breast and gave a slight bow in salute. His long, brown and grey-streaked hair hung loose over his shoulders and a sky-blue patch covered his right eye. "My Lord! Welcome at last! Now we may drive forth this Hál-spawned Shadow from the Free Lands and get on with our lives!"

"You speak too hastily, Marshal Spiridon," one of the other Matadane captains said. "The forces arrayed against us are far greater than our meager army can deal with. The Shadow marches even now—I wager the enemy marches with it!"

Spiridon frowned. "You have ever been a skeptic, Nedros. The prowess of the Haganes is reputed to be matchless, and the power of the Dawn King himself stands with us, embodied in this good Wizard."

"One Wizard and four hundred Haganes does not an army make, Marshal," Fieldmarshal Nedros responded.

Spiridon growled. "I swear I sense the odor of a coward. . . ."

Nedros came to his feet, and both men reached for their swords. All at once, a bright light flared up in their midst, cast by Odyniec's intervening staff, leaving both knights blinking.

Odyniec lowered his staff. "*Peace!* Let us not bicker between ourselves like rival clansmen—we must remember that we are allies gathered together to hinder the advance of Iysh Mawvath and his forces however we may.

"Indeed, Fieldmarshal Nedros, the numbers of the Kubruki are far greater than our own, yet the time has not come for the Dark Powers to rise. Elekar will provide strength to our arms. We cannot fail, unless you seek to fail."

The Matadane commanders moved their hands away from their weapons, grudgingly putting aside their differences for the moment.

"Thank you, Master Odyniec," Dell said after the warriors had stood down. "Now may we attend to the matters at hand?"

"Of course!" Marshal Spiridon stammered in embarrassment. "Please be seated, My Lords."

Dell and his captains took their places at the table in the center of the pavilion. Upon the table was a map of the region with Gildea Keep circled in red ink. Dell looked around the table. "Do we know anything of the enemy's position?"

"More than we might possibly have hoped, My Lord," Marshal Spiridon replied. "Lord Guthwine, himself, has been within the Shadow. I shall let him tell his own story."

The Royal Marshal nodded to Lord Guthwine, and the Elf rose to his feet to speak to the war-council. "Indeed, I have been within the Darkness—to Gildea Keep itself—and it was no simple task. However, I discovered paths seldom trodden by Iysh Mawvath's horde.

"This I know of Gildea Keep: the west side of the city is open to attack, for there is no western wall—it is guarded only by Den Jostalen. The Kubruki forces are weak there as well, for creatures of Darkness fear running water and seldom go near it, much less cross it. The Kubruki are perhaps the least intimidated of those creatures, yet still they avoid the water when possible.

"I know, too, that the Keep itself has been razed to the ground, to the last stone. . . ."

Turan the guardsman drew in a startled breath.

"And that Iysh Mawvath has raised a black temple upon its ruins. What binding spells he has laid upon it to give it strength upon the rubble, I know not.

"I also know this of the land surrounding Gildea Keep: the direst of the Dark Legion avoid the river at all cost, and I came upon few Kubruk patrols as I traveled back along the river's banks. Also, the nearest town this side of the Keep—a small fishing hamlet called Tarlas—is under the direct control of Iysh Mawvath's forces. Undetected approach to the Keep will be impossible without taking Tarlas first—swiftly and without mercy."

The captains muttered their approval of this idea.

"Lord Guthwine, did you see aught of survivors at either Tarlas or Gildea Keep?" asked Dahmus, one of Dell's chief captains. "Any who might be able to aid us from within?"

"There were a few mortals," the Elf replied. "In Tarlas, the survivors were scarce. They were mostly peasant women and children, but there were a few men—including a few of the town officials.

"Of Gildea Keep, I know not. I did not attempt to enter the city. I watched from across the river, under the cover of a sparse grove. From there, I saw many women and children, though I saw no men. Most of the children I saw were younglings. There were a few youths—including a pair that were perhaps of Lord Kradon's years.

"Even my vision, however, could not pierce very far through the Shadow."

Kradon felt eyes upon him and looked up to see Odyniec smiling at him. He wrinkled his brow in confusion, then

Odyniec's words at the temple of Manton struck him. "Lord Guthwine, could you describe these youths you spoke of?"

"One, yes," Guthwine replied. "For his appearance was unmistakable to Elvin eyes, even in the murk of the Shadow. The other I could see only vaguely.

"The first one was perhaps of your build, Lord Kradon, and fair to the eye. There was an undeniable Elvin air about him. . . ."

"Lord Quellin!" Turan exclaimed. "It could be no other!"

"What of the second?" Kradon interrupted.

"He was a large lad—perhaps a hand or so taller than yourself—and of a strong build. But other than that I cannot say."

Kradon looked at Odyniec, agape. "How did you know? How did you know he was there?"

"Who, my son?" Lord Dell asked.

Kradon felt his father's gaze upon him and turned to face him. "Brendys, Father. At the temple of Manton, Master Odyniec told me that Brendys was alive and in Gildea!"

Dell darkened in anger as he turned to the Wizard. "How dare you play upon my son's hopes! Brendys perished in the Silver Pass—the dead cannot be brought to life again."

Odyniec's gaze hardened in return. "I would beg to differ, for Fanos Pavo himself conquered the bonds of Death. I have never lied to you, Lord Dell, for that is not the way of the Dawn. There is much that I know that I do not tell, but I have never lied. In this, I have spoken what I may, and it is naught but truth. Brendys of Shalkan was brought to Gildea Keep by the hand of Elekar himself, for he is the Bearer of the Flame of Elekar!"

Marshal Spiridon, whose allegiance lay with the Dawn King, came to his feet. "The Bearer of the Flame! Denasdervien has been found?"

Odyniec gave him a slight nod.

"But why?" Dell continued, refusing to give in. "Why would your Dawn King place him in such a deadly position?"

The Wizard's gaze bore into the Hagane Lord. "For a purpose you cannot begin to understand."

He turned his face away, his eyes briefly falling upon Kradon, his visage grim.

There was a moment of tense silence before Dell spoke again. "Enough of this foolishness! Lord Guthwine, please continue with your report."

"My report is concluded, My Lord," the Elf replied with a slight bow. He returned to his seat.

Turan arose to speak to the assembled captains. "If I may, I can add to Lord Guthwine's report. An attack against the west side of the city would be futile. Den Jostalen is wide and deep enough for shipping commerce. To bring an army against that side would be suicidal."

"Perhaps," Captain Dahmus said, shaking his grey head thoughtfully. "But I think not. If the strength of our army attacks the main gate, it may distract the Kubruki enough for a smaller force to cross the river by raft and gain control of the gate from within."

Dell contemplated the plan for a moment, then nodded slowly. "I like this plan of yours, Dahmus. What say you, Marshal Spiridon?"

Spiridon nodded in agreement. "'Tis risky, but then, this whole venture is an attempt to foster a miracle."

Fieldmarshal Allard, another of the Matadane captains, shook his head. "I do not like this plan. My Lord did not send his men to be slaughtered without a hope—and that is just what will happen if the Kubruki are not deceived by the attack on the gate."

"Marshal Allard is correct," Fieldmarshal Nedros concurred. "This plan is desperate."

"What, then, do you propose?" Odyniec said, glaring at the men.

The Matadane warrior frowned back. "That we attack the main gate with full force. . . ."

"To break upon it like a weak tide against a mountain," Odyniec finished for him. "There is more sense in Captain Dahmus' plan than you realize."

Lord Dell and Royal Marshal Spiridon aided Odyniec in glaring down Nedros and Allard.

"I think it is agreed then that we will go ahead with Captain Dahmus' plan," Dell finally said. "I will lead the assault on the main gate and Marshal Spiridon will lead the infiltration force across Den Jostalen and into the city."

"You are forgetting the other obstacle, My Lord," Guthwine said. "To reach Gildea Keep, we must pass through Tarlas, and for the infiltration force to reach the western side of the city, they must have a raft."

Turan spoke after the Elvinlord. "We can travel along the east bank of Den Jostalen to the place where Den Smih forks away from it. Den Smih can be forded an hour or two down river from there. We can take Tarlas, then march upon Gildea Keep. We may be able to dismantle the Tarlas ferry and bring it with us."

"The force at Tarlas is but a small guard," Lord Guthwine added. "It could be overrun quickly, perhaps before they are able to send word to Gildea Keep."

Turan spoke again. "The greatest difficulty will be in getting the infiltration force into position unnoticed. There is little cover along Den Jostalen."

Lord Guthwine looked thoughtful. "Perhaps not as difficult as you think. All that is needed is a diversion."

"And what is it that you propose, Lord Guthwine?" Dell asked.

"Malach, one of my archers, is also a master falconer," the Elvinlord replied. "His bird, Amrein, is descended from the White Hawks of Mingenland. They still understand the tongues of Man, and the Elves still know their tongue. It is believed that the House of Trost also retains the ability to understand the tongue of the White Hawks.

"If indeed Lord Quellin still lives, we may be able to deliver a message to him through Amrein and arrange a diversion from within the city."

Dell nodded slowly. "Aye. We will encamp after taking Tarlas—we will release the bird then. We should arrive at Gildea Keep early the next morning. Lord Quellin should have enough time to prepare a suitable diversion, if he is able."

He looked at the men around the table. "Are there any questions for further discussion?"

When no answers were forthcoming, he ended, "Then let us adjourn for the night. We will need all our strength in the coming days. May the gods show us mercy."

The war-council disbanded and took their blankets.

* * * *

In the morning, the host was on the move once more. In a few hours, the army passed into the Shadow. That feat alone cost the army several horses and a handful of warriors. A driving wind swirled at the edge of the marching Darkness, like the winds of a great hurricane, throwing man and beast aside as it swept over them. Once the winds had passed, a heaviness fell upon the hearts of those who stood within the Shadow, for it was the power of the Shadow to bring despair to the heart and weariness to the mind.

The host traveled for three days in a forced march, hardly stopping long enough to eat. The warriors became exhausted—a few had even been left behind, gravely ill—but still they pressed on.

Captain Dahmus brought his horse up beside Lord Dell. His grisled features were heavy with concern and with fatigue from the ride. "My Lord, if we are not hindered, we should come to Tarlas by tomorrow morning."

Grimacing, Dell nodded. "The sooner, the better. This accursed Shadow eats at my soul!"

The concern in the old captain's brown eyes deepened as he spoke again. "My Lord, I think it best if we encamp here for the night. The men and horses have passed their limits, and another day like this will kill them."

Lord Dell looked back at his followers, taking in the evidence of their exhaustion.

"Aye, you are right, Dahmus," he replied, his voice disclosing the extent of his own weariness. "We all need rest. Call for camp!"

The Captain left, and Dell turned to the Wizard who rode beside him. "Master Odyniec, you amaze me!"

"How do you mean?" the old prophet asked.

"All of these strong, young men, including myself, are exhausted beyond all account, yet you do not seem the least bit weary!"

"What!" Odyniec exclaimed. "Just because my age counts at over seventeen hundred years, I must be old and weak! I wager I could stand you on your head if I put my mind to it."

Dell's eyes grew wide. "*Seventeen hundred years!*"

Odyniec shrugged. "Thereabout . . . I lost count sometime during the Third Age."

Dell was whelmed with awe. "Either your Dawn King is most powerful indeed, or else your magic is greater than I deemed."

The Wizard seemed chafed by the Hagane Lord's observation. "I do not deal in what you call magic. Magic is stolen power, twisted to evil. To use what you call magic, one must call upon the very power of Hál. The Wizards of Athor are empowered only to do those things which Fanos Pavo wills."

Dell shook his head. "Your ways are strange to me."

"And right they should be," Odyniec replied sternly.

Lord Dell and Odyniec dismounted, handing their reins to one of the men-at-arms.

* * * *

The night was long for Kradon. Not only did the curse of the Shadow drop a chilling pall upon his heart, but he also could not let the words of Odyniec go. Part of him wanted to believe the Wizard, to believe that Brendys was still alive. But common sense said that it was impossible. Even if Brendys had survived the flames, the fall would have killed him instantly.

But then, when did common sense ever enter into it? he thought. *Did common sense bring our families, noble and common, together to begin with?*

He sat up, unable to sleep. Across the dying campblaze, he could see Asghar kneeling, head bowed, hood hiding his features. The Dwarf propped his axe up before him with one hand, and with the other, marked Dwarvin runes in the dirt. Kradon could barely hear Asghar muttering something in his own language.

For a moment, Kradon thought about asking the Dwarf's opinion regarding the Wizard's words, but quickly reconsidered. It would have been rude to interrupt Asghar's meditations.

But the concern was unnecessary. Asghar raised his head and looked at Kradon. His eyes glimmered in the glow of the dying embers. "My Lord, you should be asleep. You will need your strength."

Kradon gave him a wan smile. "I could say the same of you, Captain Asghar."

"The Kjerek are a people of the night," Asghar replied. "And so shall they remain until every Kjerek in Milhavior knows of the Bearer of the Flame and the return of Denaseskra renamed."

"Then you believe Brendys is alive?"

Asghar's gaze did not waver. "I must."

Kradon turned his face away. "I wish I had your resolve."

"Then you will," the Dwarf replied firmly. "Now sleep, My Lord. Very soon, many good Men will die for a dead nation. Such forces gather even now at Gildea Keep that I cannot foresee victory without the direct intervention of Kolis Bazân. You will need your strength."

Kradon nodded silently and laid back down. Whether Asghar returned to his meditations or also took to his blankets, he did not know. He fell asleep almost immediately, feeling suddenly relieved of a burden.

* * * *

When the Dusklight rekindled, the army broke camp and resumed their trek. That morning saw the combined host of Matadol and Racolis fording Den Smih to draw nigh upon the fishing-village of Tarlas on the banks of Den Jostalen. Royal Marshal Spiridon sent scouts ahead to determine the numbers of the enemy.

Four of the seven scouts came pounding back several minutes later.

"Report," Spiridon barked.

"They are waiting for us, Marshal," the lead scout replied. "Somehow they discovered our march and have fortified the town. There are no Kubruki that we could see, but there is a guard of Dark Elves about five hundred strong."

"Skud!" the Royal Marshal spat. "How did they discover us? We found no patrols!"

"There are more fearsome things in the Darkness than Kubruki or Dark Elves, Marshal Spiridon," Lord Guthwine replied. "Drolar and Jaf dwell in the Night Hours . . . and they do not suffer the bonds of mortal existence. They come and go as they please, visible or invisible, and they do not suffer the Kubruki's fear of water."

"Nevertheless, they are but five hundred strong," Fieldmarshal Allard put in. "We are five times their number."

"These are Dark Elves, Fieldmarshal," Lord Dell replied. "I fear their arrows as much as I covet those of our Elvin allies."

Kradon approached the lead scout. "Where are Novosad and the twins? I do not see them with you."

"My Lord, Novosad desired to get a closer look at their fortifications," the scout replied. "I could not dissuade him. The twins went with him. If anyone can slip them past the senses of the Dark Elves, it would be Copanas. And Lehan, his brother, has the eyes of a hunting bird."

"Truly," Lord Dell added. "And Novosad is a master swordsman. Yet it will take the power of the gods to keep them from discovery. It will be a sore loss if they are found out.

"Come, let us encircle our enemy and put an end to their trespass. Warn all to remain out of range of their archers . . . I want no one harmed before we attack. Upon my signal, we shall ride down upon them, with our Elvin friends among the front lines."

The scouts rode off to spread word throughout the host.

Chapter 14

Novosad and Copanas knelt behind a hedge on the bank of the river, staring out at the nearby buildings. They were clad only in their breeches, for they had swum the river to the northeastern edge of Tarlas. Their weapons lay about on the ground around them. A stirring in the water drew their attention to the river. Copanas' twin slowly pulled himself onto the bank.

"Well?" Novosad asked, brushing his sodden, shoulder-length, dark hair out of his face.

"Nothing," Lehan whispered in reply. "They know our army cannot cross the river here, so they have not spared warriors to guard this side of town. They have fortified the southern edge, where the host will attack."

Novosad grinned. "Then let us see what mischief we can make for them!"

Lehan grimaced. "You're mad."

Novosad shrugged. "Perhaps, but I wish to know if any of the townspeople yet live. It may be that we can find allies here."

Lehan and his brother glanced at each other uncertainly, then looked back at Novosad and nodded their reluctant assent. Novosad and Copanas slung their swordbelts over their shoulders, while Lehan fit an arrow to his longbow. Lehan stood up and bent his bow, his sharp eyes swept the area, piercing the Shadow better than most Men. When he was as certain as he could be that the way was clear, he nodded to Copanas and Novosad.

They rose quickly to their feet and leapt over the shrubs, scurrying behind the nearest dwelling. Lehan followed them, stationing himself at the corner of the building across from the others. It smelled like it may have been the village stable. Lehan peered around the corner of the building, then motioned the others on.

In unison, they slipped out of cover and edged along the buildings towards the main street. As Novosad and Copanas reached the far corner of their building, they could see the Dark Elves fortifying the southern reaches of the village. The Dark Elves' pale skin cast forth a deathly glow which illumined nothing, eerier than even the Dusklight of the Shadow. Even as the scouts observed the enemy's fortifications, a pair of Dark Elves came out of a house only a short distance from the alley in which they hid.

Novosad and Copanas dashed across the alley to where Lehan stood, bow ready. They could hear a shout from one of the Dark Elves in a language they could only assume was Machaelonese— harsh and foul sounding, despite the musical voices of the Elves—followed by a rustling sound. The scouts were sure they had been discovered.

Copanas glanced back over his shoulder and noticed a stairway running up the side of the building to a balcony overlooking the river. He motioned his companions towards the stairs, then followed himself. They made it up the steps just in time. The Dark Elves entered the alley just as Copanas slipped onto the balcony and behind the wall of the building.

The Hagane scouts crouched against the wall of the building, hardly daring to breathe for fear that the Dark Elves' sharp hearing would discover them. Below, they could hear the sounds of the immortals searching amongst the barrels and crates scattered throughout the alleyway. Finally, the search ended.

The scouts listened as the Dark Elves argued with each other. Though they could not understand the words, it seemed that one was certain he had seen something, while the other tried to convince him that he had been mistaken. Eventually the voices faded out of hearing as the Elves went back on their way to the southern end of the village.

The scouts waited for a few minutes, then rose to their feet with the intention of heading back down the stairs and continuing their search for survivors, but a new set of voices halted them again. From an open window overlooking the balcony, they could hear two men speaking. One had the fair voice of an Elf, the other had the sound of a Man, elder in years. The Man spoke fearfully as one begging for his life, but his words could not be distinguished.

The scouts edged towards the window, Novosad in the lead. When he reached the window, Novosad peered cautiously around the sill. The pane was open, but the curtain was drawn, though cracked just enough that all three of the scouts could peer through if they huddled close. In the Dusklight, no shadows were cast upon the curtain, concealing the presence of the scouts. Confident that he and his companions were hidden well enough, Novosad motioned for the twins to look.

The voices were coming from behind a door on the other side of the room. Within the room, staring in fear at the closed door, was a young maiden clad in a thin, ragged robe. She was young, though Novosad was certain she was not much younger than himself, perhaps twenty-two or twenty-three years. Like most Gildeans, her hair was darker in hue, as were her despairing eyes. She moved away from the door as the voices came nearer, towards a bed at one end of the room.

The scouts could hear clearly now the words being spoken.

"I beg you, Lord Chol, return my daughter to me," the Man begged.

The Dark Elf responded in a derisive tone. "My dear Governor, why would I wish to return her?"

"I beg of you, My Lord," the Man persisted. "She is my only child. . . ."

"Silence, mortal!" The door slammed open, and an old man tumbled into the room. Within the doorway stood the Dark Elf. His bearing was as fair and noble as any Elf, but his skin was ashen in color, like all of those who had fallen with Thanatos. A dark grey scar hooked down below his left eye, marring his deceptive beauty.

He pointed towards the girl. "Here is your daughter, old man. Look upon her . . . she has served me well, like the willing cow she is."

"*Liar!*" the maid cried. "You took me from my family and made me your whore! Hálspawn! Let me go back to my people . . . if I am to die this day, I would rather die beside them than beside a living wight!"

A strange smile crossed the Dark Elf's lips. "Indeed? Then your wish shall be granted."

In almost a single motion, Lord Chol drew his pale sword and dragged the girl towards himself. As the Elf raised his sword to strike her down, Lehan bent his bow, aimed, and let loose his quarrel. With a hiss, the arrow pierced through the Shadow and the Dark Elf's throat.

Lord Chol's sword dropped to the floor with a sharp ring. He tried to cry out, but could only manage a strangled gurgle, before falling dead to the floor.

The Town Governor and his daughter were both too shocked to cry out. They stared in horror at the dead Elf for a moment, then turned their eyes to the open window, startled to find three mostly-naked men standing outside.

"This way!" Novosad hissed, motioning to them. "Before more come!"

The girl helped her father to his feet and together they climbed out the window onto the balcony. Novosad motioned for Copanas to lead the way back down the stairs. The girl and her father went after him, followed at last by Novosad and Lehan. At the bottom of the stairs, the Town Governor turned to Novosad.

"Who are you?" the old man whispered. "I have not seen you before. How did you come here?"

Novosad told Lehan to watch the street, then replied to the Governor. "Your Grace, my name is Novosad and these are Copanas and Lehan. We are scouts from yonder host, which by now is preparing to lay siege to this village."

"That much I gathered," the old man testily replied. "But whose host is this? Has King Treiber won free from Gildea Keep? Do the armies of Gildea ride against the Shadow?"

Novosad frowned darkly. "Nay, Gildea remains conquered. Indeed, Treiber is dead. The host which rides now was brought from Racolis in the north by my Lord, Dell of Hagan."

The old man embraced his daughter in joy, but refrained from shouting aloud. "There is now hope, Titha!"

Novosad remained grim. "Hope? Perhaps . . . but little."

The young woman looked him in the face. "Little? Have you not come in strength to drive the foe and this Darkness from our land?"

"We have come," Novosad replied flatly. "But in short numbers. There was little time to muster an army. We estimate the Kubruk legion encamped at Gildea Keep will outnumber us nearly four to one."

Titha grew pale, even in the Shadow. "Then we are doomed!"

Novosad watched as hope drained once more from her eyes and his heart was stirred. She was lovely in a simple fashion, but his eyes did not judge for him. Something within him could not bear to see her desolate, and he took pity upon her. "Do not lose all hope, yet. We may be few, but we still have allies who are more powerful than the Kubruki, no matter their numbers."

He knew she had sensed his heart, but he could not read her emotion, whether it said, *Thank you!* or *Do not pity me!* He looked at her for a moment, suddenly becoming very conscious of his lack of clothing. Feeling his cheeks flush, he turned back to her father. "Your Grace, are there other survivors?"

"Aye," the old man replied distractedly. He, too, had noticed the look that passed between the Hagane warrior and his daughter. He waved his hand towards the small street directly across from them, from which they had come. "They are being held in a shelter beneath the stable. There are a few men who are still strong, but most are weakened from maltreatment. These Dark Elves have no regard for human life."

Novosad nodded grimly. "They will have to do. I intend to distract the Dark Elves from within, while our warriors attack from outside."

An angered shout went up from within the building. Lehan looked back towards the stair and said, "Then we had better move quickly . . . the distraction is beginning without us!"

The young warrior fit another arrow to string and raised his bow just as a Dark Elf appeared at the head of the stairs. He let fly his shaft, striking the Elf in the heart. The Dark Elf fell back against the balcony railing, then collapsed forward and tumbled down the stairs.

Novosad drew his sword and motioned Copanas to take the lead. He looked at the Town Governor next. "Go on. You and your daughter follow Copanas, Your Grace. Lehan and I will protect our rear. Go!"

As Copanas and the Gildean nobles started across the main street, they could see the Dark Elves at the far southern end of the street beginning to mill about, startled by the outcry from Lord Chol's abode. Several of the immortals saw the humans dashing across the street and ran after them with a speed only an Elf could muster. Novosad and Lehan came up behind their companions, and Novosad cried out, "Go! We will hold them back!"

Copanas turned and ran at full speed, the Governor of Tarlas and his daughter following much more slowly behind him.

"Beware!" the old man called to the young warrior. "There are two guards within!"

Copanas did not pause to acknowledge him, but ran until he stood before the side entrance to the stable. He drew his sword and started to reach for the latch, but hesitated. He backed away from the door and swung his foot up hard, knocking the latch up and throwing the door open. There was a loud grunt as the door smashed one of the Dark Elf guards against the stable wall.

The second guard came through the open doorway, sword drawn, but Copanas slew him before he could pass the threshold. The Hagane scout dived through the doorway and rolled up on one knee, facing the first guard. Hatred burned in the Dark Elf's eyes as dark streams ran from his nostrils and mouth down his pale, white face.

In a moment of fury, the Elf lunged at him, moving with blinding deftness and agility. Copanas managed to jump out of the way, the Dark Elf's blade missing his head by inches. He came back up to his feet and brought his sword to bear on the Elf.

Steel rang on steel as the Elf's blade clashed against the Man's. Copanas was taken aback briefly as he realized that though the Dark Elf had far superior speed and reflexes, his swing had nowhere near the power of his own. The Elf's smaller, lithe form did not possess the brute strength of Man.

In his fury, the Elf pressed his attack without relief. Copanas gave way under the attack, biding his time, hoping the Dark Elf would tire himself. But his hopes were in vain, for Elves did not tire as Men. Copanas found himself wearying quickly beneath his foe's assault.

Suddenly, the Dark Elf stiffened and his head snapped back, a look of shock on his pale features. Copanas seized the moment and slashed with his blade, cleaving the Elf's head from his shoulders.

The body fell forward, a hayfork thrusting up out of its back. Titha stood across from the Hagane scout, eyes wide, hands covering the lower half of her face. Her father stood behind her, with his comforting hands on her shoulders.

Not a warrior maiden, to be sure, Copanas thought. He gave her a reassuring smile and said. "Good work, M'Lady."

The sound of human voices and hands pounding on wood drifted up from the floorboards. Copanas looked around. "Where is the entrance to the shelter?"

"Over there," the Governor replied, pointing to a large trunk set in a corner.

Copanas could see the outline of a door in the boards beneath the trunk. He trotted over to the chest and shoved against it, but it did not move. He pressed his back against the box and pushed with all his strength, bracing his feet against the floor, but his feet only slid out from beneath him. The trunk would not budge.

He tried to open it, but discovered it was locked.

"How did the Dark Elves move this?" he asked the Governor. "I know they do not have the strength of Men."

The old man shrugged. "I do not know. I never paid heed. My mind was ever on my Titha."

Copanas sighed and gazed for a moment, the pounding of the trapped villagers echoing in his ear. Then he realized *this* pounding was not coming from beneath him. His eyes darted to a nearby stall.

* * * *

Novosad stared around the corner of one building, while Lehan stood near another. The Dark Elves had not dedicated many warriors to the eradication of the handful of rebels within the village, trusting five to perform that task, while the remainder kept vigil against the encircling host. Three Elves had already fallen to Lehan's bow. The last two bore only hand weapons. Novosad watched as his fellow scout dropped his bow, knowing that he would not have time to knock and release before the Dark Elves were upon them. Both Men took sword to hand and waited.

Novosad jumped out at the first Dark Elf, swinging his sword down at his enemy. The Dark Elf brought his own blade up in a two-handed grip to block it. Novosad's eyes grew wide when he saw the blade. It was a double-edged weapon, an inch or two longer than the average broadsword. Both edges were razor keen and scalloped into several pointed teeth.

The Dark Elf caught Novosad's blade between the serrated edges of his own sword and flicked his wrists, ripping the longsword out of the young warrior's grasp. He swiped at the scout, but Novosad jumped back far enough to avoid serious injury. He winced as the tip of the weapon grazed him, causing a thin cut across his bare chest.

A shout from the street on the right drew the attention of the combatants. Copanas was leading a small mob of townsfolk towards them. Out of the corner of his eye, Novosad noticed that the Dark Elf, like himself, had been taken off guard by the appearance of those he had thought prisoners rushing towards him bearing hayforks and crude wooden clubs.

Novosad spun back and lunged at the Dark Elf, dragging the immortal's sword-hand to the side. He thrust his knuckles into the stunned Elf's windpipe, then firmly planted his knee in his enemy's groin. He jerked the vicious sword from the Dark Elf's weakened grasp and ripped it across his enemy's throat. The Elf fell to the ground in the silence of death.

The townspeople aided Lehan in dispatching the last Dark Elf, then started down the street towards the main force of the enemy.

"Wait!" Novosad called. "Do not attack! Lehan, send a few arrows amidst the Elves. When we have their attention, scatter among the buildings . . . make them come after us!"

The townsfolk hesitated, then rejoined the Hagane scouts.

Lehan let fly several arrows in rapid succession, without heed to aim. Some found marks, though most struck harmlessly in the barricades, but it was enough to draw forth the enemy.

* * * *

Kradon rode up beside his father as another scout came galloping back.

"My Lord!" the warrior cried. "The Dark Elves' defenses are weakening! Many of their warriors are leaving the barricades!"

"Novosad and the twins?" Kradon asked his father.

Lord Dell responded with a nod. "I should not be surprised."

He turned and called to his herald. "Sound the charge!"

Horns blared throughout the host and the horsemen surged forward. Lord Guthwine's archers led the charge, spraying arrows amidst the stunned enemy with an accuracy unimaginable from horseback. The Elves broke away as they neared the village, allowing the lancers an opening. Heavy chargers leapt over the barricades, trampling the Dark Elves beneath their hooves.

Trapped between Lord Dell's forces and the remaining townsfolk, the Dark Elves stood their ground and died.

When the battle was over, Dell called his captains together.

"We shall set camp here," he told them. "Tomorrow, we shall lay siege to Gildea Keep."

His countenance turned grim. "The odds against us shall be greater than they were against the Dark Elves this day. I fear we march to the slaughter."

"Perhaps," Lord Guthwine replied. "Perhaps not. Aid came to you unseen once already, and we still have the Gildeans to consider. Malach waits for your command to send word to Lord Quellin."

Lord Dell turned his gaze on the Elf. "Send your message, My Lord. We have come too far to turn back."

The Elvinlord inclined his head to Dell, then took his leave.

Dell returned his attention to the council. "We have already decided much of what will be done. All that remains is to choose the commander for the infiltration force. It is a desperate ploy, for we do not know the true strength of the Kubruki guarding the river. Will any volunteer?"

There was a quiet moment, but it was brief. The silence was broken by Kradon. "I will go."

Startled, Lord Dell turned to face his son. "I cannot allow that."

"Why not?" Kradon replied flatly.

"You are too young," Count Wargon, Dell's aide, interjected.

"And you seek only vengeance," Dell added.

"I have been raised from birth to be Lord of Hagan," Kradon replied quietly. "You cannot deny that I have never been rash or unwise in my decisions. Neither would I do anything to risk the lives of those around me, Father, regardless of my desire. You know that."

Dell started to respond, but the Wizard, Odyniec, interrupted. "My Lord, if I may speak. . . ?"

The Lord of Hagan hesitated, casting a wary eye on the Wizard, but nodded his assent.

"I believe, My Lord, that this task was appointed for him," Odyniec continued. "Your House is beloved by your people. You cannot lead that force, for you will be needed to lead the main assault. I believe your men would rally to your son as readily as to you, and I believe he can lead them to victory at the Gate of Gildea Keep."

He glanced at Kradon with an odd smile and added, "Besides, I think he will have more influence within the walls of Gildea Keep than anyone else."

Dell grimaced. "Are you still harping on that, Wizard? Brendys is dead."

The Wizard cast a sharp eye on him. "If you truly doubt me as much as you claim, My Lord, I will gladly return north and let you ride on alone."

A brooding silence fell for a moment, broken only when Lord Dell had made his decision. "Kradon shall lead."

"My Lord!" Count Wargon exploded. "He is just a boy!"

Dell looked at his aide, then turned a proud eye on his son. "Nay, Wargon . . . he is a man."

Chapter 15

Gowan slowly helped Brendys to his feet. Supporting the Shalkane youth with his own slender frame, he walked Brendys around the room. "The Princess says ye needs t' get yer stren'th back. That old witch's slop 'ealed ye up right well, I'd say . . . 'ardly a scar t'show ye 'uz burnt up so bad!"

Brendys grunted in reply. "I don't feel healed up . . . I ache all over, and I can't even walk on my own two feet!"

"Ye been stuck abed a-whiles," Gowan said as they turned to cross the room again. "Course ye can't stan' up yet. Ye'll get yer legs under ye soon!"

At Gowan's prompting, they walked around the room for several more minutes, until Brendys was able to stand—however unsteadily—on his own. Brendys sat down on the edge of the bed to rest for a moment, then donned the clothing which Gowan had brought for him.

"The Princess prob'ly be waitin' fer ye in th' front room," Gowan said as Brendys dressed.

Brendys looked at him with a grin. "Well, we certainly don't want to keep Her Highness waiting."

He slowly came to his feet and allowed Gowan to lead him from the bedroom.

Mattina was sitting on a couch in the front room, idly poking at a bit of mending. With the occupation of Gildea, there was little else to keep her busy, but she seemed particularly distracted today. She briefly looked up at Brendys, then to Gowan, whom she dismissed with a slight nod of her head.

Gowan responded to her with a big grin, eliciting an exasperated grimace in return, then left her alone with Brendys.

Mattina put her work aside and motioned for Brendys to sit beside her. "You are looking much stronger today."

Brendys wanted to complain about his aches and pains, but found it impossible to grumble while gazing into Mattina's face, soft and fairly glowing with pleasure. His own lips cracked into a smile.

"I'm feeling much better," he lied. He took one weak-kneed step towards the couch and fell flat on his face.

Mattina burst out laughing.

Red-faced, Brendys pulled himself up onto the couch with a groan and a grimace. He gave her a sheepish look, then laughed as well.

When their mirth had subsided, Mattina turned to look at Brendys, her glittering eyes studying his face. "I have told you about Gildea, Brendys. Now, it is your turn. Tell me about Shalkan . . . about *your* home."

"Shalkan?" Brendys repeated, taken off guard by the request. "There is really not that much to tell about it. It is as dreary a place as there ever was."

Mattina crossed her arms, pursing her lips. "Surely, it cannot be *that* dull. I cannot think of anything worse than a city where the only color is grey and the only emotion oppression. Please, do tell me!"

A second voice entered in. "Aye, tell us. 'Tis only fitting that we should know a little bit more about our . . . guest."

Quellin and Arella stepped into the room, seating themselves across from Mattina and Brendys. Mattina frowned at the intrusion, but said nothing. If Quellin noticed, he did not react.

Brendys laughed. "Very well, then. I have been outnumbered."

He fell silent for a moment, trying to decide where to begin. Finally, he spoke, starting slowly. "It's like every other place, I suppose: animals, trees, grass, stone—a lot of that—water, good fertile soil, even some small hills in the northern reaches, all enclosed by Barrier Mountain. A pretty, little valley really—nay . . . pretty doesn't really describe it."

Brendys's voice drifted into silence. He now realized that little, insignificant Shalkan was something more than just any other place. Indeed, it was home. It was home, and he missed it dreadfully. He wondered if he would ever see his father again, or Farida and Willerth. It seemed unlikely. But of course, his very presence in Gildea was entirely impossible.

He looked up. Quellin, Arella, Mattina—these people were total strangers to him, yet he found himself able to open up to them as if he had known them all his life. Taking a deep breath, he went on, telling the royalty of Gildea about his low, common life. They listened patiently for hours, until, at last, Brendys fell silent, feeling as though a great burden had lifted from him, or at least lessened.

Mattina spoke, a smile on her lips. "Your Shalkan doesn't seem to be a very dull place after all."

"Aye," Quellin said in agreement. "And you speak as though you miss it greatly—which I can understand. I would give the Crown of Trost to be in Shalkan right now. But, alas, that cannot be."

The Gildean King shook his head and sighed. After a moment, he brought his gaze back to Brendys. "You have spoken much about your father and the servants, but you have said naught of your mother . . . why?"

Brendys became uneasy at the Trostain's scrutiny. With a little difficulty, he answered, "She died when I was only four."

Quellin nodded grimly. "The Plague."

The Shalkane youth's gaze dropped to the floor. For many years, he had tried to keep the pain in his heart hidden from others, but now he could not. His voice cracked as he spoke. "I can't remember much about her—only standing at her bedside, weeping, watching her suffer. I was there when she—when. . ."

His voice faded to a whisper, then was gone. The pain of the memory was too great for him. A tear rolled down his cheek, promising more to follow.

"That was a damnation upon our race," Quellin said, shaking his head. "A retribution placed upon Men by the Dawn King for the suffering of his servants. And still we did not learn. Nor will we ever, it seems."

"If that is so, then why did he take Mother!" Brendys exploded, jumping to his feet. "She served him!"

Quellin's dark eyes met the Shalkane's, holding them with an uncanny understanding. "I thought that you believed the Dawn King a myth?"

Brendys dropped back to his seat, dragging his eyes away from the Trostain's steady gaze with difficulty. "I do."

Arella reached over and placed a hand on the youth's strong arm, her voice soothing. "We shall speak no more on this, Brendys. It is hard enough for you to be trapped in a struggle of which you have no part."

Her gaze edged towards Quellin, hardening a little. "*We* do not need to add to that burden."

Brendys shook his head. "Nay. However I came here and for whatever reason, your struggle is now mine as well."

His eyes strayed back to Quellin. "But what I don't understand is why you continue to tolerate this Iysh Mawvath! Why haven't you formed a rebellion against him?"

"With what?" Quellin returned with a dry laugh. "You have seen the Kubruki, and with the exception of you and I and perhaps a handful of youths, we have no one but women and children remaining in this city. Iysh Mawvath is a powerful warlord, and a Sorcerer as well. We have nothing to fight him with.

"At first, I thought that was the reason for which you were sent to us—as one who would provide the means for our liberation. You brought Denasdervien—what greater hope could we have than that? But when I learned you could not even draw the Flame, I knew that I was wrong."

"But that isn't my fault!" Brendys said defensively, though why Quellin's words affected him so strongly, he did not know.

Quellin gave him a contemplative look. "I wonder. . . ."

Before Brendys could respond, there came an urgent knocking at the front door and a whimpering voice. When no one else seemed inclined to move, the Shalkane youth started up to answer it. Quellin grabbed him before he was halfway to the door, pulling him away.

"Only one kind of creature stalks the streets during the Night Hours, lad," Quellin told him. "And that is the Drolar. Do not open that door!"

After a few minutes, the banging stopped and the voice silenced.

Brendys looked questioningly at Quellin. "What is the Drolar?"

"What *are* the Drolar," Arella corrected him. "None of us knows for certain. We have never actually seen the creatures, only their handiwork. But legend has it that they are demons which have taken physical form."

Brendys turned to her. "But if it is so powerful, why doesn't it just break the door down?"

Quellin put a hand on his shoulder. "It has power only outside this house. Elekar protects his own. The weakness of the Drolar is that it cannot enter a dwelling where servants of the Dawn King reside, unless they let it in."

Brendys knit his brows in confusion. "I don't understand. . . ."

"I did not expect you to," Quellin said, an understanding smile crossing his lips. "Though I daresay you will understand before long, I'm sure. Just heed my warning and do not open that door!"

He paused, then said, "This has been an unsettling night for you. Why don't you go and get some sleep now? And Brendys . . . I do apologize if anything I have said has hurt you."

Brendys avoided Quellin's gaze, but nodded acceptance of the apology, then turned and strode down the hall to his room. He was indeed weary, but he felt too nervous to sleep. A strange chill had come over him, though he could not determine the source.

Trying to ignore the sensation, he went to bed and finally drifted off.

Brendys tossed and turned in his sleep, the odd chill disturbing his dreams. A child's scream for help tore the youth from his less than peaceful slumber. He jerked up in bed and listened, but all was quiet. Then the screams came again.

"Don't be noble," he told himself. "You don't know what is going on."

But the screams continued, dragging at his conscience. Against his better judgment—and Quellin's advice—Brendys crawled out of bed and slipped on his clothes, then slowly made his way to the front door. Carefully sliding the bolt back so as not to disturb Shanor and Bipin asleep on the couches, he slipped out into the Darkness and stumbled off in the direction of the screams.

Once or twice, Brendys tripped over rocks and other small objects, for during the Night Hours not even the grey Dusklight shone. For the first time in his life, he experienced true darkness. Finally, he tripped and fell, thudding his head against a wall.

Darkness turned to flashes of red light, then all went black again. Stunned, he turned and slumped back against the building. As he struggled to gather his wits about him, two shining, red spots appeared in the Darkness before his eyes again. Brendys blinked his eyes and shook his head, trying to destroy the image. The spots did not vanish.

"It is only my imagination," he assured himself, rubbing his aching head. "I hit my head too hard, that's all."

Serpentine laughter came from the direction of the eyes.

"Oh, no, my dear, young fool, it is not your imagination!" the voice hissed. "Oh, how I have been waiting for this moment! Now my master's victory shall be complete, the curse fulfilled!"

The glowing eyes started to advance, but just as the cold metallic points of the beast's claws brushed against Brendys's arm, a bright light spilled into the Darkness. The creature sprang back with a roar of pain. In the flicker of the light, Brendys caught a glimpse of a black form huddled against the wall, covering its head with all too human arms.

Then another voice yelled at him. "Run! Back to the house! Hurry now!"

Brendys did not stop to think, but ran with all the speed his weakened body could muster in the direction of Etzel's house—a fairly straight line. A few more pairs of eyes dotted the Shadow before him, but they scattered upon the light's approach.

Soon, Brendys reached his destination. Gasping from both his run and out of fear, he threw open the door and stumbled into the house, falling to the wooden floor when he was safely within. He felt his head being lifted up, and he opened his eyes. Mattina was there, holding him in her arms, wiping the perspiration from his brow, with a kerchief.

Quellin rushed into the house behind him, carrying a torch, and slammed the door, quickly sliding the bolt back into place. He swung around to face Brendys, as pale and sweating as the youth.

"You fool! You blasted, young fool!" he cried. "Did I not warn you?"

Brendys did not argue. He had been tricked by a Drolar, and he knew it. He also knew it would never happen again.

Something troubled him, though . . . something the creature had said. The screaming had been a ruse, designed especially for him. Brendys shivered, then choked out, "It's here to fulfill the curse . . . it's here . . . it's here to kill me!"

By this time, Arella, Sherren, and Etzel came into the room, looking disheveled, having been wakened from their sleep. Shanor and Bipin were both sitting upright on their respective couches, staring at him fearfully. Of those present, only Etzel did not wear a look of surprise.

The anger drained from Quellin's youthful features. "Curse? What is this about? I could barely hear the Drolar's ramblings. . . ."

Brendys noticed Etzel's expression change. A look of genuine concern swept over her features. "It spoke? With its own voice?"

Quellin looked down at Brendys. Brendys just stared back, a little dazed, until he realized that the Gildean King expected him to answer the question. The youth met Etzel's unsettling gaze and stammered out, "Y-yes . . . it did."

Etzel looked grim. "Then it was not a Hálcor you faced, that which you call Drolar."

"If it wasn't a Drolar, then what was it?" Quellin asked. "It appeared, as far as I could tell, like the other Drolar which were out . . . and there were many."

"I did not say the form was not of a Drolar," the old woman replied sharply. "I said only the creature itself was not a Drolar. The Hálcor cannot speak, except to mimic what it has heard."

Brendys shuddered. The screams he heard had been real . . . he heard the voice of a memory, the Drolar's imitation of a hapless victim. He did not want to think about that victim's fate.

Quellin rubbed his face in agitation. "The Night Hours are not the time for this discussion. You have a tale to tell, Brendys. Be prepared to tell it tomorrow. Right now, everyone go back to bed. And for the sake of all that is holy, *stay there!*"

Brendys looked up at him and nodded.

* * * *

Iysh Mawvath sat upon his throne within the inner sanctum of the Black Temple, his head bowed forward, long pale hair draped over his shoulders, eyes closed in concentration. The chamber was round, the walls lined with grotesque statues of demonic and beastly things. Pale stones in the floor of the circular chamber formed a grey pentagram against a black background. At the center of the design was an altar formed from a single black stone. Though the Night Hours had begun long before, still the strange Dusklight shone in that room.

A passage opened up in the far side of the chamber leading to the upper halls of the temple. Past that entrance, the Dusklight ceased and Darkness reigned. Iysh Mawvath did not leave his sanctum during the Night Hours. Even after centuries in the service of Thanatos, he could not bear the utter blackness of the

Shadow in the night. The deathly Dusklight was better than naught, though at times he yearned for the true light of the sun. Yet the knowledge that he was under the Curse of Darkness laid on all of the creatures which served Thanatos kept him beneath the eaves of the Black Shadow.

The Warlord of Thanatos had doffed his armor and now wore a grey robe. His grim face was drawn and haggard. But for his tremendous size, he would have looked like the corpse of an ancient King, perished in his throne. Iysh Mawvath was troubled. Ever since he had come to Gildea Keep, he could feel a strong power within the city—a power which resisted his attempts to locate it. He was certain that power was hiding Lord Quellin, but that was the least of his worries.

Many days earlier, he had felt a sudden surge of power like a blinding light in his mind's eye. Ever since then, the image of a sword of argent flame troubled his thoughts. His head ached fiercely . . . still, that image seemed to make the Shadow less oppressive. Part of him yearned to find that power, to embrace it, to break the Darkness that he himself had conjured. But it was impossible. He had made his choice centuries ago.

Even death would not be an escape from the master to whom he had pledged his soul. Death would only hasten his descent into the Black Pits. Blood was his only hope . . . the blood of the innocent sustained him, strengthened him. It was the price of immortality.

The *clang!* of the great iron portals of the temple echoed down from the entrance hall, disturbing his reverie. Iysh Mawvath leaned back in his throne and waited. In a few minutes, he could see the burning eyes of a Hálcor in the Darkness of the entry arch.

"Why have you come here?" Iysh Mawvath said without moving. Though he spoke quietly, his deep voice echoed through the chamber like an earth tremor. "I have not summoned you. Why do you trouble me at this hour?"

"Do not use that tone of voice with me, Iysh Mawvath!" the beast spat back. The creature stepped into the Dusklight of the sanctum and approached the throne, a lithe, black shadow in the form of a man with the head of a panther. As it crossed the chamber, a red light enveloped the creature like a fine mist, growing brighter until the Hálcor's form could no longer be seen, then vanished. In the creature's place stood a grey-bearded man in grey robes similar to Iysh Mawvath's. The Sorcerer's black cloak rippled around him as he strode forward.

Iysh Mawvath glared. "*You!* I have no need, nor want of you here. Go back to the Black Pits and let the Horde gnaw your wretched hide."

The Sorcerer ignored his remark. "I shall have you know that I have been given charge of the Temple at Karuna in Shad. You may be the physical head of this Legion, Iysh Mawvath, but I am its spiritual backbone."

Iysh Mawvath gave a wry laugh. "*Spiritual backbone?* I am aware of your post, fool. I am also aware of your taste for acolytes . . . you would make even the Kubruki ill."

"And I know of your taste for blood," the other Sorcerer hissed in return. "At least my acolytes live!"

Iysh Mawvath looked bemused. "Do they?"

A look of consternation came across the bearded man's face. "I did not come here to bandy words about our methods."

The Warlord of Thanatos narrowed his eyes. "And I did not ask you here at all. State your reason and be gone."

"He is here, Iysh Mawvath!" the Great Father replied, his voice rising. "The Bearer of the Flame is here at Gildea Keep!"

Iysh Mawvath came to his feet and strode down the dais to stand before the other Sorcerer. Iysh Mawvath rumbled, "I have felt a new power within the city, but could not determine its source . . . now I know. The sword I have seen is Denasdervien. Where is he, this Bearer of the Flame?"

The Great Father trembled before the giant, causing Iysh Mawvath to smile inwardly in satisfaction. "He has taken refuge in the house of Etzel Uhyvainyn."

The Warlord of Thanatos turned and slowly climbed the dais to his throne. "Of course . . . Uhyvainyn, that meddling hag. I should have known! Lord Quellin must be hiding there as well. But you know as well as I what the witch really is—Alar, True Alar. We cannot even touch them as long as they remain within that house, not without the power of the Black Hand of Thanatos himself!"

"Perhaps not," his fellow Sorcerer agreed. "But the Bearer must come out of his hole sometime—and when he does, Brendys of Shalkan will feel my touch!"

Iysh Mawvath shook his head. "Nay, demon, not yet! There is still much to be done. This is not your time."

His voice gently resonated. "Not yet. . . ."

* * * *

Brendys lay in bed, but he did not sleep, nor had he for the last two nights. Neither had he ventured out of doors since his encounter with the Drolar, whether in the Dusklight or Night Hours. He had never been superstitious. He did not believe in curses, mystical powers, gods or goddesses, Lightlords or Deathlords, but that was quickly changing. He had felt for himself the power of the sword, Denasdervien—indeed, had been transported across Milhavior by it. He had been threatened by a demon straight from Hál, a creature which claimed knowledge of the curse against Brendys . . . a creature which reminded Brendys all too much of the beast Willerth had dreamed of the night the curse was spoken.

He had shared all he knew with Quellin and Etzel the morning after the attack. They had closeted themselves for long hours discussing the creature, but they said no more about it to Brendys.

His body ached and his mind was weary from exhaustion, but still he could not sleep. Terror kept his mind and heart racing through the Night Hours, though he knew nothing evil could touch him there. Somehow, Etzel's house was protected against the sorceries of Iysh Mawvath and his minions. Gowan had told him Etzel was a witch, but somehow the word did not seem to fit.

* * * *

As he lay there staring up into the utter blackness of the Night Hours, it seemed to him that Dusklight began to gather around his bed . . . faint, but still enough to outline objects in the room. He raised himself up on his elbows, wondering if the Night Hours had ended, though the time had seemed so short. But something was not right. There had never before been any transition from Darkness to Dusklight. It was always an immediate change.

As Brendys strained to peer through the murky Dusklight, he thought he could see something large looming near the foot of his bed. Slowly, He crawled towards the foot of his bed, and as he did, the Dusklight grew brighter. The object became clear, though Darkness still surrounded it. It was a large altar of black stone, and stretched out upon the altar, bound ankle and wrist, was a child. The boy's body was bruised and bleeding from wounds caused by a scourge. His eyes were closed as if in sleep, oblivious to pain.

Brendys stared in confusion. He had seen this before—at least twice before—only the last time the boy had been him. This child was familiar, yet different. In what way, he could not tell. Brendys tried to crawl forward to unbind the leather thongs holding the boy to the altar, but he fell short, collapsing to a cold, stone floor.

Brendys rose to his knees and stared in shock. Manacles and chains tore at his wrists and ankles, binding him to a dank dungeon wall. His bed was gone—indeed Etzel's house was gone. He was alone in a stone chamber with the altar and the boy.

A gleam of light—true light—caught his attention. To his right, point thrust into the flagstones, was a sword which could only be Denasdervien, its gleaming Silver-gold blade the only color in the grey Dusklight. A strange hissing sound like the stirring of a viper's nest drew his attention back to the altar.

In the Darkness beyond the altar, the gleam of red eyes appeared. Brendys could hear words among the hisses, words that brought a chill to his heart, and realized it was a chant. A black, clawed hand appeared out of the Darkness, hovering over the child. Suddenly, a wind began to blow in the chamber, growing stronger as the chant grew more shrill. The hand raised, poised to strike.

Brendys, in desperation, grasped for the sword, but it stood just beyond his reach. He stretched towards the weapon until blood ran from his wrist where the manacle bit, but still he could not reach it. As he brought his eyes back to the altar, the chanting stopped and the claw plunged down into the child's body.

Brendys wanted both to scream and retch, but could do neither. Transfixed in horror, he could do nothing but watch. The altar and the claw vanished into the Shadow, and Brendys found himself standing on a low hill. The sun was bright and a warm breeze was blowing. A low rumble like the growl of thunder echoed on the horizon. Slowly the noise grew in volume until Brendys could recognize it as the stamping of hundreds of horses. The ground trembled beneath his feet as a long column of horsemen and foot soldiers appeared on the horizon—a brilliant red creature mottled with dull earth tones.

When the column neared, he could make out the standard borne before all—the banner of the House of Hagan. At the head of the army rode a man he recognized as Lord Dell. Beside him was an old man in white robes and a long white beard. Following behind them were Kradon, Asghar, and Captain Folkor. Kradon and Folkor were grim of countenance, while Asghar wore his hood low in the Dwarvin manner of mourning.

Brendys tried to call out, but still could not speak. He then attempted to make himself known by waving his arms, but no one seemed to see him . . . no one but the old man, who turned to look at him, an odd gleam in his eye. Suddenly, the old man's gaze hardened, and Brendys realized he was staring behind him.

The youth turned around and found himself once more surrounded by Darkness, face-to-face with a demon. The creature was smaller than he and lithe of build. Sleek, black fur covered it from clawed foot to panther-like head. Its eyes burned like red-hot coals as it bared its fangs in an evil grin.

"From here, there is no running, boy," the creature hissed. "The Flame shall be quenched as will the Heir."

Without warning, the Drolar sprang forward, claws extended towards Brendys's throat.

Brendys screamed as a blinding flash of white light knocked him backwards. . . .

When Brendys opened his eyes, he was in his bed in Etzel's house, surrounded by the grey of the Dusklight Hours.

"Bloody Hál," he choked out. "It's not really after me at all."

Mattina was at his side in an instant, embracing him. "You're awake!"

Brendys smiled weakly. "I think we have been through this before."

"Don't mock," she chided angrily. "Etzel thought you might not ever wake up."

Brendys nodded seriously. "I believe you. . . ."

Mattina cut him off with a kiss.

Brendys's eyes widened in bewilderment. As Mattina pulled away, he asked, "What was that for?"

The girl looked away, embarrassed. "I . . . I . . . You almost died. You were asleep for a week . . . Etzel said she tried to find you, but something held her back."

"A-a week!" Brendys's mind began to reel. The dream had seemed but moments long, yet he had been asleep for a week! A wave of dizziness swept over him, and he felt he might pass out again.

Mattina, seeing him swoon, called out for her brother. Quellin came into the room, followed by Etzel. The old woman's expression was a mask of concern.

Brendys looked up into the Gildean King's deceptively youthful face. "Quellin, it isn't trying to kill me . . . or rather it is, but it's also trying to kill someone else by killing me."

Quellin glanced at Etzel, then brought his piercing gaze back to Brendys. "Calm yourself. I don't understand, Brendys. What are you trying to say?"

"The Drolar," Brendys replied, choking a little at the memory. "I saw it. It killed a little boy, or it's going to . . . I don't know."

Etzel leaned forward, her strange eyes intent upon him. "Tell me exactly what you saw, boy. Everything. The Road to the Vision Realm was blocked to me—it takes a mighty power to accomplish that. I wandered far, but could not find you. Speak . . . I must know what you saw."

Without delay, Brendys related his vision to the old woman in great detail, from the sacrifice to the attempt on his own life. When he was through, Etzel waved her hand over his eyes, and he fell into a dreamless sleep.

Etzel turned back to Quellin. "Let the boy sleep now. There are things we must discuss."

Etzel left the room without another word. Quellin glanced back at Brendys. Mattina was sitting on the edge of the bed, stroking the youth's forehead. Quellin shook his head in pity. *Lad, you bear a heavy burden . . . may Elekar deliver you from it.*

He turned and left the room.

* * * *

Quellin found Etzel in her library. The room was cluttered with shelves full of tattered scrolls and books, some written in languages he did not recognize, others marked with dubious symbols and totems. Racks containing vials of various liquids and jars of powders were scattered here and there as well. Quellin looked around nervously. The room gave credence to the rumors that Etzel was a witch.

Quellin's eyes alighted on the old woman, sending another jolt of trepidation through him. The normally imposing figure was bent as though under a great strain, the confidence and strength in her aged countenance replaced with a mixture of thoughtful concentration and fear.

"Etzel?" he said quietly. "You wished to speak with me?"

The old woman started at the sound of his voice, but she quickly recovered, a fierce power returning to her gaze. "Aye, Your Majesty. Many things of importance have been set in motion. Powers of which I should be aware are hidden from me. Dark times are coming. The Winds of Hál are stirring."

"Indeed, that much I know," Quellin replied.

Etzel's frown deepened. "Then know this as well, the last mortal bastion of light—Reanna Orilal, the Vision Realm—has fallen. It was inevitable—the Vision Realm is, after all . . . *mortal*, imperfect. Evil has finally thrust through the barriers protecting that Realm. . . ."

"You speak of things I do not know," Quellin interrupted.

Etzel sighed and nodded. "My apologies, Your Majesty. For a Man, you are learned, but such things are beyond the learning of Men.

"Reanna Orilal is a mortal Realm, yet unlike En Orilal—the world at large—it lies outside time and reality as you know it. Those with special gifts may see into that Realm. Their minds take physical shape there. . . ."

Quellin was quickly becoming more confused. "Then how do they still live in this Realm?"

"I said mind, not soul," the old woman snapped. "The mind does not give life . . . it is but a physical manifestation of the link between soul and body. The soul remains in this Realm. Only the thoughts of the gifted take form in Reanna Orilal, nothing more. Now, please, if you wish for understanding, do not interrupt."

Cowed by the strength in Etzel's ancient voice, Quellin remained silent.

The old woman continued. "In the Vision Realm, the past, the present, and the future may be seen, though the visions are random and vague to the untrained mind. The gifted can bend the visions to their will for the seeking of knowledge. However, even then what is seen may only be a possible future. Reanna Orilal may defy space and time, but only Elekar can reveal the truth in its entirety."

Quellin nodded thoughtfully. "Then what Brendys saw may or may not come to pass."

Etzel's already grim features darkened. "That is the trouble, Your Majesty. The boy should not have been able to enter Reanna Orilal without aid in the first place, nor should I have been hindered in my search for him. Unless the evil which has corrupted the Vision Realm has become powerful enough to defy even Elekar, only the hand of Elekar himself could have performed that task."

"What of the Drolar?" Quellin asked.

Etzel shook her head. "The Sorcerer who has taken that guise—for that is what the beast is—is not nearly powerful enough. If it is not strong enough to withstand me in this Realm, it would certainly be powerless against me in that Realm.

"Nay, the Hálcor was permitted to attack Brendys, and I think I understand why. This much I have gleaned from things I saw in Reanna Orilal and things the boy said of his visions: Brendys of Shalkan is the Bearer of the Flame, the harbinger of the Heir of Ascon."

Quellin nodded. "This, too, I had already determined by his weapon."

"Then understand this, Your Majesty: If the Bearer of the Flame is slain before his appointed time, the Heir of Ascon will never return to his throne, and Darkness shall rule until Elekar comes himself to claim his own. The boy must surrender to his destiny, or all is lost before it has begun. It is for this reason that he has been thrown in danger's path."

"Now you speak in riddles that no mortal may understand," Quellin responded. "If Brendys is truly the last hope of Milhavior, why present him as easy prey to the Deathlord's minions?"

"Unless Brendys gives in to the destiny laid on him, he cannot draw upon the power of Denasdervien," Etzel replied. "If he cannot draw upon the power of the Living Flame, there is no region of the entire known and unknown world that can protect him from the wrath of Thanatos."

Quellin nodded, Etzel's words finally becoming clear to him. "So he has been placed in the center of a battle between powers whose existence he has denied at every turn, in order to force him to acknowledge them."

"That is my belief," Etzel replied. "Again, these things have been hidden from me, but I *believe* this to be true. Once he has acknowledged the Flame and the Shadow, he will have taken the first step on the path to Truth, and to his destiny. However, Thanatos will use fear and hatred to draw Brendys from that path. We must be ever vigilant, lest he strays."

"Vigilance?" Quellin said quietly. "First we must defeat the undefeatable and drive back the Darkness, else our vigilance will be wasted."

Etzel barked out a short laugh. "Your Majesty, I have told you before, fear not for Gildea. Thanatos may not claim victory in Milhavior unless he himself comes forth to conquer. That he *cannot* do.

"He cannot defy his banishment. He cannot return to this Realm until his appointed time, unless the Heir is slain.

Shadows may rule, yes. But I think not. Night will break and the Dawn shall rise forth from the Shadows. Take heed and take heart."

Quellin nodded, only half-reassured by her words.

* * * *

Brendys recovered quickly from his most recent ordeal, and with a strength of heart that he had lost upon his first encounter with the Drolar. Despite the fact that he knew he was still being hunted by the creature, he found his courage strangely rallied by the knowledge he had gained in the Vision Realm. His life was no longer the only one in jeopardy.

Within a few days, he was strong enough to help with the chores. And help he did, for he had become weary of staring at grey walls all day. After pointing out to Quellin that the Kubruki were undoubtedly already aware of his presence in Etzel's house, he was permitted to assist the younger boys with their labors. But he could go no farther than the goat pens behind the house, the limits of Etzel's protection.

Goats.

Brendys followed Brumagin and Kovar out to the goat pen, little Bipin trailing quietly behind him. Brendys hated goats. To him, they were nothing but noisy, smelly beasts with no reasonable use. His father's horses may have been noisy and smelly at times, but at least they were practical. He would much rather have been helping Gowan with the fishing-boat—though boats and fish did not settle well with him, either—but for the sake of his own safety, he could not leave Etzel's domain. Nevertheless, Brendys wanted to help in any way that he could, thus he did his share without vocal complaint.

As the boys entered the fenced enclosure, Brumagin's mother, looking ragged and overworked, her dusky hair tied back with a thin strip of cloth, called to her son from a small dwelling a few yards from Etzel's goat pen.

Brendys watched as Brumagin scrambled over the fence and hurried to his mother's side. The Shalkane youth noticed a pair of Kubruk guards standing only a few yards away. One watched Brumagin closely, while the other stared in Brendys's direction, but neither moved.

Brendys allowed himself a brief defiant glare in the Kubruki's direction, knowing that the creatures were watching for him. Shortly, Brendys's gaze drifted back to Brumagin and his mother.

With a furtive glance at the Kubruki, the woman handed her son a small, folded piece of paper. "Give this t' the Man, Bru."

"Aye, Mama." The boy slipped the bit of paper into the rope around his waist.

Brumagin's small sister, Fey, came out of the cottage, dragging a dirty and torn rag-doll behind her. She wrinkled her nose as she passed her brother. "Ye smell, Bru!"

Brumagin gave the girl a soft kick on the bottom, then ran back to the goat pen.

Fey briefly fumed to her mother, then went about playing with her doll.

"What's that?" Brendys asked as Brumagin clambered back over the fence.

Brumagin glanced over his shoulder towards the Kubruki, then whispered in reply, "List o' goods. Weapons and what kind . . . we been gatherin' since they come. It's fer 'is Majesty."

"I'll take it to him," Brendys said, holding out his hand.

Brumagin pulled the scrap of paper from his makeshift belt and passed it to the Shalkane youth. "Ye're jes' lookin' fer a way outta workin'."

Brendys grinned. "I know."

He took the paper from Brumagin, then turned and started back to the house. A sudden outburst of frightened voices and children screaming halted Brendys in his steps.

From the edge of his vision, Brendys saw Kovar clamp a hand over Bipin's mouth, before the youngster could utter a sound, and drag him down amidst the goats. At the same time, Brumagin's mother frantically rushed to retrieve Fey. But she was too late. A large, scaled hand shoved her away from the child before she could pick her little girl up.

Three more Kubruki pressed into view.

Then came Iysh Mawvath.

The giant Sorcerer scooped up Fey with one hand and lifted her up to look at her, the girl shrieking in terror.

"Nay! Please, don't!" the girl's mother screamed.

She tried to pull her child away from the Warlord, but Iysh Mawvath whipped the back of his armored hand across her cheek. The woman struck the wall of her home, then collapsed to the ground and there remained, one side of her face torn and bleeding.

Brumagin started forward with a distressed cry. "Mama! Fey!"

Brendys caught him before he could get very far and held the struggling boy back.

Iysh Mawvath turned to face Brendys, and the youth froze. As he stared into the shadowed sockets of the Sorcerer's skull-shaped helm, images of his nightmare aboard the Scarlet Mariner were drawn to his mind. The rest of the dream had already come to pass, and now this. Before him stood a monster with a skull for a head.

Iysh Mawvath's pale armor gleamed with a cold light in the Shadow, evidence of his supernatural being. Brendys tried to tear his eyes from the sight, but he could neither turn away, nor blink. Fear seared his being like a red-hot brand. His heart began to pound as the Sorcerer handed Brumagin's screaming sister to one of the Kubruki and strode towards the pen.

Iysh Mawvath stopped suddenly, less than a foot away from the goat pen, as though there were some impenetrable barrier between him and the fence. Brendys could see his fierce eyes now. The giant held his gaze steady, pouring dread into his heart, until the youth gave a cry. Iysh Mawvath burst out with such laughter that Brendys felt his spine would crumble to dust.

"So *this* is the mighty Bearer of the Flame," Iysh Mawvath said in a low voice. He laughed again, freezing Brendys's heart. Still laughing, Iysh Mawvath turned and walked away, taking his guards and little Fey with him.

When Iysh Mawvath was gone, Brendys released Brumagin. The boy hurried to his mother's side, Brendys following him.

Brumagin dropped to the ground and shook his mother, tears streaming down his face, his voice cracking uncontrollably. "Mama! Please, Mama!"

Brendys knelt down beside the lad and felt the woman's neck and heart for any sign of life. He slowly drew Brumagin back from the body. "She's dead, Bru."

At first, the boy stared in disbelief, then he let his head drop against the older boy's chest and wept.

Brendys put his arms around Brumagin and tried to comfort him, but could not.

"What happened?"

Brendys looked up, on the verge of tears himself. Quellin and the others had come after the commotion had died down.

Brendys dropped his gaze down to the body, then raised his eyes back up to meet Quellin's. "He-he killed Bru's mother and took Fey. He was a giant."

Quellin looked upon the body of the woman for only a brief moment, expressionless, then turned away without a word and walked back to the house.

Brendys grew angry at the Gildean king's seeming lack of feeling. "Does the man have no heart!"

"*Brendys!*" Etzel said, her sharp voice quickly silencing Brendys. "Do not judge where you do not have the right. You do not know the grief His Majesty bears. He shares the full suffering of his people, dies with every child sacrificed by the devil-king.

"Aye, he has a heart, but it has grown cold with hatred for Iysh Mawvath. Expect no tears until Iysh Mawvath is no more!"

Brendys did not reply, but turned his face away from the woman, regretful of his hasty tongue.

Brendys and Gowan buried Brumagin's mother a short time later, and Etzel performed a brief funeral ceremony, then all returned to Etzel's house.

That night, Brendys lay in his bed, once more questioning in his mind why he was placed in such a desperate situation. He did not put out his lamp, for his fear of the Shadow had been renewed, and his dark thoughts only added to the gloom. He wondered to what purpose was he forced to witness and experience the suffering of Gildea? To what end would this ordeal lead? He closed his eyes and tried to go to sleep, but could not.

Visions of that afternoon flooded his mind, images of fear and death and sorrow. Why was this happening to him? What had he done to bring such a fate upon himself?

Brendys felt movement on the bed, and a small, shivering body huddled against his own. He raised himself up on his elbows and looked down at the child.

Bipin at first seemed surprised to find Brendys in his bed, but then realized his error. His brow furrowed and his lips quivered in a frightened frown. "I'm afraid, Brendys."

The Shalkane turned on his side, propping his head up with his left hand, and nodded understandingly. He pulled the blankets over Bipin and patted the boy's little shoulder. Bipin snuggled closer to the Shalkane.

Brendys stared at the boy, ashamed of his selfish thoughts. He understood now that he had never known what true suffering was. He had only received a small taste of what the Gildeans were going through. He was only now beginning to realize fully the hell that yet lay ahead.

Bipin stared back, his tender eyes, moist with tears, reflected Brendys's own fears and confusion.

At that moment, Brendys knew one thing for certain: one way or another, he would be the death of Iysh Mawvath.

Chapter 16

The Dusklight came and went with the turning of the days, until finally it wavered. The sensation was palpable—a spreading ripple in the air like a large stone dropped in a calm pond. It awakened all the denizens of Gildea Keep, both human and Kubruk. The Dusklight itself began to give way. No longer did it block all color—instead, the air took on a faint reddish hue.

Quellin was not sure whether to take the change as an omen for good or ill. The red haze seemed to strike terror in the hearts of all the city's inhabitants, good or evil. The Drolar ceased to roam the Night Hours and the Kubruki relaxed their vigil on Etzel's house, not daring to come near. However, a sense of dread also struck the hearts of the Gildeans with the coming of the haze—a sense of approaching death. Quellin questioned Etzel about the haze, but she refused to discuss it. She again pointed him to her library, so he gathered together an armload of scrolls and took them to the front room to study them in relative comfort.

He found Mattina sitting on a couch in the front room, a stack of mending piled beside her. She was considered a very fine seamstress among the Gildean courtiers, but none of them had ever openly admitted to that. Jealousy had abounded everywhere because she was of Trostain blood, but he knew that at that moment her mind was not on mending. She was thinking of a foolish youth from a far land—a youth that Quellin knew was far more.

Quellin sat down on the second couch across from his sister and began to study the first scroll in the pile. That particular scroll detailed mysterious events in the history of Milhavior and the Dawn Wars between Death's Legion and the Alliance of the Free Kindreds. He hoped to find some clue that could help him rise up against the might of Iysh Mawvath and his armies of Kubruki.

After a few minutes, Brendys came into the room, heading towards the kitchen in the rear of the house. He stopped before leaving and turned to Quellin.

"Kovar asked for some help this morning. You will know where to find me if you need me."

Quellin distractedly nodded to the youth. Kovar needed his help now. Brumagin had not stirred from the room he had been given.

Brendys continued on his way without another word.

Mattina's eyes raised to the corridor as Brendys moved out of sight.

Quellin looked at her, then to the corridor, then back again.

The young Princess noticed her brother's curious observation and quickly returned to her work, without a word, avoiding his eyes.

Quellin's heart chilled. His studies had revealed to him one thing thus far: if Brendys was indeed the Bearer of the Flame, his lot was not to be a happy one . . . now his sister seemed to be throwing hers in with him. He watched Mattina as she worked with her mending, his gaze never leaving her face. After a moment, he spoke. "Mattina, tell me—what is it that you see in Brendys?"

She stopped her work and gave him an innocent look. "What do you mean, Quellin?"

Quellin gave her a knowing look. "Now, don't play the fool with me, dear sister. You know very well and good what I mean. You have been ogling over him ever since Gowan dragged him out of the river!"

"Perhaps I have," Mattina returned, avoiding her brother's gaze. "What does it matter now?"

Quellin sighed. "Such a thing is not possible, Mattina. He is a commoner, and you are royalty. The nobles would never permit such a union, no matter your feelings or mine."

Mattina flashed an angry look at her brother, but did not speak. Instead, she stood up, gathered her mending, and returned to her quarters.

Quellin lowered his gaze to the scroll in his lap, with a pang of guilt and anger at himself. But he could not allow himself to back down. He could not allow his sister to share Brendys's fate.

"Why do you deny her, my son?"

Quellin started at the voice. Queen Sherren stood in the doorway through which Mattina had vanished. "It is unthinkable . . . the people would never accept such a union. It is positively scandalous."

"The people will accept what their King decrees," Sherren replied. "Do you think for a moment that the nobles were pleased that Treiber chose *you* as his successor, or that it was any less scandalous in their eyes?"

Before Quellin could respond, Sherren continued. "Of course not . . . but despite their grumbling, they would not deny their King. My son, unless the Dawn King himself frees us from Iysh Mawvath's grasp, the ruling Houses are dead. Release your sister."

Quellin lowered his gaze. Frowning, he stared off into nothing. Silence hung thick in the Shadow.

"Quellin, Mattina has set her heart," his foster mother pressed. "Will you destroy it?"

Quellin brought his piercing stare to meet Sherren's. "It is for her sake that I deny her. I have learned much of what is to be from Etzel's scrolls. This I know to be true, the Bearer of the Flame will live a life of grief and loss...."

"And you are trying to protect Mattina from that life." Sherren shook her head. "You cannot. Think, Quellin... she has scorned every worthy suitor brought before her, but now this coarse and unlovely stableboy from a land she had never heard of has won her heart, despite a bleak destiny. Do you truly believe it chance?"

Quellin could only glare back in silence, for he knew she was right. His sister's course—indeed, his own—had been set before them. There would be no turning back.

* * * *

Brendys grunted as he stood up from beside the goat he had just finished milking. He picked up his pail with a sigh, but before turning back to Etzel's kitchen, his gaze fell upon the place where Iysh Mawvath had slain Brumagin's mother and taken his sister. He shuddered involuntarily. Fey had been publicly sacrificed shortly thereafter, within sight of Etzel's house.

He recognized the gesture for what it was... a taunt aimed at himself, challenging him to defy the Sorcerer. Quellin claimed he was the Bearer of the Flame of Elekar, just as Asghar had. He could not accept that, but apparently he was the only one—even the Warlord of Thanatos believed it.

A short cry and the clatter of a pail drew his attention away from that spot. He turned to see Shanor sprawled face down in a puddle of goat milk and manure.

Grimacing, the blonde boy stood up and shook grime from his arms.

"This is humiliating," Shanor muttered.

Kovar laughed. "What's wrong, Yer Lordship? Ain't ne'er 'ad t' work afore?"

Brendys could not suppress the grin tugging at his lips. Shanor wore his nobility with arrogance, never lowering himself to common chores. He was only helping—of his own will, Brendys had to admit—because Brumagin was still in mourning.

Shanor's sour expression melted away into wonder as he stared past the Shalkane youth.

Brendys and Kovar both turned in time to watch a large hawk alight upon the fence of the goat pen with a loud scream. Even in the red haze of the Shadow, Brendys was sure the bird was pure white.

The hawk stared straight at Brendys for a moment. There was an intelligence in the bird's gaze that unnerved him. The bird began to squawk out decidedly un-birdlike sounds.

"'er name's Amrein."

Brendys looked at Kovar. The boy was still staring at the bird in wonder. "What are you talking about?"

Kovar slowly broke into a delighted smile. "She said so . . . 'er name's Amrein. She 'uz sent 'ere from th' 'aganes wit' a message fer King Quellin!"

Shanor snorted. "You're daft. Bird's don't talk . . . leastwise, not hawks."

Brendys looked from the bird to Kovar, then back again. He was at first inclined to agree with Shanor, but recalling the hawk's gaze and the sounds it made, he was not absolutely certain. "You can understand it?"

"Aye," Kovar said with a quick nod. "Don't know 'ow, but I can! An' it's a 'er, not an it."

Brendys looked at Amrein and shrugged. "All right . . . her."

The hawk returned his gaze, cocking its head curiously.

Brendys watched the bird with interest and hope. If, indeed, she had come from Lord Dell, then that much of his experience in Reanna Orilal was true. And there, he had seen Kradon, Folkor, and Asghar alive. After a moment, Brendys broke the silence. "What do we do with her now?"

Kovar gave him a wry look. "Take 'er to the King, o' course."

"And how do you propose we do that?" Brendys asked.

"Carry 'er, o' course," came the boy's reply.

Brendys once more soaked in the hawk's sharp talons and predatory gaze, then shook his head. "Not I . . . Quellin can come out here and chat with the bird himself."

"You are both daft," Shanor interjected.

Ignoring Shanor, Kovar answered Brendys with a sigh, "Cowart."

The boy started towards the hawk, but an angry hiss halted him.

A Kubruk appeared at the corner of the house next door. Seeing Amrein, the creature drew its curved scimitar and ran at the hawk with snakelike speed.

Brendys grabbed a pitchfork and leapt towards the fence, shoving Kovar back as he passed.

Amrein took wing as the Kubruk swung its weapon. The blade passed harmlessly through the air where the hawk had been perched a moment before. The Kubruk's momentum carried it forward into Brendys's outstretched hayfork. The tines burrowed completely into the Kubruk's chest. The creature crashed against the fence and collapsed to its knees, dead.

The force of the Kubruk's charge drove Brendys backwards. He lost his footing and landed hard on his back, the wind driven from his lungs. He rolled onto his knees, doubled over, gasping for breath. After a couple of minutes, he regained his composure. He climbed to his feet and jerked the pitchfork out of the Kubruk, letting the corpse slump to the ground, leaking black gore from its chest.

Amrein alighted on the fence once more, and Brendys and Kovar approached more cautiously. As they came closer, they could see that the hawk's talons were tipped with steel. Kovar stripped off his tunic and wrapped it around his right forearm, then held his arm up, supporting it with his left hand. To Brendys's surprise, Amrein hopped from the fence onto Kovar's arm without hesitation.

Brendys led the way back to the house with Kovar following him. Shanor retreated in fear of the hawk as they approached, then fell in behind Kovar. Brendys hurried ahead to find Quellin. As he came into the front room, he found Quellin sitting on a couch, staring across the room at Queen Sherren.

Quellin snapped a cold glance at Brendys as the youth entered the room. "What is it?"

Brendys hesitated, taken aback by the icy tone in Quellin's voice. "A messenger from outside has arrived."

Quellin came to his feet, his anger forgotten. "What? Where is he?"

"Kovar is bringing her in," Brendys replied. He shifted nervously under Quellin's gaze. "The messenger is a . . . a bird."

The Gildean King gaped in wonder as Kovar entered the room bearing Amrein. The hawk gazed back in silence, head cocked to get a better look at Quellin.

"*This* is the messenger?" Quellin asked.

"Aye, Yer Majesty," Kovar replied. "Her name is Amrein."

"I have heard of lesser birds used as couriers, but never a hunting hawk of this quality," Quellin said in amazement. He held his hand out towards the boys. "Where is the message?"

The bird turned its head to look at Kovar, then returned her gaze to the King of Gildea. She began to chirp and squawk in her strange form of speech.

Quellin's eyes widened. Slowly, he slumped back to the couch. "By Elekar. . . ."

Amrein continued to speak. Quellin, recovering his wits, listened intently to the tidings she brought. When she had finished, Quellin nodded.

"This much, Etzel and I determined from Brendys's experiences in Reanna Orilal," he said. "Lord Dell of Hagan has ridden to our defense alongside a force from Matadol and a company of Elves."

"Father made it through!" Shanor cried. "I knew it! I knew he would."

Quellin closed his eyes and lowered his head, what joy he had expressed before drowned by sorrow. For the first time, Brendys saw a tear form in his eye. The Gildean King drew in a deep breath and looked back up at Shanor. "Your father is dead, Shanor."

"Nay!" the boy returned. "He went for help and now they've come!"

Quellin shook his head. "Nay, Shanor, he did not. Iysh Mawvath killed him. I . . . I saw it happen. That is how I knew where the Kubruki were holding you."

Shanor stared at his King in disbelief. As tears began to well up in his eyes, he turned and ran from the house.

Quellin closed his eyes and drew in a deep breath, then looked around the room, putting behind his grief once more. "Lord Dell proposes to launch an attack against the main gate. A second assault shall ford Den Jostalen in an attempt to win to the gate from the inside."

Etzel and Arella moved into the room from an adjoining hallway.

"Then it shall be our duty to draw the Kubruki from the western side of the city," the old woman said with a nod to Quellin.

Arella looked at her in surprise. "With what? We have no arms."

"Not so," Quellin responded quickly. He produced a bloodstained piece of paper. "Brendys gave this to me the day Brumagin's mother was murdered. From throughout the city we have gathered over a hundred swords, some broken, but all serviceable. We have also over a thousand hayforks and other farming tools available."

"And there is a Kubruk outside that can vouch for the use of hayforks," Brendys added.

"But who will wield them?" Arella pressed. "Aside from Brendys and yourself and perhaps a few youths of Gowan's age, there are no men of fighting age left in the city."

"Then it falls to you and I," Etzel replied. "And to all the women and children of Gildea Keep."

As Arella started to object, Etzel interrupted. "Whose homes have been raped and pillaged, My Lady? Matadol? Racolis? Nay, Gildea. Yet the warriors of Hagan and Matadol have ridden far to sacrifice themselves for our people. The least we can do is sacrifice ourselves to aid them."

Quellin intervened with a sharp word. "*Nay!* I will not jeopardize Arella or Mattina. They shall remain here."

Etzel's gaze landed hard upon the Gildean King. Brendys shuddered as a wave of power engulfed the room. He watched as Quellin quailed back in fear, more like the boy he appeared, than the man he was. Quellin had always treated Etzel with a healthy respect, but never had Brendys seen such fear in his eyes.

"So, you would not send those you love to fight and die," Etzel snapped. "But you would send your people to the slaughter, for of what worth are they? What have they done to deserve life? What but to keep yours from being lost?

"Is *this* the King I have taken under my protection? A selfish boor who looks out for his own heart at the expense of his people? I did not believe it so, but now I must wonder."

A look of shock, then shame, replaced Quellin's fear. He slumped forward, burying his face in his hands. "Oh, Lord . . . is this a test I have failed? Indeed, when there was no threat to my heart, it could bleed for my people. But now . . . ?"

Brendys looked around the room. He saw shame on all the faces and knew that his must have shown the same, for each one of them would have hesitated to thrust another of them into danger's path.

Queen Sherren was the first to break the silence. "I am old and have not the strength for battle, but battle I shall."

Quellin leaned back, raising his head. "Aye, indeed we all must, as Etzel said. The people must see us and know that we do not ask them to do something we ourselves would avoid."

Etzel's features softened, and the power drained away from the room as though a stopper had been pulled. "Nay, not all. Queen Sherren, as you have said, you do not have the strength to wield a weapon against the Kubruki . . . there are better uses for such as you. Healers will be needed."

She looked again at Quellin. "And, indeed, Mattina should remain here. Though with my absence from this place, the house will not be protected, the Kubruki will be looking elsewhere for blood. Mattina should remain as safe as possible, for if you are lost, she will rule Gildea in your stead."

Brendys noticed Quellin glance quickly in his direction, his expression a mixture of fear and relief. The Gildean King then nodded to Etzel. "Indeed, I see the wisdom in that . . . though she will doubtless disagree."

A cold, almost cruel smile crossed the old woman's lips. "We are all forced to do things we do not wish."

Quellin glared back. Brendys wondered what unspoken words crossed the room in that gaze.

The door slammed open, and Shanor dashed into the room. Tears stained the boy's face, but they had been forgotten in a new burst of excitement. "They are here! Lord Dell's army. The Kubruki are fortifying the walls and the North Gate."

Quellin rose to his feet. "We haven't much time then. This is the hour of decision. I will force none to take up arms. The choice must be yours: will you stand with me?"

No one stirred for a moment, even Etzel, who had pressed for this action—though Brendys was certain her hesitation was intentional. Her gaze flitted searchingly across the faces of the household. Brendys lowered his eyes in shame when she looked upon him. He had already made his decision, but was afraid to speak out.

When no one else answered, he raised his eyes to meet Quellin's. "I have made this war my own for many reasons, but one above all: though I know a commoner like me could never hope to attain her, I love Mattina and would see her restored to her rightful place before the end. I will stand with you."

Brendys averted his gaze, glad that the red haze in the Dusklight hid the color rising to his cheeks. He had not failed to notice the look of astonishment that swept across Quellin's face, before looking away. Clearly, the Gildean King had not been expecting that speech from him. From the absolute silence in the room, Brendys gleaned that Quellin was not the only one shocked by his boldness.

Finally, as each found their voice, they all pledged their support, beginning with Arella.

Quellin turned to the younger boys. "Find Gowan and Brumagin. Spread out and take this message to every dwelling in the city: On the morrow, everyone who would have this city free must take up arms against the Kubruki. Those with the strength to bear swords can find arms at Brumagin's house. They should go in small numbers to fetch the blades so as not to arouse suspicion.

"Tomorrow, when the battle horns blow, they must draw the Kubruki towards the East Field, away from the North Gate and the river. Tell them to listen for my signal.

"Do you understand?"

The boys nodded in acknowledgment, then left the room.

Quellin looked next at the hawk, Amrein. "You have heard all that has been said. Return to your masters with this message: We shall be ready upon the morrow."

The hawk screamed once and launched herself through the door which Shanor had thrown open upon his return to the house.

"Brendys," Quellin started, turning towards the Shalkane youth.

Before he could finish, Brendys excused himself and headed for his room. He was in no mood for the lecture he was sure was coming. He had bared his feelings to everyone—everyone except Mattina—and knew that in doing so he may have estranged the royal lot that he had come to care so much for.

Not far down the hallway, he nearly walked into Mattina. Brendys was startled out of his thoughts. "Oh! I'm sorry. I wasn't paying attention to where I was going."

Mattina gave him a concerned look. "You seem troubled. Is something wrong?"

Brendys hesitated before answering. He was tempted to tell her his true feelings, though he was sure she knew—he was certain she felt the same—but he instead replied, "Tomorrow, we fight."

Mattina's eyes widened. "What?"

"The Haganes are already encamped outside the North Gate," Brendys answered. "It is our lot to distract the Kubruki from within."

"What is my brother thinking?" Mattina exclaimed. "Is he mad? The entire garrison of Gildea Keep could not turn the tide . . . what does he think an army of women and children can do against Iysh Mawvath. We are none of us warriors."

Brendys half-smiled. "Arella made the very same argument. It is an argument that cannot be won. Tomorrow, we fight."

"Do not make light of the situation, Brendys of Shalkan," Mattina snapped. "You don't know what Iysh Mawvath is capable of!"

Brendys's smile melted away, leaving behind a grim frown. His voice lowered ominously. "I do know. That is why I, at least, must fight."

Mattina stared at him in alarm. "Brendys, he is just waiting for you to leave the confines of Etzel's ward! He would kill you!"

"Etzel is determined, herself, to fight," Brendys replied quietly. "She told us that her ward will lift when she leaves the house. I will not be safe here or anywhere else."

His eyes fastened onto hers. "But you will. With me gone, the Kubruki will not come here."

"What do you mean?" Mattina shot back. "If Gildea is to revolt, do you think I will sit idly by while others die?"

Brendys smiled gently. "As you would have me do, you mean?"

Mattina looked away. "That is different. Iysh Mawvath is waiting for you. . . ."

"And you don't want to see me harmed," Brendys interjected. "Because you love me."

Mattina's eyes snapped back to Brendys, a look of indignance coming over her face.

"Don't look at me that way," Brendys said, his expression turning serious. "You know it is the truth. I am not the only one who has seen it."

Mattina broke into an embarrassed grin and lowered her gaze.

Brendys gently lifted her chin to look her in the face once more. His gaze was solemn. "That is why I am asking you to let me be your sword. Love is something I have never really known . . . but I confess that I have loved you since the first."

For a long moment, they stared into each other's eyes. Finally, Mattina gave a slight nod and whispered, "Very well, Brendys of Shalkan . . . you shall be my sword."

She stepped closer to Brendys and raised her lips to meet his.

Brendys pulled her into his arms and held her there. He had wished for this moment for a long time and now he savored it, for he knew it was likely he would not survive the coming storm. How strange, he thought, that he should be cast into this plight—to learn true love—only to face death. If indeed it was the design of the Dawn King, then that being was truly as cruel as Brendys had always believed.

Quellin cleared his throat.

Brendys released Mattina with a start and spun to face the Gildean King, his heart thudding in fear. "I . . . I can explain this. . . ."

Quellin strained to keep a straight expression. "I believe you already did, a little while ago."

"He did?" Mattina asked, wrinkling her brow.

Quellin inclined his head to his sister. "Indeed. Brendys told us in no uncertain terms in council that he loves you. He is either a very brave lad, or a very stupid one."

Brendys muttered, "I believe the latter is more likely."

"Mattina, would you excuse us?" Quellin asked firmly, though politely. "There are matters I must discuss with Brendys in private."

His sister glanced at the Shalkane youth, then back at him. She nodded silently and continued into the front room to find Arella and Sherren.

Quellin held Brendys in his gaze for a long moment before speaking. "Brendys, I was not convinced I should do this . . . until now."

Brendys swallowed. What discipline the Gildean King had in mind, he could only imagine.

"If, when this is over and you return home, your feelings for my sister remain the same—and likewise," Quellin continued. "You have my oath that if you wish to take Mattina's hand in marriage, you will have the permission and the blessing of the Throne of Gildea."

Brendys gaped at the Gildean King, unable to reply. He had not expected this. "Quellin. . . ."

Quellin raised his hand, silencing Brendys. "You are a young fool, Brendys of Shalkan, but an honorable fool and fool with a destiny. May the Dawn King guide your heart."

The Gildean King turned and walked back down the hall, leaving an astonished Brendys alone in the corridor.

Chapter 17

Lord Dell squinted in the bloody haze of the Dusklight as the flap of his pavilion was pulled back and Lord Guthwine entered. The Elvinlord's eyes glinted brightly, despite the gloom of the Shadow.

"Amrein has returned, My Lord. Quellin of Trost does indeed live and is now King of Gildea. He sends word that his people shall be prepared to fight on the morrow."

Dell nodded. "Then if Iysh Mawvath does not sally against us before then, we should have the element of surprise on our side."

A slight smile tugged at Lord Guthwine's lips. "Amrein brought other news, as well. There was a youth present with King Quellin by the name of Brendys."

Dell rose to his feet in astonishment. "Brendys? He *is* alive?"

"Did you truly doubt the words of Odyniec?" the Elf asked, a sage expression on his face.

"After what my son and his companions reported?" the Hagane Lord replied. "Aye, I doubted . . . what was I supposed to think?"

Guthwine smiled mysteriously. "Perhaps now you will trust the words of the Wizard? He knows much that even I cannot, without walking the Road to Elekar."

Dell lowered his gaze, a thoughtful look passing over his features. Indeed, everything Odyniec had told him thus far had proven true. After a moment, he raised his eyes towards the flap. "Kinnon!"

One of his guardsmen stepped inside. "My Lord?"

"Summon Lord Kradon and the Captains," Dell commanded. "Tell them we have received word from Gildea Keep. I would meet with them immediately."

The warrior snapped his right fist to his heart. "At your command, My Lord."

The Hagane Lord's eyes met Lord Guthwine's. "We have a council to attend."

The Elf inclined his head to Lord Dell and followed the Man out of the pavilion.

They waited until all of the captains had gathered together before beginning. When the council was arrayed, Dell arose and faced them.

"I wish to begin with an apology to Master Odyniec." His eyes strayed to his son, his voice softening. "And to Kradon. The hawk, Amrein, has returned with word from Quellin of Trost, now King in Gildea. Brendys of Shalkan, alleged Bearer of the Flame, is indeed alive and dwelling at Gildea Keep. Forgive me for doubting you."

Dell's gaze drifted back to the captains. "King Quellin also sends word that his people shall provide us our distraction. They shall draw the Kubruki away from the western reaches of the city, so that our infiltrators may cross the river in safety."

Marshal Allard frowned. "I thought only women and children remained in the city? How could they be of aid in this?"

Lord Guthwine smiled at him. "I said only that I did not *see* any men, Marshal. And do not underestimate the fighting spirit of these women. They have lived hard lives and would be willing to die for their land and their children."

Marshal Allard glared at the Elf, but remained silent.

Lord Dell turned to Royal Marshal Spiridon. "Marshal, have you selected the men who will accompany my son?"

Spiridon nodded. "Aye, My Lord. I have chosen seventeen of my best swordsmen and five Elvin archers, including Lord Guthwine. The last two places are reserved for Captain Folkor and Delvecaptain Asghar, by their request."

Dell's gaze flitted briefly to his son, a sudden shadow crossing his heart.

Marshal Spiridon continued. "The ferry raft we brought from Tarlas has been reassembled. When the attack on the gate begins, we shall be ready to do our part."

"Thank you, Marshal," Dell acknowledged. "I have commanded that a double guard be posted tonight, in case the Kubruki seek to force our hand.

"Unless there are questions, I suggest we retire. We shall have need of such strength at the breaking of the dawn as we have never known before."

Lord Dell paused to allow for questions or comments. When none were forthcoming, he rose to his feet. "May the gods go with us."

* * * *

Ere the breaking of the Night Hours, Kradon's infiltrators arose. With as much stealth as they could muster in the absolute darkness of the Night Hours, they carried the raft to the river bank and began a slow, silent journey down Den Jostalen towards the western edge of Gildea Keep. By the time they were in place, Lord Dell's forces had arrayed themselves for battle and formed ranks to assault the gate and the North Wall.

Lord Dell sat astride his charger beside Odyniec. His eyes strained futilely to pierce the Darkness in the direction Odyniec had told him the Keep lay. The whisper of shuffling robes drew Dell's attention.

"My Lord, it is almost time," he heard Odyniec whisper in the Shadow.

With a sharp hiss, Dell's sword slid from his scabbard. He raised the blade above his head, waiting for Odyniec's signal. Dell hoped in his heart that Quellin's people were prepared as well, for if their timing was off, their efforts might be in vain.

* * * *

Kradon stood near the front of the ferry. Asghar stood on his right and Folkor on his left. His gaze wandered, but in no direction could his eyes pierce the Darkness. He heard Asghar stir beside him.

"We near the wall of the city," he heard the Dwarf mutter. "Be prepared."

Kradon quietly drew his sword and unslung his shield. Prepared? How could anyone be prepared for the bloodbath to come? Nevertheless, he whispered a quick prayer and tensed himself.

* * * *

Without warning, the red haze of the weakening Dusklight burst forth. With it came a loud thundercrack and a blast of white light from Odyniec's staff. Dell's sword arm fell, signaling the charge.

Heralds sounded their trumpets and the host surged forward, sweeping around Dell and Odyniec. The cavalry halted behind their Lord as the last ranks of footmen passed. Warriors bearing tall ladders and ropes with scaling hooks rushed towards the wall under the protection of Elvin arrows. The Kubruki rained arrows and large stones down upon them, maiming and slaying many, but for every Man who died, three Kubruki tumbled back from the wall, clutching at the shafts which sprouted from their bodies.

Dell watched helplessly as his warriors expended themselves upon the assault. The Elvin archers wreaked havoc upon the Kubruki, yet it was not enough. Their numbers were so great that the fallen were replaced almost as they died. He turned an expectant gaze on Odyniec, but the Wizard shook his head.

"My strength shall be needed when we have pressed into the city," Odyniec said, rightly interpreting the man's gaze.

"*When* we press into the city?" Dell shouted above the din. "*If* is more like it. At this rate, our forces shall be crushed in short order!"

Odyniec did not respond.

Dell looked towards the river, but the ferry bearing his son had already passed from view. His gaze swept across the walls. His heart leapt both with hope and fear as more Kubruki abandoned their posts. He did not doubt the infiltrators had begun their attack. Little by little, Dell's warriors began to mount the wall, forcing the Kubruki into a melee upon the parapet.

The Hagane Lord turned his steed to face the cavalry. In a loud voice, he cried, "Arms at ready! The gate shall be ours!"

* * * *

Kradon felt the ferry bump to a stop against land and knew they had passed the city wall. As the Dusklight weakened the Shadow, Kradon found himself face-to-face with a Kubruk warrior. Before the creature could raise an alarm, Kradon whipped his sword from its sheath and across the creature's throat.

The trumpets of the host sounded from beyond the North Wall, signaling the assault. Cries sounded from within the city as well, but Kradon's eyes could not pierce that far into the murk.

The youth pointed his sword in the direction of the North Gate. "Marshal, take your men and press towards the gate. I shall seek out King Quellin."

"Not alone you won't," Folkor rumbled.

Asghar hefted his axe and stepped to the sailor's side.

Lord Guthwine spoke a few words in Elvin to his archers, then turned towards Kradon. "I am honor-bound to your father to protect you, and so I will."

Kradon nodded once, then said, "Let us go."

Men, Elf, and Dwarf headed off at a trot in the direction of the battle within the city, while Royal Marshal Spiridon and his warriors, with the four remaining Elves, made with all stealth towards the North Gate.

Kradon marveled that the Kubruki had left that part of the city so badly undefended, but it was not long before he and his companions came into view of the battle. A roiling mass of Kubruki pressed slowly eastward, leaving behind them the tattered corpses of the women and children who dared defy them. Many of their own kind also lay dead upon the field, slain by sword or axe or less noble, but no less deadly weapons.

A golden light beyond the line of Kubruki broke through the eerie red haze. Kradon pointed towards the light. "This way! They will need our aid!"

His companions close behind, Kradon charged forward. As they ran, Guthwine let fly arrow after arrow, each Elvinsilver shaft blazing with argent fire as it dropped among the mass of Kubruki. Kradon, Folkor, and Asghar fell upon the rear guard, slaying several of the reptilian creatures before they were noticed.

A Kubruk swung its curved scimitar at Kradon, but the youth deflected the blow with his shield. The force of the swing still knocked Kradon to the ground. He rolled to the left, avoiding another attack. With an upward thrust, Kradon spitted the creature through the sternum before it could pull its weapon free from the earth.

The Hagane youth climbed to his feet and glanced around to gain his bearings. Catching sight of golden light once more, he pressed on, slicing indiscriminately at every Kubruk within reach. Finally, he broke through the enemy lines and nearly stumbled over a pair of scythe-wielding children. A quick survey of the area brought bile to his throat. The mutilated bodies of hundreds of women and children were strewn about the visible portion of the field, piled atop each other and a far smaller number of Kubruk corpses. The Haganes had come to free Gildea Keep, but the last remnant of that city was fast dwindling to extinction.

With an enraged cry that startled both Kubruk and human, Kradon plunged back into the melee. The humans, child and adult alike, recovered more quickly than the dull-witted Kubruki and renewed their assault, dealing out several deathblows before their enemies could react. Kradon lost track of time as the battle raged on, intent only on destroying as many of the invaders as possible. It was not until the Kubruki began to withdraw towards Keep Hill that he noticed Folkor, Asghar, and Guthwine had rejoined him.

As he moved to pursue the retreating creatures, Folkor grabbed him by the arm.

"Let them go!" the sea captain yelled over the din. "They are regrouping their forces, and we need to do the same or we shall be overwhelmed."

"I can see our forces gathering about a Man wielding an Elvinsword," Lord Guthwine said, staring off towards the source of the light they had seen. "That would be King Quellin. We should join them there."

Kradon nodded, then called to all within hearing to follow him.

* * * *

Before the blackness of the Night Hours fell into the murky red Dusklight and the battle for Gildea's freedom began, the defenders of Gildea Keep had armed themselves, prepared to fight and die for their home. Brendys had not slept much, anticipation and anxiety fueling his restlessness. He did not hesitate to rise with the others when the time came.

While he was dressing, his gaze fell upon the Elvinsword, and he once again felt drawn to the weapon. Despite the fact that he could not draw the sword, its hidden power still sent forth a call to him, plaguing his mind until he acknowledged it. He found a belt long enough to use as a harness and fastened Denasdervien to his back, then threw on his cloak and joined the others in the front room.

Quellin had girt Kalter once more. No longer was he dressed in peasant attire, but was instead garbed in the same clothing that he had worn during the Fall—light-green tunic, red hosen, leather boots, and the tan cloak bearing his family's coat-of-arms, though their colors were muted to various shades of grey in the Darkness. He had also donned the battered and fire-tarnished silver crown once belonging to his late liege-lord, Treiber.

Brendys watched the Gildean King through the dull candlelight as he stared blindly out a northward window. Finally, Quellin turned to his companions. "By now, the others will have taken up positions. When the Dusklight comes, we must be prepared for battle. Brendys, you, Gowan, and Kovar guard the northeastern corner of the house. Brumagin and I will take the northwestern."

"And I, Your Majesty?" Etzel asked in a stern voice.

Quellin barked a short laugh. "My Lady, I would not deign to instruct you, who have instructed me for greater benefit. Defend what position you will and in your own way."

"I thought you would see it that way," came Etzel's satisfied response.

"All right, time is short," Quellin said, motioning his arm to the door.

With quiet acknowledgement, Gowan and Kovar hurried out the door.

Brendys started to follow his younger companions, but Mattina grabbed him and embraced him with a kiss.

"I love you," she said in his ear, her voice quavering slightly.

Brendys was glad for the darkness of the room as he blushed. He looked at Quellin over Mattina's shoulder, but the King's youthful face was unreadable in the shadows. Drawing Mattina away, he looked into her face with a smile. "You've given me all the reason I need to live."

He turned and walked out of the house, using the wall of the building to guide him to his post. As he joined Gowan and Kovar, he said slowly and quietly. "Do you think we will make it through this?"

Neither of the boys replied, but the smell of nervous sweat gave Brendys the answer to his question.

They waited in silence for the last few minutes before the bloody dawn they knew was coming. Soon, the hazy Dusklight burst forth into existence, and with it came the sound of horns and battle cries. The armies outside the city walls were charging. Shortly after the cries of the first charge, Brendys could hear the sounds of a second assault from the direction of the river.

He could see the faint shadows of Kubruki moving across the North Field from the North Wall to the river to meet the challenge. He glanced towards Quellin and saw the Gildean King nod in return. Quellin drew Kalter from its sheath, and its golden fire blazed to life.

Raising his sword, Quellin cried out in a loud voice, *"For Gildea!"*

His battle cry was repeated in a roar of voices as his people surged forward from hiding places throughout the city. Brendys and his companions drew their own weapons, but held their ground. The green light of Volker, Quellin's Elvinknife, pierced the red haze of the Dusklight as Gowan drew the weapon from its sheath. Brendys believed he could almost hear a faint hiss from the Stajouhar gemblade.

The Kubruki reacted quickly to the new threat. The force which had started towards the river turned to meet the Gildeans. Even as the Gildean people swept forward to engage them, Quellin, Brendys, and their companions continued to hold their ground. The Kubruki smashed through the wall of peasant women and children with savage ferocity.

Quellin shouted out a command, and the Gildeans began to withdraw to the South Field, the Kubruki following. The Kubruki who passed near Etzel's house seemed to lag, as if slowed by a heavy burden. Etzel's ward had not yet collapsed entirely.

Brendys slashed at the Kubruk nearest him, but his sword clattered off the beast's buckler.

The creature swung the stave of its spear up, striking the youth in the jaw.

Brendys fell back, stunned. He could taste the saltiness of blood in his mouth. As he struggled to keep hold of his senses, he saw the Kubruk plant its large feet in front of him and lift its weapon in the air. He fixed his eyes upon the point of the spear and tried to roll out of the way, but his body would not respond to the commands of his mind.

In a flash of green light, the Kubruk suddenly bellowed in agony, then dropped sideways to the ground, a trail of smoke rising from its back. Gowan started to reach a hand down to Brendys, but another Kubruk came at him from behind, brandishing a scimitar. Gowan fell forward atop Brendys as the creature swung its weapon.

"Gowan!" Brendys cried. He rolled out from under Gowan's limp form, rising to his feet. With a powerful thrust of his own sword, he drove the Kubruk back into the wall of Etzel's house. The creature's scimitar fell from its grasp as it collapsed.

Before Brendys could pull his weapon free, he was driven to his knees by a blow from behind. With a sharp ring, the Kubruk's blade shattered, unable to penetrate the thrumming token of power strapped to the youth's back. Brendys threw himself against Etzel's house, facing his foe.

The creature lunged forward with bloodied claws stretched forth. In a flash of light, the Kubruk was hurtled aside as it was struck by a ball of argent fire. Brendys look toward the source of the fire and saw Etzel standing several feet away, hands outstretched.

The old woman hurried forward and knelt beside Gowan. She carefully picked up Volker and slid the Elvinknife into its sheath at Gowan's belt. She glanced up at Brendys. "I will tend to the boy. The battle is not yet over here."

She lifted Gowan in her arms as if the youth were but a rag doll and stood up. As Etzel disappeared into her house, Brendys rose to his feet and jerked his sword from its victim's carcass.

"Bren'ys!"

Brendys spun around to see Kovar being beaten back by a Kubruk nearly twice the boy's size. He had all but forgotten the other boy in the press of the battle. Before he could react, a piercing scream filled the air as a bird plunged from the sky full into the face of the Kubruk, its talons burning with an Elvin fire. It took Brendys a moment to realize it was Amrein the hawk. While the Kubruk was distracted, both Brendys and Kovar drove their weapons into the creature's body.

As the Kubruk toppled over, Amrein alighted upon Kovar's outstretched arm. Brendys noticed thin streams of blood running from where the bird's Elvinsteel-tipped talons had pierced the boy's arm, but Kovar did not seem to notice. He conversed calmly with the hawk, unmindful of his pain.

Brendys looked across the battlefield. The Kubruki had pressed back towards the North Wall. The gate had clearly been won, and Lord Dell's forces were now pouring into the city.

He surveyed the open carnage in stunned silence. He had seen violence in his life, but never the utter devastation he was witnessing now. The murders of Brumagin's mother and sister both sickened him, yet strengthened his resolve to fight, but what he saw now—the butchered corpses of women, children, even Kubruki— numbed him to his core.

Kovar's voice summoned a small amount of life back into him. "Bren'ys? Are ye a'right?"

Brendys let his sword slip from his grasp. He looked down at his blood-smeared hands and fell to his knees. His words caught in his throat, but were forced out with a choked cry. "What in Hál am I doing here!"

Wracking sobs shook him as he covered his face with his hands. He could here Amrein's scream and the beat of her wings as she took flight. He could hear Kovar cry out, "Bren'ys, they're comin' again!" He could hear the sounds of battle draw nearer, but he did not move, nor stop weeping. At that moment, he wished nothing more than for oblivion to take him. He could sense movement around him and could hear Quellin calling to him, but his mind would not respond to the summons.

The Gildean King grasped Brendys's shoulders and shook him hard. "Damn it, boy! Get up!"

Brendys raised his tear-clouded eyes to meet Quellin's soul-piercing gaze, but did not flinch.

Quellin leaned closer and hissed, "So, you would betray Mattina after all?"

Mattina? Betray her? Brendys angrily slapped the Gildean King's hands away from him. Grabbing up his sword, he rose to his feet. "You bloody son of a... !"

The traces of a grin played at Quellin's lips. "That's the fire you need, boy . . . now use it!"

Kalter lit the Shadow once more as Quellin turned to face the oncoming foe.

Brendys glared at the Gildean King for a moment, letting anger boil within him, yet still afraid to face the carnage again. He cast a last glance towards Etzel's house, then turned and leapt towards the rush of Kubruki with a cry, not allowing himself any time to think about his actions. A wave of Gildeans swept around Etzel's house to join the fray.

Soon, the battle crashed down around him. Brendys lost all sense of time. How long the battle raged, he did not know. Heedless, he struck out at every Kubruk which came within his reach, swinging his broadsword with both hands like a berserker, afraid that if he allowed himself to think, he would lose himself to despair again.

When at last there was nothing left for him to swing at, Brendys allowed himself to survey the battlefield once more. The remnants of the Gildeans had been joined by Lord Dell's knights, who were now wandering about the field, searching for wounded among the bodies of the fallen.

His gaze wandered towards Quellin, but what he saw left a hollow feeling in his gut. Quellin stood over Brumagin, his expression twisted in sorrow. Etzel was crouched beside the boy.

The old woman reached out and closed Brumagin's unseeing eyes. Her quiet, raspy voice reached Brendys's ears. "May the Dawn receive you with mercy."

Quellin stared down at the child's body. "I tried to protect him, but there were too many, and he wished for death."

"You cannot protect everyone, Your Majesty," Etzel replied, her voice firm, but not unkind.

Brendys felt himself being shaken from his numb reverie and a familiar voice calling his name. But for the voice, the air had become deathly silent. Slowly, he turned and looked down into the face of another youth. The youth's face was grim, smeared with sweat, grime, and blood.

"Brendys?" the young man said. "Brendys, what happened? Are you all right?"

Though his voice cracked from long hours of yelling, it was a gentle, cultured voice that Brendys recognized. He looked closer at the face before him. Beneath the blood and grime, it was a face he knew.

His lips moved silently for a moment before he spoke. "Is it over?"

With a shake of his head, Kradon replied, "Not yet."

Brendys drew a deep breath and struggled to keep his tears from returning.

A brawny hand clasped Brendys's arm, and he looked down into another familiar face.

"You led us quite a chase, my Kjerken," the Dwarf said. "Yet you do not seem surprised to see us."

"I saw you all with Lord Dell's army many days ago, Asghar," Brendys replied, bringing a puzzled look to his friends' eyes. "There was also an old man in white. I . . . I think he saved my life."

"Indeed, he did."

Brendys turned to face the speaker. Lord Dell stood beside the man.

"I am Odyniec," the old man said.

Brendys swallowed nervously. He found the old man's gaze only slightly less unnerving than Etzel's. "You must be the Wizard that Kradon told me about before our ship was destroyed."

"I am," Odyniec replied with a nod. "You have walked where ordinary mortals have never walked before, and I sense you have seen more than you wished."

"I never wished to see *anything*," Brendys replied bitterly. "I was delivered here against my will, and only ill has come of it."

Quellin interrupted him, his gaze as piercing as the hawk's. "Only ill, Brendys? Nothing good?"

Brendys opened his mouth to respond, but bit back his reply and bowed his head in shame. Slowly, he raised his eyes to the door of Etzel's house. The thought of Mattina drove out the last of his fear. "Nay, you are right. There has been *some* good, and for that I would suffer a thousand wars."

"My Lord!" Attention turned to three approaching Hagane warriors. Novosad and the twins saluted Lord Dell.

Dell inclined his head in return. "Report, Novosad."

"The Kubruki have retreated to the first ward upon the hill," the scout replied. "My Lord, the Sorcerer has joined them and is rallying them for another assault. I have never seen the like of him before."

"And you may never see the like again, I fear," Odyniec responded. "If he has come forth from his temple, then he is fully prepared. If we are to. . . ."

Novosad cried out. "'Ware, My Lord!"

Brendys spun around in time to see a wounded Kubruk rise up from amidst the surrounding carnage and, with the speed and agility of a serpent, strike out with its weapon. Brendys watched, horror-stricken, as the point of the Kubruk's spear burst out from Kradon's chest. His friend's head snapped back briefly, his features contorted in agony, then lost nearly all expression.

The Kubruk jerked its bloody spear from its victim's body, and Kradon fell forward into Brendys's arms. Brendys staggered and dropped to his knees, still holding Kradon. He looked up to see the Kubruk leap towards him, but Novosad thrust his serrated blade through the creature's heart before it could claim another life.

Brendys lowered his gaze to Kradon's slack features. Kradon choked, startling the Shalkane youth, for he thought his friend was already dead. Kradon's lips moved, but Brendys could not hear what he was saying. He moved his ear closer to his friend's lips, straining to hear the words.

Kradon choked again, then rasped out, "*Engen kellim . . . Arzola . . . dellis el . . . boradis. . . .*"

He coughed blood once more, then his entire body went limp in Brendys's arms.

Brendys turned his gaze back to his friend's face, wondering what his words meant. Kradon's lifeless eyes stared back, his blood flowing freely from the wounds in his chest and back, darkening Brendys's hands and tunic as the Shalkane youth pulled him close. Brendys wanted to cry, but his tears were gone.

"Master Odyniec," he heard Lord Dell say, the pain in the man's voice mirroring the pain in his own heart.

"His spirit has already passed into the Dawn," the Wizard replied gently. "There is nothing I can do for him now."

Nothing. The word echoed in Brendys's mind. With the power of the Dawn King at his beck and call, there was nothing the Wizard could do? Brendys felt anger building up within him, hammering his heart and mind, seeking escape. Unable to contain the inferno within, he threw back his head and released a scream of rage. When the sound died away, his head dropped forward once more.

Silence fell, but only briefly. The door of Etzel's house creaked open.

"What happened? Is it over?" Mattina asked. "Have we won?"

There was only a short pause before Brendys heard her call his name. Her hands touched his shoulders only briefly before she was pulled away again.

"Back inside, all of you," Quellin bit out. "We are far from victory."

His voice softened. "Brendys, go with them. There is no more you can do."

Brendys gently laid Kradon's head on the ground. Grasping the hilt of his sword, he rose to his feet. He saw that Arella had joined them, standing near Mattina and Sherren. Arella's exhausted face wore the same grim signs of battles fought that everyone's did, but for a few scratches, she seemed otherwise unhurt. Queen Sherren looked harried, the blood of the wounded she tended staining her arms and clothing.

His gaze remained longest on Mattina. She had clearly been assisting Sherren in her work, but in his eyes her beauty could not be marred. Her face was a mask of concern and fear. Brendys knew her heart bled for him, and he knew what she feared.

Her fears would be justified. Brendys had chosen his course and would not be swayed from it. He swung around to face Quellin. His words carried an edge as sharp as any blade. "It is over. It ends *now!*"

He turned and took a few steps in the direction of Keep Hill before Quellin grabbed his arm.

"Brendys, you can do nothing. . . !"

The Shalkane youth jerked his arm away. "Except fight!"

Before he could continue on, Asghar and Folkor restrained him.

His eyes remaining firmly on Brendys, Quellin motioned them away. "Brendys is right. It must end now, one way or another."

He was answered by silent nods.

Lord Dell stepped towards him. "We must gather our forces, even as the enemy gathers his strength. I will send word that your people are not to join in this battle. They are few enough as is . . . I would not have more die in a hopeless cause."

Quellin nodded assent, and Lord Dell dispatched heralds to muster his warriors.

The Gildean King's gaze fell upon Asghar, Folkor, and finally Brendys. "I would have you all stand with me."

Asghar shook his head. "I will not stand behind a wall of Men, brave and skilled though they may be."

"I would not ask you to, Captain," Quellin replied. "Iysh Mawvath stands at the head of his army. I intend to face him myself."

"Then I shall be honored to stand with you," the Dwarf returned.

Folkor muttered his agreement.

Quellin looked once more at Brendys. "And you?"

Brendys felt some of his anger die away. He nodded, swallowing back his grief.

Quellin sent a dark glance in the direction of the women. His gaze sent a message to them as clear as any words. Mattina, Sherren, and Arella retreated to into Etzel's house, not daring to argue.

Etzel, who remained outside after Arella and Mattina returned to the house, and Lord Guthwine moved forward to join the group. It did not take long for the remainder of Lord Dell's host to gather. Soon, they were marching in rank up the road to Keep Hill, Quellin, Dell, and Odyniec at their head.

As they approached the first ward, the army came to a halt. The Kubruki stood among the ruins of the wall, but did not appear prepared to continue the fight. Several yards to the fore stood Iysh Mawvath.

The giant's ghostly armor gleamed with a ruddy light in the bloody murk of the Shadow. Silently, he waited, the shaft of his pole-axe planted firmly beside him. As Quellin, Dell, and their allies halted, Iysh Mawvath stirred.

The Warlord of Thanatos raised his left hand. Many forms began to coalesce in the red haze around him, a legion of shadows shaped like men, but with cat-like heads. In the skies above him circled creatures even more dread in aspect: half man, half-bat, with taloned feet and hands.

Odyniec leaned toward Quellin and whispered, but not so quietly that Brendys could not hear him. "Drolar and Jaf. I knew they would appear before the end, but their numbers are greater than I imagined."

"My sword and Lord Guthwine's arrows are all we have that can slay these creatures," Quellin muttered darkly in reply. "This, then, *is* the end."

The Wizard shook his head. "Do not give up hope yet. Strike the head from the serpent and the body shall die. Fight to delay the enemy. I can deal with Iysh Mawvath, but you must force him to make the first move."

Brendys watched Quellin's head dip in acknowledgment. Odyniec pushed his way past Brendys and disappeared into the ranks of Lord Dell's army. When Brendys turned back towards the enemy, Quellin had walked forward several paces.

"Who are you, boy, that you dare invade my domain?" Iysh Mawvath rumbled.

"*Your* domain?" Quellin called back. "I know this city to be mine. I am Quellin, Lord of Trost and successor to the throne of Gildea.

"As you are surely aware, Lord Balgor failed in his mission to sway me and paid with his life. Now, I give you the same choice that you gave my liege-lord, Treiber: surrender or die. You and your legion may leave Gildea and return to your dead lands in peace. If you remain, I will destroy every one of you. What say you, Sorcerer?"

Brendys rushed forward to Quellin's side. "What are you saying? Are you actually willing to let this murderer go free?"

A familiar chill ran down Brendys's spine at the sound of Iysh Mawvath's low, rumbling laugh. His gaze snapped towards the Sorcerer to find the giant looking towards him.

"Your Dawn King has failed you, even as he failed your King," Iysh Mawvath rumbled across the field. "Even now, my legions march upon this city in countless numbers, and before you stands the means of your destruction. Your precious Bearer of the Flame, the boy upon whom all your hopes ride, stands powerless.

"Your options are few: pledge allegiance to me or burn in the Black Pits. What say you, Quellin of Trost?"

Brendys looked from Iysh Mawvath to Quellin. The Gildean King's youthful features were set in grim determination.

"You want an answer, Iysh Mawvath? You may have it. *Go to Hál!*" Quellin shouted back. He raised Kalter and a golden flame ran down its blade. "*Kindone Getheirne un hason!*"

With that single cry, the two armies leapt towards each other. Brendys found himself swept forward beside Quellin. As the Drolar neared, a mounting sense of dread surrounded him, but his mind remained focused on one task, Kradon's blood reminding him of a debt to be settled. He followed in the wake of Quellin's advance, harmlessly batting away claws and fanged maws as Drolar lunged at him.

Soon, the tide of battle separated him from Quellin. At last, he could see Iysh Mawvath's pale form only a few yards away, but that sight was quickly replaced by a sea of black as he was dragged to the ground by several Drolar. Icy talons dug into his limbs and body, bringing a shriek of agony to his lips.

Brendys tried to break free, but the demons held him in grips of iron. The panther face floating before his own moved closer, until all he could see were a pair of burning, red eyes set against a black veil. The creature's breath smelled strongly of rotting flesh, causing Brendys to gasp.

"Iysh Mawvath cannot have you," the creature hissed. "You are *mine!*"

Brendys quickly forgot his pain at the sound of the Drolar's voice. The creature's bestial face drew back, allowing Brendys to see the claw poised to strike. In place of the creature's hand was an artificial appendage. The claw was roughly hand-shaped, but in place of each finger was a pair of curved, black blades.

Brendys watched in horror as the claw plunged towards him. The single-bitted blade of a Kubruk axe suddenly appeared between him and impending death, deflecting the black claw. A second sweep of the weapon caught the Drolar in the chest, flinging it backwards. As it flew through the air, the creature melted into the Dusklight and vanished.

Folkor's broad arms also entered his vision, wielding a heavy Kubruk mace. Together, the sea-captain and the Dwarf swept the remaining Drolar away from Brendys. Folkor's strong hand drew the youth to his feet, then returned to the task of driving back the grasping claws of Drolar and Jaf.

A path slowly cleared before Brendys, forming an opening to Iysh Mawvath. Several warriors fell to the Warlord's pole-axe before Brendys plunged forward. With a cry of rage Brendys swung his sword at the Sorcerer, but Iysh Mawvath swept the weapon aside with his own, then delivered a backhanded blow to Brendys's head. The giant's plated gauntlet cut into the youth's face and spun him around.

Brendys dropped to the ground, face-first, stunned from the blow. A heavy weight fell upon his back, and a vision of Iysh Mawvath's axe driving through his body flashed in his mind. But even as he felt the impact of the giant's weapon, a bright light flooded through his closed eyes, and a burning sensation spread across his back. A metallic shriek split the air, accompanied by a sound like glass shattering and a tortured scream, almost immediately silencing the battle around him.

Slowly raising his head, he saw Iysh Mawvath sprawled amidst the shards of his shattered weapon, his armor scorched black.

The Sorcerer stirred, then began to rise.

Weakly, Brendys tried to stand and failed, but tumbled backwards out of the giant's reach.

As Iysh Mawvath came to his full height, the shadowed sockets of his skull-helm fell upon the youth. Brendys could feel the depth of the hatred emanating from the Warlord. "Now you die, Bearer of the Flame."

A white flame blossomed several feet behind Brendys, driving back the Shadow. Odyniec stood at the center.

"Nay, Man of Death!" the Wizard cried forth. "Your power is failed. Gildea is taken from your hand. Your master is defeated again."

Rage filled the giant's voice. "Odyniec! Fool of Athor! I shall not be denied!"

He stretched both hands out towards the Wizard, chanting in a vile tongue. Iysh Mawvath's blackened armor began to emanate a deep Darkness, focusing around his gauntlets. Sable fire erupted from his outstretched hands, writhing towards Odyniec.

The Wizard swung his staff down under his arm, grasping it with one hand, and pointed his free hand at Iysh Mawvath. The Athorian runes carved around the staff's head began to glow. The white flame which engulfed Odyniec gathered around his hand and shot out, striking and twisting about the black fire.

A vision flashed before Brendys's eyes, a dream he had seen before, though the faces he had seen were not the same. He shook his head, trying to destroy the vision, but realized that no longer was he seeing the picture in his mind, but was witnessing the event in reality.

For only a few brief minutes—though it seemed an eternity—the two foes struggled against each other in a great battle of power, the dark flame slowly pushing back the argent. Finally, in one sudden flare, Odyniec's white flame consumed that of Iysh Mawvath, striking the Warlord of Thanatos full in the chest, knocking him to the ground again. This time, Iysh Mawvath was even slower to rise.

As the Sorcerer climbed to his feet, a Shadow began to form behind him—a Shadow blacker than even the horrid Darkness during the Night Hours—gradually taking the shape of a great, black hand, rising up behind the Warlord of Thanatos. Brendys joined Lord Dell's army as the Shadowhand moved forward.

Odyniec stood dumbfounded, his arms hanging loosely at his sides, his grip on his staff weakening. The white flame which surrounded him flickered and vanished.

Quellin called to the Wizard. "What is that?"

"'Tis the Hand of Thanatos, himself," Odyniec replied in a defeated voice.

Brendys fell to his knees, his eyes fastened in terror upon the thing before him. His mind shrieked in a last refusal to admit the devastating power rising before him. *Nay! It **can't** be true!*

The Shadow began to creep over Iysh Mawvath. The Warlord spun around to face the shade and immediately dropped to his knees.

"Nay! I can destroy them!" he cried. "No, I beg of you, My Lord. . . ."

Brendys saw Odyniec turn his face away as the Shadowhand closed about the giant, a bloodcurdling shriek rending the air. When the Hand disappeared, Iysh Mawvath was gone. The Drolar and Jaf faded in the Dusklight, leaving the remnant of the Kubruki to defend themselves.

For a moment, utter silence reigned over the field, then a terrible wind began to blow. Quellin shouted for the warriors to gather the wounded and take shelter indoors.

"I fear this night," Quellin shouted at the Wizard, his voice muted in the raging wind. "I want everyone inside—now!"

Odyniec nodded, his aged features were burdened with a terrible weariness. Grabbing the nearest warrior at hand, he said, "Warn everyone to lock their doors and shutter their windows!"

As the Dusklight vanished and the Night Hours began, Brendys, Quellin, and Odyniec rushed into Etzel's house, shutting and bolting the door behind themselves.

Chapter 18

No one in Gildea Keep slept that night. The wind moaned like the spirits of the dead, and spectral children could be heard crying from all reaches of the city, unearthly voices which sent fear into the hearts of the people. Crashing sounds were heard above the wind, coming from Keep Hill, like huge stones being broken and tossed about. The Gildeans huddled together in their homes, vainly trying to keep out the frightful sounds.

* * * *

Odyniec sat alone on a small couch in a chamber adjoining the front room of Etzel's house. His shoulders were slumped and his head bowed as he leaned forward, rubbing his hand through his beard. Like most in the city, there was a burden on his heart.

"Master Odyniec, you look sad."

The Wizard looked up to see Lady Arella standing in the doorway. He nodded slowly and answered. "Aye, My Lady. Indeed, I am."

The woman stepped into the room and came to sit beside the old prophet. "Why? For whom do you grieve?"

Odyniec smiled weakly. "My sorrow is for Iysh Mawvath."

Surprise registered on Arella's face. "I do not understand. Why should you grieve for *him?* A viler creature I have never known."

The Wizard sighed at memories of a distant past. "We were very close once. Very close. He was not always as you have seen him. He was once a great man."

His voice quieted to a whisper. "A great man."

Arella placed a hand on the Wizard's arm. "What happened to him, that he should become such a monster?"

"The Black Hand of Thanatos was laid upon him," Odyniec replied. "The Deathlord deceived him into studying the Black Arts. His greed for power overcame him and soon destroyed him. The Hand of Thanatos made him what he was and now has taken him away, and there is no hope remaining for him."

"Oh, Len!" the Wizard cried suddenly. "Len! Why did you not heed my warnings?"

Arella watched for a few minutes longer as the old Wizard wept, more confused than when she had first spoken to him, then she left him alone once more.

* * * *

Brendys sat on one of the couches in the front room, dressed only in his breeches, with Etzel and Mattina on either side of him, tending to his myriad wounds. He winced in pain as Etzel began to apply a portion of her pungent-smelling salve to the burns on his back.

"I don't understand what happened," he said with a groan. "Iysh Mawvath should have cut me in two. Did Odyniec blast him?"

"Nay, a power far greater than the Wizard's saved your life," Lord Guthwine replied from across the room. The Elvinlord approached the youth, holding Denasdervien. He displayed the sheathed weapon before Brendys, revealing the gash in the scabbard where Iysh Mawvath's axe had struck it. The ragged wound in the black leather still hid the blade from view.

"The sight was indeed a wonder to behold. When the Sorcerer's weapon struck Denasdervien, a great column of white fire burst forth, engulfing Iysh Mawvath," the Elf said, grasping the sword's hilt. "This blade is empowered by Elekar himself. Iysh Mawvath could not stand against it."

After he finished speaking, Guthwine pulled Denasdervien from its sheath.

Brendys cowered back, expecting the blast of argent fire that he had experienced twice before, but his fear was belied. He stared in wonder at the weapon in the Elf's hand. Its mirrored Gloriod blade gleamed in the Shadow with the same deceptive color he had seen in the signet rings he and his father possessed.

"How did you do that?" he said, looking up at the Elvinlord. "You say it belongs to me, yet I could not draw it."

A mysterious smile crossed Lord Guthwine's lips. "*Engen kellim Arzola, dellis el boradis.*"

Brendys started to rise, startled by the Elf's response, but Etzel held him firmly in his seat. He had been sure that no one but he had heard Kradon's last words. "Kradon said that. . . ."

Guthwine gave a single nod. "Aye. My ears hear many things."

"What does it mean?" Brendys asked.

"It is part of an old Athorian proverb, though Lord Kradon spoke it in his own tongue," Lord Guthwine replied. "In the Common Tongue, it says, *Look to the Dawn, and all is possible.*"

Before Brendys could respond, another voice, a weary mortal voice, chanted in a sorrow-laden tone:

Look to the Dawn, and all is possible,
Though Night shall come and Darkness reign,
Still Dawn must rise and Shadows fall,
Renewing Light and Life again.

As Lord Dell fell silent, he bowed his head, a single tear running down his haggard face. "Dawn may come again, Elf, but my son will not. The gods have failed me."

"Did you expect otherwise?" Guthwine replied gently. His tone and bearing were not condescending, and his eyes reflected understanding.

Dell did not respond.

"But what does that rhyme have to do with the sword?" Brendys asked in confusion.

The Elf turned back to Brendys, sliding Denasdervien into its sheath. "With the sword? Nothing, directly. It has to do with *you*. Only two mortals may draw this weapon from its sheath, and you are the first."

Guthwine handed the short sword back to the Shalkane youth. Brendys drew in a sudden breath as he took the weapon. The gash in the scabbard was gone. The sheath had been restored to its original condition, battered but whole. He tested the hilt, but the weapon remained firm in the scabbard.

"How do I draw it?" he said, looking up at the Elf.

"Lord Kradon has already given you the answer," Guthwine replied. The Elvinlord's handsome features took on an unaccustomed grimness. "I feel I must warn you, Brendys of Shalkan. I see you standing at a crossroad. The way ahead, though not without strife, is bright and clear, but the paths to either side are dark. I cannot see your path should you turn aside."

Brendys lowered his gaze, a bitter frown crossing his lips. "I know what you are saying, Lord Guthwine, but the road you would have me walk only leads to death."

Etzel roughly slapped a pad over the burns on the youth's back, causing Brendys to yelp, then motioned for Mattina to finish binding the pad in place. She rose to her feet and glared down at Brendys. "I am surrounded by fools! Lord Dell blames his gods for Kradon's death, and you blame the Dawn King, because it is convenient. Choose what road you will. I wash my hands of you."

She walked across the room to stand beside Quellin. Brendys was surprised that Mattina's brother had not already entered the conversation, but it became clear that Quellin was not even aware of the debate. His gaze was fixed firmly on the door, his boyish features trembling both in fear and anticipation.

"Dawn is coming," Etzel told the Gildean King. "It is time. There are things you must see, things you must understand. We must go."

Quellin looked up at her and nodded.

Arella, understanding what they meant to do, grabbed her beloved's arm. "Quellin, you can't—it is too dangerous! You do not know what's out there. You could be killed! The Drolar may still be out there."

Quellin did not look at her, but softly replied, "I *must* go . . . whatever may come."

He briefly turned his haunted gaze on his sister and Brendys before walking to the door. As he stepped outside, he was nearly toppled by the powerful wind pounding against his body. Etzel followed him out of the house, taking his arm to steady him.

"Come with me," she said, turning him towards Keep Hill. She did not speak loudly, yet Quellin could hear her every word, even over the shriek of the wind.

He looked up and saw a great cloud rising up like a great pillar from the South Field. Occasional bursts of white flame could be seen within the cloud, and the shadows of great boulders being flung down and crushed. In fear, he hesitated and stepped back a little, but Etzel pulled him onward again. He stumbled forward unable to resist her unnatural strength.

Under her firm hand, Quellin accompanied her to the top of Keep Hill. They walked around a great, empty pit which had once been filled with the rubble of Gildea Keep and upon which Iysh Mawvath's temple had stood, until they came to the southern edge.

Quellin's heart raced furiously as he stared up at the towering column of smoke and fire. He wanted to hide his eyes from the sight, but could not.

"As you have seen the Hand of Thanatos, look now upon the work of Elekar," Etzel said, raising a hand to the pillar.

Quellin turned to her, gaping in awe. In the presence of that power, he suddenly felt small and insignificant, like a child in the presence of a King. "Why is this being shown to me?"

The old woman looked him in the eye. "To teach you, Son of Trost. Look not too harshly upon young Brendys's denial, for you yourself shall one day doubt Elekar, even after you have seen his hand at work."

"Never!" the King of Gildea returned with an adamant shake of his head.

Etzel nodded. "Yes, Quellin. It must be so. But Elekar's hand will not leave you."

"How do you know this?" Quellin asked her, regarding her with trepidation. "Who are you, Etzel? *What* are you? Radnor knew something about you, didn't he? That is why he sent us to you, isn't it?"

Etzel laughed. "You are learning already, Son of Trost."

A light began to grow within her, and her age seemed to melt away. The glow became so bright that Quellin was forced to turn his face away.

Etzel spoke again, her voice now young, almost musical, and yet still her voice. "Yes, Quellin, Radnor knew about me. He was quite clever as a lad. He tricked me into revealing my Elvin name—Uhyvainyn."

Awestruck, Quellin stared at her, unable to speak. This *witch* was Uhyvainyn, one of the Alar—denizens of the High Realm— who was said to have taken Trost, the father of Quellin's royal House, from his cell in the dungeons of Gildea Keep, after his betrayal of the Gildean people. She had taken Trost into the High Realm, for his sons planned his death and would have cast blame upon Gildea, the new King.

"I must leave you now, Son of Trost," she said to Quellin. "You shall see many great things when I am gone, but of them you must never speak. What you see is for your eyes, and none other."

The light that was Etzel Uhyvainyn slowly diminished into a faint glimmer, then that too vanished.

The wind steadily grew stronger, and Quellin was forced to the ground. Raising his head, he watched as streams of smoke swirled out of the cloud, flowing over the entire city, creeping along the ground. Finally, the billowing mist drew back into the pillar. All at once, the entire column spilled down upon the earth, covering the whole South Field and Keep Hill, surrounding Quellin and filling the pit behind him.

The wind became louder and shriller, and Quellin clamped his hands over his ears. The cloud gathered back into a pillar and shot up into the sky. The Darkness cracked in a white blaze as the column pierced through its sun-choking bounds. The blasting gale died immediately, and deathly screams replaced the whistle of the wind.

* * * *

Brendys, Mattina, and the others waited impatiently for Quellin and Etzel to return, but neither came back to the house. Fear for them grew stronger, for that night was fast growing into a nightmare.

As the hours passed on, the wind grew stronger and stronger, finally rising to a high-pitched whistle. Suddenly, the wind broke, and shrieks—as of those dying an agonizing death—shattered the air. Then, just as suddenly, the screams stopped. Shutters burst open, breaking even the strongest bolts, and the bright rays of the sun filled every room of every home.

Brendys and his friends hurried out of Etzel's house to find Quellin and the old woman. They feared the worst, but still hoped that the pair had survived the eerie night. As Brendys and his companions searched for Quellin, Dell's warriors combed the city for signs of the remaining Kubruki, but there were none to find. The bodies of the slain, both friend and foe alike, were gone, and so also were the Kubruki who had survived the battle.

Not only had the corpses of the fallen vanished, but the ruins of the Keep and Iysh Mawvath's temple had been cleared away. Even the stones which had collapsed into the Lower Halls within Keep Hill had been removed, leaving a gaping pit in the center of the mound. All signs that a battle had ever taken place at Gildea Keep had simply vanished.

After a long search, Brendys and his companions finally found Quellin standing on the southern side of Keep Hill. Etzel was nowhere to be seen.

Arella went directly to her beloved's side. "Quellin, where is Etzel?"

Quellin's emerald-green eyes were wide and unblinking. He slowly shook his head and mumbled something indiscernible.

"Is she dead?"

Again, the Gildean King shook his head. Life returned to his visage, but he still seemed a little dazed. Pointing with his hand, he directed the companions' gazes to the South Field. Thousands of graves covered the entire field between the wall of the city to the base of the hill where Quellin and his companions stood.

Quellin led the others down from the hill to the South Field. The field was surrounded by a low wall, built from the broken stones of the Keep. An arch was constructed in the center of the wall, and upon the topmost stone were engraved strange symbols, blackened as if scorched by fire into the stone.

Brendys stared at the markings for a moment, then asked, "What do they say?"

Odyniec stepped forward and read the words aloud. "*Here lay the dead of Gildea and their allies who were slain in battle for their freedom and for their King. Evil shall not enter herein, lest that Evil be destroyed. This shall forever be a haven of safety for the Children of Elekar and shall be preserved by the power of the King of the Dawn, so that all shall remember the valor and the faith of Gildea. Henceforth, let this place be known in the tongue of Gildea as **Sharamitaro**, the House of Sorrow.*"

Quellin turned to Brendys. "Now do you understand? You have seen with your own eyes the Hand of Thanatos and you now look upon a work that no mortal hand could devise in a single night. It is time for the Bearer to take up the Flame. Will you not swear allegiance to the Dawn, Brendys?"

Brendys paused before answering. For him, the name of the Dawn King meant only suffering and loss. He had seen his mother and his truest friend die in agony; he had watched as Brumagin's mother was murdered and his sister carried away by Iysh Mawvath to be sacrificed to the Deathlord; he had witnessed the terror, the suffering, and grief of the Gildean people. How could he ever bend his knee to a being as merciless as the Dawn King?

"No," he replied with a grimace.

Quellin opened his mouth to speak, an answer ready on his lips, but he stopped himself. Instead, he shook his head sadly and said, "Alas, after all the wonders that you have witnessed here, still you choose to remain as a blind fool."

Brendys again shook his head. "Nay. It is true, I can longer deny the powers I have seen, but neither can I swear allegiance to a being who had the power to prevent this from ever happening."

Quellin looked away, his gaze becoming distant. "You will see the truth someday, Brendys. I only fear what it will take."

Without another word, they entered the stone ring. Quellin led them to a row of seven mounds raised at the center of the field. Names were placed at the foot of each, and below those were set the charges of their Houses. These mounds were the graves of King Treiber, the five Lords of Gildea, and finally Lord Kradon of Racolis.

Brendys stood before Kradon's grave beside Lord Dell, staring at the stone engraved with his friend's name. It was hard for him to believe that Kradon was actually dead, but the blood staining his tunic would never let him forget the agony of his death.

The agony in his own heart was immeasurable. Not only had he lost a friend, but a brother. While Kradon was alive in Racolis, the distance between them was far, but easily traveled. Now the distance was such that Brendys could not span it in a lifetime.

Mattina started towards Brendys to comfort him, but her brother held her back.

"Leave him be, Mattina," Quellin told her. "Brendys will heal with time. But right now, there is nothing that you or I or anyone else can say or do to ease his pain."

Mattina nodded and stayed at her brother's side.

Quellin turned his gaze to the man standing next to Brendys. A change had come over Lord Dell. He seemed older and weakened. The light of life was gone from his eyes. His face was hard, and his eyes stared sightlessly towards his son's grave. As with Brendys, only time would bring his healing.

"Sire!"

Quellin turned to see Shanor coming towards him. He shot a nervous glance at Radnor's grave, then reached a hand towards Shanor to stop the boy from coming nearer.

The boy halted and looked down at the mound. Seeing his father's name at the foot of the grave, he choked out, "Papa. . . ."

Shanor fell at the foot of the mound, weeping.

Quellin knelt down beside him, gently placing his hands on the boy's shoulders. "Be strong for him, Shanor, for when you are come of age, you must take his place as Lord of Horack-Gildea."

Shanor looked up at him, wiping the tears from his eyes with the backs of his hands. "You said you saw it happen."

Quellin lowered his gaze, frowning. "Aye. After I saw Arella safely to . . . to Etzel's house, I came back to scout out the situation. I saw Iysh Mawvath interrogating your father. The Sorcerer was searching for me, but Radnor would not tell him where I was.

"Iysh Mawvath tried to use you to force Radnor to talk, but your father sacrificed himself instead. I followed the Kubruki to you, and the rest you know."

Quellin sighed. "I should have told you right away, but I could not bring myself to it. I suppose that I have given you reason enough to hate me, just as your father did. But I could not bear to break your heart, Shanor."

"Sire, Father didn't hate you!" Shanor said, sitting up straight. "He loved you like a brother—I heard him tell my mother that many a time. He was afraid for you, that is all."

Quellin gave the boy a lopsided smile. "I wanted to comfort you, but alas, instead it is you who have comforted me. You will make a wise Lord when the time comes."

Shanor threw his arms around Quellin's neck, and Quellin squeezed him tightly.

The Gildean King stood up and looked around the field, his smile fading. "Let us leave this place to the Dead. I have many visits to make. The Living shall have need of me."

Quellin and his companions left Sharamitaro, leaving Dell alone. The Lord of Hagan remained at his son's grave long into the night, until Queen Sherren, his kinswoman, brought him back to the house of Etzel Uhyvainyn, Alar of the Dawn.

* * * *

Quellin, Mattina, and Arella spent the rest of the morning and afternoon visiting the women and children of his city, ministering comfort where comfort was needed. Many children had been orphaned by Iysh Mawvath's invasion and the liberation of Gildea, many women had lost their children, and all had lost their fathers and husbands.

When Quellin had finished in the city, they all returned to Etzel's house. He took Arella into a room adjoining the front room, and stayed there into the evening.

* * * *

Mattina sat down beside Brendys in the front room, wrapping her arm around his. "Are you all right, Brendys?"

Brendys looked at her, gazing long into her emerald-green eyes, losing himself in their depths. Her eyes had been the first thing he had noticed when he had first met her, but now with the Shadow lifted, they held him captive. Finally, he nodded with a smile. "I'm fine, or I will be."

He turned his gaze back to the front door. "Right now, I am thinking of Lord Dell. He is taking Kradon's death very hard."

"And you are not?" Mattina responded, a little surprised. "You were ready to march on Iysh Mawvath alone for vengeance's sake . . . indeed, you were foolish enough to attack him yourself."

Brendys shrugged nervously. "Aye, and I learned from that mistake. I have had time to think. I hurt—the gods know I hurt—but I have to go on . . . Kradon would want it that way. But Lord Dell . . . it is like he has given up on life altogether. Like he is dead already."

Mattina rested her head upon his shoulder. "Let us not speak anymore about death. I have had my fill of it. Can you think of nothing pleasant, or at least something a little less gloomy?"

"Very well," Brendys replied. "Perhaps you can tell me what Quellin and Arella are talking about. They have been in that room for hours."

"I do not know as it is any of your concern, but if you must know, they are discussing the future stability of Gildea," Mattina answered.

"Future stability of Gildea?" Brendys repeated. "I would think it is rather soon to be worrying about that."

Queen Sherren entered the room, walking towards the front door, on her way to retrieve Lord Dell. "Not so, lad. It was my Treiber's belief that the stability of a nation depends greatly upon the stability of its ruler, and the only stable King is a married one. Quellin listened well."

Brendys's blue eyes widened. "You mean. . . ?"

The door leading from the front room opened, and Quellin stepped out, holding Arella's hand. "Aye. That is precisely what she means. In two weeks from this day, Arella and I shall be wed. I will announce the marriage to my people upon the morrow."

Brendys stood up, assisting Mattina to her feet, and gripped Quellin's hand. "That is wonderful! I only wish that I could stay for the wedding."

"We were rather hoping that you would," Quellin returned, with a cursory glance at his sister. "It will take a few days to bring a ship here to take you to Ilkatar, in any case. Will you not stay? For two more weeks?"

"Yes, Brendys," Mattina pleaded. "Just for two more weeks?"

Brendys looked at her and his heart melted. Despite his desire to return home, he replied, "Since you asked, I suppose I will stay."

* * * *

In the morning, when his people were gathered together, Quellin announced his wedding. Two weeks later, the Gildean people put aside their sorrow and lifted their spirits to great celebration. Quellin, son of Quiron, Lord of the House of Trost, King of Gildea, wed Arella, daughter of Haran, Lady of the House of Horack-Gildea. And so began a new era in the history of that land and of all the lands.

Over the next two days, those from foreign lands who had aided in the liberation of Gildea went their separate ways. All but Brendys began their journeys homeward on the first day after the wedding. Brendys would be the last to go.

Quellin and his people gathered at the North Field to bid farewell to the departing army and their friends. The Gildean King shook hands with Dell, Folkor, and Asghar, and bowed deeply to Odyniec and Guthwine. "May Elekar keep you on your journeys. You will always be welcome as my guests at Gildea Keep—when a new Keep can be raised, that is."

"I promise you a new Keep by next spring," Asghar replied. "A Kjerek-built fortress that will stand against any foe."

Quellin smiled in gratitude. "I certainly hope so, my friend. I never want to go through this again. For the Throne and for my people, I thank you, Captain."

He bowed to Asghar, then faced the army of his foreign allies, clapping his fist to his heart in salute. He raised his voice so that all could hear. "My friends, I cannot thank you enough for what you have done for my people; but rest assured, when we are able, we shall repay our debt to you . . . and with glad hearts."

Novosad, chief of Dell's scouts, stepped forward from the ranks of the host. "Your Majesty, I am certain that all of my comrades would agree with me when I say you owe no debt to us. We all knew the risks we would face when we came. Lord Dell gave us the choice of remaining behind at Hagan Keep, but we came anyway. We rode forth to aid friends in need—friends do not ask payment of friends."

The young warrior fell silent, an expression of nervous embarrassment coming across his features.

Quellin took notice of the man's expression and responded. "Your words are gratefully received, but I perceive there is more on your heart. You may speak freely."

"Your Majesty," Novosad began nervously. "There is . . . there is a certain lass in the village of Tarlas that I would take as wife. . . ."

"And does she share this feeling?"

"I . . . I believe so, Your Majesty," Novosad stammered in reply.

"Then of what concern is this of mine, other than to congratulate you on your own victory?" Quellin responded with a confused laugh.

A ragged chorus of scattered laughter ran through the crowd.

Novosad lowered his head for a moment, then returned his gaze to Quellin. "She is the daughter of the Town Governor, Your Majesty."

Silence fell upon the crowd.

Dell turned quickly to Quellin. "I must beg your pardon, Your Majesty, for. . . ."

Quellin silenced him with a wave of his hand. He gave Brendys a sidelong glance, eliciting an embarrassed blush, then replied, smiling, "Lord Dell, I have already made worse breaches in protocol than to grant the hand of a noble's daughter to a common soldier."

Removing his signet ring, he held it towards Novosad. "Present this to the Governor with my command that if she be of the same mind, his daughter be wed to you."

The warrior stepped forward and took the ring, then bowed. "Thank you, Your Majesty."

Quellin looked to the young warrior's Lord. "Dell, your people have a greater honor than many whom I have known, and it makes me all the more determined to pay my debt. This is but the first portion. Many of your youth died for the sake of my people, including your own son; thus I swear to make amends to all of those who lost their sons for our sake, as I am able."

Dell bowed to the Gildean King and replied in a solemn voice, "If that be your wish, Your Majesty."

The Lord of Hagan turned and rejoined his army.

Lord Guthwine came to stand beside Brendys and gave him a slight nod. "You are slow to learn, Bearer of the Flame, but you are not entirely without hope—at least, I do not believe so."

Brendys gave him a questioning look. "What is that supposed to mean, My Lord?"

Guthwine opened his mouth to answer, but Asghar grunted a reply before the Elvinlord could speak. "The Elf means that you are an idiot, but he likes you anyway."

The Elf nonchalantly raised a brow. "That is a subtle way of stating it."

"Subtle!" Brendys burst. "Just how stupid do you think I am?"

Captain Folkor clapped him on the shoulder. "Don't ask stupid questions, Bren. Farewell, and give my respects to your father."

He and Guthwine then joined the Hagane host.

Asghar twirled a thick finger in his red beard. "Farewell, Brother. I am stricken to part with my Kjerken, but alas it must be so."

Brendys curled his lip. "Don't make so much of it, Asghar—you hardly know me."

Asghar shrugged. "What is there to know that I do not know already? You are my Kjerken—to me and my people, you are Kjerek. No Jontn has borne that honor in my lifetime. Bear it well, my Kjerken."

"I will," Brendys replied. "Whatever it is. Farewell, Asghar, and may we meet again soon."

Lord Guthwine brought Asghar's horse to him, and with a furtive glance at the beast, the Dwarf mounted up.

Dell, his army, and the Wizard, Odyniec, started on their journey north back to Racolis, while the Matadanes and Guthwine's people traveled westward to their own lands. Asghar and Folkor rode with the Hagane host as far north as Delcan. There, they went their own ways—Folkor traveled eastward to his home on the banks of Den Fantiro in Ovieto, and Asghar journeyed northeast to the Crystal Mountains.

* * * *

The morning following the Haganes' departure, Brendys was escorted to the fishing-village of Tarlas, where he boarded a ship that would take him to the Shipyard of Ilkatar. Brendys was accoutered in the blue and green colors of the House of Trost, clothes with a fine cut more befitting a noble, than a Horsemaster's son. His black hair was cut short after the manner of a knight, only barely hiding the scar on his temple. Indeed, Quellin had named him his squire before the assembly of his people and had offered Brendys the opportunity to train for knighthood, but the youth would not be turned from returning to his home in Shalkan.

Quellin, Arella, and Mattina went aboard with Brendys to give their final farewells.

The Gildean king shook the youth's hand. "Brendys, lad, you are a stubborn ass, but I do not regret that Elekar sent you to us, whatever his reason. Nevertheless, you must return again."

"Aye, you must," Arella quickly agreed. "But, please, come by ship—do not make Gowan fish you out of the river again."

Brendys smiled politely. "Thank you, and I will—come back, that is—but I don't know when. It could be a long time yet. But I promise, until then, I will send word to you from Shalkan."

Quellin nodded. "You do that, lad."

At a look from his sister, the Gildean King took his wife's arm and started for the gangplank. "Come, Arella. I think Mattina would rather say her farewells alone."

Mattina took Brendys's hands in her own. "Do not be too long in returning. I do not know how long I can wait."

"Oh, you will wait, all right," Brendys replied, drinking in the depth of her emerald eyes, the smooth contours of her face, as though he feared he might forget them. "The question is, how long can *I* wait?"

Mattina wrinkled her brow in confusion. "What do you mean?"

The ship's captain gave word that he was ready to sail.

Without responding to her question, Brendys kissed Mattina, then took her gently by the arm and turned her towards the gangplank.

Mattina gave him a strange look. "Is that the best you can do?"

The Shalkane youth nodded. "Aye—for now. But it will get better. Remind your brother of his promise."

Mattina knit her brow. "What promise?"

Again, Brendys avoided the question. "Good-bye, Mattina."

Brendys led the Gildean Princess to the head of the gangplank, where she disembarked and joined her brother and sister- by- marriage on the shore.

Brendys waved as the anchor was weighed and the ship moved away from the single dock. When he could no longer see his friends, he went below to ride out his long journey home.

Chapter 19

Brendys gazed out across the fields of Ilkatar, where autumn was already falling, towards the great form of Barrier Mountain. Soon, he would be home.

Eagerly, the tired youth spurred on the horse he had borrowed from the Shipyard of Ilkatar. When he had arrived in Ilkatar, he was met by Gwydnan, who told him that word had come from Shalkan that he was dead.

The Shipyard Manager ordered Brendyk's horses returned to him. Gwydnan had told his superior he was a fool, but had followed his orders nonetheless.

Brendys's road steadily angled uphill as he entered the dark confines of the Western Pass. As he came out of the old mountain pass, he settled his steed into a slow trot and headed down the dirt road. A few hours later, he came within sight of his father's farmstead.

Brendys checked his mount's stride and breathed deep the pungent smell of horses. This was the only life for him. Nothing else would ever do. Brendys urged his horse on once more, not stopping again until he came to the stable. There, he dismounted and led the animal into the barn.

Brendys unsaddled the horse and brought him to an empty stall, brushing him down and feeding him. As he passed Hedelbron's stall, the old grey poked his head over the door and nudged his master. Brendys patted his horse's muzzle, then tossed him an extra fork-full of hay, before leaving the barn.

The youth started towards the house, the sight of it quickening his pace with every step. When he was about halfway across the stableyard, a young boy came out of the house. Brendys felt a lump forming in his throat.

The boy stared at him for a moment in shocked silence, then called back through the front door. "Master Bren'yk! Master Bren'yk! It's 'im! It's 'im! I told ye 'ee ain't dead!"

The boy ran towards Brendys, followed closely by Farida and the Horsemaster.

The youth knelt down, receiving Willerth with tear-filled eyes, embracing him. Brendys looked up at his father and whispered, "I'm home."

Glossary

People and Creatures

Aden (Ay-den): A human youth from Shalkan. Orphan once taken in by Brendyk.
Adina (ah-DE-nah): A human youth from Shalkan.
Agidon (AG-id-on): A Man from Fekamar. A Fekamari nobleman.
Ailon (AY-lon): A Man from the early Fourth Age. A High Steward of Milhavior.
Alara (ah-LAR-ah): Immortal denizens of the High Realm from which the Elves originated.
Allard (ALL-ard): A Man from Matadol. A Fieldmarshal in the Matadane army.
Allic (ALL-ik): A Man from Shalkan. Innkeeper's assistant at the *Green Meadow Inn*.
Amrein (AM-rayn): A hawk belonging to Malach.

Analetri (ah-nah-LET-ree): The Sea Elves.

Aragon (AIR-ah-gon): A Man from Gildea. Lord of the House of Gildea.

Arella (ah-REL-ah): A Woman from Gildea. Lady of the House of Horack-Gildea. Sister of Radnor.

Ascon (ASK-on): A Man of the Third Age. First King of Ascon. First High King of Milhavior.

Asghar (AZ-gar): A Dwarf from the Crystal Mountains. Companion of Brendys.

Balgor (BAL-gor): A Man from Qatan. Lord of the House of Robel-Rigus.

Beelek (BEE-lek): A Man of the Third Age. First King of the land now called Ilkatar.

Berephon (BARE-eh-fon): A Man of from Gildea. Son of Runyan the Bard. Narrator.

Bernath (BER-nath): A Man from Gildea. Lord of the House of Gildea.

Bipin (BIP-in): The childhood nickname of Berephon.

Braya (BRAY-ah): The goddess of life.

Brendyk (BREN-dik): A Man from Shalkan. Horsemaster.

Brendys (BREN-dis): A human youth from Shalkan. Son of Brendyk. Prophesied Bearer of the Flame.

Brugnara (broog-NARE-ah): A Man from Fekamar. Father of Willerth. Brendyk's stablehand.

Brumagin (broo-MAH-gin): A human child from Gildea.

Caletri (ca-LET-ree): The High Elves.

Champa (CHAM-pah): Horse owned by Rister.

Chol (KOLE): A Dark Elf from Nightwood.

Copanas (co-PAN-as): A Man from Racolis. A scout in the Hagane army. Twin brother of Lehan.

Dagramon (DAG-rah-mon): The Dragon-Riders of Krifka.

Dahmus (DAH-moos): A Man from Racolis. A Captain in the Hagane army.

Danel (DAN-el): A Woman from Shalkan. Brendyk's wife. Brendys's mother.
Deciechi (deh-SEE-eh-kee): A Man from Gildea. Guardsman of Henfling.
Dell (DEL): A Man from Racolis. Lord of Hagan Keep.
Deran (DAYR-an): A Man from Racolis. High Priest at the Temple of Oran.
Derslag (DER-slag): A Man from Gildea. Lord of the House of Gildea.
Dinugom (DIN-yoo-gom): A Man from Ilkatar.
Drolar (DRO-lar): The Elvin name for a demonic being shaped like a man with the head of a panther.
Ekenes (EK-en-eez): Horse owned by Brendyk.
Elekar (EL-ek-ar): The Elvin name for the Dawn King, ruler of the High Realm.
Elgern (EL-gern): A mysterious farmer from Ilkatar.
Erwin (ER-win): A Man from Gildea. Horackane guardsman of Quellin.
Etzel (ET-sel): A mysterious woman from Gildea.
Evin (EH-vin): A Man of Shalkan. Great-grandfather of Brendys.
Evinrad (EH-vin-rad): A Man of Shalkan. Grandfather of Brendys.
Evola (ay-VOLE-ah): A Man of the Third Age. Second King of Ascon. First High Steward of Milhavior. Brother of Ascon.
Fanos Pavo (FAH-noss PA-vo): The Athorian name for the Dawn King.
Farida (far-EE-dah): A Woman from Shalkan. Brendyk's house servant.
Faroan (far-OH-an): Elf from Dun Rial.
Fey (FAY): A human child from Gildea. Sister of Brumagin.
Folkor (FOLE-kor): A Man from Ovieto. Captain of the *Scarlet Mariner*.

Gerren (GAYR-en): A Man of Gildea. Captain in the Gildean army.

Goffin (GOFF-in): A Man from Shalkan. Local drunk from Ahz-Kham.

Gowan (GOW-an): A human youth from Gildea.

Graemmon Laksvard (GRAM-mon LAK-svard): Warlord of the Dwarves during the Third Age.

Gramlich (GRAM-lik): A Man from Qatan. King of Qatan.

Grintam (GRIN-tam): A Man from Gildea. Royal Marshal of the Gildean army.

Grotan (GRO-tan): A Kubruk from the Blackstone Mountains. War-Chieftan under Iysh Mawvath.

Guthwine (GUTH-wine): An Elf from Dun Ghalil.

Gwydnan (GWID-nan): A Man from Athor. Mysterious kitchenhand at the Shipyard of Ilkatar.

Hagan (HAY-gan): A Man of the Third Age. First King of the land now called Racolis.

Haran (HAYR-an): A Woman of Gildea. Lady of the House of Trost. Mother of Quellin and Mattina.

Hedelbron (HED-ell-bron): Horse owned by Brendys.

Heil (HILE): The god of the sea.

Henfling (HEN-fling): A Man from Gildea. Governor of Gerdes.

Igin (IE-gin): A Man from Shalkan. Innkeeper at the *Green Meadow Inn*.

Iysh Mawvath (EESH MAW-vath): Man of Death. Warlord of Thanatos. Sorcerer.

Jaf (JAFF): The Elvin name for a demonic being shaped like a man with the head and wings of a bat.

Joahin (JO-ah-heen): Elf of the Caletri kindred. Chief of all Elves since the Third Age.

Jontn (YON-tin): The Dwarvin word for Men.

Kanstanon (kan-STAN-on): A human child from Ilkatar. Stableboy at the Shipyard of Ilkatar. Ward of

Gwydnan.

Kerebros (KAY-reh-bross): A Sorcerer of Thanatos. Shapeshifter in the form of a three-headed wolf.

Kjerek (KYARE-ek): TheDwarvin name for the Dwarvin race.

Kjerken (KYARE-ken): A Dwarvin title of honor given to Brendys by Asghar.

Klees (KLEESE): A Man from Qatan. Lord of Robel Keep.

Kosarek (KOH-sar-ek): A Man from Racolis. King of Racolis.

Kotsybar (KOT-sih-bar): A Man from Shalkan. Brewer in Ahz-Kham.

Kovar (KOH-var): A human child from Gildea.

Kradon (KRAY-don): A human youth from Racolis. Lord of the House of Hagan. Son of Dell.

Krifka (KRIFF-kah): A Sorcerer of Thanatos. Emperor of the Dagramon.

Kubruki (koo-BRUH-kee): A reptilian race originating in the Under Realm, but now inhabiting the Mortal Realm.

Languedoc (lan-gweh-DOK): A human youth from Shalkan.

Lehan (LEH-han): A Man from Racolis. A scout in the Hagan army. Twin brother of Copanas.

Lenharthen (len-HAR-then): A Man from Athor. Iysh Mawvath's former name.

Lorella (lo-REL-ah): A human youth from Shalkan. Languedoc's sister.

Malach (MAL-ak): An Elf from Dun Ghalil.

Manton (MAN-ton): The god of justice.

Mattina (MAH-teena): A human youth from Gildea. Lady of the House of Trost. Sister of Quellin.

Mikva (MIK-vah): A Man from Gildea. Doorwarden of King Treiber.

Molden (MOLE-den): A Man from Racolis. Guard-Priest at the Temple of Oran.

Nathon (NAY-thon): A Man from Shalkan. Glazier in Ahz-Kham.

Nedros (NED-ross): A Man from Matadol. A Fieldmarshal in the Matadane army.

Nerad (NEER-ad): The Athorian word for a Wizard's apprentice.

Nibys (NIE-biss): A Man from Ilkatar.

Nisbud (NIZ-bud): A Man from Fekamar. A Captain in the Fekamari army.

Novosad (NO-voh-sad): A Man from Racolis. A scout in the Hagane army.

Odyniec (o-DIN-ee-ek): A Man from Athor. Wizard of the Dawn King.

Omusok (OM-yoo-sok): A Man from Ilkatar.

Oran (OR-an): The god of the sky.

Quellin (KWEL-in): A Man from Gildea. Lord of the House of Trost.

Quiron (KWIE-ron): A Man from Gildea. Lord of the House of Trost. Father of Quellin and Mattina.

Radnor (RAD-nor): A Man from Gildea. Lord of the House of Horack-Gildea.

Rasheth (RAW-sheth): An Elvin title equivalent to chief or king, held by Joahin since the Third Age.

Reanna Orilal (ray-AH-nah or-il-AL): The Elvin name for the Vision Realm.

Rister (RISS-ter): A Man from Ilkatar. Horse-trader.

Roby (ROH-bee): A Man from Ilkatar. Dockhand at the Shipyard of Ilkatar.

Rodi (ROH-dee): A Dwarf from the Podan Peaks.

Runyan (RUN-yan): A Man from Gildea. The most famous Bard of Milhavior.

Saereni (say-REH-nee): A small mortal folk not yet revealed the other mortal folk.

Sedik (SEH-dik): The god of the earth.

Shanor (SHAY-nor): A human child from Gildea. Son of Radnor.

Sherren (SHARE-en): A Woman from Gildea. Queen of Gildea. Wife of Treiber.

Spiridon (SPEER-id-on): A Man from Matadol. Royal Marshal of the Matadane army.

Tasic (TAZE-ik): Dockhand at the Shipyard of Ilkatar.

Taskalos (TAS-kah-loss): A Man from Matadol. King of Matadol.

Thanatos (THAH-nah-toss): The Athorian name for the Deathlord, ruler of the Death Realm.

Tinsor (TIN-sor): A Man from Ilkatar.

Titha (TIH-thah): A Woman from Gildea. Daughter of the Governor of Gerdes.

Tonys (TOH-niss): A Man from Ilkatar.

Treiber (TRAY-ber): A Man from Gildea. King of Gildea.

Trost (TROST): A Man of the Third Age. First King of the land now known as Gildea.

Turan (TOO-ran): A Man of Gildea. Guardsman of Treiber.

Ubriaco (yoo-BRIE-ah-ko): A Man from Gildea. Lord of the House of Gildea.

Uhyvainyn (oo-hih-VAY-in-een): Elvin name of a High Alar.

Umbrick (UM-brik): A Man from Gildea. Captain in the Gildean army.

Venloo (VEN-loo): A Man from Racolis. Temple Priest at the Temple of Oran.

Verak (VAY-rak): A Man from Shalkan. Carpenter in Ahz-Kham.

Wargon (WAR-gon): A Man from Racolis. A Hagane nobleman.

Willerth (WILL-erth): A human child from Fekamar. Son of Brugnara. Servant of Brendys.
Zanyben (ZAH-nib-en): The head of the Wizards of Athor.
Zoti (ZOH-tee): The god of death.

Places

Ahz-Kham (oz KOM): A town in Shalkan. Home of Brendyk and Brendys.
Alaren Orilal (AH-lar-en or-il-AL): The Elvin name for the High Realm.
Algire (AL-jire): A town in Gildea.
Anatar (an-AH-tar): The Great River. Spans the breadth of Milhavior.
Ascon (ASK-on): The High Throne of Milhavior, located in the Northeast Quarter.
Ascon Keep (ASK-on keep): A city in Ascon. Capitol of Milhavior.
Athor (AY-thor): The Holy Isle, home of the Wizards, hidden from the mainland. One of the Free Lands.
Bale Keep (BALE keep): A city in Matadol.
Bascio Keep (BASS-kee-oh keep): A city in Delcan.
Bhoredan (bor-eh-DON): An island nation in the Southwest Quarter of Milhavior. One of the Free Lands.
Bulkyree (bull-kih-ree): A nation in the Southeast Quarter of Milhavior. One of the Dark Lands.
Caladin (cah-LAD-in): A nation in the Southeast Quarter of Milhavior. One of the Free Lands.
Charneco (KAR-neh-ko): A nation in the Southeast Quarter of Milhavior. One of the Dark Lands.

Chi Thanatos (KIE THAH-nah-toss): The Tower of Death, fortress of Thanatos located in Machaelon.

Dahl Keep (DAL keep): A city in Matadol.

Delcan (DEL-kan): A nation in the Southwest Quarter of Milhavior. One of the Free Lands.

Den Fantiro (DEN fan-TEER-oh): A river in the east of Milhavior.

Den Inkanar (DEN in-KAY-nar): A river in the south of Milhavior.

Den Jostalen (DEN jo-STAH-len): A river in the south of Milhavior.

Den Smih (DEN SMEE): A river in the Southeast Quarter of Milhavior.

Dun Ghalil (DUN GAH-leel): Greyleaf Forest. An Elvin forest in the Southwest Quarter of Milhavior.

Dun Rial (DUN ree-AL): An Elvin forest in the Northwest Quarter of Milhavior.

Ecavan (EK-ah-van): A town in Kahadral.

Elnisra (el-NIZ-rah): A town in Shalkan.

En Orilal (EN or-il-AL): The Elvin name for the Mortal Realm.

Erutti Keep (eh-ROO-tee keep): A city in Delcan.

Fekamar (FEK-ah-mar): A nation in the Northwest Quarter of Milhavior. One of the Free Lands.

Gerdes (GER-deez): A town in Gildea.

Gildea (gil-DAY-ah): A nation in the Southeast Quarter of Milhavior. One of the Free Lands.

Gildea Keep (gil-DAY-ah keep): A city in Gildea.

Hagan Keep (HAY-gan keep): A city in Racolis.

Hàl (HAWL): The Athorian name for the Under Realm (or Death Realm.)

Iler Hill (IE-ler HIL): The hill upon which Hagan Keep sits.

Ilkatar (IL-kah-tar): A nation in the Northwest Quarter of Milhavior. One of the Fee Lands.

Kahadral (kah-HAD-ral): A nation in the Northwest Quarter of Milhavior. One of the Free Lands.

Lake Xolsha (LAYK ZOL-shah): A lake on the border of Gildea and Qatan.

Lewek Keep (LOO-ek keep): A city in Delcan.

Lind Keep (LIND keep): A city in Kahadral.

Machaelon (maw-KAY-el-on): The barren land between Milhavior and Mingenland of old; controlled by Thanatos.

Maelen Orilal (maw-EL-en or-il-AL): The Elvin name for the Under Realm (or Death Realm.)

Matadol (mat-ah-DOLE): A nation in the Southeast Quarter of Milhavior. One of the Free Lands.

Milhavior (mil-HAY-vee-or): The continent north of Machaelon and Mingenland given to Men by Elekar at the end of the last Dawn War.

Mingenland (MEEN-gen-land): The continent in the far south where Men and Dwarves originated.

Neza Bokân (NAY-zah BO-kawn): The Gate of the Arches. A minor portal into the Silver Mountains.

Neza Edvêjga (NAY-zah ed-VAY-ga): The Gate of the Golden Trove. A portal into the Silver Mountains.

Nordin (NOR-din): A town in Fekamar.

Ona Orilal (OH-nah or-il-AL): The Realm Complete. The Elvin name for all of creation.

Ovieto (oh-vee-EH-to): A nation in the Southeast Quarter of Milhavior. One of the Free Lands.

Phelan Keep (FEE-lan keep): A city in Caladin.

Podan Peaks (POH-dan PEAKS): A Dwarvinholt in the Northwest Quarter of Milhavior.

Qatan (kah-TAN): A nation in the Southeast Quarter of Milhavior. One of the Dark Lands.

Racolis (RAK-oh-liss): A nation in the Northwest Quarter of Milhavior. One of the Free Lands.

Racolis Keep (RAK-oh-liss keep): A city in Racolis.

Shalkan (shal-KAN): A little country located in a box canyon at the heart of Barrier Mountain in the Northwest Quarter of Milhavior. Formerly the fortress retreat of a forgotten king.
Sharamitaro (shay-ram-it-AR-oh): The House of Sorrow. A cemetery honoring the fallen at Gildea Keep.
Tarlas (TAR-las): A fishing-village in Gildea.
Wegant Keep (WEH-gant keep): A city in Matadol.
Wills Keep (WILZ keep): A city in Kahadral.
Yasgin (YAZ-gin): A town in Gildea.
Zhâyil-Kan (ZHAW-yil kon): The original name of Shalkan.
Zirges Keep (ZER-geez keep): A city in Qatan.

Things

Crorkin (KROR-kin): Black Elvinmetal. Has the power to slay by only the merest scratch.
Denasdervien (day-nass-DER-vee-en): The Living Flame. Also called the Dawn Sword or the Flame of Elekar. Weapon of the Bearer of the Flame and the Heir of Ascon. Formed of Gloriod and Crorkin.
Denaseskra (day-nass-ES-kra): The Black Flame. The original name of Denasdervien, forged of Crorkin by the Dwarves to slay Elekar.
Elvingold (EL-vin-gold): Gold Elvinmetal.
Elvinsilver (EL-vin-SIL-ver): Silver Elvinmetal.
Golven (GOLE-ven): A summer month in the Milhaviorian calendar.
gona **(GO-nah):** The Gildean G.
Gloriod (GLO-ree-od): Silver-gold Elvinmetal. The most powerful of all Elvinmetals, unbreakable by any amount of force.
Kalter (KAL-ter): Quellin's Elvingold sword.
Kjerekil (kyare-EH-kil): The Dwarvin language.

Stajouhar (STA-yoo-har): Green Elvinstone. Has the power to burn wounds with an unseen flame.
Volker (VOLE-ker): Quellin's Elvinsilver and Stajouhar long-knife.

Phrases

"Engen kellim Arzola, dellis el boradis!" **(EN-gen KEH-lim ar-ZOH-la DEH-liss EL boh-RAD-iss):** "Look to the Dawn, and all is possible!"

"Kindone Getheirne un hason!" **(KIN-done geh-THAYRN un HASS-on):** "May the Dawn guide our hands!"

"Kuntok ê, Kolis Bazân!" **(koon-TOK EH KOL-is BAY-zawn):** "Hear me, King of the Dawn!"

"Mondone, Kiloni Velarin!" **(MON-done, KIL-oh-nee veh-LAR-in):** "Hail, Lord Quellin!"

"Mondone, Treibeirne Delorin!" **(MON-done tray-BAYRN del-OR-in):** "Hail, King Treiber!"

"Omdi kosumni udinor uktur!" **(OM-dee koh-SOOM-nee OOD-in-or UK-tur):** Nonsense phrase spoken by Odyniec.

"Shilnuk!" **(SHIL-nook):** Untranslated Kubruk word.

"Shilnuk kubu mok!" **(SHIL-nook KOO-boo MOK):** Untranslated Kubruk phrase.

"Shilnuk nik Pragu!" **(SHIL-nook NIK PRAH-goo):** Untranslated Kubruk phrase.

"Skud!" **(SKUD):** Untranslated expletive.

About the Author

Jonathan graduated with a B.A. in English from Southern Illinois University at Edwardsville and is publisher and Editor-in-Chief of Athor Productions. Inspired at a very early age by the works of J.R.R. Tolkien and C.S. Lewis, he became an avid reader—and later, writer—of fantasy and science fiction. As well as writing fiction, Jonathan also designs role-playing and trading card games.

CPSIA information can be obtained
at www.ICGtesting.com
Printed in the USA
FFOW04n0320150515
13332FF